a novel

inspired by saint dominica of cornwall

Ann Foweraker

Dominica

a novel inspired by saint dominica of cornwall

ISBN: 978-1-909936-33-1

Paperback Edition 2026 Pendown Publishing
Cornwall, United Kingdom

Set in 11pt Gentium book basic
Pendownpublishing.co.uk

Cover Art Work
Front – ***Marion Kemp Pack***
Back – ***David Thomas***
(from a window in the church of St. Dominica)

dominica

Legend tells us Dominica was the daughter of an Irish King who came up the Tamar river with her brother in AD 689 and created a religious settlement on its bank, in this small corner of Cornwall.

The question is: What *could* this woman have *possibly* done to not only be acclaimed as a saint, but then be kept in mind for over 550 years so much so that, in October 1259, their new stone-built parish church was dedicated to her?

A Celtic saint for this place alone.

What did she do?

A novel – inspired by Saint Dominica of Cornwall

Ann Foweraker is best known as a contemporary novelist. However, to write this novel, she was drawn back to the 7th century by the enigmatic patron saint of the 13th century Parish church in St. Dominick, where she lives. Ann weaves a plausible tale of the life of Saint Dominica, set into the fabric of early medieval conditions and threaded with threats, trials and triumphs.

Contemporary novels by Ann Foweraker

Divining the Line
A story of family, love and loss - and divining.

Nothing Ever Happens Here
Crime meets romance in this light thriller set in Cornwall.

Some Kind of Synchrony
A light thriller where gritty reality & strange events meet.

The Angel Bug
Science fact and fiction in light thriller set at the Eden Project.

A Respectable Life
Psychological thriller set in the tranquil Tamar valley.

CONTENTS

Foreword

My reason for writing this novel goes back to about 2010. It was a late Saturday afternoon and I had just finished doing the sacristan duty, which entailed setting up the altar and the bread and wine ready for the Holy Communion service the next morning in the church - of St. Dominica - the parish church of St. Dominick in Cornwall. As usual I completed my time in the church with a little reflection and prayer at the chancel step.

The sun was coming in through the window to one side of the tower behind me, shining through the leaves that flickered in the breeze, and painting the interior of the church with moving patterns of coloured light from the stained glass window and then, into this reverie came the thought, loud and clear: **'What did she do?'**

'What did Dominica do for the people that they remembered her for over 550 years? So much so that when they built their new stone church, in the middle of the 1200s, they named it after her? St. Dominica - a saint known only to them in this little piece of Cornwall beside the Tamar,'

And then this thought: **'You could write her story'.**

My immediate reaction was - Oh no! I do not write historical novels! For one thing, they are way too hard, for two, I have no idea what she could have done and for three, I was in the middle of writing a very contemporary novel, at that time.

After about nine years of trying to ignore this idea of writing Dominica's story, while writing and editing other books, I felt she was still nagging me to write it. So I finally gave in and bumped it up my 'book ideas list' from number nine to number six.

I began researching whenever I could. Firstly the legends - there are a few versions, **but only one involves both Dominica and our area.** You'll find more about these at the end of this novel.

Then I began researching the times and what I could find out about life in Cornwall, in particular, at the time the legend puts her here – from AD 689.

This was hard! This is deep in the Early Middle Ages, the time that used to be called 'the Dark Ages' mainly because of how little was known of those times. There are few proper relevant records, not even a lot of helpful archaeology and it was a time of flux – especially on the borderlands of Saxon Wessex and Dumnonia, as the Celtic kingdom covering what is now Devon and Cornwall was then known.

Earlier, in the reign of King Centwine of Wessex, AD 676 - 685, the Saxons had invaded Dumnonia and then ruled the area right down to and including what we know as Exeter - but had then lost much of that area again during a time of instability in Wessex. So by the time this story arrives in Britannia, the old British kingdom of Dumnonia stretched from Land's End to a line lying roughly along the border of today's counties of Somerset and Dorset with Devon.

The Saxon Kingdom of Wessex had, from AD 688, King Ina (also written as Ine and Ini) at its head - a Christian and pious king, who gave up his throne in AD 726 to go to Rome and live out the rest of his life as a monk there. He was also a thorough ruler, who drafted a set of laws that were later incorporated into King Alfred the Great's famed law code, when that was created more than 150 years later.

King Ina comes into the legends – so I researched him and his influence where it concerned Glastonbury and Cornwall.

When looking at my main characters' origins, I also researched what being an Irish King of that era actually meant, again because the legend says Indract and Dominica were the son and daughter of an Irish King.

Then I delved into what is known about **early medieval monasteries,** both Irish and British, as our protagonists would come from the former type, and set up similar in Dumnonia.

The first thing I found out, very quickly, was that *I had to forget everything that I thought I knew about medieval monasteries* – for everything I knew was really about an entity and life-style that only came into being a few hundred years later than the date this book is set at.

I have always had a fascination for history, vernacular history in particular, yet I found I actually knew nothing relevant of this time. The monasteries we hear most about, in school for instance, are those of the High to Late Medieval period, with the latter eventually dissolved under Henry VIII, and as such would have been virtually unrecognisable to the people of Dominica's time - and, most certainly in Cornwall, where things were different again to more eastern areas of Britain.

I spent a couple of years researching the history of the time, from a vast array of resources including published books, serious internet-based history platforms and up-to-date theses for PhD and Masters qualifications.

I also delved into scientific analysis of the ingredients of the herbal mixtures, poultices and potions probably used, and their actual effects on bacteria, viruses and well-being – combining this with the nature of diseases and ailments verified to that specific era and their usual outcomes.

I was even able to look into the weather! How amazing is it to be able to find out notable weather events and trends that were relevant to the dates and areas that Dominica's story is set in?

Eventually I began to form ***an idea of what she could, possibly, have done*** ... and sketched out my ideas to make a storyline.

Needless to say the characters did their usual thing, of saying and doing things I hadn't planned, or just arrived, when I hadn't known they were even going to be there.

However, as usual, I let them have free rein - I have learnt this is the best approach - but it also meant that I was constantly having to stop and research whether what my characters wanted to do or say was right for the Early Middle Ages ... it was exhausting. I ran down so many really interesting rabbit holes, sometimes spending half a day before being sure of a paragraph - which in the end might not even have got through the first edit - so it is no wonder it still took me nigh-on five years to get the first draft finished - where two is normal for me - and I may still have some mistakes.

And then there was the issue of place names! By that I mean what to call places, depending on who was talking, depending on where they were living, and at what point in the timeline This was a complex matter in a story where different peoples meet and become ruled by, or subjugate, others and where, because of the change of the dominant language, names get changed. For those who know the actual areas there is an explanation of my choices of various alternative names to those more familiar to you today in Author's Notes. For everyone there is a starter under ***Orientation*** for names used and their modern names.

There are also some maps to help out as the story moves around geographically - as some of my early readers said they would like them.

All of this is to say: this book is a novel - based on a piece of legend specific to the parish of St. Dominick in Cornwall - yet as historically accurate to the times it is set in, as it is understood to be in the present day, and as I could make it.

I hope you enjoy the journey Dominica has taken me on in trying to answer that first question 'What did she do?'

Dedication

To everyone who keeps the church of Saint Dominica in the Parish of St. Dominick, Cornwall, open, welcoming and alive – no matter when you lived, or live, or will live.

The 13th Century Church of St. Dominica, St. Dominick FSF1995

ORIENTATION

The majority of this novel is set across 55 years between AD 667 and AD 722, and moves from Eriu (Ireland) to Dumnonia (Devon and Cornwall) touching on many places between there and Rome (not listed) including Glestyngabyrig (Glastonbury) in Somersaete (Somerset).

This, is a time of political and linguistic flux - so a short list of some of the places mentioned in the story is given here to help give you some bearings, with reference to current and other past names.

Places in order of appearance:

Eriu** (to the natives) - **Ireland

***Hibernia** - Ireland (to the Saxons and much later)*

***Drom-Eanaigh** - meaning 'Great ridge in the marsh' It overlooks The Blackwater River (originally called The Great River - An Abhainn-Mhor) with the winding Goish river valley between it and **Drom-Mhor** - likely the reason for the marsh. It is on this ridge that I created the court of King Conall Ua-Faelain of the Deisi Muman.*

*Today there is a 13th century castle on this ridge called Dromana (an anglicised spelling of **Drom-Eanaigh)** with the more recent Villiers Town down in the valley.*

***Drom-Mhor** - Meaning 'Great ridge' now anglicised to Dromore. There are Ogham tombstones on its lower slopes. On this ridge I created the Monastery of St Declan and St. Brigid. Initially as a daughter monastery from (the real) St. Declan's monastery at Ardmore (Aird-Mhor) on the coast about 20 miles away, but independent by the time of the story.*

***Eochaill** - the port of Youghal - at the mouth of the Blackwater River, Co. Waterford.*

Dumnonia - Devon and Cornwall (roughly, at this time)

***Kernow** - Dumnonia West of the Tamer.*

***Dewnen** - Dumnonia East of the Tamer.*

***Tamer** - Tamar (river) the boundary between them.*

In Kernow: Cornwall

Tamerkam *- their main stronghold overlooking the Tamer - and also for the whole area ruled by Cador and Keynae, which, by the Domesday book would be named as the 'Manor of Haltone'.*
Halhtun *- original Saxon spelling of Halton.*
Bo Barr *- created name meaning homestead of Barr. [Baber area of village of St. Dominick]*
Bo Etherick *- a name meaning 'homestead of Etherick'. [Bohetherick, hamlet in St. Dominick parish]*
Ventonpemps *- created name meaning 'five springs'. This covers the hamlet of Ashton and all that area belonging to what, by the Domesday book, would be called the 'Manor of Aissetone'.*
Kellyventon *- created as a very early name for Callington meaning 'spring in the woods'.*

In Dewnen - Devon

Tamerunta *- Tamerton (Foliot) - taken from their legends, at the end of a creek issuing just down river from where the Tavy joins the Tamar.*
Porthkudh *- created name for Mount Batten meaning 'hidden port'. Plymouth did not exist at this time, nor even Sutton. This had been the main port of the bay since before the Romans. Later to be called 'How Stert' by the Saxons.*
Escancastra *- Exeter (from contemporary records).*

In Somerseate - Somerset

Glestynabyrig *- Saxon name for Glastonbury.*

Worldwide - a thin place

'A thin place' is the Celtic name given to a place where the veil between heaven and earth becomes almost transparent - where a sense of God's peace and love can be experienced.

You can find out about more place names, and the reasons for my choices in this story, in Author's Notes

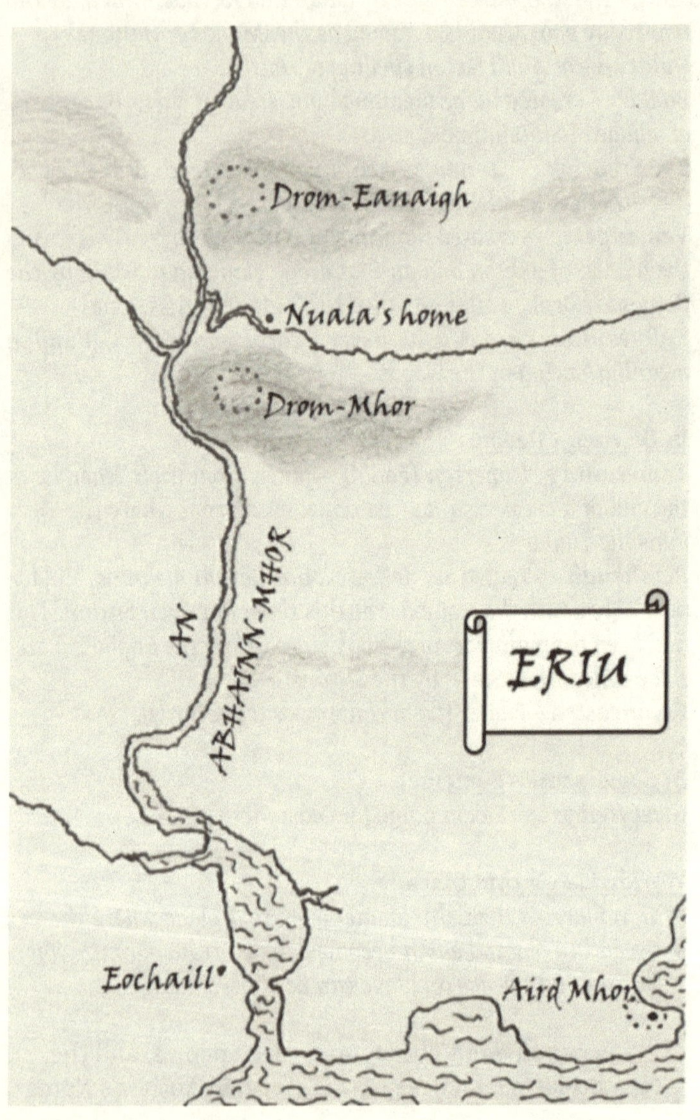
Drom-Eanaigh
Nuala's home
Drom-Mhor
AN
ABHAINN-MHOR
ERIU
Eochaill
Aird Mhor

Part One

At Drom-Eanaigh, the stronghold of King Conall, above The Great River in Eriu

Chapter 1

The Arrival - *circa AD 667*

Queen Affraic moaned again as her belly tightened and heaved - her body was ready but the babe wasn't coming and, Nuala, the midwife and healer, was starting to sweat. Nuala ran her hand across the Queen's belly again. Something was very wrong, she could feel feet off to the side, maybe a shoulder across from there, she needed to get the babe to turn head-down again otherwise they could both die.

'Why is it so bad this time? I don't understand!' Affraic asked Nuala between breaths - she had safely delivered her of three sons, now aged ten, eight and three years. 'It's never been so bad or so strong before.'

'My Lady,' Nuala began, then glanced at the other women in the room, she could see in their eyes that they knew something was wrong too and were subtly backing away, as if distancing themselves from what might be going to unfold. What Nuala realised for certain was that the birthing stool was not the place for the Queen to be, and rose up from her kneeling position.

'Ladies,' she said addressing the Queen's closest women with as much strength of conviction as she could, 'come and help lift the Queen to her feet, she needs to be on the bed.'

What her Lady actually needed was for the babe to change its position. Only yesterday it seemed fine and head-down, lined up but, as it had not sunk down into the final position, the delivery didn't seem imminent, and Nuala had returned to her home. Today it was wrong. The contractions had begun suddenly and were very soon really strong so by the time the messenger had brought Nuala up, from her home by the ford, the Queen's ladies had her sat on the birthing stool.

Affraic cried out as they pulled her to her feet and supported her.

'My Lady, we have to turn the babe, it is not quite aligned to come out,' Nuala said as they steadied her. 'Help the Queen to kneel on the bed,' she commanded the high-born women, and, said more gently, to the Queen, 'My Lady, rest your forehead upon this pillow, lift up on your knees.' The Queen let out a howl as another spasm overtook her.

A banging on the door frame jolted through everyone. Eyes widened as they all looked at the door.

The King himself shouted, 'Woman! What is happening?' Which shook them again, now all eyes were looking at her. So Nuala rose quickly and went to the door, opening it a piece.

'Sire, the babe will not come – it is laying the wrong way - crossways. We are trying to turn it.'

'Can this be done?'

'I have done it once before, sire, I pray it will work again today.'

'And if you cannot?'

Nuala stared at him, her mouth not working, she felt her head shake a fraction - if she could not they would certainly lose the mother and child but to say it out loud would be a bad omen. She saw him reach his own conclusion, his eyes widening in fear.

'Pray!' King Conall commanded her, 'and I will go and pray too - this child will be a gift to God if all goes well, but, whatever, save my wife!' He turned and strode away.

Nuala went back to the Queen, who was still supported by her ladies but now sobbing. Maybe she understood now too. Nuala spoke softly to her, 'My Lady, I am going to turn the child between the pushing, it may hurt but try to let it happen, try not to fight it.' All the while she was running her hands over the Queen's belly, feeling a foot here, a shoulder there. She spoke to the women, 'All of you, support the Queen, here, hips and shoulders, do not let her fall while I press!'

She stood on the bed, leant across, began to press into the belly, pushing hard down one side but using her other hand to feel for movement on the other. The ladies had to brace themselves to hold the Queen so she did not fall over. The Queen howled that she had to push again and Nuala told her to open her mouth and give many small gasps, to lessen the effect. Once it had subsided Nuala tried again and felt the weight change. Telling one woman to 'press here and hold it just so', she moved to the other side and massaged the Queen's belly, pushing up again and again.

There was movement, the foot she had felt travelled up the side. She moved back to the first side, pushing carefully but firmly on what she could now feel was a head, told the lady to 'press and hold it just so' and again returned to the other side. She ran her hands up the Queen's belly pressing towards the centre and as she did so she felt the belly change shape. There was a gasp from the woman she'd told to press on the Queen's side and she straightened, taking her hands away. 'No!' Nuala snapped, 'Press!' but it was too late, the last movement reversed, the babe aligned diagonally again. Nuala felt like crying, like screaming at the stupidity of the high-born woman, but a glance showed that the other woman had realised her mistake.

Taking a deep breath Nuala spoke quietly to the Queen. 'My Lady, we are so nearly there, so nearly in position. After the next squeezing my Lady, I want you to breathe open-mouthed, to try to relax your body into the hands that are holding ...' The Queen's groan cut her short as she went into contraction, Nuala pressed, hoping to use it to shift the babe more upright as it tightened, or at least to prevent the babe from moving fully back into the crossways position. As the contraction eased Nuala looked at the woman, saying, 'Come, press here.' She did so, keeping her eye on Nuala as she returned to shape and press as she had before. Nuala pressed and pushed, for a second she thought that it would not happen again, and then the movement, a fluid, animal ripple under her hands. A quick glance told her the lady pressing was ready for this and pressed in more as the babe moved under her hands to the head-down position.

'Quickly, my Lady, lift up,' Nuala said to the Queen, and indicated for the ladies to lift the Queen upright. It wasn't quite done yet. 'We need the Queen to walk around,' she said, and the ladies helped her off the bed to stand supported by them. After a short while of walking the Queen in a circle Nuala rested her hands on the Queen's belly and it all felt right, completely right, the head engaged. They walked her to the birthing stool, where Nuala oiled her hand, knelt before the Queen and checked; the Queen was ready and the crown of the head was in place.

Nuala breathed a sigh, and smiled. 'When you need to push my Lady, do.'

The babe arrived a little blue but, with a slap, soon took her first breath. The Queen was washed and tidied by her ladies, while Nuala checked and cleaned the babe. The Queen was then settled in the bed to receive her daughter.

'She's beautiful,' Affraic said, gazing down at her daughter with her crown of ebony hair already drying – all memory of the agony lost in the wonder of her babe.

Eventually, when all was ready, a message was sent to the King's chapel for him to come back. The King arrived, knocking gently this time – for even a King takes care on entering a birthing chamber. He smiled to see his wife, alive and with a babe nestled in her arms and was beside her in a few quick strides.

'A girl at last,' Affraic said, her voice full of wonder.

His smile was broad. 'And I see she has your hair,' he said stroking the fuzz with his forefinger.

'What shall we call her? I'm thinking after your mother?' Affraic said softly, her gaze fixed on the child.

'No, my love, we must name her for the Lord,' he said. Affraic looked up at him, puzzled. 'Affraic, my love,' he said, laying his hand on her hand, 'When all was not well I prayed for your life, for the babe's life. I prayed like I have never done before – I, and all at the monastery. I made sworn oaths before others, to God - she is promised to the monastery.'

'What? What? You gave away my child before she was born? A girl! You know how much I have wanted a daughter - how could you?' her voice cracking, 'How could you?'

'I wasn't to know she was a girl, my love, I only knew I wanted you to live. I have made a solemn, witnessed promise to God. I cannot turn back.'

Affraic looked down on the babe. When she looked up there were tears in her eyes, 'Then you must promise me that we'll keep her here until she is of age, until fourteen, that we will not give her up to the church until then!'

Conall gave a rueful smile, 'We can do that, as long as her life is dedicated to the Lord, then my oath to God will be honoured,' Conall said looking down at the tiny bundle. He leant down and kissed Affraic on the forehead, and the same with the babe. 'Welcome to Drom-Eanaigh, Dominica.'

Chapter 2
Flanna – circa AD 667

Almost two whole days had passed and yet the Queen's milk had not come in, the babe suckled and pulled away to cry, time and time again.

'Nuala, what is wrong - I had plenty of milk for each of my boys?' Affraic asked. 'There seems to be nothing coming through, and the babe whimpers so.'

Nuala sighed as she had already suggested that they use a wet-nurse but the Queen, in some grip of delusion, had refused the idea. 'I fear my Lady that you are so weakened by the birth that your body hasn't the strength to make the milk. She will need someone else to suckle her.'

'Oh! But she is my daughter, it breaks my heart to let her go.'

'Many do so even without need,' Nuala said gently, 'but without this, you may always be without her. My Lady, I know, I have seen, that sometimes, after a birth, a mother's thoughts do not run straight. They are confused by feelings too strong to discern. You must choose for the good of Dominica, not your heart.'

'Not now, later maybe, the milk may still come through,' Affraic said, not looking at Nuala, dismissing her.

Nuala left the Queen and took herself to the king's meeting-house. She knew he would be there with his men, eating the noonday meal. She stood outside for what felt like a long time, gathering her courage to speak to King Conall. Taking a deep breath, she stopped a servant who was heading into the house, and told him to say the wise-woman needed to speak with the King.

The man first looked her up and down and then nodded. He returned a while later telling her to go in. The low light meant that she had to take a moment to locate the King –

but after a nervous pause, she did and worked her way around the room to bow before him.

'What is it woman?' he asked.

Straightening, she glanced at the other men lounging on either side of Conall, 'It is about the Queen my Lord, and the child,' she glanced at the men again, with the King following her glance before understanding her meaning.

'Move away,' he said, chopping his hand at them left and right. They clambered to their feet and moved away. The King raised his eyebrows at her questioningly.

Nuala stepped closer and spoke in a low voice, 'My Lord, you know that the babe does not feed, that the Queen has no milk. I fear the birth has weakened my Lady too much to give milk. I have given the remedies I know – herbs steeped in milk that help the milk flow, but to no avail. I fear for the babe, and the Queen,' here Nuala hesitated, conscious that her next words must not be taken the wrong way. She then went on rapidly, 'I believe the Queen is not in her right mind, just now, I have seen this happen after giving birth before - it passes, but right now – she will not listen to reason, and ...'

'And?' he asked impatiently.

'And the babe must have a wet-nurse now, or she may not survive another day.'

He stared at her a moment, 'Hmm, leave it with me, I think I can make the Queen see reason.'

A little while later, Conall sat with Affraic as she tried to comfort Dominica at her breast, the babe crying, the mother in tears.

'Affraic, my love, I know I agreed we could wait this one time, but now I *must* take Dominica to the monastery for baptism.'

'No, not yet,' she said tearfully, 'You know I so much want to be there to hold her, please, and they won't let me go in the church yet, the time has not passed.'

'I know, I agreed as she was bonny and looked so strong, but she is not thriving now, is she? Yet you are so determined to keep her to yourself,' he stood and turned back to her. 'Would you risk her dying unbaptised?'

'No, but ... can they not come here?'

'It would make no difference – you would still have to be outside the chapel.'

'No ... the milk will come, it always has, it is just slow,' she turned her liquid blue eyes to him, magnified by tears.

He nodded, a grim smile on his lips. 'Tomorrow then, if the milk has not come in by tomorrow, we give her to a wet-nurse or I take her for baptism - she cannot survive without milk.'

Affraic dropped her gaze to the little one, 'I know,' she whispered.

A little while after he had left her, Affraic said, 'Nuala, the King has given me no choice, I must have a wet-nurse for Dominica,' she pursed her lips and looked away, her eyes filling with tears. 'Is there anyone suitable?'

There were three – but only one in the full flush of milk – Nuala's own daughter, Flanna. Nuala thought hard. Maybe, if she could persuade the Queen, it didn't have to be at the expense of her grandson. The usual pattern was for the natural child to be fed milk from a goat, while the child of the high-born woman took the mother's milk – and Nuala didn't want that for her Brannon.

'My Lady, my own daughter gave birth just last month, my Lady, but I beg you, let her still feed her son too if you take her to be a wet-nurse for Dominica - she has plenty of milk.'

'Your daughter - Flanna?'

Nuala nodded.

'I remember Flanna from when I first came here and she used to help you. Maybe I wouldn't mind it being Flanna too much, and yes, as long as Dominica has all she needs first – then he can suck too. I will talk to the King today.'

'Thank you my Lady.' It was the best she could hope for – Flanna's situation would soon have become known if the King had demanded a wet-nurse to be found immediately.

'Sire,' Nuala bowed low before the King. She'd been summoned by two of the king's men and so was not certain of the reason.

'You, your daughter and her babe are to come and reside here, in the Queen's quarters. Now. Today. Get your daughter here to feed the babe as soon as you can. The rest of your family, all of it, will be moved up to the court, a place will be provided for you all, and then you can join them there.'

Nuala had no option but to accept, though she wondered what would become of her old homestead, her plants and her goats.

By the evening there was a milky peace in the Queen's quarters - one of the two chambers adjoining the royal household. Affraic sat entranced as Dominica hungrily suckled at Flanna's breast, the milk sometimes escaping the corners of her little mouth. Brannon, Flanna's babe, lay wrapped quietly beside Flanna in a basket on the floor. Indract, the three year old prince, played with a pile of sticks near his mother's feet, stacking them up and then toppling them by rolling a stone at them. When they were all knocked down he stood and, seeing his mother's lap free of the babe scrambled up for a cuddle, sticking his thumb in as she pulled him close, her eyes turning once again to the babe while she absent-mindedly stroked the boy's hair.

Nuala stood to one side, by the fire, warming a pot of milk with herbs steeped in it that she wished may still help the Queen come into milk. Though, glancing at Affraic, she was certain that it would not help; there was a washed-out look to the Queen's skin that didn't look right or healthy at all.

As the week passed and then another, Dominica grew stronger and began to put on weight, plumping out. At the end of the third week from the birth, the King called for Nuala again.

'Sire,' Nuala said, bowing low. She had a feeling she knew why she was there this time, but it didn't help.

'How goes it with my daughter?'

'Sire, she feeds well and grows.'

'And my dear wife? She does not fare well, does she?'

'No, my Lord. I fear she does not.'

'Fear! What is it that ails her?'

Nuala looked at her feet. She knew he would be seeking this, but she had no answer. 'I don't know, sire,' she said in a low voice.

'Why not? Is it not your duty to know – are you not the wise-woman here?'

'I do what I can to help, where I can – but I do not know the cause, I have not seen this before, so I do not know how to treat this malady.'

Conall paced the room, then his head swung round to face her again, 'Go to the monastery, my men can take you, they have healers there, bring one back.'

'Yes, my Lord.'

'And I will send word that prayers must be said for her health. Yes, I'll do that.'

Nuala had never been to the monastery before, but she knew that the monastery was indebted to the King, as it had been his grandfather who had called for it to be founded on Drom-Mhor and had given it that land. She had seen it from outside the boundary only, had seen the top of a tall building standing proud of all that surrounded it.

Built on a great ridge of land, across the wide valley from the King's court, the monastery had an earthen rath like a lys - but no palisade. And this boundary bank had just a gap - no proper gateway to be barred. Inside the rath she could see the huge building, the monastery church. It was a marvel to behold, especially as they drew close, like the trees had joined themselves together to make walls. To either side, visible through the gap, were the more familiar round houses, some small, some larger.

As they came right up to the gap a monk stepped out and greeted them. They slid from their sturdy mounts and one of the warriors asked for Nuala to be taken to the Abbot. The monk looked at Nuala with hard eyes, but did not question the men. Instead he told the one who had spoken to leave his weapons with the other, then led them toward one of the larger round-houses and told them to wait. After a few minutes another monk appeared and asked the purpose of their visit.

'The King ...' Nuala began.

'Not you,' he made a dismissive gesture with his hand. 'You!' he said, his eyes fixed on the man behind her.

'The King wishes this woman to speak to the Abbot,' the warrior said.

The monk's eyes widened as if in surprise, but he turned and went back into the building. After a short while he returned, looked at the warrior and nodded, standing back to let them pass, avoiding eye contact with Nuala.

Inside, the round-house had been divided, so that portions to each side were blocked off. Ahead, behind a table sat the Abbot or, at least, an older man with a monk's robe on, though his was also of a lighter shade than those she'd seen the other monks wearing.

Nuala bowed.

The Abbot tipped his hand. 'Speak sister,' he said, his voice gentle and soft.

'My Lord the King has sent me to ask after a healer. His queen is ailing and he would have assistance. He also sends a gift and asks for prayers for Queen Affraic's health,' Nuala glanced at the warrior who placed on the table a small pouch that chinked as he set it down.

'Why did he send you?'

'I do not know, my Lord, just that I was bidden.'

'Just Father,' the Abbot smiled. 'I hear that the Queen had a difficult confinement. Are you the wise-woman who delivered her?'

Nuala was surprised, but tried not to show it, 'I am, Father.'

'I believe God worked through you. Both survived and I am told this is unusual in these circumstances.'

'Indeed, Father.'

'I will send Sister Ciar back with you, she runs the women's infirmary. Tell King Conall, prayers will be said.'

'Yes, Father.'

Nuala and the warrior waited in the courtyard and eventually a woman appeared, attired in a similar way to the monks, except that she also wore a simple veil, covering all from her forehead back and seemingly just tied beneath the loose fall of itself at the nape of her neck. She carried a basket and looked only at Nuala. 'I am Sister Ciar, and I am ready.'

'Welcome sister, I am Nuala,' the wise-woman said, 'you are to ride with me, it would seem.'

On their short journey Sister Ciar asked many questions about the birth, and the health of the Queen since. After a while she was very quiet. Their route took them down to the valley and across the ford. As they turned to ascend the hill on the other side of the stream they passed Nuala's homestead and Nuala felt a pang for it as it looked sad and alone. The sister remained quiet all the long slow trek up the hill.

They were nearly at the court when Nuala, unable to remain silent any longer, asked, 'So, sister, do you have any idea what ails our Queen?'

'I am praying for enlightenment. Maybe when we meet, God will help us,' Sister Ciar said, but her reply didn't fill Nuala with confidence.

Chapter 3
God Mother - circa AD 667

Sister Ciar looked at the sample of urine in the small semitransparent glass vessel she had brought with her. The urine was dark, yet cloudy and smelt strongly of a strange odour, not the usual smell. She passed it over to Nuala.

'What do you make of this?'

'I do not know – but I know it doesn't smell right. And you, do you know?'

'I do not, but I think something inside is poisoning the Queen.'

'*Don't* say *that word*,' Nuala shushed, her eyes wide with fear. 'All our lives will be forfeit! *I* understand your meaning, but to most ears, poison is only something *given* to kill.'

'Ah, I see, I am with those who do not think that way so much, I forget. Yes, there is something in the Queen that is ... She has a pestilence of the waters.'

Nuala gave a nod, adding, 'And, can we help? Is there a herb that will drive away this pestilence?'

'I do not know for sure. I know plenty of cooled boiled water may help. Let us try that first.'

'Also, the – derangement? I thought that the Queen suffered, as many do after childbirth, from the melancholy, but now it is something different. Now she says she sees things that are not there, says people talk to her who are not even alive any more. Can this – pestilence have got into her thoughts too?'

'It is possible. I have experienced something similar with very old women, whose lives are nearly at an end, but not with one as young as the Queen. Maybe giving birth opened her up to this pestilence and it has taken root. I may need to go back to the monastery to study some of the herbals there.'

'I will arrange it,' Nuala assured her.

Sister Ciar returned to the monastery that very day, leaving Nuala to care for the Queen. She no longer had any concerns for the babe; it was obvious she was doing very well. Nuala ordered water to be boiled, and as she was not the one standing over it, decided that the saying of the Our Father four times over would suffice for the time that it should bubble before drawing off, covering and leaving to cool.

When the pot of cooled water was brought to her she poured some into a horn cup with a nicely thinned lip that would make drinking it from easier, and brought it to the Queen.

'You? You, here again?' Affraic said, gazing at her as if she was amazed to see her.

'Yes, my Lady, I have brought you a drink.'

'Where is my babe?'

'Nearby, she is being fed, I will bring her to you as soon as you have finished your drink,' Nuala said soothingly, offering the cup up to the Queen.

'Not thirsty. I want to see her.'

Nuala wondered again at the wisdom of excluding the nursing babe from the Queen's quarters, but Sister Ciar was worried that the condition could be catching, and would not risk them being all together.

'Drink first, it will help you feel strong enough to hold her.'

'Strong, huh? Strong,' and she reached for the cup. Nuala had to steady the Queen's hand as it shook so much.

'So good, my Lady, so good, here take some more,' Nuala held a second cup, this laced with herbs that would help the Queen sleep. Affraic reached out her hand and Nuala, feeling guilty, helped her drink it.

Affraic rested back. She seemed to have forgotten the babe and the promise, she began to sing to herself, an old song about love and battle. Nuala pulled a cover across her

Lady's shoulders and moved off to sit near the wind-hole where a fresh breeze found its way in.

Sister Ciar returned the next day. She brought some dried herbs and seeds with her and had a list to be collected.

'Nuala, can you collect these herbs for me, I have brought with me the ones that are from far away.'

Nuala looked at the piece of parchment the sister held up. 'I'm sorry, sister, I cannot read.'

'No? I am sorry - you are so skilled I didn't think. Listen,' she said, pointing to each one, 'feverfew, do you have that? And lus-Brigits, but they should be easy?'

'Yes, sister, they are. I can be back with them by the afternoon, if I go right away.'

'Do that – and I will begin my work with these precious seeds from distant Nubia.'

'What are they?'

'I'm not sure exactly, but they are called 'the buried grains'. To work they must be brewed to make a drink that will then cure some pestilences that nothing else can touch. It doesn't work on all pestilences, but for some it has an almost miraculous effect. This handful is all that we have left at the monastery from the small sack I brought back from Rome - we can but pray that this time it will work.'

Nuala was pleased to be out in the fresh air. As she set off down the hillside towards her old place she noticed the grain harvest was all gathered in. Once home she knew where to find most herbs that grew in the area, and within her own garden grew others that were not so common. She checked on her own place first where, in such a short time, the wild plants had encroached, almost smothering some of the more delicate herbs. She noted damage to her hut too; it looked as if a cow or horse had used it to rub up against and had cracked the daubed wall. Perhaps she'd be able to get it repaired, she had a feeling that she would need it again one day. She noticed her goats were in the field nearby and called to them; they came slowly regarding her with their slit-eyes. They looked healthy enough, and she knew that Flanna's eldest boy was coming down to milk them and drive them into their compound at night and let them out in the morning. She sighed and turned back to collect the herbs.

She could have picked lus-Brigits from anywhere, its sunny face and jagged leaves were common, but she knew those in her herb garden area should be clean, at least safer than those near the outer rim of the court. The feverfew, however, would only be found in her garden. It was hard to find in the wild, though it was said to be found in special places. She had planted it from seed gained from a trader in such things. With sufficient herbs in her basket she returned up the hill to the King's lys.

*

Two more days passed. Nuala and Sister Ciar spent all their time with the Queen, while, at sunset, the King would come, ask them of the Queen's progress. He had asked if he could touch her without the pestilence coming on to him, and Sister Ciar had said it would do the Queen good, and that the King only had to wash his hands three times, in the name of the Father, the Son and of the Holy Ghost, in clean running water afterwards and he would not get this pestilence.

Nuala noted how the sister brought into all her dealings with the sickness her faith in God – then realised she had done something similar when using the Our Father to time the boil, though when at home she would sing the song of the water to the same effect.

*

On the seventh day of brewing the potion was ready. It had a sour-ale taste and an unusual slightly greenish tint, but was not offensive. For the Queen they watered it more, as they were still giving her plenty to drink as this seemed to have helped a little, and gave it to her four times a day. Each day they repeated the dosage.

For the first three days Affraic remained distracted and weak. The fourth day of this treatment brought the same result and Sister Ciar wondered if this pestilence was the wrong type for a miracle to occur.

On the fifth day, however, Nuala arrived to find the Queen looking bright-eyed. She turned to Nuala and demanded, in a voice stronger than it had been for weeks, 'Bring me my daughter!'

Nuala looked to Sister Ciar, who nodded and, coming over towards Nuala, said softly, 'We can bathe the babe afterwards.'

The King was delighted and amazed to find his wife sitting up and looking better, and to listen to her talk and make sense again. He praised both Sister Ciar and Nuala and left them in a good mood.

There was only enough of the brew left for two more days, so they administered it on the two following days and hoped that its work had been done. With great relief they saw improvements in the Queen's health not only that day but in the days following. Nuala wondered how these 'buried grains' were obtained, and tucked the knowing of them in her mind for a later time when she could ask the herb trader – for knowledge of healing herbs was her life.

The Queen then asked to see her son Indract as well as the babe. Indract came in, quietly and gently. Dominica lay in a small crib beside Affraic, who didn't want her out of her sight now she was feeling better.

'Come here brave boy,' she said to Indract, he climbed up to sit with his mother on her bed, 'come have a cuddle.' He snuggled into his mother breathing in deeply, sighing out softly. 'Ah, I have missed you Indract,' she said giving him a squeeze. 'And what do you think of your little sister?'

Indract did not reply. 'Ah, my lovely, she'll be big enough to play games with you soon, don't you worry. Do you know her name?'

'Domca,' he said with a triumphant grin. His mother ruffled his hair, 'Ahha! Domca! Sweet boy. Nuala, did you hear he calls her Domca – so sweet.'

'He does. I think Dominica is a bit of a mouthful when you're only three summers.'

The Queen remained well as the days passed. Flanna came often to feed Dominica and care for her, and Sister Ciar began to think of returning to the monastery. One evening the King announced that the day of churching was close and that, as the Queen was recovered, they would have the churching and the baptism together as the Queen desired, though, as she was still very weak, he had spoken to his uncle, the Abbot, and he had agreed to come over to the King's chapel for the church blessing and baptism.

*

When the day arrived, the Queen seemed worse again, she appeared to glaze over and forget what she was saying more than once. Nuala and Sister Ciar shared a concerned glance, but only they seemed to see the difference in the Queen as yet.

'I was worried about this happening,' Sister Ciar said in a hushed voice.

'Why?'

'The herbals say the brew should be given for a whole moon cycle. We had only enough for seven days. Maybe that was not enough and the pestilence has come back.'

Meanwhile the Queen's ladies fussed around Affraic, preparing her, modest but regal, for the blessing of the church – the blessing of thanksgiving and praise for a safe delivery – and for the baptism of Dominica.

The whole court was decorated; flowers had been taken from the wild and their stems poked into the edge of the thatch, so every home was ringed in flowers. The King's chapel was well swept and fresh lady's bedstraw and silver rush were strewn for their scent, the paved aisle was washed and polished with a sweet smelling oil.

The Abbot and Abbess arrived riding on ponies accompanied by three monks and three sisters. The Abbess, Mother Mara, in charge of the women's side of the monastery of Saint Brigit and St. Declan, had rarely visited the court of Drom-Eanaigh.

'Conall, you remember Abbess Mara? She will, God sparing, take care of Dominica when she enters the monastery, so she will stand Godmother to the child,' the Abbot told his royal nephew, 'and I will stand Godfather.'

'Who will you be having as the second Godmother?'Abbess Mara asked.

The King hesitated – but the Queen spoke up clearly, 'The other Godmother shall be Nuala.'

'But, but,' Conall stuttered turning to face her, 'Surely, your sister? Or mine?'

'They are not here – and neither would I, or Dominica, be here without Nuala – can't you see, husband? God has meant this to be!'

The King turned to the Abbot, but he seemed to be praying, his hands folded, his eyes turned to the ground. He looked back to the Abbess.

'As the Queen says – let it be Nuala,' he said.

The next day the Queen began complaining of pains in her lower back, and she would not be comforted. The rambling speech returned the next day and her urine went back to being dark, but now even it was darker, a bluish-purple hue and stinking, despite her drinking good amounts of clean fresh water. They prepared a draught that would ease the back pain, which helped a little, but nothing they tried took away the other symptoms. Sister Ciar prayed almost continuously.

As the days passed the Queen's symptoms changed – added to the pain in her back, which had now spread, she was both feverish and frequently shivering, often complaining of the cold, while her forehead burned. The strength she had regained was lost again, she trembled and complained of being tired, though she did little more than lie in bed.

The King called Nuala and Sister Ciar to stand before him, 'Why is my Affraic sick again? I thought she was cured!'

'We cannot say, sometimes ... ' Sister Ciar began.

'Has a curse been laid on my wife? Is that it?' he said, his voice sounding strangled.

Sister Ciar straightened and said clearly, 'My lord King, only God had the power over life and death!' Then she continued, more softly, 'But maybe, maybe God just wanted the Queen, your Affraic, to be at Dominica's baptism, and had healed her for that occasion alone.'

The King didn't look as if he wanted to believe her – but he gave a nod and turned away from them.

A few days later, the Queen's face, hands and feet puffed up, as if stuffed with food, when in reality she couldn't even bear to eat a thing as she said everything tasted foul. Within hours she was vomiting liquids – and even in that, there was a strong stench like that of urine.

'I have seen these signs before, they signal the end, it seems God is ready to take the Queen into his care,' Sister Ciar said sadly. 'I will go to the King to prepare him.'

Chapter 4
Muirenn - circa AD 668

After the funeral King Conall could not think clearly let alone live with the children near him. Whenever he saw the babe the anguish of losing Affraic, the woman he had fallen in love with even before they had been matched, would come back to him. It was no use, he decided to send the babe and Indract, both, to stay with Nuala and her daughter. Dominica still needed the wet-nurse, and Nuala was as trustworthy as any to care for young children and they would always be nearby anyway.

Besides, Conall now had other pressing matters of the kingdom to deal with. He'd already had a message from King Caipre of the Ui-Liathain clan, urging a treaty, to stop the cattle-raiding between their peoples. Caipre offered an alliance, sealed with a marriage to his daughter.

Conall pleaded that he was in mourning but the response from King Caipre had been 'treaty first, there is always time later for mourning', and a reminder of the value of 'being united against the common enemies'. So it was that just six moons after they had laid Affraic in the ground King Conall set off to visit the Ui-Liathain - accompanied by his best warriors, their leather gleaming, their weapons sharp - just in case.

He need not have feared for Caipre was truly seeking a treaty not a fight, as they rode up they were welcomed with open arms, showing no weapons were held, and on foot. Conall dismounted and the kings clasped each other in a friendly embrace. Once they were in King Caipre's court house, food and drink were brought and then the Drom-Eanaigh party were told that there would be a feast in King Conall's honour later, but for now they were invited to a guest house, to rest and clean the dirt from their journey.

When later they all returned to the king's court house, now set up for the feast, King Caipre introduced Conall to his queen, Cobblaith, and his sons; Baetan, Cuan, and Faelan, and his daughters; Conchenn, Muirenn and Sheenagh. Each bowed before retiring to sit around in a circle. Food and mead were brought - with no talk of business allowed until after the feasting. Conall could not help but glance at the middle daughter, Muirenn, her red-gold hair framed a sweetheart face, with skin like milk. The elder daughter, Conchenn was beautiful too, but tall and dark and so all too reminiscent of his beloved Affraic. Indeed, he found he could not look at her without thinking of what he'd lost.

At the end of the feast, King Caipre dismissed everyone, leaving only himself and Conall.

'Come now, let's talk about marriage and unity,' he said.

Conall leant back, showing his upturned palm to indicate that Caipre was to speak first.

'I am tired of having to defend the border with you, I admit I have enough problems coming from Ui Maic-Caille, but they are savages, and who would want to marry with them? To seal our alliance I would offer you my eldest daughter, my beloved girl, Conchenn. Accomplished, she can both read and write, and she is devout and knows how to be a queen,' he raised one eyebrow.

'Conchenn ... is indeed lovely. And a blessing to you. But, please, understand, she reminds me of my loss.'

'A good woman will help you overcome your loss ...' began Caipre

'You misunderstand me, when I look upon Conchenn I am reminded of my lovely queen Affraic.'

'All the better then, surely,' cut in Caipre.

'No! It cuts me to the quick. She is too close in resemblance – tall and dark of hair – whereas, your middle daughter, Muirenn, she does not remind me of Affraic at all, and is lovely in her own way.'

Caipre sat back, his brow furrowed, 'I'm not sure she is ready to marry yet,' he said, 'she is old enough but not accomplished in ways that Conchenn is.'

'That is as may be,' began Conall, finding that the more Caipre pushed for Conchenn, the more he wanted Muirenn, 'but I cannot grieve every time I turn to my new wife. It will be Muirenn or none.'

'Then we will talk with Muirenn and see what she thinks of the proposal - don't look like that - I love my daughters too much to give them no say when there are alternatives, but she is a God fearing woman and will listen to my wishes attentively.'

After further negotiations it was decided that Caipre, Cobblaith and Muirenn would pay a visit to Drom-Eanaigh before decisions would be made. Conall returned to Drom-Eanaigh and set about preparing the his court for the visit. In the days that followed buildings were repaired, animal pens taken down and rebuilt outside the fortifications, ways made wider and cleaner, despite it being the muddy end of spring. Inside the court the late Queen's rooms were redecorated, cleaned and hung with new carpets brought in by traders from distant lands. Wines from across the sea were obtained and their amphorae stood in a line, waiting for the visit.

As the great feast of Pascha approached, celebrating the risen Christ, so did the day of the visit. Indract was moved back to the King's household and placed in with his older brothers under the care of a servant woman for his well-being. He was now four years old, and quiet around his brothers who were so much older, even the younger one more than twice his age, and so different from him. They were full of teasing and pranks and would launch themselves upon each other and wrestle until they laughed. Even when they were gentle with Indract he was no match for them and usually ended up in tears. Tears, it seemed were not acceptable to them or anyone else, and resulted in teasing and mocking. When things got too much for him he would sneak out and run to Nuala's house, where they would be kind to him, give him sweet things to eat and then take him back to his place in the court.

The King commanded the whole court be decorated for the day of the arrival of the Ui-Liathain royal party as it had last been for Dominica's baptism, so once again flowers edged the thatches, and sweet herb plants were strewn where walking on them would release their perfume.

Conall felt nervous as no king need be, but in his mind's eye the beauty of Muirenn had increased. He thought about her far more than he expected, and the notion that she might refuse him caused him consternation. He had scouts stationed along the route, with orders to ride back fast when they saw King Caipre's entourage approach, so that he could be ready to receive them. In the event, a scout came flying in through the gates just as the sun touched the distant hill.

Just as King Caipre had, Conall met the party at the gate to the lys, he and his men on foot. He welcomed them and led them through to a newly built house, set aside for their use, furnished with the best he had. He bade them refresh themselves and invited them to join him in his king's court house when they were ready, all the while stealing looks at Muirenn, looking radiant yet humble in a simple hooded riding brat over her dress.

The feast that night had to be modest, by reason of it still being the Lenten season. Yet Conall made sure that every luxury that could be allowed was included. Muirenn was as beautiful as he'd recalled. She was also quiet and modestly glanced away if she saw him looking her way. He began to be concerned that she was not keen on the match, and even saw himself as he might appear in her eyes, a man much older than her, not quite as old as her father but, even so. And Caipre had said he would let her have her say on the matter.

Next morning dawned bright and clear - showing Drom-Eanaigh at its best. The morning began with a service for Pascha in the king's chapel, to celebrate the resurrection of Christ, after which the day became joyful as gifts of dyed eggs marked with a cross were given to children and a good breakfast was had by all.

Afterwards Conall offered to show the party around Drom-Eanaigh, but King Caipre said he'd rather rest and that Conall should take Muirenn on a tour, accompanied by one of her ladies, of course. Conall couldn't have asked for more, and led Muirenn out of his court house and around the inner courtyard, which was still looking flower-bedecked and festive.

'All the houses and buildings inside this area are solely for the use of my court and the families of my best men. In the outer court are the homes of my ollomain, we have many skilled in poetry, in music, in our histories and in law. The Deisi are good people, devout, hard-working and hard fighting people, I keep the best nearby the court.'

'The flowers are a pretty thought,' she remarked.

'In your honour,' Conall smiled, and led her onto the rampart and round to the view where the bank and palisade stood above the steep slope that led down to the bank of the river behind the fort.

This view was always magnificent - you could see right across to the hills and mountains showing hazy blue in the far distance. Then deep below the river flowed dark and wide, living up to its name of the Great River. Another turn had them looking towards the monastery, across the wide valley that the stream had caused as it wound its way to the Great River, and even from here the monastery church, a substantial tall building, was impressive. 'We have close ties with the monastery, my uncle is Abbot there,' Conall explained, 'and my daughter will go there when old enough.'

'And do you have your wedding ceremonies there?'

'We haven't,' Conall began, he turned to look at Muirenn. Was she suggesting their marriage vows should be taken there? She blushed prettily as if reading his mind. 'But I see no reason why not?' he finished.

He guided her further round. Below the stronghold another area was set around with a low stone bank. Within this were huts with smoke pouring from them and the sound of metal being beaten, others had large pits beside them. There were more huts further down the hill, where the stream meandered, and where linen could be seen stretched out beside the stream. These were working areas, and a place where livestock could be gathered and defended from cattle-raids, Conall explained. Almost back to the gate Conall paused, pointing out how the land to the north and east was fertile and well farmed. A number of smaller earth-banked raths visible in this area sheltered one or two homes with smaller outbuildings, showing a prosperity and a number of men of goodly rank, all living under the protection of the King of Drom-Eanaigh.

Muirenn gazed across the landscape as if she just thought it wonderful. Her eyes were smiling as she turned to Conall. 'It is a beautiful land, though I would miss the sea,' she said, leaving Conall none the wiser as to her intentions; leaving him still feeling on edge.

After the Pascha feast Caipre took Conall aside, until they too were walking the ramparts.

'So, this is where you brought my daughter to do your wooing?'

'Well, I suppose I hoped the land would speak for itself.'

'But *you* didn't speak for yourself! My Muirenn says you did not speak of how you favoured her, or wanted her to be your wife. You left her wondering whose choice she was, mine or yours.'

'But, she's my choice. I thought I had made that clear to you before?'

'To me, yes,' Caipre laughed, 'But I did not tell her that!'

'And I didn't know of your omission!' Conall gritted his teeth, he didn't like the turn this was taking, and certainly didn't like being laughed at in his own court, 'besides, I am much out of practice in wooing, having been completely content with my beautiful late wife for many years.' This was a jab back as it was well-known that Caipre had sired many children on women that were not his wife.

'Don't take on so! You have until we depart to convince her!' Caipre laughed.

So it was that Conall once again walked with Muirenn, the lady accompanying them still keeping well back.

'You recall when I came to your home, and was introduced to you all?' he began, she nodded in reply. 'It was then, when I first set eyes upon you, that I knew I wanted you to be my wife. Why your father did not tell you of this I do not know. He would have your older sister wed to me, but I asked for your hand, yours alone, sweetest Muirenn. I will do anything I can to make you happy here. We can have a good life, it is a prosperous place, and the court can be merry when we have good things to celebrate - and you may bring your own ladies with you for company - will you consent to be my wife?'

'My father told me he had made the arrangement to align our courts, but said I would be able to make my own final decision,' she said quietly. She gazed out across the great river. Conall gazed at her, willing her to say yes. After a long pause she turned her pale eyes towards him, 'I decide, yes, my Lord. Yes, I will wed you.'

Chapter 5
A Wedding *circa - 668 - 669*

The bridal party was accompanied by many cattle being driven into a special area fenced off for them. These were Muirenn's cattle, not a gift to her husband to be – her wealth that she kept with her as she moved on to be a Queen.

The ceremony was to take place in the Abbey Church and she would stay in a newly built round-house of her own on the days before the wedding.

Conall thought back to his first wedding. It had been far simpler than this one, with the ceremony held in the King's chapel, under the watchful eye of his father. His father had arranged the marriage – but he and Affraic had already known each other, had met on many occasions and had both been longing for the match. They hadn't really thought about estate, though Affraic had her cattle-worth brought into the Drom-Eanaigh herd as was customary, and continued to be customary, their line belonged to her children and not to him. *That* wedding had been simple and joyful – this one seemed to be getting more complicated by the day.

The Abbey had to be the venue, Muirenn was definite about that. The Abbot had been less keen and it had taken a substantial gift for the way to be smoothed. Then Muirenn wanted musicians, both in the Abbey and in the court to entertain the guests, and the guest list kept growing, as she decided she needed to become acquainted with all the neighbouring kings and their wives. She said she knew her place, and the most noble folk from his kingdom should be there too, to acknowledge their new Queen.

The wedding day dawned bright, the autumn colours shining warmly on hill and in vale. The bridal party set off amid orchestrated cheers from the people, riding down to the ford, across and back up to the Abbey. The marriage vows were taken in a quiet and solemn fashion, and Conall took Muirenn as wife. No musicians had been permitted inside the Abbey, but the sisters and brothers sang a holy chant that sufficed.

Once the wedding party was back at Drom-Eanaigh the celebration commenced with all and everything the new queen had desired. Seated at the high table with King Caipre and his wife, Conall looked at his beautiful new wife and rejoiced to be such a lucky man, to have been blessed with marriage to a woman that made him feel so happy.

*

Three moons and Christmas-tide passed and all seemed well in the court. The King was very content with his choice of wife, and she seemed to have settled in well. Conall decided it was time to bring his whole family back together and sent for Nuala. She made a bow before him.

'Nuala, how goes it with Dominica? I see she runs and plays well enough.'

'Yes, my Lord, she is nearly a year and a half old and is good, bright and playful.'

'Then, as my daughter, it is time for her to return to the family and live with her new mother, the Queen, and her ladies.' Nuala felt herself freeze and an ache struck her across her chest. It was hard to know if it was because she loved Dominica and wanted to keep her for herself, or because of an unknown fear for her with the new Queen – Muirenn had not so much as spoken a word to her, even when she and Indract were brought to her to be introduced before the wedding.

'As you wish it, Lord, but maybe, she is still so young and there are no other young children amongst the queen's ladies to give her company, and perhaps the Queen will not want the trouble of caring for her?'

'Nonsense, the Queen is a caring woman, prepare Dominica to return – and as for a company – Indract can return too. He can stay with her until he is ready for training,' Conall said, his annoyance at his order being questioned obvious. Nuala bowed as acquiescence and left.

Indract had been so happy to be returned to Nuala after the Queen's first visit, Nuala wasn't sure whether even he, at five years, would want to go to live with the Queen. Nevertheless, she made the best of it when she prepared them both, telling them of the better things, the rich surroundings, the good food that would be theirs when they went to live with the Queen.

Nuala brought Dominica and Indract dressed in their best to be presented to the Queen, and found the King there too. She bowed low, saying, 'My Lord, my Lady,' she turned to Dominica and Indract, hoping that, as she taught them, they would bow and say the same. Indract, catching her eye, presented a good formal bow, and said, 'Father, my Lord, my Lady.' Dominica stuck her thumb in her mouth and swung her little body from side to side.

'Dominica ...' Nuala said quietly but firmly. Dominica slowed her swing, but then just looked at her feet. 'She is so young yet,' Nuala offered.

Conall turned to Muirenn, 'See, my dear, they will greatly benefit from your teaching and care.'

'I do see,' she said. 'Tomnat, take them into my chamber,' she said addressing one of her ladies. A short dark-haired woman came forward and silently took each child by the hand, tugging Dominica when her little feet seemed to stick to the floor.

Nuala went back to her home in the court. It seemed so empty, too vast for her. Flanna and Coleman had returned to Nuala's holding when Dominica had been weaned, and were living in her old home, caring for her goats and growing what they needed in her plot. Coleman came and went as and when he was needed at the fort. Like many of the king's men when not at war, he practised his skills and went out on patrols when ordered. Brooding on her situation, Nuala tidied the space, though there was not much to be done. Then she fetched her basket, swept her brat over her shoulders and headed out of the court and down to visit her old place.

Coleman was away on a patrol and Flanna was happy to see her mother.

'Mother! Good to see you! But where are the children?'

'The King has decided that the Queen will care for them.'

'And, I can see, you are not happy about that! Come in, tell me what worries you.' For all her failings in learning the lore of plants, Flanna had a kind heart and a good sense of other people's feelings. They sat in the sun with their backs to the wall of the old house each with a wooden drinking bowl in their hands.

'I worry for Domca. You know she is like a ray of sunlight, yet she stood like a little thundercloud, and there wasn't a kind word towards her. I might be wrong. I hope I am wrong, but I do not think she has endeared herself to the Queen and ...'

'And what?'

'It might just be my imagination, but the King, well, he looked at Domca when she came in – but then looked away and didn't truly look at her again.'

*

Muirenn thought that she would give it another month, making it look as if she had really tried. To be honest, she would have gladly given the children straight back to that woman to care for, but she was mindful that they were the King's children and her standing was not sealed until she gave birth, and that seemed likely to be no-time soon as her bleeding had started again. She was frustrated to tears and as usual her ladies comforted her, made all sorts of excuses, the move, the excitement, the water, the food – anything they could think of to make her feel better that she would not be carrying news of a baby on the way.

Muirenn had already tried talking to the King about having to look after the children; 'I am as kind as a mother to him but he does little but whine – the boy is a milksop – surely he would be better being with his older brothers now, so that he can grow up,' she had said of Indract, who, indeed had been whiny and sad. And of Dominica, 'I am as gentle as a mother to her, but she only gives me hard looks – anyone would think she blames me for her mother's death – instead of herself.' That had been a step too far, she realised, as a shadow had, for a moment, passed over Conall's features. She'd forgotten herself - forgotten that he had loved his late wife.

After a while she tried another tack, she complained, in guise of fear, that Indract had 'run-away, telling no-one where he went – and she had been fearful for his life!' She well knew that he had just run round to the wise-woman's place, no doubt to be fussed over and given sweetmeats, and she had brought him back – but the fact was he *had* run away.

Something her ladies said started an idea in her mind. Excuses and reasons. When the next month there were the usual cramping pains she made up her mind. When the ladies again found reasons for her failure to become pregnant, she mused aloud, wondered, whether having other babies around was good or bad for the chance to become with child. It didn't take much for someone to say, 'Oh, yes! I've heard that, having a young baby prevented a new child being conceived', and that idea - fanned into a flame – became the tale that the young children of a dead mother would, somehow, prevent a new child being born. Muirenn smiled secretly to herself when she heard the idea, the rumour, the old-wives-tale, being sported around the court.

After a particularly pleasant coupling Muirenn stroked Conall's chest and murmured to him, 'They say that the reason we have no child starting is because such young children of another wife are too close to me.'

'They? Who are 'they'?'

'Oh, you know, it is old folk-lore, and is known to be true in so many cases, ask anyone in the court.'

'Why do you believe these tales?'

'Because, because, I am sure there is something. Month after month I bleed, yet I am fit and young and you – are so virile,' she paused to kiss him, 'I cannot tell what, but sometimes I feel that Dominica curses me – she stares at me with such a look – they say it is why we have no child of our own.'

'They again?'

'They? Oh, my ladies - they have seen her, and she is still so young it could be true?' Her hand swept down his chest and came to rest on the top of his thigh. Conall moved and adjusted himself a little, 'Send them away, my King, and you will see, for half a year, try it for just half a year - and all will be good between us and God will bless us,' she said sliding her body onto his.

Chapter 6
***Cairech** - circa AD 670*

Over the next few days Conall had discreet questions asked about these folk-lore tales, and Muirenn's words were confirmed. Meanwhile Muirenn wasn't herself. He couldn't say she was sulking but her smiles seemed short or rare. But when he came to her and said, 'I will send them back to the wise-woman for their care,' like the sun from behind a cloud, Muirenn's face changed back to that of an angel, and he found himself relieved.

'And you'll send that woman away - out of the Royal court? She has her own place does she not - by the ford?'

King Conall looked at his beautiful young wife. He hadn't realised she'd learnt about such mundane things.

'Yes, she has, but her son-in-law lives there now. She has lived here for the past few years, and we all benefit from her care.'

'She can still do that,' Muirenn smiled sweetly, 'we can call her if we need her - but we don't actually need her type *within* our court walls, do we?'

'I'll think on it,' he said slowly.

'Send men to Nuala the wise-woman's old home down by the ford.' Conall commanded his steward the next day, 'Restore the main house Coleman and his family live in, build her two more houses, one for her with three bays and one for her medicines, as she has here - then make it all defensible, a ditch and bank with palisade, and a gate that can be barred,' he added, thinking it must be a safe place for his children, 'And a shelter for a guard to live in, a stable and store houses.'

'Yes, sire, when do you want this done?'

'Now man! Send enough men to make it complete by the new moon.'

'My Lord.'

'And send Nuala to me – I will tell her what must be done.'

'Sire?' Nuala bowed low to the King.

He sighed. 'It is time for you to return to your own home. I have ordered it restored and a new place for yourself, with a healer's hut, as you have here. I will also give you a servant to do the heavy work for you. You are to take care of Indract and Dominica for now, they will live with you, at least until after the Queen has a child of her own.' He looked hard at Nuala to see if she divined the reason behind the orders – and saw a flash of recognition in her eyes. This woman must know of the old-wives tales as well as any.

'As you will, sire.'

'Whatever you need to care for them will be given. Remind them often that they are still of the Royal household and merely in your care. I will arrange all other matters for them, you understand?'

'I do, sire. When will this happen?'

'As soon as the building is complete – I have set many men onto it. It should be done by the next new moon.'

'Thank you, sire,' Nuala nodded, 'May I go now to collect plants from my herb-bed there, I will need them for the future and they may be lost in the building work.'

'Yes, do it quickly. Your son-in-law and his family will come back to live in the court with you while work is being done - they can help you.'

'I will, I shall go today, my Lord.' It would be a relief to be home in some ways – she would not have to walk so far to find the herbs she needed and the peace of her old place would be welcome. Inside the royal compound was always busy and in the summer filled with dust or, in the winter, with mud. But she was concerned that the new Queen had really taken a dislike to the children – and even to herself – and that did not bode well.

Just after the new moon the King sent notice that the new compound was complete, and Nuala and her family set off to their new home. She had watched from a distance how the plot that had been her simple home, became something much larger, something that only the land-owners and lesser nobles had – and, indeed, even more than some of those as the palisade was raised on the earthen rath.

She carried a large basket with food for the day and held Dominica's hand to help her walk along. Indract followed with Flanna and her family, most carrying something – though any weighty possessions were on a cart following on. It wasn't that far - the King's court could still be seen on the rise way behind them, and the Monastery matching it across the valley.

Nuala surveyed her old home as she approached. Where before there had only been her hut and a small shelter for animals, now stood a small-scale lys, a miniature fort.

As she stepped inside the gateway she smiled at her old home, now freshly thatched and newly daubed and washed in a dusky pink, ready for Flanna, Coleman and their growing brood. She noticed the other new buildings, a slightly smaller round-house also washed in pink, a smaller place for her herbs and potions, washed white, as was a long lean-to shelter beside the gate, meant for the servant, Dugan, that King Conall had sent with them. Then, almost all around the inside of the rath, were more storage areas, the top of which also formed a raised walk-way, so those inside could see out over the tall palisade of sharpened stakes.

'It's a grand job they've made of it,' Flanna said, returning from her mother's old house.

Nuala smiled, 'I'm glad you are happy - and Coleman?'

'Oh, he's happy enough,' laughed Flanna, 'he's all for the quiet life.' Coleman, her husband and already one of the King's warriors, was to be a guard on his own home, employed by the King to defend the place should anyone think a king's children were easy pickings for ransom. He'd have a second warrior sent down each night to support him, and Dugan was to help in daylight hours being an old warrior himself, should it come to it. There was even a beacon set up to alert the king's court day or night of any trouble, though it would be a rash raiding party that tried anything in the daylight as the new place was within sight of the court where lookouts were always posted and from where warriors on fast ponies were sure to arrive quickly.

Nuala and the royal children soon settled into life outside the court. As she had been bid, each Sunday she took them up to the King's chapel for prayers, and each Sunday she reminded them who they were, like a catechism. 'Who are you?' she would ask, and the children replied, 'We are Indract and Dominica, son and daughter of King Conall Ua-Faelain, a king of the Deisi, loyal king to the High King of Muman'. Though in truth it was mostly Indract and even him saying his sister's name as Domca, and Dominica saying bits here and there, but Nuala felt her duty was done.

Nuala found it pleasant living with the two young children again and taught them as she worked. Indract was not so interested in everyday whys and wherefores, but loved to collect things; stones from the stream, snail shells, types of seed-pods, always finding something interesting in them that no one else did. But this could be helpful, if she showed him a herb and asked him to find more he was assiduous in his searches and always found more than even she knew grew locally.

Dominica followed Nuala, lamb like, thumb in her mouth, always wanting to be in her skirts, seeing what she was doing, pointing her little fingers and asking all the time 'what's that?' and 'why?' What surprised and delighted Nuala was that, later, she seemed to remember everything she had been told, for when she turned three summers, she began to speak clearly, telling Nuala the names of the herbs and what they were used for as they gathered them.

Outside both children played with Brannon, Flanna's child born just before Dominica, a flame-haired little boy, stocky and freckled whereas Dominica and Indract were dark and grew tall like the willow. Their games were childish; chasing one another, building houses with sticks and throwing stones into pools, but this suited Indract, who had not enjoyed the short time he'd been in the court with his much older brothers. They had teased him and their play-fighting had frightened him, though they had laughed and tickled him too, he preferred gentle play.

The three children each had a toy they loved, a stick-horse which Dugan had made. He'd found sticks with one much larger end and had carved, into this part, a horse's head. Then Nuala had added reins woven from wool. The children would go riding on their stick-mounts outside the compound, yet under Dugan's watchful eye, Indract, as the eldest, in the lead, planning where they were going and what they would be doing.

Occasionally the King would ride by and call upon Nuala asking how their health fared. One day, just after the celebration of Samhain and just before Indract's seventh birthday, he called to see him alone.

'Indract, now remember, you are a prince of Muman, it won't be long now before you will return to the court to learn to be a warrior,' Conall said thinking of Muirenn's gently swelling belly.

'Yes, sire,' Indract said, looking at the ground.

'Look up boy! You are a prince – behave like one and look at me – your father - not your feet!'

Indract looked up, as far as his father's mouth, mumbling, 'Yes, father.'

'At me! You'll not make a warrior if you can't look a man in the eye.'

'Don't want to be,' Indract burst out, looking his father right in the eyes.

'Don't be stupid! You are a prince of Muman and you need to be a warrior.'

'My brothers can do that! I don't want to – I want ...'

'Want! Want? You will do as you are told!'

'Nuala, I warned you that the children were to be brought up as royal children - that they had to know their duty.'

'Yes, sire. I have made sure they know who they are. My Lord, ask them yourself, they can tell you that they are your son and daughter – children of your royal family,' Nuala said.

'Yet Indract doesn't want to be a warrior – and he behaves like a slave.'

'He has learnt respect sire, that is all. He knows you are both his father and his King and shows you respect,' she hesitated a moment then plunged on, 'Maybe, sire, he is not made for battle – he even shies from rough play with Brannon, instead he takes great care in observation and ritual. Maybe, sire, as your third son, he is instead called to serve you by serving God?'

King Conall looked at her for a long moment. 'He prays?'

'Dutifully for you every day and ...'

'And ... woman?'

'And he makes up his own prayers, perfectly proper prayers that he commits to memory, for I have heard them more than once.'

'Hmm,' Conall turned a full circle, returning to face Nuala, 'And Dominica?'

'Grows apace, she has a quick mind and a good memory,'

'Is it time for her to have teaching from the Abbey?'

'Possibly, if one of the sisters could come here it would work, maybe they both could take lessons?'

'Maybe, maybe,' Conall said, wondering if his prayers were being answered at any rate.

'And Dominica? Will you see her?'

'Not today, maybe later, after ...' he left the rest unsaid. The child when last seen showed signs of being as beautiful as his first wife had been, her black hair and her clear blue eyes shining Affraic's soul out at him. Maybe after his new child was born to Muirenn, maybe then he'd be able to face Dominica.

*

He had never heard a woman scream so, not even Affraic that last time when everything had gone wrong. Muirenn had with her a woman from the Ui-Liathain, an old woman who had helped at the birth of Muirenn's father, it was said. He paced, thinking to himself he should be past this worrying. This was women's work, he would be as well to get drunk and find out about it all later. It was no use, he had to know, once again he found himself standing at the closed door, hearing screams and demanding to know what was wrong. No one answered. He thumped against the post again, and this time a woman he did not recognise opened the door a crack.

'What is the problem?' he asked.

'Nothing you can help with sire,' she said and made to close the door. He put his hand to it and stopped it closing.

'Do you need the wise-woman here – I can send for her?'

The door flew open and the wizened old woman stood there, her eyes bright and piercing. 'I am all the wise-woman needed sire. Now leave this place – your presence is affecting the Queen and she cannot give birth and think about you!' With that, the door was pushed shut and something or someone leant against it.

They found the King asleep with his best warriors in his court house. The fire had burned away, the flagons were empty, drinking horns lying on their sides. They slept where they had sat down, slumped against each other.

'Sire, sire?' a hand gently touched his arm. 'Sire, the babe is born.'

‘What?’ Conall stumbled, ‘Wha? Oh, the bairn?’

‘Come sire – the wise-woman says you may come now.’

‘Is all well?’ Conall said, struggling to his feet and pulling a hand across his face to check it was still there.

‘Yes, sire, praise God.’

Muirenn was sitting up in bed, her hair had been done and her face looked fresh and beautiful. Tucked in the nook of her arm was the babe, wrapped tightly but the top of its head showing a down of pale rose-gold. Conall felt the dregs of the ale in his mouth, the grime of the day and night in the corners of his eyes, and wished he’d delayed enough to freshen up.

‘Ah, my Lord, come and see your beautiful daughter,’ Muirenn said, no sign that she’d been screaming with pain not eight hours since. Conall looked on as Muirenn pulled the cloth from around the babe’s face. A face so pale, set with a rosebud of a mouth, lips pursed - his heart squeezed with love.

‘Beautiful,’ he said, he looked at Muirenn, ‘beautiful,’ he said again. Muirenn smiled happily.

*

Three moons passed, the child had been baptised at the Abbey and named Cairech, and all was settled at the court when Conall announced that it was time for his son and daughter, Indract and Dominica, to return.

Muirenn looked unhappy at the idea but could find no further cause for delay, saying only that she could not care for them, being too occupied with Cairech. They would need a woman to look after them. Conall said for it not to trouble her, and sent for Nuala, Indract and Dominica to return.

Nuala was also unhappy; she now had no wish to return to the court, but had little choice. A house was made ready and the return journey was made, with Conall sending his men to help bring whatever she needed with her.

They settled into life back into the royal court, with Indract becoming quieter and quieter, and Dominica staying closer to Nuala than ever.

One summer evening, Cairech, now four moons old, would not settle, her cries becoming whimpers as she coughed and wheezed. Her little face was bright red, her forehead hot to the touch.

'What is it?' Muirenn asked the women, 'She was good this morning, was she not?' They shook their heads, they did not know, but such things happened to children, to babies, and were sometimes fatal.

'Send for the wise-woman,' one suggested, wishing the old midwife had not returned to the Ui-Liathain.

'Oh, her? I don't trust her – they say she was the one who killed the last queen,' Muirenn sniped.

'No, no, where did you hear that? That's wrong – she saved her, at least at the birth,' another said.

'See, even you agree. Is there no-one else?'

'It would take hours to get someone else, and Nuala is here in the court.'

'Very well, send for her,' the Queen sighed, 'I cannot bear to hear Cairech cry any more.'

Nuala came into the room, and bowed extra low to Muirenn, 'Lady?'

'Help Cairech, if you can. She is so hot, and cries so pitifully.'

As Nuala moved forward, they saw that she was followed by Dominica, holding on to her dress. Nuala bent over the crib and placed a hand on the babe's forehead. With all eyes watching her, she removed layers of covers and picked up the child, then taking her to the wind-hole she hooked up the covering, letting in the light and fresh air. All the while Cairech whimpered.

'When did she last feed?' Nuala said turning to the Queen. Muirenn turned to a woman in the dark-side of the room and asked, 'Well?'

'Before noon, Lady. She wouldn't take any more after.'

'She has a fever, and maybe a sickness. Are you well woman?' Nuala said addressing the woman in the shadows. The wet-nurse stepped forward, it was obvious she was not well - her face had a sickly sheen.

'Leave the room ... in fact, that goes for all of you, leave,' Nuala said firmly.

'I'll not leave you with Cairech alone, I will stay,' Muirenn said.

'As you wish,' Nuala said as she placed the limp child back into the crib.

'What are you going to do?'

'Try to get some healthy liquid into the child – are you dry?'

Muirenn looked away, 'Yes,' she murmured. She'd deliberately handed over to a wet-nurse to return her body to normal as soon as she could. She had hated the bloated feeling, the leaking and the dependence, though she loved her daughter dearly she'd also been told that the sooner she stopped feeding the more likely she'd be to conceive the son who would secure her place and her family in this kingdom.

'Then send your ladies to see if there is another woman locally who can wet-nurse, right now. Someone healthy! Failing that, have them bring fresh goat's milk, boiled then cooled quickly.' In the meantime I will bathe her to bring down her fever.'

As it got dark outside Muirenn left them, saying she was going to pray. By the morning Nuala's eyes were heavy, she had bathed the babe, and then had dripped cooled boiled goat's milk into her mouth, so each drop was swallowed easily, all through the long hours. The crying had stopped, but that was not always a good sign, Cairech no longer felt hot but each breath sounded laboured, a rasping wheeze. Nuala's head drooped and she rested it a moment on her arm ... and slept.

She startled awake - before her she saw Dominica's small hands hovering close over the babe's face and, simultaneously, heard the door scrape open.

'No! No! No!' Muirenn screeched as she raced across the room, her eyes wide and angry, she slapped Dominica so hard that her little feet left the floor and she landed heavily in a heap – Nuala reacted immediately, gathering the small girl up to protect her from Muirenn whose arm was already raised again.

'Didn't you see?' shrieked Muirenn in Nuala's face, 'Little witch! She was smothering her! And you? You let her! What have you done to my Cairech?'

Only then did she look at her babe - the infant's previously flushed skin was now normal, her breathing steady and sweet. 'Oh?'

'Sleeping peacefully, Lady, the fever broke sometime in the early dawn,' Nuala said, though wondering when the painful wheezing in the little chest had ceased.

Muirenn stared at her, dislike written all across her face, 'Well, praise God, my prayers were answered then! So now you can go, and take that little witch with you. I know what I saw! I saw her, I saw what she was trying to do – my child is not safe with *her* in this place, so get out now! Get out!'

Chapter 7
Dugan - circa AD 670 - 675

Nuala was brought before King Conall by an escort of two warriors. As soon as she was brought in he dismissed them.

'Nuala, my wife brings accusations against you – and against Dominica.'

'What of, sire?' she asked, feeling sick to her stomach.

'That you would harm Cairech - that Dominica is jealous and would harm Cairech.'

'Sire, I did all in my power to heal the child, and it worked. Dominica says she was praying for the babe – that her hands were not even touching the babe's face, just feeling the breath. I do not think, sire, that she has the guile at such a young age to make up a lie such as that.'

'Hmm, well, I would believe you, both, but I am going to have to return you to your own compound, for your own safety ... and my peace. I have thought on what you have said about Indract and deem it possible. I will send gifts to the Abbey and ask them to send a teacher to your compound to begin their studies after next Pascha.'

Nuala smiled and bowed as she said, 'As you wish it, sire.' She was glad to be going out of harm's way and back to where she preferred to be.

*

The gifts sent to the Abbey, it seemed, included a pony, too old for war but sure-footed and able to carry a sister from the Abbey down to Nuala's compound daily. Sister Magda arrived the first day after the Pascha celebrations, unheralded, except by the compound's dogs, and rode up to the gate. Dugan, recognising one of the Holy Sisters, helped her dismount and took the pony off to care for it. Nuala, hearing the commotion, stepped out of her healer's hut into the bright daylight to see the sister turning this way and that, observing all.

'Sister!' she said, 'Welcome! Am I right in thinking you are here to teach the King's children?'

'I am. Sister Magda,' she touched her simple wooden cross, 'and you must be Nuala?'

'I am, please, come and take a drink, a herb brew?' Nuala said, leading the way towards her own hut.

'Thank you. Where are the King's children?'

'Out, playing with Brannon, my grandson, watched by his mother, they are safe.'

With a bowl of drink in their hands they wandered out to where they could see the children grouped around something they were playing with in the grass.

'Tell me a little about them,' Magda said, lifting her chin a touch towards the children.

'You know their history, about their mother?'

Magda nodded.

'Since Dominica's birth they have been with me, on and off. I confess I love them as my own. Indract is eight years. His father would have him learning to be a warrior but he is a gentle boy, more interested in studying things than playing rough, and he is devout in his own way. Dominica was four last summer and, as you know, is already promised to the church when she reaches fourteen.'

'A little late.'

'It was her mother's wish and King Conall will abide by it. She is quick, learns well and is always trying to help.'

'Not bad qualities in a girl.'

'No, indeed. When shall you want them for lessons, they each have their chores to do too.'

'Chores for the King's children?' Magda queried with a smile.

'I believe it is good for them, keeps their feet on the ground,' Nuala said, looking defiantly at Magda, then adding, 'but you agree, I can tell.'

She was rewarded with an emphatic nod. 'Humility is a virtue, and our Lord calls us to serve.'

As neither child could read or write Magda had them begin their studies together. She would sit between them by the door of the hut, and turn from one to the other. Sometimes she made them write in the earth with sticks or fingers, sometimes she gave them a slate smeared with mud and made them use the quill of a feather to make their marks. Nuala would hear them chanting back lines that Magda gave them to say. Later Magda would write lines for them to learn. It was the first time that Nuala had seen the mysterious words of the Our Father written down; all the ordinary people only learnt them by heart.

As the summer came Magda moved their classroom out of the hut to the shade of a large willow tree beside the stream. They had been using this new space for a week or two when Brannon fell from the branches. He was unhurt, barring a scrape and a bump on his elbow, but Magda was angry with him for 'scaring the life out of her', as she put it. He stood there sheepishly rubbing his elbow until she told him to go away.

His face turned crimson and he folded his scrawny arms, saying, 'No, I want to learn, I can tell you the letters, I want to know the words, the Lord's words!'

Magda was so surprised, for the second time in as few minutes, that she laughed. 'Go on then,' she said, writing a letter on the mud-slate.

'It's an *ah*,' he stared back defiantly, 'and the next to come is *bay*, then *kay*.'

'Oh, and how would you be knowing that?'

'Domca shows me - but I want to learn all the mysteries.'

Magda looked at Dominica, who blushed under her scrutiny, 'I see, and your mother and father, do they not want you to be a warrior or a farmer?'

'Dunno,' he looked up at Magda, 'but they've others to do that.'

Magda smiled, 'I will speak to them, and if they are happy, yes, young Brannon, you may learn the words of God.'

***

'Mother Nuala,' Dominica said one day, when she was just about eight years old, 'why does Dugan carry a dark bag in his belly?'

'Dugan? I don't know what you mean child - he carries no bag on his girdle, only his knife.'

'No, it is inside him, a dark bag and it grieves him.'

'Well, it's true he has asked if there is anything I can do to help the burn in his gullet, and that is linked to the belly.'

'It is not a good thing. Mother Nuala, I can feel his pain when he helps me up on to the pony.'

'I'm sure you can,' she said, eyeing Dominica as if it were the first time she had seen her, 'I'll see if I can do anything.'

'Dominica, come here child,' Nuala said later as she sat by the fireside. Dominica came from where she was sewing by the light of the doorway to sit beside Nuala.

Nuala smiled before saying, 'I spoke to Dugan today and you are right, he is troubled by a pain, and so I felt his belly to find the place the pain comes from. Dominica, he has a hard lump inside of him. I have felt these before. There is seldom anything I can do, though sometimes, just sometimes, the herbs may make it shrink or be less painful, more often than not the lump grows until it kills the man.'

'Can't we pray that the Lord takes away the lump – like in the Holy Book?'

'We are not our Lord, are we?'

'But Sister Magda says that all his disciples were sent out to preach the word *and* heal the sick.'

‘That is as maybe, but I am not even as holy as Sister Magda ...’

‘Can we try the herbs mother, Dugan is a good man.’

‘I can try those and you should be with me when I give them. You can say your prayers for his healing – as you saw his pain.’

Dugan came into Nuala’s healer's hut and gazed around at the bench with her grinding stones on it, the bunches of herbs, and the pattern-marked leather pouches, hanging from the roof. In all the years he’d been with them he’d not once stepped into this hut as Nuala forbade anyone, except herself and Dominica, from entering. Over the central fire steamed a metal pot, fragrant with herbs.

‘Dugan, be seated, I have a potion for you that may ease the pain,’ Nuala said, her voice melodious and soothing. Dominica loved to hear it, so reassuring, so gentle and yet, at the heart, something strong.

‘Yes, willingly, if you can help at all,’ easing himself down on to the low stool.

‘Here, lift your leine, I will rub some of this salve on to your belly. Do you feel how it is cooling?’ Dugan nodded, the aroma of mint filled the air. ‘Now take this, drink it all but make it last twelve sips, one for each of the Apostles, while Dominica prays to our Lord for your healing.’

He looked up from the bowl he was about to drink from to see Dominica emerge from the shadows, with her palms pressed vertically flat together as Sister Magda had shown her how to pray, before going to stand behind him.

Dominica closed her eyes and began to pray, her voice very small, her rehearsed lines hesitant, ‘Dear Lord who healed beside Galilee, hear our prayer and heal our friend Dugan here today.’ All of a rush she felt herself warm-up from head to toe and her hands drifted apart and turned palm upwards. Her voice suddenly became stronger and vibrant, ‘Lord God, Father of all mankind, Jesus Christ, saviour of all mankind, Holy Spirit guider of all mankind –

reach out your hand now and touch your servant Dugan, restore him to health,' Her hands lifted, the hollows of her palms felt filled with pools of heat, then they came together, as if cupped in a space over his head. 'In the name of the Father, the Son and the Holy Spirit, glory be to God, now and forever, Amen.' Her hands tipped towards each other, as if pouring something from them.

The silence after she stopped speaking was resounding, the crackle from the fire the only thing to dare to fill the void. Dugan brought the bowl down from his lips – his eyes were wet with tears. 'I felt it move, inside me,' he whispered. 'The pain, it slipped away.'

'Thanks be to God,' whispered Nuala, still looking at Dominica – the child standing stock still as if in a trance with her hands, now palms down, hovering just over his head.

With a long inhalation she seemed to come to herself and, quickly, as if she didn't know why her hands were outstretched she brought them back together into the pious prayer stance.

Nuala wondered whether she should say anything to Dominica, or not. She had never seen anything like it. The child had seemed to make the dark space inside the hut light up. She had heard of the healing power of the Holy Spirit but she had also been told of how the old healers, the heathen druids, had raised their hands to the skies and called upon their gods to bring healing. She decided to bide her time, and speak only if she thought danger might come towards Dominica. After all, she had been the only witness; Dugan had only heard the girl's voice.

Chapter 8

Brother Indract - *circa AD 676*

The years passed. The Queen had other children, two sons; Caipre and Quillan, and she was well pleased with herself and them. She knew her place was assured and never felt the need to care for the King's other children. Indeed his older boys were nearly men now and only occasionally seen in the court when they were back from patrols or riding the kingdom doing their father's bidding. She was wise enough to be courteous to them both always, for should her husband die they might rule in his place and her care could be in their hands.

Indract had grown tall in those passing years and labouring on the land alongside Coleman and his older boys, when not at his lessons, meant he had filled out too. He knew he was a son of the King, and he kept a part of himself slightly aloof, but also understood how the monks also also laboured for their food and how they needed to be strong for when they set out on their journeys to spread the word.

He had impressed Sister Magda with his natural piety, his careful observations and his willingness to set his hand to any task that did not include violence. She had mentioned his maturity to the Abbot and he was now set to join the monastery after Pascha in the year when he turned twelve - and Brannon would go with him, even though not quite nine, he would accompany Indract as a potential lay brother, at least until he was older. Though most of the monks were from the nobility, or at least high-born, the monastery was wise enough to recognise ability in those who were of lower birth, and Sister Magda had told them of this boy's aptitude.

The day came when Indract was to go to join the monastery, and at noon the King came with an entourage of four warriors, including Indract's older brothers. They brought a war-pony for him to ride, dressed-out as if ready for battle. 'For you are going to battle the Devil,' Faelan, his older brother said, laughing. Brannon, meanwhile, was hoisted up behind Domnall, Indract's eldest brother, and they set off across the ford and up to the ridge on the other side, up to the Abbey.

Indract glanced back often, glad he had said all his goodbyes earlier as he watched the people he cared most for in the world grow smaller in the distance – Domca, Nuala and Flanna. Brannon glanced back too, sad to be leaving his mother and his home, but brimming with excitement at the journey he was making, a journey into a new type of life with more to learn everyday.

As was usual the mounted party were met at the entrance to the Abbey grounds and were invited to dismount. No weapons were allowed within the grounds, not even the King's, and so the warriors stayed with the ponies and kept all the weapons with them.

Indract and Brannon stood side by side and looked around them. What they saw was not unlike the King's court, except that in the centre stood the church. This was like nothing else in the area as it was a tall rectangular building, and so much more imposing when you were up close to it - far more than it seemed when looking across the valley.

A monk came out and greeted the party, and led them to meet the Abbot. As they walked towards a large round building the Abbot emerged and hastened towards them.

'King Conall. Welcome,' he said, and glancing at the others added, 'and more than one of your sons, I see?'

'Greetings Abbot,' Conall smiled and nodded, 'Yes uncle, you recognised Domnall and Faelan aright, on whom I would ask a blessing, and here is young Indract, come to join you here.'

'Welcome all, indeed, and our young lay-brother-to-be, Brannon, too,' the Abbot's eyes twinkled, as if mentioning the humbler boy's name amongst those of the others made him smile. 'We will go to the church and thank God for his mercy, his guidance and his wisdom in bringing these two young people to his work, after which, they will pass into the monastery, so now is a good time to say any farewells you have left to say.'

Indract turned to his father. Conall hesitated, then stepped forward and, placing a hand on Indract's shoulder, looked him in the eye. Indract looked back, fearlessly.

'Farewell, son, may God be with you - and remember to keep us all in your prayers.'

'Amen, father. May God be with you too,' Indract said with a smile.

The ceremony was simple; the boys knelt at the altar steps and the Abbot prayed. He asked them if they willingly gave their lives into the hands of God and whether they promised to follow the rules of the monastery. Both agreed. Someone came forward with two simple robes, which were handed, one to each of the boys, and it was over.

'Go with Brother Finnachta,' the Abbot said, indicating the young monk who had handed them the robes.

As they left Conall turned, nodded at the Abbot, then hesitated before saying, 'Uncle...'

'We will look after him, Conall. He could have a great future here - someone needs to take my place one day.'

At that Conall nodded again, this time with a tight smile, then turned and left, Domnall and Faelan trailing behind.

Outside the church Finnachta pointed lightly at himself and said, 'Finnachta, but Finn to my friends and brothers.'

'Indract.'

'And I'm Brannon! Happy to meet you.'

Following Finn's glance, they turned to see the King and the older princes leave the church and stood watching as they reached the ponies.

'Come on you two,' Finn said, 'I'm to take you over to our cells.' With that he set off leading them across the courtyard, past the building the Abbot had come out of, towards the side of the compound. There he headed for a largish round-house. 'This is the house of postulants and novitiates,' he explained as they stepped through the doorway.

Once inside, as their eyes became accustomed to the dimness, they saw it was divided all around the side into sections, each about as long as a tall man is tall, with simple wattle walls and a sort of door formed by a rough cloth hanging.

'Here's yours,' Finn said, tugging aside the cloth at one bay. Indract looked inside at a space that held a rough bed, a mat and a stool with no room for much more. 'I'm in the next one,' Finn added. 'And you little raven,' he said turning to Brannon, 'are over here, by the door.'

In the centre of the building was a hearth, with tree trunks arranged in a square around it to sit on. 'Brother Seamus is in charge of us all, and sleeps in that cell there,' Finn added, pointing to a very slightly bigger cell just inside the door, but on the other side of to Brannon's. 'Put on your robes, I will show you where everything is, then I'm to take you to meet him.'

Once they had been shown around the monks' side of the monastery, starting with the gardens and fields outside the rath, and knew which building housed the Abbot, the choir monks, the scriptorium, the infirmary, the hospice, the stores, the latrines, the laundry, they came to the kitchen and the refectory. Pleasant cooking smells filled the air as they drew near.

'It is after nones now,' Finn said with a smile, 'everyone will be in the refectory.' He paused. 'I know we've been talking freely, but that was a dispensation for me – to explain things. The rule, generally, is for there to be no unnecessary talk, but the rule inside the refectory is for silence, so if Brother Seamus wants to speak with you he will take you aside. Come on.' He led them into another large building. It was full of people but, save a single voice reading from the bible, it was quiet, bar the scrape of spoon on bowl or shuffle of feet as monks moved around.

Finn beckoned them forward and led them to a much older man, his hair greying. Finn stopped, bowed his head a little, and tipped his hand towards Indract and Brannon. Brother Seamus smiled, and beckoned the pair to follow him, which they did, and he led them back outside.

'Welcome Brother Indract and Brother Brannon. I will be your teacher and your guide for your first years here. Until you are ready to move on.'

'Thank you, Father,' Brannon said.

Brother Seamus smiled at him. 'Brother is fine for me, but do call the Abbot 'Father'. Are you hungry? Of course you are. Come, come and eat before we join with the others for today's lessons.'

The first chance they got to actually talk to the other postulants and novitiates was back in their dormitory near the end of the day. They had a short time between vespers and compline where they were permitted to converse. Nothing rowdy, of course, despite the fact they were all young men and boys whose contemporaries would have been horsing around, but it was a time to get to know each other anyhow.

Sitting around the fire, bathed in the light from it, Brother Seamus began with a prayer which he brought to a close with, 'Amen.'

The group replied, 'Amen,' and as one pushed back their hoods from their heads, Indract and Brandon hastily copied their example.

Brother Seamus looked around his pupils, 'Brothers we welcome into our fellowship, Indract and Brannon,' indicating each as he named them.

The group looked towards them and nodded, smiling. Each of them seemed to be waiting for someone else to speak first. Indract wasn't sure what was acceptable to say or whether he should begin, he glanced towards Finn for guidance but even as he hesitated one of the other brothers spoke.

'Cormag,' he began, pointing himself, and looking straight at Indract. 'Is it right that you are the King's son – from here?'

'Um, yes. I am.'

'That's very unusual. I too am a King's son, of the line of Sill n Aedo Slaine of the Ui Neill - but even I am not on home turf – I was told it is expected to go where your lineage is unknown.'

'Not unknown for long,' Brannon murmured under his breath to Indract, but perhaps not quietly enough as Cormag's dark eyes flashed in his direction.

'Me too, a King's son, away from home,' added Finn quickly, 'but what of it? It is not a requirement - to be sent away from home.'

Brother Seamus sat tall and watched. Indract felt he was expecting a reply, maybe it was a test?

'I have been away from home most of my life,' he said, 'even though within sight of it. Here, this place, in God's place, is my only home now.'

Brother Seamus gave the slightest shadow of a smile and his stance relaxed. There was a pause, as if there was a gathering of breath or a silent jockeying for position for who was going to speak next.

'Welcome, both of youse, I'm Ainmire,' a narrow-faced novitiate spoke up, 'and this place is my home now too,' he added, finishing with a smile towards Indract. Indract nodded and smiled back.

'And I'm Niall. Welcome ... um, brothers, yes, both, welcome,' another piped up. Indract could have sworn this pale, sandy-haired brother coloured-up with the effort of talking in the group.

'I'm Fergus,' said another, 'And this is ...'

'I can speak for myself, man, I'm Kellagh.'

'And welcome,' Fergus finished.

There was another pause. Brannon glanced at the two who had so far been silent, wondering who would speak first. One straightened as if he would say something, but as he did so a smirk flashed across the face of the other and he spoke instead, 'Durragh,' he glanced at the one who had straightened, then back to Indract, 'the final one of us nobles in this group to welcome you.' Indract and Brannon nodded to him.

This last brother smiled and tipped his head a little, 'Brothers, welcome. I'm Teagan – not high born, but by God's grace given bardic gifts for His glory, for which I give thanks and praise. I am delighted to say, welcome.'

Brannon beamed. At last here was someone who was not of high birth; maybe there was a real chance for him to become a choir monk. 'And, I'm Brannon and ...' he began.

'And *what* are you boy?' Cormag interrupted.

'I'm just ...'

'My brother,' Indract intervened.

Unasked questions hung in the short silence that followed this, then Brother Seamus said, 'And now brothers, it is time for us to walk to Compline.'

Chapter 9

***Guda** - circa AD 678*

The King was now a frequent visitor to the compound, pausing there whenever he had need to pass that way, so Dominica had told him many times how she missed Indract desperately, and had also pleaded her case to go early into the Monastery. Truth was, she missed Brannon especially; it was as if her twin had been taken from her.

So it was not a surprise when the dogs heralded the King's approach one early evening, barking in what Dominica always called 'their welcome voice' with tails wagging. This time, however, he brought a stranger with him, for riding in front of a warrior was a girl.

Dominica stared at her - Muirenn and Cairech's red-gold hair was beautiful but not a rare colour, not like this girl's. Her white-blonde hair was unlike anything Dominica had ever seen; it shone like a beacon.

'Father, my King,' Dominica said, greeting Conall with a bow as Dugan took hold of the reins.

'Dominica, I have brought you a slave, to keep you company.' Conall said, 'She's from over the sea, a Saxon.' Just then Nuala ducked out of her healer's hut. 'Ah, Nuala, someone to help you in your home, and company for Dominica.'

'Thank you, Sire. Won't you take some refreshment?'

'No, I must return speedily,' he said, a smile on his face. He nodded to the warrior, who then let the girl slide down from his pony. 'She's named Guda,' he added and with that he took back his reins and turned his mount and they rode off at a canter, back to the royal court.

Guda stood still where her feet had landed and looked straight at Nuala.

'Come Guda, come and have a drink,' the wise-woman offered gently. But Guda remained where she was. Nuala thought, then mimed, beckoning to her, and drinking, while repeating the words. The girl broke a small smile and followed. Dominica followed her, looking closely at the girl's hair, as they entered Nuala's home.

Over the next few months Nuala and Dominica taught Guda Goidelic and Dominica learnt a lot of Anglisc. They also learnt that Guda was fifteen summers old, that she had been captured in a raid on her village by the river, the Irish currachs having travelled up the estuary, deep into Saxon lands. Dominica, still fascinated by Guda's hair, was amazed to hear that her hair colour was quite usual in Guda's village. It sounded like King Conall had bought her from her captors when he'd been visiting their court beside the sea. More than that she did not know or couldn't say.

She told Dominica more about the land she came from, and about the Gods that watched over them; Woden, Frigg, Thunor and Tiw. For her own part, Dominica told her about the one true God, Father, Son and Holy Sprit. Guda wasn't sure that they sounded more powerful than her gods, and Dominica set her heart to convincing Guda of the truth.

After a couple of months it became evident that, though ostensibly she was there to help Nuala and be company for Dominica, these were not Conall's true reasons for bringing her to them. As a warrior told Dugan one day, it had been Muirenn who banished the girl from the royal court, after finding King Conall was taking too much interest in her.

A month later, while visiting the compound one evening, Conall, clearly in a foul mood, ordered everyone out of Nuala's hut except Guda. It didn't take much imagination for even Dominica, as she sat with Flanna and her family around their fire, to understand what her father was doing with the fair-haired Saxon slave girl

This was just the first time; over the next month the visits for Guda became more frequent and Dominica found herself growing increasingly angry. After much persuasion from herself she felt that Guda was starting to turn to the one true God - but her father's behaviour was undermining this as it was not Christian at all. Dominica was determined to say something to him, King or not!

She tried to talk to Sister Magda about it, but the holy sister shushed her, and wide-eyed asked her what she knew of such things. Dominica, who had made it her business to understand all that she saw in nature as well as all that Nuala could teach her, didn't even blush as she told the sister that humans made their children in much the way that dogs did.

Sister Magda, blushing, lifted her eyes to heaven and said, 'Dear child – you must not say this to anyone else, ever, for your father is the King. God has given him – dispensations. Even in the Holy Bible we can read of times when God, in his wisdom, has given women to Kings, slaves even, to take to their beds to further God's plan.'

'But Guda isn't happy about it!' Dominica said, standing, 'That can't be right!'

'We will pray for her,' Sister Magda said, 'kneel down child.'

One afternoon, shortly after that day, Dominica found Guda sitting by the stream alone.

'Guda!' Dominica said in greeting, 'Sister Magda says we should pray together.'

'What for little sister?' Guda retorted, 'That the King drops dead?'

'No! No, that wouldn't be right.'

'No? But then he'd leave me alone, wouldn't he?'

'But, but, maybe God has a reason for it ... maybe he has a higher purpose. Maybe you will have a child who will be a great prophet.'

'It is you who is the child!' Guda snapped. 'If the King gets a child on me – my life will be done – his wife will see to that.'

Dominica felt ashamed - of God, of her father - and ran to Nuala crying. Once Nuala had calmed her enough to understand what was wrong, she said, 'We can help in ways that are better than prayer at this time, Guda is right, Muirenn would have her put to death if she felt threatened.'

So Nuala tended to Guda's fears in more practical ways, teaching her what she needed to know, which herbs to take to make sure she didn't get with child, while Dominica, still angry, listened and made mental notes of all she heard.

When her father rode up Dominica now no longer ran to greet him. She expected him to come to her and ask her the reason, so she could tell him exactly why! However, he didn't even ask for her! Just ordered anyone who was inside Nuala's hut to get out - except for Guda.

So Dominica changed her tactics: she greeted him when he arrived and, each time, beseeched him to allow her to go to the monastery early. Usually he just replied, 'No,' and strode past her but one day he paused and turned.

'I've provided you with company, what more do you want?'

'Company for yourself, more like!' Dominica blurted out.

'What?'

'You take Guda as your whore of Babylon, woe to him that does that!' Dominica said, her face red and her hands on her hips.

Conall laughed, 'Much more of that and I *will* forget my promise and have you carted off to the monastery early!'

Chapter 10
To the Monastery – *circa AD 681 - 683*

After Dominica's fourteenth birthday, King Conall came for her himself with an escort of warriors, as he had for Indract. They led a pony draped in a fine cloth, decorated with a pattern in blue along the edges. Despite Muirenn's objections he was determined to see his daughter into her new life with recognition of her status.

The procession was watched by Dominica and Nuala as it made its way slowly downhill towards them.

'It is really happening,' Dominica said quietly.

'Yes, but you've always known this, and you are happy, aren't you?'

'But not to be leaving you, and here,' Dominica scanned around her home. 'I love here, I love you, mother Nuala.'

'And you, you have been – everything I could have wanted from a daughter, you know as much herb-lore as I and,' she shook her head, 'and you just have the knack of knowing what is wrong and what is best.' Nuala said, though in truth she knew there was more to Dominica than learning and understanding.

Suddenly Dominica whirled round and knelt before Nuala, 'Bless me, before I leave.'

'It's not for me to bless you child ...'

'Do it, please, use the old blessing your mother taught you, the one I have heard you give ... to the older folk.'

Nuala was taken aback, she had tried to keep this old lore from Dominica. 'I can't – it is ...'

'Please, I want to hear it given me.'

Nuala looked at the approaching procession and made a choice, 'Bless you, daughter, may the four powers in water, earth, air and fire keep you safe, may the wisdom of the three ages of woman sustain you, may the gods ...' she faltered, 'Father, Son and Holy Spirit, go with you,' she ended, bringing herself and her words back to the safety of the Christian gospel.

The entourage arrived and Conall dismounted swiftly. He came towards Dominica with some blue fabric looped over his arm, and Dominica moved to meet him. His eyes never left her as they came towards each other and, when they were face to face, he smiled and nodded.

'You will soon be as tall as your dear mother, and you look so like her already. This,' he said, lifting his arm which held the material, 'was your mother's favourite brat. It made her blue eyes so bright – I know it will do the same for you.' His voice had become uneven; he swallowed. 'I have saved it for you, for when you were tall enough to wear it. It is yours now. Wear it today as you ride to the monastery.' He opened the brat wide; its darker woollen fringe flittered in the breeze. He swept it around her, drawing the corner across before releasing the pin, and re-pinning it for her at her shoulder. The bronze brooch shone like gold in the sunlight against the deep sky blue of the beautifully woven wool.

To Dominica, the comforting weight of the brat felt like a hug. 'Thank you,' she said, feeling suddenly tearful, 'thank you, but, father, they won't let me keep it.'

'I know, but they'll look after it, don't worry,' he said, his own blue eyes seeming brighter near the brat.

Though Magda had described the monastery and life there to Dominica, she was still unprepared for the sheer size of the place. It was, she thought, at least as big as her father's court, but grander in that the main building, the church, was huge. Dominica also noticed the other difference between the King's court and the monastery's - a lack of a fortified boundary - there was only a simple earthen rath, more to keep out animals rather than marauders, and with no proper gate, just wicker hurdles to close the gap against any wandering creatures.

The King was greeted at the gateway and the whole party was asked to dismount. A monk then escorted Conall and Dominica slowly to the doors of the monastery church, an awe-inspiring rectangular building of wood, unlike any Dominica had ever seen close-to before.

Her father came and stood beside her. Looking down he said, 'Dominica, from now on you belong to God. He had but lent you to me, and I know it has not been an easy time, but now you are going into the church I ask that you pray for me and for your blessed mother.'

'I will father,' Dominica said, but the mother image that came into her mind was of Nuala.

They stepped inside the building and she took in the grandness of the church. Two rows of timber pillars supported cross beams that supported a thatched roof far higher than she'd ever seen before, and along the sides there was a line of small wind-holes, that didn't let in the wind at all as they were all covered with something that gave them a warm glow and filled the inside of the church with a pale light. At the far end stood an altar dressed in a brilliant white cloth, surmounted by a simple cross flanked by candles – it was perfect.

Dominica knelt before the altar and there, before the Abbess and God, made a promise to learn the ways of monastic life. Then with her father looking on, she was blessed and given a plain robe as a symbol of being a postulant. When she stood and turned it was to see tears in her father's eyes. He then abruptly nodded and left. He was no longer her father – she was now only a child of God.

Sister Magda came and stood beside her, gently leading her away to show her where she would sleep and what her duties would be. Dominica was so glad to see a familiar face, as she was suddenly feeling lost, even though she was so close to home.

The brothers' dormitories and those of the sisters', made up of groups of round houses, were separated by being set either side of the church. Behind these and around the sides of the compound were more buildings, Magda pointed some of them out - for cooking and eating, for study, for meetings, for storage, for laundering, for sheltering animals and - the latrines.

Magda then took Dominica to the dormitory house, where she was shown her cell, a space on one side, separated only by a wicker hurdle from the next cell and from the centre of the house by a coarse cloth curtain.

'This is your space to sleep in,' Magda said, pulling the cloth hanging aside for Dominica to see. 'Every nun has one similar, from the lowest to the highest. You also keep your monastic robe and clothes here when not wearing them. Look, your second robe is there, and two leines to go beneath them and an apron for rough working. Your worldly clothes will go into store until you make your vows.' She let the cloth drop again. 'The postulant and novitiate's house has up to twelve in, including the novitiates' nun, who will be your guide and teacher through the years until you make your final decision.'

'Is it not you, Sister Magda?'

'It is not. Had I been the novitiates' nun I could not have come traipsing down to you each day as I would have had my many other charges to teach. It is Sister Maire...'

'Good day sister, what is it that I am?' Sister Maire said as she appeared in the doorway.

'In charge of the novitiates sister,' Sister Magda said, giving a polite smile.

'And this is the little princess I take it. Well, miss, you'll have to get used to a different lifestyle here - no-one to get you dressed or wait on you here.'

'No sister,' began Dominica, 'I mean, yes, sister. I know, and I've never had anyone to dress me - except when I was very little.'

'And you needn't answer back either!' Sister Maire snapped.

'Sister Maire, she *has* had a humble upbringing, I have seen for myself,' Sister Magda said.

At that Sister Maire raised her eyebrows as if in disbelief, 'Huh!' then turned to Dominica, 'Put your robe and apron on and follow me. I will take you to where the others are working. They are in the herb garden.'

Dominica changed into the robe swiftly but fumbled with the sacking over-tunic until she got it over her head, but then had to tie it up on the run while following Sister Maire as she left the house. She led Dominica out of the monastery entrance and round the side of the rath, following a beaten earth path through the top of a number of small fields, to a sunny spot where a group of girls could be seen. All were on their knees, bar one, who swiftly dropped as soon as she was seen. They walked past all the other girls, and stopped just beyond the last one.

'We are weeding,' Sister Maire explained. 'You will work along this path,' indicating one of the paths between the rows of herbs next to the last girl. 'Try not to take out any herbs - concentrate on taking out grass. I'm sure you can recognise that at least,' Sister Maire sneered.

'I know all the herbs, well, maybe not all...'

'Did you not hear me earlier? Or did you not understand? You will learn your manners.'

Dominica didn't quite know whether to answer or not but, as Sister Maire continued to glare at her, she mumbled, 'Yes, sister.'

'Pardon? Did you say something?'

'I said – yes, sister, um, sorry sister. I – I will remember.' A quick glance at the nearest girl and her slow blink, told her she had done the right thing.

'I will have my eye on you,' Sister Maire said, and as good as her word patrolled up and down behind the whole row of novitiates as they worked.

When the time to return to the inside of the monastery came, the girl lined up beside Dominica for their walk back to the house, to clean-up before going to the refectory. They were far-enough back from Sister Maire that she couldn't hear them.

'Brigit,' the girl introduced herself in a low voice, 'You must be Dominica! There's been lots of talk of the King's daughter coming here.'

'I am. Is that why Sister Maire doesn't like me? Because I'm the King's daughter?'

'Sister Maire seems to think us all too high and mighty for our own good, and will set herself against you until she is satisfied she has reformed you, made you humble – like she is.'

'But I was told there are others here similar to me, from royal households?'

'Yes, I'm one. From the Ui Barriche. But my father is far away, which makes it easier for her to forget, I think.'

'But I don't understand why Sister Maire has the wrong idea about me. Sister Magda knows all about my life,' Dominica said letting her voice rise.

'Shh!' Brigit hissed, her eyes looking forward to where Sister Maire had paused and turned. Then Sister Maire turned back, led them round through the entrance to the rath and into the monastery court, and then the line of girls wove its way back to the novitiates' house.

After they had removed their aprons and washed their hands they lined up again and were escorted to the refectory. There they sat on simple benches at a table that was little more than a wide bench itself and were served a bowl of pottage and a wedge of bread. A grace was said by a nun standing at a lectern and they began to eat in silence. The pottage was made from soaked oats and a few vegetables, but with not enough herbs to give it a proper flavour – in Dominica's opinion. It was, at least, warm. The nun opened a book and began to read from it, slowly and without intonation, all through their repast.

When they had finished, she closed the book and gave a blessing. All the novitiates stood together and filed out of the refectory, with Dominica gravitating to walk beside Brigit. Dominica was bursting with questions, but it was obvious that talking was not an option – not yet at least, and that was one of her questions – when could they talk? She already knew from Sister Magda that it was not a silent order, but that 'idle chatter' was discouraged. But Dominica thought wanting to know what the rules were, wasn't exactly idle chatter.

When they were safely back in the novitiates' house, Sister Maire left them. This was the time they were able to talk it seemed, yet even then it was all done quietly as if Sister Maire might hear them from wherever she had gone.

Most of the other girls gathered round Dominica to welcome her, and most were older than her. To Dominica's surprise they also seemed to know that she'd been promised to God from birth, though none knew how her life had been spent since then. Seven of the girls were from a noble background and said they'd felt the deprivations of the monastery sorely at first. But they told her that she'd soon get used to it, that it was better never to answer Sister Maire back and that life in the monastery was safe. They explained how, though it was a double monastery, the monks and the nuns saw little of each other except during prayers. There was also a girl, maybe eight or nine, who said nothing but hung back on the edge of the group.

Dominica noticed, however, that there were a couple of other, older girls who did not come to greet her, and wondered why, so later she went to them to introduce herself, 'Good evening sisters,' she began, 'I am Dominica and I'm ...'

'We know who and *what* you are!' said one sharply. 'But rank means nothing here.'

Dominica was taken aback, 'Oh! I'm sorry, sorry - I was just wanting to greet you.'

'As the newest here, you should wait for the senior ones here to address you first.'

'But, I was just ...'

'She knows no better, the entitled always assume they have the right,' the other said. Dominica didn't know what to say or do, she ended up giving them both a nod and backed away, muttering, 'Sorry, sorry.'

*

After a few months Dominica had found out all the things she had wanted to know, and had settled into the routine of the life. The girls who didn't greet her that day were both lay-sisters, from poorer households, favoured by Sister Maire as it seemed that she started life as one too.

The times for prayer punctuated days in which they worked or studied almost every hour of daylight. They took turns working in all the aspects of the daily life, the cooking, the serving, the laundry, the gardening, the cleaning and the infirmary. They were helped and guided in these tasks by a number of older lay-sisters who worked at these tasks always. Dominica liked working with these women. It reminded her of home - there was no putting on of airs, no snide remarks - these women seemed to genuinely like each other. She liked working in the infirmary and the garden most of all as both of these places made her feel useful and at home. However, she still struggled to make friends with any of the other girls apart from Brigit. It was as if they dared not be friendly while she was so obviously not favoured by Sister Maire.

**

There was a great deal of excitement in the novitiates' house as Lent drew to a close over a year from when Dominica entered the Monastery. Five of the novitiates were to take their vows at the great Pascha celebration – and move out of the novitiates' house into one of the nuns' houses – and Brigit was one of these.

Dominica was happy for Brigit, but sad that she would not be with her friend and confidante much in the future. Ever since that first day they had shared so many of their thoughts, joys and questions; now she'd have no one to share everything with. Still none of the other girls wanted to be close to her.

***

After Pascha-tide when Brigit had gone from the novitiates, Dominica fell quiet, talking little, eating less. At first Sister Maire told Sister Ciar triumphantly that Dominica had learnt not to be so bold, to be meek, at last. However, as time went on Dominica's eyes dulled, she seemed listless and even when working in the garden didn't raise her head from her work to gaze about the countryside as she had so often been told not to do. Sister Maire noticed this also and one day went to the infirmary to speak with Sister Ciar.

'Sister.'

'Greetings sister.'

Sister Maire sighed, 'It is about Dominica. I am – now – a little concerned about her. I think she is not well,' she began and then explained the girl's demeanour and how withdrawn and pale she was becoming.

Sister Ciar thought for a moment then said, 'I have been praying for an assistant, and I can say, of all the novitiates, Dominica is the only one who knows what it is to care for someone as if by nature, and her knowledge of herbs is excellent for one so young. Shall we see if she would like to do more in the infirmary, where I can also keep an eye on her own health?'

So it was that at Pentecost of that same year, with Mother Mara's blessing, Sister Ciar came to the novitiates house to speak to Dominica.

Dominica stood waiting, head bowed, before Sister Ciar - as she had been told to do by Sister Maire.

'Sister Dominica, I have been praying for an assistant in the herbarium and infirmary, and Mother Mara has granted that you may join me there, even though still a novitiate. I hope this is good news to you?'

Dominica looked up, her eyes suddenly shining, and with a smile lighting-up her face, 'Thank you, sister, thank you, I will try my best to make you happy with my work,' she said warmly, quickly adding, 'and God, of course.'

Chapter 11
***Herbarium** - circa AD 684-685*

Dominica started to work with Sister Ciar in the infirmary and the herbarium most of the work-day time, though she still lived with the other novitiates and was with them for prayers, study, in the refectory and for weeding-work.

One day, early in this time, Sister Ciar and Dominica were working side by side carefully planting individual herb seeds in soil sifted through a wicker basket, when Sister Ciar asked softly, 'I suppose you are missing home?'

There was a short silence before Dominica replied, 'I miss mother Nuala, it is true, but - it's not the ache I feel at missing Sister Brigit, and she is even nearer.'

'And why Sister Brigit?'

Dominica felt her lips twitch as if she were about to cry and bit her lower lip to stop the tremble. She drew a breath, 'She - we were such friends, I have never had such a friend, a girl, that is. I grew up surrounded by boys, especially my brother and milk-brother. I love them dearly but this was different.'

'How so?'

'We shared so many thoughts, she made me feel less alone, and she taught me so much about girls and helped me understand their anger and – and their lies. When I asked her, why someone felt angry, or felt sad, to me, she seemed to know the kind of thoughts that made them like that. All I knew was that I could feel it like waves, but I didn't know, I didn't understand what drove it.'

'Why did you say nothing to Sister Maire? She came to me as she was concerned for you.'

'I wouldn't dare, sister.'

'It is her duty to care for the novitiates.'

Dominica, looking down, shook her head; the thought of telling Sister Maire she felt bereft was too scary to think about, even now.

Sister Ciar was quiet for a while, busying herself with tidying the area. 'And who was sad?'

'Little Sister Bronagh.'

'But I thought - she seems happier now? I cared for her here when she was first brought in, and she smiles at me when we meet. I know she says nothing, but she has said nothing since she was found.'

'Brigit told me that - not a word! But her smile is just to make us happy, it doesn't go inside her. The waves of sadness and anger stop it going inside her, I think.'

'Poor child, she has all right to be angry and sad.' Sister Ciar sighed. 'How she alone survived that slaughter and got away we may never know.'

'Slaughter? What happened?'

'All we know is she was found struggling along the riverside, higher upstream from Drom-Eanaigh, half covered in mud and dried blood, from a scalp wound, and nigh on starving. The King sent men to follow the river up to see if they could find where she came from – and they did, a *very* long way upriver.' Sister Ciar stopped, as if not sure whether to go on then, after a sharp intake of breath, she continued. 'They found a silent farmstead. In a heap in one of the huts they found the bodies. All ages, from elders to babes brutally killed, some even ....' she shook her head. 'There was nothing left that could be taken, not even a cup or a fowl, and no one to say who did it - or why. It was the only place she could have come from.'

Dominica was silent, taking in what she had just been told, then she said slowly, 'The King would punish those guilty, if they knew who did it. Couldn't she write it down, sister?'

'She doesn't get writing study, as you know, she is but a lay-sister, she doesn't need it.'

'Of course. But, what if I showed her the letters? I used to do that with my milk-brother and he is here now, maybe on the way to becoming a choir monk as he is clever with reading and writing. If it helps her speak, or at least to write her own words, would that not help her?'

Sister Ciar was quiet again. Dominica was getting used to the unhurried pace of the way Sister Ciar seemed to weigh-up words before deciding whether they should be said or not.

'Maybe, maybe. I will speak about it with Mother Mara.'

When Sister Ciar spoke about the writing lessons with Mother Mara, she agreed, and it was also agreed that Sister Bronagh would come to help more in the herbarium, where her small nimble fingers were adept at working with seeds and small plants. During part of each working time in the herbarium Dominica would help Bronagh with her letters, patiently teaching her the letter shapes, their names and their sounds – and how they made the words that might be needed to break the spell of silence.

To begin with Dominica tried to teach the alphabet as she had been taught it, and as she had then passed it on to Brannon. But Bronagh seemed puzzled by the letters, as if she wasn't sure what they were for. Then Dominica had an idea. She wrote out the Our Father, carefully and neatly. Pointing to each word she began to read it to Bronagh. Within a line Bronagh was nodding along with the words, as she heard them and as though they meant something to her. Dominica stopped, went back to the beginning again and started repeating it, pointing to the words. She glanced at Bronagh - she had a smile on her face and her eyes were shining.

Dominica pointed to a letter, said the sound, and the next, and the next – then ran her finger along the word, putting the sounds together to make the word. She glanced at Bronagh and repeated the process. Bronagh smiled and nodded vigorously. She understood! After that the teaching became easier with Bronagh hastily taking the stick to make her marks and to shape the letters. Soon the two of them were beginning to form a bond.

Step by step, Dominica was restored to health. She loved working beside the thoughtful and knowledgeable Sister Ciar, learning more herb lore, especially of plants, powders and seeds from far distant lands which she had learnt about and brought back. In fact, hearing about those far distant lands was inspiring in itself, for Sister Ciar had herself been on a pilgrimage to the Holy See in Rome with the Abbot and a group of other monks and nuns, at a time when the Abbot had been himself just a choir monk.

She spoke of their peregrination without boasting; of the difficulties, the long days of walking, the vast monasteries they stayed in overnight and the kindnesses they had experienced along the way. And she spoke of the Holy See, of the expansive tall buildings made in stone, with amazing columns like huge stone tree-trunks, carved and decorated. Of the colours, the heat, the magnificence of St. Peter's and other churches nearby, and of the stench and danger of the areas outside the Holy See, in the ravaged parts of the once great city. Dominica was entranced, the thought of leaving everything you knew to make a journey into the unknown both fascinated and frightened her. She plied Sister Ciar with questions over the weeks and months, to keep her talking, but sometimes Sister Ciar would simply say, 'Not today,' and then they'd slip into a comfortable silence.

One day Dominica was working in the herbarium alone at a simple task set by Sister Ciar, to bunch and tie herbs and hang them to dry. She was singing to herself as she worked, to begin with almost under her breath as she was singing one of the songs mother Nuala had taught them all, a folk song, not a hymn or psalm. As the song rose to the crescendo of the final chorus she let her voice rise just a bit, so the words became clearer – then she heard a little, almost simultaneous, echo, and turned. Bronagh was in the doorway, a basket of fresh herbs on her arm, with the sweetest sound of the song on her lips. Dominica couldn't help but smile, and repeated the chorus a little louder, and Bronagh joined in.

'Sweet Bronagh, that was lovely! You have your voice!'

Bronagh smiled and nodded, then she opened her mouth as if to say something, but ... nothing came. Her eyes welled with tears.

'No, no, don't cry! It's all right, but at least we know the sound *can* come,' Dominica said, taking the basket, dropping it to the floor and giving Bronagh a swift hug. 'Come, let's bunch these up now,' picking up the basket and drawing Bronagh to the bench.

Over the succeeding months Dominica worked with Sister Bronagh at improving her writing and reading – though the latter was hard at first as it was impossible to know if Bronagh could understand words that were written as she couldn't say them out loud. One day, Dominica had an idea, and explained that they would play a game. She would write down an instruction for Bronagh to act out and Bronagh could then do the same for her. It would be fun, she said. Bronagh smiled and nodded. Dominica wrote, 'Stand on one leg' and showed the slate to Bronagh. She studied it a moment then stepped back and stood on one leg. Dominica clapped her hands in joy, and Bronagh joined in.

'Now, Bronagh, you write something for me to do.' Bronagh wrote, 'Sit down' and turned the slate, Dominica looked around and immediately sat gently on a stool. They both laughed and clapped! Dominica next wrote, 'Run to the door'. Again Bronagh studied the instruction for a moment then, with a quick glance at Dominica, she picked up her skirts and made a short dash to the door, spinning to see the reaction and almost falling onto Sister Ciar as she came in.

'Sisters?' the older woman said, her voice serious.

'Oh! Sister – look, it is how we know Sister Bronagh is reading aright. Look!' Dominica wrote: 'Put your hand on your head' and showed it to them. Sister Bronagh glanced at Sister Ciar as if asking permission, and was given a nod. She placed her hand on her head. 'See! Isn't it wonderful? Dominica exclaimed, 'You write now Bronagh!' Bronagh took the slate and wrote, 'Put your hand on your foot', turning the slate for Dominica. Dominica laughed and bent down to place her hand on her own foot, then stood again, laughing, 'See, sister!'

'I do indeed see. It is such good progress,' Sister Ciar said beaming at Bronagh. She then looked thoughtful, 'Maybe we can teach Sister Bronagh how to make healing potions and balms from our herbal recipes, after all.'

***

Dominica had been at the monastery for about four years by this time. Lately the weather had been unusual - cold, windy and wet all summer - and then, only last week, there had been the red rain, like an omen. Everything pale it fell on took on a pinkish hue and, as it dried, everything was left masked in a fine layer of red dust that tinted fingers when touched.

This day it was dry, but particularly chilly for the season, so she was hugging herself as she walked, briskly, from the herbarium to the dormitory.

Brannon spotted her crossing the space beside the church and ran after her calling, 'Have you heard? Indract is sick ... He ... they think he may die!'

Dominica spun to face him, 'No! Where is he? I must see him.'

'In the small infirmary, the brothers are caring for him - they may not let you...', he began but Dominica was running, so Brannon ran after her.

Together they arrived at the door of the small building where only those who were very sick were cared for.

Chapter 12

The Sickness - *circa AD 685*

When they reached the infirmary, Brannon, catching his breath said, 'Let me,' and opened the door, before calling inside, 'Brother Tighe, I ask after Brother Indract.'

'Brother, you are best to go and say prayers for his everlasting soul,' a voice said from the dark and stuffy room.

'No!' Dominica cried, pushing past Brannon, 'No! I *must* see him!'

'No, sister!' A man moved to block her way, 'for you may fall ill too.'

'I am not just *a* sister – I am Indract's sister! And well versed in healing. Let me see him!'

'She is! And she's King Conall's daughter,' Brannon added in case Tighe hadn't taken the hint.

The monk looked sad and resigned, 'Very well. But just you, Brother Brannon you must leave,' he instructed, before turning to Dominica, 'Just look and speak to him, don't touch him, here, cover your nose and mouth with this,' He handed her a piece of damp cloth fragrant with the scent of water-mint and wild garlic. Dominica nodded as she understood the herbs being used, one gave a cooling scent, the other helped to cleanse the air breathed in through the cloth, just as it also cleansed wounds.

Dominica's eyes had quickly grown accustomed to the gloom - with the darkness kept at bay by just one candle. She could now see Indract laid on a bed, his eyes closed as if already dead, his neck swollen and his breathing harsh, the air full of smoke and the smell of incense. Still driven by concern for Indract, she turned to the monk and said in desperation, 'Why is there no fresh air in here, no light?'

'It keeps evil at bay, sister, you should know that.'

'But this patient needs clean air to breathe, and light is good unless it hurts the eyes. Let in some light, let in some air! Let me see him!' The monk hesitated, but Dominica turned on him gathering her strength to be bold, 'Indract may have given himself to God but be assured he is still the King's son – has the King even been told?'

The monk shrugged, 'The Abbot knows', he said, but began to untie and pull away the wicker-and-hide shutter from the wind-hole, allowing both light and fresh air to stream into the building.

Dominica went close to Indract. Noticing that his eyelids and lips were almost blue, she looked at his skin - it had a greyish tinge and looked shiny and damp and his neck looked puffed up. 'What do you think ails him?'

'It is the strangling sickness,' he sighed, 'the second brother with this affliction this past week. Both had been ministering outside. Brother Josef passed yesterday.' They stepped away from the body lying so still, breathing with such difficulty.

'The strangling sickness? I thought – I thought only children...?'

'I have only seen it this bad in our area once before. It comes in different guises.'

'What have you tried already to help him?'

'There is nothing to be done. It is the hands of God if it takes them or not.'

'And ...' Dominica paused, 'how many does it take – in this guise?'

'Most children, most older men, and about half of the rest.'

'But Indract is not a child nor old.'

'But very ill, sister, very ill.'

'Let me bring something for him, for his soreness of throat.'

'He cannot swallow, there is a growth, like a skin across the back of the throat.'

'Really? I have never heard of this - let me see!' Reluctantly the brother, cloth at his own face, returned to Indract's side and gently pressed on his chin with a smooth stick to open his mouth so that Dominica, cloth still pressed to her face, could see into the back of the throat. There, indeed, was a greyish-white skin stretched across much of the back of Indract's throat that vibrated with his stentorian breathing. The brother relaxed the pressure and Indract's mouth returned to its partially closed position. He then stepped back and dropped the stick into the fire.

Dominica's head whirled with everything she knew about easing sore throats, but almost everything meant swallowing a liquid. Then it came to her: steaming. Children who suffered with the night croak were often eased by steaming - maybe this would help a bit. 'Steam!' she said suddenly. 'Brother, may we try making the air vaporous with herbs that might help breathing, clear mucus, or open airways?' She thought he would refuse, but then he said slowly, 'Why not, it might help, and it won't hurt to try.'

Dominica beamed behind the cloth still at her face, 'I will fetch the herbs, if you will prepare the water to boil,' she said and left the sick room. She rushed over to the nuns' infirmary and called for Sister Ciar. There was no answer, so she just went into the herbarium and collected any herbs she remembered were good to open airways, to ease breathing. With small bunches of each wrapped in a piece of cloth she hastened back to the monks' infirmary, and didn't even hesitate at the door.

Brother Tighe had raised the fire to make flames, and the bronze pot above it was obviously warming well. So Dominica unwrapped her herbs and crushed them in her hand and, as she dropped them into the water, said a prayer over each one.

'Sister, if we are to make it vaporous in here, as you wish, we need to close the shutter again.'

'I am sorry, Brother Tighe,' she responded, 'forgive me, I was rude and spoke in fear and haste. You are right. To keep the vapour in we must close up,' adding, 'I'll help you.' Knowing how tricky they could be to close-up alone. While she helped Brother Tighe reposition and re-tie the shutter she was thinking of how she had seen mother Nuala sit someone with a cloth over their head and a cauldron of hot herb-filled water between their feet.

'Do you think we can make a little tent over his bed head, and bring bowls of the hot water giving off its vapour and put them inside it?' she suggested.

Brother Tighe nodded and left. He returned after a few moments with four sticks, twine and a cloth. With these they fashioned a small tent that covered Indract's head and shoulders. Dominica poured the hot fragrant water into a wooden bowl and tucked it under the covering, beside her brother's head.

'And now, we can only pray,' Brother Tighe said. So that is what they did, in silence, standing well back from the foot of Indract's bed.

After a long while, in which they changed the hot water twice, a bell clanged, and Brother Tighe looked up, 'Vespers,' he said.

'You go, brother. I will remain here until you return.'

Brother Tighe nodded, lit a torch and set it in a sconce to make a little more light in the room. He then left them, stepping quickly out into the sunset-lit evening.

For a while Dominica just stood there, then she filled the second bowl with hot water and swapped it for the one that was cooling under the tent. She poured the cooled water back into the pot to heat up again and returned to Indract's side. She looked in at him. The torch and the candle between them still gave a poor light and it was even darker under the cloth. It was so hard to see anything, so she brought the candle nearer to see his face. There seemed to be no change, but she thought, hoped, that his breathing sounded less harsh. She tucked the cloth down again, set the candle nearby and resumed her prayers, working her way through the liturgy of Vespers, though part of her mind was wandering, searching for any helpful knowledge she might have from all she'd gleaned while growing up with mother Nuala.

In the semi-darkness Dominica felt as if she was almost sleeping on her feet. Her words stopped, she felt herself become unnaturally still, and she knew she had to pray - pray in her own words, not those of the service she was missing. She stood beside Indract and lifted back the cloth from the tent - right back so that she could see his face in the dim light. She began as she had many years ago, her hands pressed together, and prayed, 'Lord God, dearest Father have mercy on Indract. Loving brother, dearest Jesus, Son of the Father, comfort Indract. Life-giving Holy Spirit pour your healing power into Indract.' Her hands were hot, their palms burning, her hands drifted apart, palms upwards. As she continued to pray, she felt her arms rising, her hands come together as a cup and then her palms turn down. 'In the name of the Father, of the Son and the Holy Spirit, Amen.'

Once again, she came back to herself to find her hands hovering over a person's head. Indract's eyes gleamed back at her and she snatched her hands back to her sides. His eyes closed again and she realised all she could hear was the crackle of the fire - she couldn't hear Indract breathing! She panicked and touched him; his eyes flew open. 'Are you? Can you breathe?' she said. He nodded slightly, raised a shadow of a smile, and closed his eyes again.

Dominica carefully removed the bowl of water, and replaced it with another, telling Indract not to move as there was a bowl of hot water near his head. Gently, she put the tent cover back in place, explaining what it was for to the silent Indract.

Moments later Brother Tighe returned and, coming straight over to her, asked, 'How is he?'

'I think - I think the steam might have helped,' she said. 'His breathing is quieter.'

Brother Tighe picked up his face cloth and covered his mouth, then went close to Indract, and listened. He lifted the flap of the tent, he listened again. 'This is good. He's breathing, his chest is moving, but the noise? Huh? Gone.' He collected another smooth stick, 'Hold the candle,' he said to Dominica, and pressed on Indract's chin to open his mouth - instead it roused him, his eyes opening. Brother Tighe smiled, 'Brother Indract, will you open your mouth for me to see inside?'

Indract opened his mouth wide and Dominica lifted the candle and held it so that its light illuminated the back of her brother's throat. Brother Tighe looked, and looked again, then said in a hushed tone of wonder, 'Praise be to God, the strangling skin - it's gone!' He stood up and shrugged. 'Gone!'

Indract stared past Brother Tighe, straight into Dominica's eyes, and it was as if some kind of understanding passed between them.

Chapter 13

The Thanksgiving Plan - *circa 686 - 687*

As Dominica came into the herb garden to collect some early mint he was sitting on a stone bench in the sunny corner, where the wind skipped over the wall and left a pool of calm. His head was back, eyes closed, face full-on to the sun.

'Indract!' Dominica said, her joy in seeing him filling his name.

Indract opened his eyes and pulled himself upright. 'Domca!'

'What are you doing here?'

'Special dispensation, and I knew you'd turn up at some time.'

'Oh?'

'I wanted to tell you of my plans.'

'Plans?'

'I am planning a peregrination, with the aim of reaching the Holy See in Rome and maybe even the Holy Land, as a thanksgiving for my healing – you see, while I was so ill, I had a vision of travelling and sharing the word.'

'That's – um. That's wonderful, a, a - a grand plan,' Dominica said, but inside her stomach was flipping as images of places described by Sister Ciar flooded back.

'Dominica. It was a miracle. I was made well through a miracle.'

'Yes! Yes, it was!'

Indract smiled. 'And?'

'Um, and, um, yes, a pilgrimage to say thank you, um, seems right.'

'No, that's not what I meant. *I saw you that day*. I saw you praying in - *such a way.* You know when I opened my eyes I thought you were an angel - you were glowing and there was light all around you ...'

'From the candle-light – behind me.'

'It wasn't behind you, it was to your side, barely noticeable. When I looked hard I could see it wasn't an angel - it was you, with your hands raised up and like they were tipping something over me. You understand?'

Dominica was silent. She didn't know quite what it was she had done – only that it had happened a couple of times – and healing had happened.

'Domca, you must come with me on the peregrination – you were there in my vision.'

'If God wills it, I would gladly go,' her reply came instantly – yet the simple words belied the way her blood sang through her.

Indract broke into a smile, his face appearing suddenly younger and more healthy looking. 'Brave sister! I hope there will be a full twelve of us from the monastery. Best get yourself ready for a journey, for I am sure this is what God wants of us.'

*

The idea of the peregrination was approved by the Abbot and Abbess, though there was hesitation about Dominica travelling unless other sisters were willing to accompany her. Prayers were said, and the word put to the sisters to pray for guidance as to whether they were called to go too. Dominica hoped that Brigit would leap at the chance.

One day, when she was last to leave the church after matins, Dominica noticed Brigit just ahead of her. She sped up until they were side by side though, with her head bowed, Brigit seemed to not notice.

'Brigit,' Dominica said, barely above a whisper.

Brigit lifted her head a little and slowed her pace so a gap appeared between them and the sisters ahead of them. 'Dominica, what is it?' she whispered back.

'I was praying you'd come on the peregrination.' But seeing Brigit shake her head firmly. She added, 'Why? Why not?'

'I have a terrible fear of the sea,' Brigit whispered, 'You know I grew up beside it, love to look at it, be near it - but to go out on it? No! I have nightmares, often, where I am drowning, I could never go.'

'But God would keep you safe ...'

'Aye, he does, he sends me the dreams to warn me not to go!' She gave a small huff of a laugh, shook her head, and looked at Dominica sadly, 'I'm sorry, I can't go, much as part of me wants to, I can't, please don't ask me.' She ducked her head again and walked faster to catch up to the other sisters.

Regardless of the hesitation surrounding Dominica's participation in it, the organisation of the pilgrimage was still happening. The plan called for two of the monks, Indract and Cormag, who were already deacons under the Abbot to be ordained to provide the pilgrims with the Eucharist and to serve any who had need on their peregrination, and Dairmut to be made deacon to aid them. All of which which meant a bit of a delay in their planned leaving date.

Indract had drawn together those men who said they had felt the call to go on the journey. Most were young men, like himself, most had been novices with him, about half from a noble background - a few sons of kings, others from high-born families. There was just one older man, brother Dairmut who had been on a journey like this before, and one much younger; Brannon, who was not even a monk yet, but all in all they were eleven and Dominica would make it twelve.

It was an important thing in the monastery, with the decision making presided over by the Abbot, as most of those going were monks. There were those within the monastery who had gone out on peregrination or pilgrimage or both and had returned to spend their days in the monastery, bringing with them wisdom and learning. There were also many who they remembered who had not come back, some through God's calling for them to stay and work in other parts of the world, some through disasters which had befallen them. Planning was an important part of trying to avoid the latter – and the plan called for them to depart just after Pentecost with the improving weather.

**

A full five years had elapsed since Dominica had come into the monastery, and over a year since she had healed her brother. The next Pascha she would be able to take her vows, if she felt ready to by then, and if Mother Mara also thought her ready.

In the midst of Lent, and her preparation time, Mother Mara sent for Dominica. When she arrived she was bidden to enter, and was surprised to see her father standing there.

'Sister Dominica, your earthly father has come to speak with you before you take your vows,' Mother Mara smiled tightly, 'I shall leave you here with him as he has something he wishes to speak with you about,' with that she nodded her head towards the King and left her room.

Conall was silent for a moment, looking at his daughter. He closed his eyes a second and shook his head a fraction. 'Daughter! Dominica. How you've grown - you look *so* like your dear mother, and you look well. '

'Thank you, father. You look well too,' she replied, giving a bow of respect.

'I know it is time for you to think about taking your vows. I am come to ask you to think again. It was my frantic prayers to save your lives that have forced this way of life on you. And, yes, your life was spared, but, really, not your dear mother's - not both of you. So, as I see it, you have done enough. You do not have to throw your life away on vows not of your choosing, when a daughter of a king can have so much.'

Dominica stared at him for a moment, 'I am very content with my life here.'

'But think, you could wed a king, have a high status, run your own royal household.' When Dominica did not immediately reply, he went on, his speech speeding up, 'And you are, oh, you have become such a beautiful young woman, do you not want a husband and a family of your own?'

'Father, are you in need of a daughter to seal a treaty?'

'No! How could you think that of me?'

Dominica heard his words with a straight face but *his* face had already given him away.

'There *is* a fine man, a king, who I would be happy to see you wed, it is true, but I am only thinking of your future. A royal life would surely be so much better than to be ... be not much more than a servant?'

'Any servant of the King of Heaven, is higher than any earthly king,' Dominica said in a tone that suggested she'd learnt this dictum, but also believed it.

'Is that your final word? I can't understand why you'd want to shut yourself away, do nothing, see nothing, be nothing.'

'I shall take my vows and be a bride of Christ, but I will also travel, see and experience much, I shall go on a pilgrimage to Rome and, if God wills it, I will be important to Him.'

'Going away?'

'With Indract and others, to preach the word wherever we go, to heal the sick and help the poor. To do as Jesus taught us to do.'

'Nonsense! We will see about that!' he said, and strode from the room.

Within a moment or two Mother Mara had returned. 'Are you all right? You look shaken?'

‘Mother Mara, my *earthly* father would have me forego my vows, so he can wed me to a king to settle a treaty, *and* he seeks to prevent us following the vision of the thanksgiving pilgrimage too.’

Mother Mara was silent for a few moments, standing with her hands pressed together When she spoke at last it was to say: ‘Maybe this is why you were in your brother’s vision – so you could not be led away from God’s work by your earthly father’s will.’

Chapter 14
Nuala - circa AD 688

There was an energy in the monastery as the date for the start of the peregrination approached. Even those not going seemed to have a spring in their step. The older monks, who had been on a pilgrimage and returned, rekindled memories, eyes twinkling in reminiscence, and passed on nuggets of wisdom to the ones about to go. Warnings were also given, with downcast eyes and shaken heads, as if recalling those times was too hard, but necessary. And there was prayer - from the day after Pascha a prayer had been included for the peregrination, offering it to God as a means to do His work in the world. Even though Dominica was only included in the essential meetings, she still picked up on the excitement of the unknown which was permeating the place.

Three weeks after taking her vows, and four before they were due to leave, news came to the monastery that the wise-woman was sick - after all, when the wise-woman of the court herself is sick who else could you turn to? In this case, as Nuala was a woman, Sister Ciar was called for. As soon as Dominica heard she asked to accompany her, and this was granted as Sister Bronagh was now skilled enough to deal with day-to-day herbarium needs.

Though she had thought of Nuala and her home many times, walking down the long slope towards the small-holding by the ford brought back so many memories for Dominica. As they neared she recognised the tree Brannon had fallen out of when trying to learn his letters, the place where the water-mint grew in profusion along the edge of the stream, the place where the stream was dammed a bit and they had swum as children when hot and dusty.

Nothing much seemed to have changed as they arrived. The pink of the outside plaster was faded, the thatch looked darker, yet still sound, but when Flanna came out to greet them the six years since they last met had aged her - her flame-red hair faded, her face coarsened.

She was wringing her hands as she approached, calling, 'Sister, thank the Lord. I don't know what to do, and mother is beyond telling me now.' Suddenly she stopped moving and looked, 'Domca? Dominica – is it you?'

Dominica ran to Flanna and they hugged. 'Oh Flanna! Let's go and see mother.'

Nuala was lying in her own house. As soon as they stepped in Dominica could hear Nuala's breathing, harsh in the quiet. As her eyes became accustomed to the dimness she saw her lying on her simple bed, the covers drawn up to her neck. She rushed to her side as Sister Ciar set her basket in a clear space near the door.

'Mother Nuala,' Dominica said softly, 'It is Dominica – Domca.' She put her hand on Nuala's bony hand and stroked it gently. As her sight gained in the dimness she could see how sharp Nuala's face had become, how sunken her cheeks. A tightness gripped her chest and her eyes filled with tears. She touched Nuala's forehead with the back of her hand, feeling for a temperature, but only feeling the skin tacky. Nuala's eyes did not open.

'She's been like this a day now,' Flanna said.

'Why didn't you call for me before?' Dominica said, a little sharply.

'She wouldn't let me, said – said it was ... said it might be catching and *you* had important work to do ... whatever that meant.'

'Hmm, well it might be catching,' Dominica said, stepping back from Nuala, annoyed with herself that she had let her emotions make her forget her training. 'How are you feeling yourself?'

'Fine.'

'How did it start? What did you notice to begin with?' Dominica asked, holding her hands behind her back and leading them both towards the door where Sister Ciar was standing quietly.

'The cough, she tried to hide it – would rush out, cough outside. Soon she'd not join us at all in the house. She got terrible thin – you can see that, but even when eating well - though lately she wanted very little. '

'Sounds as if she was trying to protect you all.'

'Mm, maybe – and she got terrible pale. Skin see-through like. I asked her what it was, and what was she taking for it.' Flanna shook her head, her lips turned down, 'She said rosehip syrup for the cough. That's alright if it was just a cough – by then even I could see it wasn't. Then mother set herself in the house, wouldn't let anyone in, not me, not anyone. I was to leave her some food at the door and shout to her. She took it in everyday until the day before yesterday. And that's when I came in – that's when I sent word to the court.'

'Thank you, Flanna,' Sister Ciar said gently as they all stepped outside. 'We will take over her care. Please could you make a fire up for us, out here, and set a pot to boil water, as soon as you can?'

'Yes, yes, I will get that done - I've hot pot-boiler stones in my hearth, they will speed it up. Thank you sister,' Flanna said, sending a sad smile towards Dominica as she hurried to get the water ready.

'I'm sorry,' Dominica said, 'I should never have gone so close or touched her without care like I did.'

'I understand, but as soon as we have hot water you'll need to clean your hands. Fortunately Nuala didn't cough whilst you were standing over her.'

'What is it? Do you know?'

'Possibly. I'll ask Flanna a bit more – but it sounds like the wasting, it is something that fills the chest with water and blood and wracks the body with coughing till blood comes out, and night sweats that drain the body of strength. If it is that - pray it will not spread - for it can run through families when the weather is wrong.'

'How do you catch it?'

'I don't know, but maybe it's in the blood from the cough or maybe the sweat? We need to be careful.'

Dominica looked at her hands, then tucked them back behind her, 'I'll get my hands clean. I am sorry sister.' A sound came from within the house, a piteous sound between a cough and a gurgle; Dominica shivered.

After taking hot water and washing her hands well with it, Dominica walked outside the rath and threw it where no-one would accidentally touch it. It was then that she realised she had felt nothing when she touched Nuala's forehead, other than a clamminess quite usual in the sick. So often when she was treating people she had a sense of their pain, a flash of colour that helped her to find the right thing to help heal them.

Wearing a wild-garlic and mint dampened cloth wrapped across her nose and mouth and tied behind her head, Sister Ciar took a bowl of warm water into Nuala. She peeled back the cover and gasped a little to see the woman's body. This woman who was so strong and vital the last time they'd met, was now so thin that all the bones stood out, as if looking straight through the translucent skin at the skeleton beneath. The chest wheezed unsteadily up and down burbling wetly - Sister Ciar drew the covers up again. Carefully she bathed Nuala's face and talked to her gently - she was under no illusion, Nuala was dying and there was nothing she knew that could help, and only a little that may make the pain easier.

Sister Ciar came back out of Nuala's house. 'Dominica, we need some fresh herbs to strew in the house, and to boil to steam.'

'I should be able to find most of what we need round here. Nuala always kept a well stocked herb garden and the valley here is full of water-mint.'

'I had hoped you would say that, as I must go back to the herbarium to fetch a potion to help Nuala's pain. You can do what is needed while I am away?'

'Yes, sister, and I will be careful too.'

'And keep the door open – fresh air to breathe may help her, I don't know, but light and air help defend against so many things that grow in the dark.'

Dominica collected baskets full of the herbs for strewing, blessing the fact that the season meant that they were growing well. She set the pot to boil with wild garlic and water-mint and took the rest into the house. She talked to Nuala as if she were aware and well, while strewing the herbs and trampling on them to let their sweetness fill the air. As she did she thought of the last time she had been in a sick room alone where they had been sure the patient would die, and decided that while Sister Ciar was away she would pray – as she had done before. Indract had called it a miracle and Nuala needed a miracle.

Quietly she closed the door so no-one would disturb or see her, then stepped to the foot of the bed. She began with learnt prayer, reciting the words that she said everyday as a sister. She tried to find that strange calm but it wouldn't come. She prayed for it, for that calm, for that feeling. Nothing. She prayed telling God how good Nuala was, how she helped so many people. Her hands pressed so tightly together her fingers whitened and grew cold. She remembered that her hands ended up high up and tipped over, so desperately praying she raised her hands, and tipped her palms downwards, 'Please Lord, in the name of your son, heal Nuala.' Even as she acted out the prayer she knew it wasn't the same – whatever had happened before had left its mark in her, and she knew this was not it. This time she was only channelling her own wishes. 'Why? Why not heal this good woman, Lord?' she cried, 'It's not fair! It's not right! I don't understand? Why one but not another?' She turned, walked to the door and pushed it open, and as she did so she heard a sound from the bed. Not just a wheeze, a sound that sounded like her name, she stared back into the room. With every sense tingling she heard it again, 'Domca?' She rushed to the bed, ignoring the danger she grasped Nuala's hand. 'Mother Nuala!'

'Domca,' the eyes were large in the shrunken face and wet with tears. 'Glad, happy...' she struggled to speak.

'Save your strength, you will get better.'

'Won't. Too far.' She swallowed, clamped her lips, tried to shake her hand free, her eyes widened and Dominica saw fear there and realised Nuala was scared for her, unable to prevent the cough. Dominica stepped back fast, clamping her cloth over her face as Nuala's body arched and a cough barked from her. Her whole body sighed as she sank back down, looking towards Dominica. 'Happy,' she said again. Dominica listened. 'for you. I see ... good work. Gift.' She seemed to gather some strength, breathing in, 'Blessing. On me.'

'Mother...'

'On me...'

Dominica stepped forward, tears were running down her face unheeded, she made the sign of the cross on Nuala, touching forehead, breastbone, shoulder to shoulder. 'May the Lord bless you and keep you ever safe in his arms, may he make his face to shine upon you and welcome you into his joy forgiving all things in his great mercy,' Dominica paused, drew in a breath like a sigh, and went on quietly, reciting words she'd heard Nuala say to those who were near passing on to the next life: 'And may the wise women of all ages be with you, the powers of earth, water, air and fire fill you, and mother earth welcome you home, Amen'

'Amen,' Nuala breathed.

At that moment the dogs started barking, telling Dominica that Sister Ciar was back, with a squeeze of

Nuala's hand she headed out, bringing the cloth to her face once more and wiping the tears away before meeting Sister Ciar as she came across the courtyard.

'How is she?' Sister Ciar asked.

'Struggling. She spoke a little, but...' the tears began again.

'I know. Don't worry, I'll ease the pain, I have brought a potion that will help.'

The steaming pot of herbs was set by the bed, while another was set to boil on the fire outside, Dominica had cleaned-up and checked on Nuala again.

'Her breathing is smoother, though still bubbling,' she began, 'but her face, she seems at peace?'

'That will be the potion.'

'What is in it? I don't recall us doing a potion like this?'

'It's about time I told you of this one. It uses Bethlehem lungwort, to ease the mucus, foxglove to steady the heart and the female buds of the healer's hemp to take away the pain, and bring ease to the mind - all in a honeyed oil. We will make some when we return so you understand the quantities, it can be dangerous if made carelessly.'

'Flanna?' Dominica called at the open doorway.

Flanna came out quickly, 'Mother?'

'She's sleeping peacefully, but – she won't last.' Dominica swallowed the ache in her throat.

Flanna's mouth pulled down and she shook her head, 'Thought not.'

'Um, I was wondering – where she caught it? Who did she treat that had something like this? I - we are worried it might spread?'

'Not here. No. I think it might have been back near Saint Brigid's Day, a message came from her sister's family, asking for help as she was sick and there was no-one to help her - as she was *their* wise-woman.'

'Nuala has a sister?'

‘Had – an older sister. Mother nursed her until she died. But that is over in Laigin at Loch Garman,’ Flanna explained but, seeing Dominica’s puzzled frown, she added, ‘Mother said her sister was taken there by the old king’s daughter when she was wed. It's a place on the coast where the sun rises and where they trade across the sea.’

‘I see,’ Dominica said softly, picturing mother Nuala caring beyond reason for her sister. ‘When she wakes I will let you know, so you can say your goodbyes.’ Eyes filling with tears again she turned and went back towards where Sister Ciar was stirring the herbs in the pot.

‘Take this in, change it for the other one,’ she said as Dominica arrived.

‘As long as, uh, as long as it hasn’t spread to the family, it sounds like it won’t spread. Nuala nursed her sick sister across on the sunrise coast. I suspect she didn’t realise she had caught it until the cough began – and then she knew what she had to do.’

'Brannon should know,' Dominica said the next day, suddenly thinking of her milk-brother.

'He knows,' Sister Ciar said, 'but for the safety of all he's not to come down.'

Dominica rocked back, 'But I am here!'

'And you are a healer, we have different dispensations and responsibilities.' Dominica was silent. 'And have to accept different risks,' Sister Ciar added quietly.

When Dominica went in to Nuala’s hut just a little later she knew instinctively that Nuala had gone. It was as if there was an unnatural stillness, as if everything within the room was waiting, even the air. She stood still herself. Let her mind’s eye reflect on the wonderful mother and teacher that Nuala had been to her, and then, with a long soft sigh she went to tell Sister Ciar.

Dominica and Sister Ciar cleansed and wrapped Nuala’s body themselves, making sure that there would be no chance of anything spreading to others who may come near, or those carrying the bier later.

A place was prepared in the graveyard, part way up the slope to the monastery where a small wicker chapel, used for funeral services alone, stood between a wooded area and the graveyard itself. Permission had been sought for Brannon and Indract to attend, and had been granted. Dominica hoped they'd be there waiting.

At noon on the second day, Coleman, Dugan and Flanna's two older sons, lifted the handles of the bier and the rest of the family, including Dominica, fell in line behind them. They crossed the ford and began to make their way slowly towards the little chapel. As the path took its gentle turn on the slightly steeper part of the slope Dominica caught sight of more people following behind them. A stream of people was heading downhill from Drom-Eanaigh, and the first were nearly at the ford.

By the time they had reached the graveyard the people from Drom-Eanaigh had caught up with the funeral procession and there, near the little wicker chapel, were Brannon, Indract, Sister Ciar, and - to Dominica's surprise - Abbess Mara, waiting for them.

When all the mourners were gathered in front of the chapel, Abbess Mara asked Brannon and Indract to stand on one side of her, and Dominica and Sister Ciar on the other, and then she began the funeral service.

She spoke to the people in their native tongue of the thresholds of our lives, as Saint Brigid had done, of birth and death, of the gift of healing that Nuala had been given, of the resurrection through Jesus and the joy of everlasting life, and then turned to the words of the service proper in Latin.

Looking around Dominica recognised many faces but also quite a few new young ones, recognised some of them as people she knew had come to Nuala in their times of need, and now they came to give her their love and respect. Dominica could not stop the tears sliding down her face, feeling bereft and helpless, yet at least knowing she wasn't alone in her love for Nuala.

Chapter 15

To Britannia - circa AD 688

Considering the last encounter Dominica had with her father, she was surprised to see King Conall himself come to see the pilgrims off. He stood beside the Abbot, the family resemblance clear and, as they approached to receive his farewell, she heard the last snatch of words addressed to the Abbot's ear by her father, '... your choice, on your head be it.' He turned his head and looked straight at them. Beckoning Indract forward he threw his arms around Indract and hugged him in that gruff way men have of it, completed by a firm pat on his back. When Dominica stepped forward he looked her up and down, as if he wasn't sure who he was seeing.

Dominica could feel her lips twitch to pull down and cry; she told herself it was foolishness as for years she had hardly known her father, and put it down instead to her sorrow over Nuala, which had not left her.

'Daughter,' he finally said, offering his hand. She stepped forward and he drew her into a gentle embrace. 'Daughter,' he repeated.

'Father.'

'Would that you were not in the church, that you were in the world and could be wedded. Your mother would have liked that - you know you can still stop this foolishness.'

'This is my life, father, the life God has planned for me. I have taken my vows and there is no turning back.' He released her and turned back to Indract, 'Then you must take care of your sister as much as God does, as much as I would will it.'

'I will father,' Indract said, straightening his shoulders.

They joined the others in prayer and received the blessing for the journey from the Abbot and Abbess, only eleven of them though, as Brother Tirechan had been taken sick and was unfit to join them.

As they turned to make their way to the riverside, Abbess Mara drew Dominica aside. 'Sister Dominica, I have something for you to take on your journey.' She gave Dominica a tightly rolled, wrapped and tied package, 'You may wear it when you get to where God wants you to be – you know that blue is the colour of Our Virgin Lady, she will be with you,' she smiled, 'God bless you.'

Dominica opened her mouth in wonder, 'Thank you, Mother. Thank you.'

Then, with many fervent wishes of 'God Speed' from all those gathered and allowed voice at this time, they boarded the flimsy crafts and pushed off from the bank, the flow of the river helping to take their string of coracles away. With Dominica, hugging her scrip and her new bundle, looking back now and again, wondering at Mother Mara's words.

The journey from Drom-Mhor to the small harbour at the mouth of The Great River was light and easy, the flow of the river helped them on their way. Towards dusk they came to the settlement of Eochaill, set amongst great dark yew trees, with just enough light to see their way. Leaving two of their number with the drawn-up coracles, a lit rushlight and their staffs to see off any who would rob them, the party headed towards the security of the church.

The priest of the area had been told of their coming, and someone must have told him they were on their way from the town quay as a rushlight burnt brightly at the door of the church.

'Brothers!' he said, 'Welcome to the house of the Lord.'

'And peace be with you brother,' Indract replied, his voice mellifluous as usual.

'Come, come in.'

'We have left two brothers with our goods, and would send for them before it darkens any more.'

'A good idea, yes, though Eochaill has many good people, we are too close to the harbour and that always has outsiders.'

'Sister,' Indract turned to look at Dominica, 'stay here, we will bring everything here. Maybe you can help the Father with some preparation of a little food?'

Indract didn't notice the look that the father gave when he heard the monk standing at the back was in fact a woman. Yet, maybe it was shock at his words, for, as the others left, he said, 'There's not much to be had. I have very little, only enough for my own needs in my house.'

'But father, I know the monastery at Drom-Mhor has made arrangements with you for food and drink for this night,' Dominica said.

'That is as may be, possibly.'

'Father, I know, I was with those that made the plans and sent the means,' Dominica said, softly but firmly. 'I trust the means are in your hands?'

'I have them,' he began.

'Then we can go now. You must know where we can get what we need, even this late?'

In a flurry and something a little like panic, his face flushing pink, he said, 'I will go – you, you cannot come with me!' He bustled off, leaving her in the small dank church alone, by rushlight.

She walked around the place, carrying the rushlight carefully to look into all the corners. The altar was well kept, and a delicately carved wooden cross stood upon it. Finding a holder to stand the rushlight in she knelt and prayed for safe deliverance, for if this was the result of well laid and financed plans, she felt they needed God's guidance more than man's.

A clamour of voices and shuffling heralded both the priest and a burly man and woman, carrying bundles, shortly followed by the brothers and the other provisions for the journey. Dominica hastily stood and took the rushlight back to the centre sconce to light the place better.

While the man and woman laid down the bundles and left again, the priest fetched out more rushlights from one bundle and lit them in sconces around the walls, casting many shadows. The brothers sat themselves down confessing themselves parched.

Indract asked the priest if they could have some good water to drink while they waited, and the man, almost as flustered as before, glanced at Dominica before suggesting someone came with him. Indract nominated Finn, who with good grace and a stretching of his long limbs followed the priest out. Dominica caught herself watching Finn as they walked past her.

'Are we to sleep in here?' Cormag said, heavily laying on his high-born accent, and looking disparagingly around.

'Seems so,' Indract said, glancing around. 'There'll not be anywhere else at this time of night and it's only for this one night.'

Cormag grunted his disapproval and strode up towards the altar where an odd short piece of wall seemed to set aside a separate space. 'Then I choose here,' he stated.

Indract cast his eyes around the Church, 'Would it not be better for our sister to have that – separated space?' he suggested quietly.

Cormag stared back at him, 'I knew she'd cause us trouble brother.'

'Indract, I don't mind where I am, really,' Dominica said.

'No, you must have that space,' Cormag said, striding back into centre of the church, 'I won't be the one to stop you in your foolishness.'

'Good,' Indract said, and set Teagan and Brannon handing out a blanket each to wrap themselves in for sleep later.

Eventually food was brought, a large steaming pot of vegetables and oatmeal, and a hard bread was drawn out of the other bundle they'd dropped earlier, to sop it with. Yet, after grace said, they ate well of it, seated in a circle on the ground before the altar.

They gathered at the front of the Church, on their knees facing the altar and began the evening prayers, but Dominica found herself so irritated by Cormag she had to spend much of her time asking God to forgive her anger and help her to forgive him for his behaviour. By the last Amen she had come to some kind of peace – certainly enough to sleep despite the rough and dusty ground.

Dominica woke to the sound of snores and the unpleasant smell of farts. Her mouth tasted of the dust on the floor and, though it was dark, she could see light under the doors. She rose, stretched and folded her blanket quietly. Her plan was to find somewhere secluded and quiet to wash her face and see to her morning toiletries. Taking her bowl with her, she stepped quietly out the side door and at once saw the priest in his night attire. From his stance, he had to be relieving himself behind a short wall to the rear of his house, obviously meant for the purpose. She ducked back before he could see her. She guessed that behind the wall was a latrine of some kind, so bided her time and then went to see. As she had suspected the rough wall enclosed just three sides but was facing toward a bank of shrubs and beyond that the river. The walls held a simple seat with a hole in it, suspended over a stinking pit with a trickle of water running through it. She used it and went to the well, set closer to the priest's home, and drew some water to cleanse her face and rinse her mouth of the dust.

When she returned to the Church the brothers were waking, and soon, after they had also gone out of the side door and returned, Indract called them to morning prayers and they knelt. This time she could pray with a clear conscience - her anger at Cormag had disappeared overnight.

The ate some bread dipped in warmed water to break their fast and then they dragged their supplies back down to the coracles. They thought they would only have a short journey to make to the harbour, however, the tide was coming in, so the brothers had to paddle hard. Even so, they got to the harbour in time to find the currach and load their supplies before the tide turned.

The master of the currach was taciturn to say the least - he only spoke to Indract and that to tell him where to put the goods.

They knew that the journey to San Dyfed's would take the whole day and that by night-fall they should be there, but the currach, though bigger than any other vessel Dominica had ever seen, still seemed small. It was wide enough to sit three abreast near the centre, with space for the sailors to pass, but they had the pilgrims sat in pairs on the benches, leaving room for themselves to sit and row.

'You will sit down and stay in your places,' the master said, 'No matter what! You could cause the currach to unbalance if you moved around.' Only he and his crew, five young men whose faces told their relationship, were to scramble around the sides and haul on the ropes or the oars. Dominica had no problem with this, settling herself as far to the back as she could, while Indract sat at the front. Brannon came and sat beside her and he reached out and squeezed her hand briefly, his bright eyes glinting in the morning light, full of the excitement and wonder of the trip.

Dominica thought the vessel small when they were safely in harbour but, as soon as they left the protection of the bay and met their first true waves, fear climbed up her throat and she had to dig her nails into her palms to stop herself crying out. As the rhythm of the waves settled, she gripped the edge of the bench instead, to try to stabilise herself.

As the sun rose to its zenith the weather changed. Dominica saw the currach master looking past her, and saw the solemn nod he gave to his men. They too looked across the top of the pilgrims' heads to behind the currach. Dominica gave in, and twisted around to see what they could see. Behind the currach the sky was roiling up with dark clouds. Almost as she turned round again she felt the wind lift. The large square sail snapped forward in a tight bow and the currach lurched. All the brothers were starting to rise now, turning around.

'Sit yourselves down!' the man yelled, his voice whipped by the wind that now hurtled the currach along and moaned as it pushed the sail. He shouted again, this time to his men, who scrambled to pull the sail down. As it slid, protesting, down the mast the wind snatched at it again, knocking one man to sprawl over two brothers. The wind shrieked the sail out taut and then snapped the mast clean off – the sail and the wood flung out to sea, the master, knocked flat and, only by good fortune, into the bowels of the vessel, not overboard.

The wind took a breath, a very small silent pause, then the rain began. The waves joined in the game, tossing them higher and deeper than they had before. The men struggled to get the currach to turn so that it faced into the waves, but they managed it.

Indract and Finn brought the currach master close to them. Indract looked back at Dominica, and held up a hand red with blood. She dived into her bundle and fumbled until she found a bandage. She tried to stand to go forward but immediately was overcome with sickness, it was all she could do to avoid puking over the brothers in front of her, her spew only narrowly missing them. They grasped hold of her and almost passed her from one pair of brothers to the other pair until she reached Indract and Finn, where she bound the currach master's head as best she could, her stomach heaving.

As she turned to try to get back to her place she saw she wasn't the only one suffering so. Ash-green faces and robes splattered with their meagre breakfast greeted her as the brothers helped her scramble back again.

The storm was well upon the boat now. Dominica could see from their faces that the currach master's sons, or cousins or whoever, were not the men who knew how to guide the currach to the port they sought. They fought with the wind and the waves well enough, it seemed, pulling oars in rhythm, but they didn't look to where the sun would be and peer over the side into the water, as the master had done. Then something else cracked and snapped. All heard it, but Dominica saw fear in the sailors' eyes – *they* knew what it meant. The man behind Dominica and Brannon, who had been crouched down holding a long steering paddle, was flung sideward. The handle of this paddle, falling loose from his grip, tumbled into the space behind them.

Within minutes the currach began to roll as it began to turn itself sideways to the waves. The oarsmen struggled to hold the currach straight, but it was impossible. Everyone held on tight to anything that didn't move and began to pray out loud. The waves started crashing over the sides, drenching everything. Breath shut out by the coldness of the water, gasping already when the second wave came, Dominica was sure they would all drown and thought of Brigit and her dreams.

Cormag suddenly stood up! Dominica saw Indract try to pull him down but he couldn't hold him. Cormag dragged himself up to the rim, hauling himself by a rope left tied when the mast went. They saw him hold out his arm over the sea and his mouth moved as if he were shouting, but they could hear nothing. A roll, and a huge wave crashed into him and he was flung back into the bottom of the currach. They heard his cry then – a howl that penetrated the storm and filled the hollow of the craft.

One of the sailors hauled out an oar, staggered past Dominica with it trapped under his arm, dragging himself along holding the sides of the currach. She watched amazed as together he and the steersman held it and forced it into the waves. Nothing changed. The currach rose up and teetered on a wave and as it did a cry of fear escaped from all of who should have been praying. At the last moment, just before everyone and everything should have been tipped out into the raging water, the currach turned, spun even, and ran down the face of the wave. As Dominica felt the movement she opened her eyes, turned her head, to see the look of triumph on the two young men's faces as they both fought to hold the oar in place.

Almost as swiftly as it had come, the rain began to ease and, shortly after, the wind dropped. The waves, still of a fearsome size, seemed to bear the currach forward without oars or sail. Two of the other men came and helped lash the oar so it needed less effort to hold and was less likely to throw them overboard, then took over from the others. Those relieved of the task went forward and spoke with the master who had returned to himself. Dominica turned her head this way and that. The thin line of coast that had been visible off to their left before noon, had totally disappeared. Every way she looked the sea rolled out to the edges of her vision, nothing but sea and a tumultuous sky.

The fear subsided but with it went that surge that fills the body and makes it overcome its own feelings. The cold shook everyone, teeth began to chatter and the cold of the water seemed to reach tendrils from sodden clothes right into bones. Dominica leant into Brannon, and he, shivering too, drew her close.

She could now hear Cormag's moaning. With every jolt of the currach as it dropped off a wave he gave a pitiful cry. Indract turned and caught her eye, but shook his head when he saw her start to move. He had Cormag wrapped in his arms, supporting him. She didn't know what to think, what damage had been done to him when he fell, yet it sounded bad and would need her care when they landed.

Dominica wondered how long the journey would take without the sail, so twisted in her seat to call to the new steersmen.

'How long brothers until we see land?'

They kept their eyes focused on.the dipping prow and beyond, but one spoke, 'Can't tell you. Never been this way before.'

She turned back and leant into Brannon again, the small patch of warmth where their forms met seemed to radiate slowly into the core of her body. In her mind she saw the wrath on the face of Sister Maire had she seen her so close to a brother, even if lives were in danger and the cold were one of the enemies. Each of the brothers had edged close enough to lean on one another, as if drawn like iron to a lodestone.

In this small calm, and exhausted, Dominica slept, and she dreamt. She dreamt of a river. A river like The Great River, she dreamt of sailing up it with Indract in a coracle until it flowed in a great loop, a double bend in the river that nearly met itself but then, when it straightened, there, slightly raised on the bank, was a shining place and in that shining place He stood to welcome her.

When she woke it had been dark, but now there was a thin line of light off to her right, getting brighter by the moment. While she slept someone had taken blankets from their packs and given them to the brothers. One was draped around her and she was still leaning up against a sleeping Brannon. She turned her head. The oar was held by one man only now – the waves felt sleek and smooth, yet they still seemed to be moving forward.

Later the master spoke to Indract - Dominica could see that both were concerned, so many shakes of the head, and glances out to sea. She amazed herself at her lack of thought. If the currach should have been in San Dyfed's by sundown, and now it was sunrise, where were they?

The sun rose, bright and gleaming across the shining sea. Indract led them all, men and monks, in a prayer of thanksgiving for their survival, and the pilgrims sang a hymn as the men went back to their work of pulling on the oars.

Around noon the master pointed forward and shouted. 'Land!' As one the passengers began to rise, until waved down again by his hand and an angry shout. 'Sit down you fools! You'll not capsize us now after we've survived and all!'

The sailors were all staring towards the land. Dominica could tell from their faces and their puzzled glances at the master that it wasn't the land they were expecting. She thought about the storm, the rudderless turning and the force of the waves and thought that to be where they had expected to be would have been a miracle.

The men set to with the oars again and pulled for all they were worth. As they drew nearer two higher land masses appeared with a lower one between, and before that a small island. There were small coves visible they could have aimed for but didn't, and other small boats around the area - but the master did not hail them as she thought he would.

Gradually the currach drew nearer, came between the island and a great hill, and then, there through a gap to her left, Dominica could see the water stretching inland – it was the mouth of a wide river. *'This is the river'*, a voice said within her head and the hairs on the back of her neck stood up as a tingling ran around her frame. She looked at the river with new eyes.

Still the master steered the currach on, straight up the middle of the river, not hailing any other, not close enough to hail anyone on the shore. He said something, and the men rested their oars. He stood and gazed around, then they set to again, heaving, sweating, dragging the currach up the river. By the look of the glistening mud-banks the tide was about half up, or half down, but the master seemed in a hurry, as he kept cajoling the crew to go harder at the oars.

After a narrower piece, the river spread wide and magnificent again, then ahead the river seemed to split in two. As they neared the divide the master leant on the makeshift steering oar and began to push the prow towards the right-hand fork, then he leant again and the currach turned sharply right - towards the mouth of a creek all overhung by heavy trees.

It felt like the currach was suddenly going faster as it was swallowed by the great green mouth of the creek, with just enough water beneath it, judging by the narrowness of the waterway and the mud either side.

There was a little jetty ahead. As the boat reached it, with skill and a lightness of foot, one of the men leapt upon it, pulling a mooring rope behind him - just as a man shouted from higher up the bank and came running.

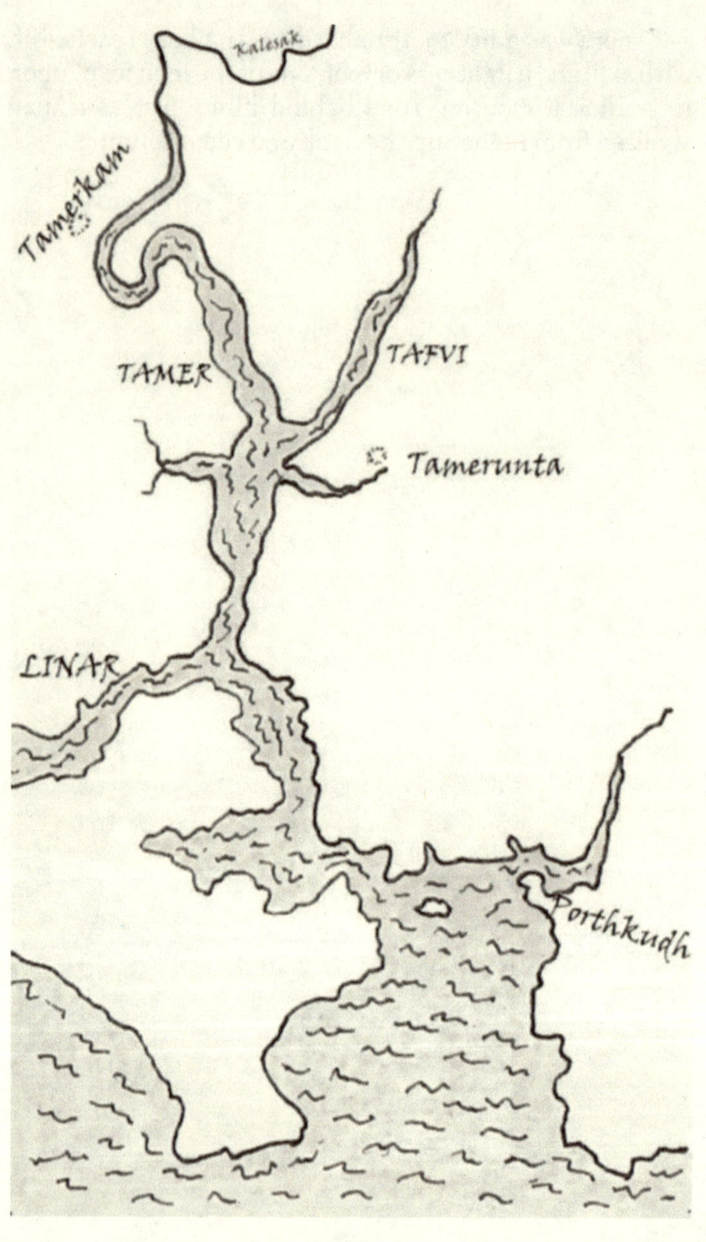

Map 2 - after the storm, in Dumnonia

Part Two

In the valley of the Tamer River, Dumnonia

Chapter 16

Tamerunta *- circa AD 688*

More men came running and shouting. Dominica's heart raced – until she saw the first man bend to help fasten the currach up.

'Stay put until I say,' the master addressed the pilgrims, and stepped up onto the jetty. The master spoke to the men on shore, and they came and helped lift Cormag up from where Indract still held him. Dominica could hear his groan as they moved him. Then it was their turn. One by one, stiff, cold and splattered with vomit, they clambered out of the currach.

Once everyone was on shore, Cormag being carried by Indract, Dairmut and two of the local men, the master seemed to collapse in on himself, as if he was keeping himself upright only until the currach was safe. One of his men caught him, and he and another of his crew supported him. They made their way unsteadily as they were led towards the homesteads

Dominica and the other brothers followed, she with her healing scrip over her shoulder and wondering what language these people were speaking, as she didn't recognise it. They soon came in sight of a very large round house, like a meeting house from home. As they neared a man, quite obviously the chief of the settlement, left the doorway and came forward swiftly to the currach master. Dominica couldn't understand him, but she could see the concern on his face, his giving of fast orders to his men. Then she saw the master taken inside and a woman running towards the house.

She and Dominica arrived at the doorway together. The comely woman smiled at her just before she darted ahead into the building. Even before her eyes got used to the dim light she turned to the sound of groans, and made out Cormag lying on a pile of skins over on one side.

The woman had gone the other way to the chief and the currach master, now sitting down. Dominica headed for Cormag and was joined by Brannon as she picked her way around the circle.

'Brother Cormag,' she began, 'where does it hurt?'

'Leg,' he gasped, not even opening his eyes.

'Brannon, I must see the leg,' she said, feeling it improper to draw back the monk's robe herself. Brannon nodded and carefully drew back the robe, feeling the tug of the salt-soaked coarse cloth then wincing at the sight of the blood, flesh and bone, the leg at an unnatural angle.

Dominica drew in a ragged breath. She needed more light, but what she could see filled her with dread. An injury beyond anything she had come across within the monastery, though reminiscent of one she had helped Nuala deal with when Dominica was still quite young. What concerned her was that the young man had not survived, even with Nuala's care - some malodour had begun to emanate from the wound and turned itself on the heart and soul of the man, draining his life away.

'Come,' a woman's voice said in Dominica's own tongue, 'we will get him carried to a better place.' Dominica looked up at the woman she'd seen earlier. 'I'm Liaden, Eudaf's wife and the healer here,' she added as she waved some men over to her.

They laid him in what Dominica recognised as a healer's house from the drying herbs and the cleanliness as compared with the big-house.

Cormag had fainted again when they had moved him - all for the best.

'Sister Dominica, the healer on this pilgrimage - and *so* glad to meet you. How is the currach master?'

'Segan's head will hurt, but he will live. Let's look at this one to see if we can say the same.'

'You know the currach master?'

'Ha! Yes, you could say the wind has blown him this way before, he's my cousin. He brought me here when I was out of favour at home in Eriu.' They worked as she spoke. A pair of bright candles were brought to light their subject. 'Mother of God!' she breathed as the damage was revealed. The skin and flesh had been ploughed down to the bone just below the knee on his inner right calf. This portion of his leg lay at an impossible angle, the knee itself jutted out awkwardly to the right of the line down from his thigh.

Liaden called a girl to boil water, gave Dominica an over-apron to wear instead of her vomit splattered robe and left her to clean the area around the gash, whilst she went to speak with her husband. He had already given the guests a drink, called for food to be prepared and showed the monks where they could wash their faces and hands.

Indract took control of the monks' activity, designating Dairmut, Brannon and Teagan to bring up their bags so each could get out their spare robes. He then asked the currach master to ask the chief if there was somewhere they could shelter, but Eudaf understood him and spread his arm wide, indicating the area they stood in. 'The big-house is yours as long as you need it,' he said slowly in Indract's tongue.

'Thank you, God bless you and all yours!' Indract replied, his voice loaded with wonder, 'He surely must have sent us to you here. I am Indract, son of King Conall of Drom-Eanaigh, servant of God and, with my sister and brothers, on a peregrination to see where God wants us to do his work.'

Eudaf laughed, 'Well, king's son, I hope you can manage with the little we have to share.'

‘The Lord lived a simple life and we thank you. You will all be in our prayers this evening.’

Liaden and Dominica stared at the strangely bloodless wound, but then decided that it looked that way through being washed by sea water so much. Dominica had used boiled water to cleanse the skin from particles of cloth that had stuck to the wound with the mixture of sea-salt and blood, but had been wary of disturbing the edge of the skin or touching the portion of bone visible.

‘The skin feels cold yet,’ Dominica said. ‘At least there seems to be no infection.’

As they talked Liaden recognised an experienced healer and was as happy as Dominica to know another. ‘Agreed, but we may have to do something drastic to marry the flesh to let it heal. I cannot conceive of how it will come together over the bone as it is.’

‘And then what of the leg? It can never work like that?’

‘Well,’ Liaden paused, ‘we will see. It might pull back into place. I have seen it done once before a long time ago, and have done many small ones on elbows or shoulders, but...’

‘But?’

‘There was no wound to consider, we may need your prayers, sister.’

Dominica looked down - if her most fervent prayers for the woman she loved most in the world had no effect, what good would they do for Cormag? But pray she would - they all would.

Cormag stirred and groaned. They both looked at each other, then to him. ‘Would that he’d stayed asleep,’ Liaden said softly. Dominica nodded. The pulling of the leg would be painful.

‘Maybe he will need ale to help? We and the brothers would give mead to a patient before trying something that might be painful.’

'Are you thirsty brother?' Liaden asked. A mute nod. Liaden sent the girl to fetch strong ale. When it arrived they supported Cormag and helped him drink. He was thirsty. Water was what his body craved, but the ale slipped into his parched and hungry body easily. They kept plying him with more, a half cup at a time, until they felt his body relax and he drifted off into an exhausted ale-induced sleep.

Liaden went and returned with Indract and two of the strongest men in the village. She carefully instructed them what to do, how to hold the thigh, how to hold the calf, how to take care not to wrench the wound.

Dominica took Indract aside and told him she had said they'd pray. Indract looked at her, 'You pray - like you did for me,' he whispered back.

'No, I will pray *with* you. That was only when we were alone. Besides I only ask healing in the name of the Father, Son and Holy Spirit - we can all do that.'

Indract looked at his sister hard, then relaxed as if deciding something, and nodded. He looked on in curious fascination as the two men took up position, Cormag groaning as they gently tried to get their bodies in a straight line with each other with the leg between them. He was so transfixed that Dominica had to nudge him into prayer when they were ready to try to pull the leg straight.

'In the name of the Father, Son and Holy Spirit we ask for healing for our Brother Cormag,' Indract began, then, 'Our Father ...' which was taken up by Dominica. As the Amen sounded Liaden counted down in Cornish, 'Tri, diw, onan. Lemmyn!' The men heaved, Cormag's body arched and he screamed. Simultaneously Liaden pushed the top of the lower leg outward, whilst Dominica held the thigh firm against her to help it remain in position - suddenly the two halves of leg aligned.

'Gently now, release,' she shouted to the sweating men over Cormag's wail. Instantly the cry cut off, but only because Cormag had dropped back into blessed oblivion.

'Thank the Lord,' Dominica whispered, catching Liaden's eye.

With the men's help Cormag's damp robe was carefully removed without disturbing his leg. Liaden shushed the men out with thanks, and asked Indract if he would leave or remain. He chose to remain.

They began to work on the gash, bleeding a little again now. They swabbed the bone, the raw edges and the surrounding skin with garlic and mint steeped cooled water. Taking a slightly curved bronze needle and a fine thread of nettle-fibre from inside a clean cloth, Liaden turned to Dominica. 'If you can draw the wound together I will try to sew it up.'

Dominica stared, 'I've never seen a needle like that.'

'It was Eudaf's mother's. It *is* special! She said she found them hidden in a piece of leather in one of those buildings made by the foreign people when she was a child, a long way from here.' Dominica nodded, it looked very special, so fine and strong.

She turned her attention to the wound, and wondered aloud if there was skin enough to marry together. It was as if the skin had shrunk or had been cut short. Working with clean hands, as Nuala had taught her, she found the lower edge easily. The top edge seemed thickened, but then she realised it had rolled under and stuck to itself. 'We will need both of us to get this unstuck,' she said.

They worked together. Dominica, carefully washing it as she went, unrolled the skin and flesh flap, Liaden holding the unrolled section close to the bone to stop it trying to re-curl. With a sigh Dominica flattened the torn end onto the bone and looked at Liaden. They both knew it would take a miracle for the ends to hold together.

'Indract! Bring the candle closer! We need better light for this!' He did as bid immediately, watching intently.

After a painstakingly tense time Liaden stood straight and wiped the sweat from her brow. 'We can do no more,' she said looking down at the ragged long stitches, 'let's get it covered, then we can see if Eudaf has found four straight sticks for us to make a frame for the leg to hold it in place.' After a word or two she left Dominica to spread honey over the patched wound and cover it with a clean cloth pad, tied on with strips of fine nettle cloth.

The sun was going down by the time the four poles had been bound around the leg, holding it rigid. They'd wrapped a length of open-weave cloth around the leg first and softened the ends of the rods, with pads of cloth filled with dried wound-moss, before the rods were placed front, back and either side and bound in. There was no way Cormag could bend his leg or for the joint to slip out again. They left him well covered and warm to sleep.

It was only then that Liaden had time to take Dominica to get cleaned up properly and she was glad to get into a fresh leine and robe, but also very hungry and thirsty. She didn't have long to wait, as Liaden brought food for both of them, everyone else having eaten.

'Tell me, where are we?' Dominica asked when her hunger had been eased, 'I know we can't be at San Dyfed's. The journey should have been only a day, and we were blown so badly by the storm and we were much longer at sea than that.'

'We call our place here Tamerunta. You came in by the mouth of three rivers. The greatest is the Tamer, one side is Kernow and on this side, Dewnen, but in truth they're all one people just divided by a river.'

'Do you know the river well? As it travels inland?'

Liaden looked curiously at Dominica, 'Not myself, but some of the men, the river-men, take coracles up further. They would know. Why do you want to know?'

Dominica hesitated, then smiled and replied, 'It reminds me of the river that runs past my home,' which wasn't exactly telling a lie, as she felt again the certainty that this river was the one in her dream.

Chapter 17

The Settlement *- circa AD 688*

True to their word the whole community of Tamerunta made them welcome. On the other side of the creek to the main group of homes, where it was but a stream and made easy to cross by stepping stones, there was a small clearing. With Eudaf's permission Indract thrust his staff into the soil there and bound a rod across it to make a cross, then he and Brother Dairmut heaved a rock from nearby to set beside it to stand on.

The head-man, Eudaf, and the people of the community, were invited to share in a service of thanksgiving for the survival of all those aboard the currach and for God's blessing on the people of the settlement - and nearly all came. Eudaf told them that many years ago, when he was just a small boy, their settlement had been visited by another holy monk, teaching them of the love of this God, which was welcomed but, without a constant presence, what they knew had melted in with their traditional beliefs.

In his prayers Indract thanked God for bringing their peregrination to these open people, and vowed to provide a long-term Christian presence, even if some of them were called to move on.

He called the pilgrims together in the big-house. All the brothers were there, except Cormag, still being cared for in the healer's house, and Dominica, who was caring for him.

'Brothers, we have thanked God for his goodness in carrying us to safety. I believe we should be thanking and praising God for bringing us straight to the first place he wants us to do his work. The people here are ready; this land was tilled many years ago, but weeds have sprouted. I propose we seek to create a small monastery and church here, preach to these people and all around who will hear and bring them back to Christ.' Indract looked from face to face. 'Has the Lord spoken to any of our number already?' No one spoke up. 'Then pray on this and after Nones tomorrow we shall see if God has answered our prayers.'

The next day, after their service of Nones and their daily meal, they gathered again - this time Dominica was with them.

'Brothers, and sister, let us pray again over this settlement and try to discern God's will for us and these people.' All bowed their heads. 'Dear Father, brother Jesus, guiding Holy Spirit, show us your will for us and your children in this place. Fill our hearts and souls with your grace and power to hear and do your will. Amen.' The 'Amen' sounded back and then there was silence, a silence that stretched into long minutes, yet did not feel uncomfortable.

After a long while, Teagan said softly, 'I see a great oak tree, so great a tree that under its branches is the whole settlement.'

Silence.

'Mm, the tree is the love of Jesus and sanctity of God,' Finn said quietly, 'it shelters and sustains the people here.'

Various voices added 'Amen'.

Silence, a warm meditative silence.

'*Your work is not here.*' The words drifted like a ghost through Dominica's consciousness, words only meant for her. A shiver ran round her frame. She said nothing.

After another long while Brother Dairmut concluded with, 'We thank you, Lord, for your love, your care and your guidance. Be with us all in the work you would have us do here in Your name. Amen.' 'Amen,' came the response in something like a sigh of satisfaction.

They decided to ask if they could stay, and if they could be allotted an area where they could clear land and build a monks' house to house themselves and church for prayer, clear land to grow for their needs, but help work the settlement land to earn their sustenance until their land yielded. In return they'd build a church and teach all they knew.

Eudaf was very happy to hear their ideas a few days later, going so far as to suggest the area below the settlement, across the creek, that was not used, and agreed to set it before the Tameruntaʼs council of elders before the summer solstice.

Every day Dominica spent time with Cormag, treating his wound, cleaning it and re-dressing it, and Cormag was recovering well, the wound showing no signs of infection, for which Dominica thanked God.

Cormag gazed at Dominica when she was concentrating on tending his leg, noticing her as a woman. A woman, not a hindrance to their journey. A woman, not just a nun. Daughter of a king; almost as high-born as himself. She had a beautiful face, that turned a smile to him as she looked up to say how well he was healing.

Finnachta had cut and fashioned a pair of crutches to help Cormag move around and, with the help of Niall and Dairmut, a high bench that he could sit back onto and raise himself from without assistance. Even so he was reluctant to step outside the healer's hut, fearing he looked crazy lurching with a caged leg or, worse, that he might fall and be unable to get up unaided. So Cormag was impatient to have the restrictive frame removed, but Liaden was wary of removing it too soon, knowing that the wrong move could cause the knee to jump out again, that it took time for the sinews that hold the knee in place to strengthen.

*

The day before the solstice Eudaf told them they had use of the land he'd spoken of, and led them to mark it out with peeled and marked sticks pushed in the ground. They were pleased and grateful. The land began on the small flat area where they had planted Indract's staff as a makeshift cross, but beyond was not too steep, had access to other water sources and plenty of woodland, much of which they would have to clear, but which would also provide their building materials. Eudaf also offered a loan of tools, over and above the few the monks had brought with them. They felt truly blessed and their evening prayers reflected this.

As soon as the permission was given, the monks began work to fulfil their plans. The land was marked out by those who had created the plan, and the first of the trees fell to their axes. Rocks were prised from the sides of the valley and brought to make into door-steps, hearth-stones and a raised area where the altar would stand. Each day some of the monks would spend time in the fields tending the crops as directed by Eudaf, or preparing the ground that would become their own source of sustenance eventually.

Dominica accompanied Liaden on her gatherings, picking herbs and berries, learning the native tongue from her, and the names for those plants she knew by other names, and the properties of plants new to her. She helped too in the drying and the preparations Liaden made, always learning more.

One day, as they were putting crumbled dried herbs into a pot she asked, 'Tell me, Liaden, how are these small pots made? What are they made from?'

'They're clay! And yes! I never knew of such as these back in Eiru. I had seen something similar, ones that had come from distant lands, but not like this, never so simple. Here you can get them made for you in sizes you want - small bowls, pots and cups – they make them round the coast a bit from here. If you want larger ones to stand in the fire they have to come from further down in Kernow, something special about their clay, so it is strong but doesn't crack in the heat.'

These walks with Liaden also took her to visit many of the out-lying homesteads, where Liaden greeted the people, enquired after their health, and introduced Dominica as a holy sister and a healer too, and that became her time to spread the word and encourage those who showed an interest in learning more.

One day, after yet another blustery squall drenched them, Dominica asked Liaden, 'Is it always as wet and grey as it seems to be here?'

Liaden stopped shaking the rain off her cloak, 'It hasn't always been so. I would say the weather turned bad about four or five years since, colder too. I know some plants do not show as early as they did, and some of our harvest has been ruined by both rain and wind three years out of the last five.' With a final shake she hung her cloak up. 'Did you ever hear of the red rain where you were from? About five years ago.'

Dominica thought back, she would have been about sixteen years, helping in the infirmary, and yes, there it was, a short time before Indract was so sick - no wonder she'd forgotten. 'Ah! The blood rain - they called it! I remember it had caught some of our leines set to dry and turned them pink. Some thought it an ill omen, even in the monastery.'

'Same here. I think it *was* an omen - of bad weather to come,' Liaden grimaced.

**

One day, shortly before the leg braces were to be removed, Dominica was gathering the old dressing for boiling when Cormag snapped at Liaden, 'Woman, get me something to drink!' Dominica looked up, and moved to go, 'Not *you* Sister Dominica,' he added.

'But I will fetch it,' she said, 'for we are *guests* and you are in Liaden's healing house.' Cormag's face darkened, but he said nothing.'

Outside, Dominica apologised to Liaden for Cormag's words. 'He was raised as a prince. The humility of monastic life has not yet entered his heart. I suspect it was not his choice.'

'Sister, do not excuse him. *I* suspect he wanted me out of the house before *you* left.'

'What do you mean?'

'You have not seen the way he looks at you when you are tending his wound. A half-starved wolf is less hungry. Take care sister, especially if God does not lead his heart.'

Once the skin had healed enough Liaden nicked the threads and, with expert fingers, drew the pieces of fibre out. A few days later, when the holes were calloused over, she deemed it time to remove the frame. There were sores where the padded ends had dug into Cormag's flesh, and his injured leg looked thinner than its pair, the one semi-wasted, the other extra exercised. The wound, however, was a really ugly scar, still ragged in appearance and discoloured, not that it should matter when the miracle was that it hadn't become infected.

Cormag left no time in getting to exercise the leg, still using one crutch to help to begin with, but already complaining that his knee was stiff making his gait uneven. Liaden and Dominica assumed it was the weakness of the muscles, but as his leg strengthened it became obvious there was something wrong.

As Cormag tried to walk without a crutch the only way he could make the foot, indeed the whole lower leg, obey him was to swing his upper leg to bring it forward, the knee stiff and unresponsive, the foot falling flat-footed and without the normal spring. There was no great pain, just an unwieldy gait that dented Cormag's pride and made him feel old. Liaden had tried to reassure him that it was early days, and that his healing had many moons to go yet. He knew he should be grateful that he lived, but in his heart he blamed Liaden for his affliction.

Early summer evenings became the time the monks and Dominica would welcome the people to join them at their cross for a service, and they came - when it wasn't wet - and stood where they looked towards the foundations of the new church being built a little further up the rise behind the cross. Here each of the pilgrims would take it in turn to teach about the love of God, the love God has for all creation and the forgiveness of sins by trust in the Lord Jesus Christ and through baptism in water and the Holy Spirit.

As the summer wound on more people came, sat quietly and listened to the good news. One day Eudaf came to Indract whilst he was helping prepare vegetables for the pot, 'Brother, I have had some people ask me where this baptism could be got?'

Indract rejoiced in his heart, and said, 'It is available to all who would have it. As soon as they have accepted Christ and repented of past sins they can be baptised.'

'Then brother, maybe we should have a baptism day. I will ask who wishes to do this thing.'

'Praise the Lord! May he go with you.'

After compline Indract turned to the brothers. 'Today we were asked to provide a baptism for those who wish to be baptised into the family of God.' There were murmurs of 'praise the Lord', and 'alleluia' in response.

'Where would we do this baptism? The creek here is not suitable to get into the water, too steep and muddy, as are the banks of the main river hereabouts,' observed Durragh.

'It needn't be the river. We could make a pool in the stream,' Dairmut said.

'You love work, brother!' Fergus replied, a laugh in his voice.

'Loves to see us sweat, more like it,' chipped in Kellagh. Indract fixed him with a stare. He dropped his eyes, 'Sorry. Brother Dairmut, I will help dig it if that's what we'll be doing.'

'Me too, Brother Dairmut.'

Dairmut smiled at the pair, little more than overgrown boys. Their quick tongues got them into more trouble than they meant. 'Aye, if we do?' he raised his bushy eyebrows and glanced towards Indract.

'What are you thinking?'

'That a nice clear pool would be an asset. We could make a few more ordinary ones below – to grow the fish as we did back home.'

Indract smiled, 'Why not indeed! It is a good thing to have. You have an idea of where?'

'Yes, it would work in that smaller stream, across from the church. It is below our water supply and would take no water out, just divert it a bit. There's likely rock enough in that rise behind it.'

'Sketch it out for us, and you can be in charge of seeing it done. When should I say to Eudaf that the baptism pool will be ready?'

'Give us a month, brother, there's a fair bit of rock to move. Say we will be ready by the next full moon.'

'Will your two volunteers be enough? Brother Cormag has not been assigned a proper role since his return to us.'

'But Brother Cormag,' Cormag intervened, 'will not be volunteering for such physical work as yet, brothers. I fear my injuries will not yet sustain heavy physical work, neither digging nor the cutting and dragging of trees. I can offer up extra prayers for all our labours as a suitable contribution if it is willed?'

'Ah! Brother. Of course,' Indract said slowly, smiling round the circle at the others, 'but you will be able to do some light work, so we can release those able to do the heavy work, thank you Brother Cormag. You may take on the burden of the kitchen duties assigned to other brothers, as that will be suitably light during your convalescence.'

Cormag also glanced at the brothers, and saw they were in accord with Indract's suggestion. 'As it is willed,' he said tightly.

'You'll not be alone in your task. We now have a local lad, Erbin, helping out and he does the heavy lifting, and of course Sister Dominica also helps with the cooking when not tending to the sick.'

Cormag merely nodded, but inside he grinned.

Chapter 18

Onward - circa AD 688–689

A week later Dominica went to see how the work was going with the baptism pool and was amazed at the amount of rock shifted from the hillside. The rocks were now waiting in piles near where Brother Dairmut had decided to create a dam, a good body's length downstream from a very small waterfall.

'Good day sister,' Dairmut called as he looked up from where Fergus was levering a slab of rock away from the side.

'Good day brothers. I have brought you a drink.'

'Kindness itself sister,' Fergus said with an extra fierce tug on the rod. Dairmut turned and reached forward to steady the slab of stone that had loosened, 'Kellagh!' The brother stacking rocks scrambled back and helped Brother Dairmut ease the block forward and over onto its face.

'It is a blessing that the rock breaks just so,' Dominica said.

'It is that sister. I had seen the way it parted when we sought hearth-stones and thought it was god-given.'

Dominica smiled. She loved the cheerfulness of these brothers and the freshness of the open air. She walked back with her empty ewer towards the kitchen hut, her face now solemn as she thought about yet another time in that small space preparing the meals with Cormag and Erbin.

Dominica had been careful ever since she found Cormag assigned to the kitchen work, as Liaden suggested she kept a wide space between herself and Cormag, and made sure not to be alone with him. She was, however, impressed by how hard he worked at the tasks set, and began to wonder if she was wrong about him.

Cormag's leg had definitely not healed properly. He struggled to decide which was the better way to appear - walking firmly with a crutch, or an ungainly hobble without. Moreover he wondered how Dominica saw him.

The next time she visited the works, the small pool was nearly empty, the water diverted by a channel around one side. The brothers had laid the blocks of stone across the stream-bed in a wide dam, brought up as high as the stream sides which had been strengthened and edged with slate slabs. The main pool, just below the little waterfall, had been dug deeper and enlarged so that it was as wide as two men abreast and as long as a tall man. Below the first dam they had created three more pools, each awaiting their own shallower dams. The brothers were so cheerful in their work that she recognised the difference between them and the studied, hard work Cormag put in back in the kitchens.

The night of the full moon was coming up soon. The final time she visited the pools, the water was running back in its old course. The top pool had two sets of blocks inside, making rough steps to descend in and out of it, and was lined with thinner slabs. The pool was clear, full and trickling over the rim where Brother Dairmut had set one larger slab a tad lower and protruding, making a lip. It cascaded down into the pool below, stirring up the unlined bottom as the pool began to fill.

'It will clear soon enough,' Dairmut said, noticing her frown, 'and besides – it will be for the fish to spawn in – and we must yet put a layer of small stones and plant it with weeds for them and that will help it stay clear.'

'I was just remembering all the pools were clear.'

'Indeed, some things take more time.'

The day of the baptism was a special day. Seventeen adults had been having lessons with brothers Niall and Finnachta and were ready. The whole settlement made a procession and followed them out, across the stepping stones, up to the praying place below Indract's staff cross.

There prayers were said, before those ready for baptism were led down and across to the new pool. The villagers gathered and watched as Brother Dairmut stepped down into the pool, the water up to his waist. Those ready for baptism stood facing the stream and him.

Indract had crossed the stream higher up and spoke to them, and the gathered people, from the other side. He began. 'As our Lord was baptised in the flowing waters of the river Jordan, so you are to be washed clean of your sins in these waters. Blessed be the water that flows here, let it flow through the lives of these, your children come to baptism, and make them new people, new followers of your way, beloved by God, we ask this in your name dear Jesus. Amen.'

'Amen!' rang back from all gathered. Indract nodded to the first in the line, he stepped forward and down into the water.

Dairmut beamed at him, 'Eudaf, I baptise you in the name of the Father and of the Son and of the Holy Spirit.' He took hold of Eudaf's elbow, placed a hand on his head and ducked him under the water. Allowing him to surface he shouted out, 'Praise be to the Lord!' and the monks replied, 'Glory to His name!' Dairmut, nodded to Eudaf, and he took the steps up the other side to stand beside Indract - a new man in Christ.

***

Their first Pascha at Tamerunta was a joyous occasion and so many had been baptised that day that the number of baptised in the area had grown to over forty. So many blessings; the monks' house made, so that the meeting house in the settlement was free once more, the church was roofed over and ready to use. Lessons were being taught to the locals, Dominica even finding time to help some of the brothers who were struggling to learn the local language which she seemed to have picked up so easily with Liaden's guidance. The stream was planted with water weeds and the first fish added to the top fish pool awaiting the miracle of new life. And another small miracle of life, a tiny spur and leaf-bud appeared on Indract's oak staff, just above where the cross rod was bound to it, so they left it there to see if it would grow.

About two weeks later Dominica and Indract stood on the headland overlooking the confluence of the two rivers, Tafvi and Tamer gazing towards the more distant Tamer. My brother is a good man, Dominica thought, loving of the Lord, a little grandiose in his duties, as if he cannot forget he is the son of a king, but good none-the-less; she turned to look at him.

'Well, what is it?' Indract asked, 'and why did we have to come so far – even if you needed a word with me in private, why here exactly?'

'Brother,' she hesitated knowing her words could cause consternation, 'maybe this isn't the place that God called us to be?' looking at him intently, as if in that look she could fill him with what she had felt, what she was experiencing.

Indract looked at her pale face, 'What do you mean? We are doing God's work here, the people have listened. Just look how many were baptised at Pascha.'

'Yes, yes, we are, you are, doing really well here, but, you know,' she faltered. She knew her visions and sensitivities could be considered suspect by some, but Indract had seen his own vision and had seen her on this journey, so surely he understood more than anyone, 'I believe God wants us, or maybe me, elsewhere – further up-river.' She wasn't brave enough to tell him her deep down conviction that God was calling her, alone, for this mission. They had made this journey, this crazy, dangerous, God-driven journey, together – how could she abandon her brother's care? She still recalled the way her father had admonished Indract to look after her.

Indract sighed. He recognised the Holy Spirit worked through his sister, gave her the gift of healing at times and even visions, so maybe she was right. 'So where do you think the Spirit wants us to go?'

'Up-river, the far river over there,' pointing to the Tamer, 'I saw that river, and we were sailing up it in a coracle until it flowed in a great loop, a bend in the river that nearly met itself and there, slightly raised on the bank, was a shining place and in that shining place He, Jesus, stood to welcome us. I will know when we get there, God will guide us.'

Indract was silent, staring out over the water. Dominica held her breath. He then looked back at her and nodded. 'So be it,' and smiled at his sister, 'we can go up-river Domca, just you and me though, that will be best.'

Chapter 19

Rising tide - *AD circa 689*

One of the larger oval-shaped coracles was borrowed, the local river-men consulted and the day set. The brothers had been told this was a peregrination, a God-prompted journey of just a few days - the only query had come from Brother Cormag who took Indract aside to suggest that he should come too. Brother Cormag was the last person Indract wanted along on Dominica's vision-led journey and so he said no, the two of them were enough.

Dominica arranged for supplies for themselves and took with her, as always, a small scrip with her most regularly used herbs and potions.

Though word had gone round, as it will in a small community when something new is afoot, the two of them had made no big thing of their leaving. However, so many of the villagers traipsed the fair distance along the creek-side to the headland, that Indract felt moved to say something.

'Brothers and sisters, it warms our hearts to see so many of you wish us well on our Christian mission. May the Lord bless our travel as he leads us to spread the word. May we come back safely rejoicing in the glory of God's wisdom.' The brothers added the Amen, taken up by the people.

The rivers were spread wide and thin at this point, both sides glistening with mud and seaweeds. They walked the coracle to the edge of a slightly deeper channel and both stepped carefully aboard while the coracle still partially rested on sandy mud. Indract seated himself at the front with the oar ready, and Dairmut and Fergus eased the coracle down into deeper water. Once there was enough water beneath them, Indract began to work the oar in a figure of eight shape to draw the shallow boat forward, in the way he'd learnt as a boy on the river at Drom-Eanaigh.

Dominica, sitting tight and keeping her balance, turned her head to see the whole company staring after them as they were suddenly caught-up in the rising tide, the water flowing stronger up the river than down. Indract worked the oar steadily to take them across the draw of the tide flowing up the Tafvi, the river flowing closest to Tamerunta, and over into the main channel of the Tamer.

Once there, he drew breath and called over his shoulder, 'All well, sister?'

'All well, brother!' Dominica called back. All well, all very well. Her heart was singing, she felt so alive and the pull of the vision was even stronger than the pull of the rising tide on their small vessel.

Indract's oar-work was more a case of keeping the coracle in the centre of the flow, less about trying to make them move faster, which gave both of them time to survey the land on either side of the river. At most points where a creek entered the river some signs of habitation were visible, maybe smoke from distant fires, or people on the riverside.

The sun was hot on Dominica's back and bright as it reflected off the ripples that ran ahead of them with the rising tide, and with the little craft moving quite swiftly it was as if it knew it had a purpose.

The main flow of the incoming tide took the outer curves of the river, so they were swept from one side to the other, the river widening and narrowing only slightly, but always showing a long bright stretch ahead of them.

Then the river suddenly seemed to narrow more than it had before, drawing them off to the right, suggesting a bend ahead, but now ahead all they could see were hills and trees. They were swept hard right, very close to the shore and another creek, with a settlement hidden amongst the trees. A few men on the shingle beach above the mud line watched them keenly as they passed.

The river drew them on, but now the distance was even more curtailed, always as if the trees blocked the way – yet moved as they moved, to reveal more river. Then a slightly longer view, much narrower, before the blanking off by trees, the sweep of the channel taking them off to the left hand bank side now, the visible distance even shorter.

They seemed to be swept in a never ending curl, hard to the left-hand bank until they passed a huge hill on that side and then, like a dawn, they came into a straighter stretch, the channel not so hard by the left, a wide creek issuing, a shingle beach in view ahead, a lone man.

'We are getting near,' Dominica called to Indract as she echoed the voice she heard in her head, and as her blood began to sing and her heart to race - Indract started to work the oar to bring them towards the shingle beach. The man started to run along the bank towards them.

'Not yet! Not just here!' Dominica called, 'I will tell you where - it's not far.' Indract stopped working the oar and the river drew them out and onward, past the man, past a smaller creek. Dominica knew that the pull she felt in her head was still leading them upriver. Then, still within sight of the man who had turned and followed their progress along the bank up to the edge of the small creek, the voice said, *'Here!'*

'Here! There – look, that little shingle bank on the left, just ahead, there!' And Indract worked the oar to draw them the little way from the faster channel to the sluggish edge of the river. Drawing the coracle in safely onto the mud edge beside the shingle. Indract hopped out, pulling it further onto the mud and steadying the coracle for Dominica to step out too. They made the coracle safe by lifting it and putting it above the water line, tucked out of sight amongst the reeds that lined the bank from here on upriver.

Dominica sighed as the tension left her body. She looked around. Mostly oak trees, their spreading branches dipping down towards the water's edge, and a narrow track, made by animals maybe, leading up through the trees.

Picking up her scrip she started up the track, Indract hastily following. 'Domca, let me go first, in case ...'

'It's fine, Indract, there's no harm here. Not just now.' The trees thinned and they stood in a glade, sunlight streaming in. Dominica moved swiftly toward the centre of the clearing and spun around, arms out-stretched. The feeling was strong but no words had come. She closed her eyes and listened to her body, then opening them walked further up the slope and stopped where it felt settled. She raised her arms and head to the sky again and stood a moment - it felt so right. Opening her eyes and glancing round she noticed a long ridge of a single stone protruding from the grass. A long stone maybe? Long fallen.

'I think this is a holy place, Indract, one of the old-people's holy places.'

He came to stand beside her, 'Odd that Our Lord would bring us here then?'

'Who knows His purpose? But you remember how Nuala told us that before the monastery was made at Drom-Mhor, folk-lore said *that* place was where the old-people had their circle, and that the first monks set up their preaching stone right at the centre of it.'

Indract nodded, but before he could speak he noticed the way Dominica looked wide-eyed past him, turning his head he saw a group of men had entered the far side of the clearing.

'Pray!' Dominica hissed and clasped her hands together. Indract, resisting with all his will the urge to turn around and face them, clasped his hands too. 'Thank you Lord for bringing us to this place, Amen!' Dominica said loudly in the tongue she'd learnt at Tamerunta. 'Thank you Lord, Amen.' Indract replied, even as he sensed the men had stopped their advance just a little way off.

Turning slowly to face them fully, Indract spread his hands and smiled, 'Welcome, brothers. I am Brother Indract and here is Sister Dominica. We come in peace and love to share the good news of Christ Jesus. Would you bring us to meet your chief man?'

Dominica smiled at them gently whilst observing the three of them carefully. One, obviously a warrior or guard, the other two seemed to be just villagers, though one looked like the man who had run along the beach, so maybe a lookout.

'Where do you come from?' demanded the larger man, hefting a formidable axe.

'Just now from Tamerunta, nearer the sea on the ...' began Dominica

'I know where Tamerunta is! What place do you think you are in now?'

'The place that the Lord God has sent us to be, to meet with the people here,' Indract spoke the words he'd prepared before his journey, clearly and calmly.

'Huh!' the axe man was obviously unimpressed. The lookout man said something to the axe wielder that they could not hear. He grunted again then, glaring at Indract and Dominica and moving quickly towards them, he snarled, 'With us, now! Follow them!' using his battle-axe to point at the other two, then using it to herd Dominica and Indract forward as he stepped in close behind them.

Chapter 20
Tamerkam *- circa AD 689*

Lookout man led them along another path through the trees higher up the clearing which, after rising a bit, dipped steeply down emerging at the creek-side at a point where it was shallower and large stones had been placed as stepping stones. With monk and nun hitching their habits a little to help them see where to place their feet, they stepped from one stone to the other, landing dry on the other side.

From here they walked parallel to the river a short way then turned up a wide track that wound gently round, always rising. They passed a valley running off to the right, curving around the foot of the steep hillside, and still they walked on. To their right a bank seemed to close everything off, until they came to a gap. In the gap stood another warrior, dressed the same way and equipped with a similar axe. Seeing them he merely lifted his chin in a motion to pass and the small party went forward.

As they walked the steep path between the openings the ditch, behind the unkempt bank, could now be seen and a taller bank beyond it. Through this they could see what they assumed to be the settlement ahead on the crest of the hill, their view at this point just showing the tops of buildings. Then, as they crossed a large flattish area, pock-marked by hooves and dry dung, the view revealed a scatter of different sized round houses, a meeting house, a forge and more enclosures beyond.

Dominica glanced back for a few seconds, looking away from the buildings and back towards the river. From here the river was laid out below them, she could see the tight bend that hooked right around to the place they'd seen 'lookout man' standing on the shore, and the other bend looping lazily back on itself beyond. Nothing could come upriver without them knowing a long time before it arrived – plenty of time to send down a greeting party.

Lookout led them straight towards the meeting house. Before they reached it, however, a well-dressed man came out, a tall woman with him. Lookout stopped, hesitated just a second, then went on.

'Father, they are here,' he said, standing aside so the man could meet Indract and Dominica.

'We come in peace and ...' began Indract.

'Welcome, we were told you were coming,' Cador said. *For a second, Dominica wondered if God had sent him a message in a dream.* 'The Tamerunta river-men said you were planning to come up river,' he added.

Dominica almost laughed out loud at herself, then realised no-one but her knew where they were going – and not even she knew exactly where, until they arrived.

'Then God be praised we have arrived at the right place,' Indract said.

Dominica whispered, 'Amen'.

'Come in. We shall share some food and drink and you can tell us of your journey. The river-men say you came all the way across the sea,' Cador said after proper introductions had been made.

'Indeed,' Indract said as he followed the head man in. Dominica made to follow but she was held back by a hand on her arm.

Keynae, Cador's wife shook her head. 'Men's business - we will leave them to it - follow me,' and walked off. Dominica glanced at the door to the meeting house. She wasn't used to being left out but, deciding Indract would tell all when she saw him later, turned and followed after Keynae.

The woman walked fast, not waiting, and Dominica felt a little slighted but followed quickly, endeavouring to catch up without actually breaking into a run. Running had been seriously frowned upon at the monastery and she tried to hold on to the dignity of her role, at least until she knew where she stood.

Keynae ducked into a round house, letting the leather flap drop, so that Dominica had to lift it herself to follow. As she did she realised she must be in the head man's own home. The layout was as she had seen in many homes but it was more comfortably furnished. Some beautiful woven hangings separated off different sections and there were fresh rushes on the floor. Simple but decorated earthenware pots stood against a wall and on the hearth an impressive metal pot stood and steamed gently. Stepping close Dominica could see the tops of a number of pots simmering within it - this was a treasure.

'That pot was my mother's and her mother's before,' Keynae said as she reappeared from behind one of the hangings, 'My father was the Big Man at Kellyventon. Like a fool I fell for Cador at a spring gathering as he was handsome and my father, like a fool, let me wed him,' and she laughed.

Dominica wasn't sure how serious she was, because of the laugh, but smiled and said, 'I can see why - he still is.'

Keynae stopped and stared, 'Sister? Are you supposed to notice such things?'

'Noticing is just observation, and he must have been besotted by you too,' Dominica added, as it was true - the head man's wife looked both beautiful and formidable.

'And I dare say you'd turn men's heads if you weren't in a habit,' Keynae returned, 'and maybe even though you are!' Both women found themselves smiling. 'Come, take something to eat – we can talk about why you have come here.'

Seated beside the fire and eating some warm honey-cake and with a cup of mead to hand Keynae heard how Dominica had been promised to the church before she was born and of the scary journey that had brought them to this coast, instead of the one they were headed for.

‘I understand that Tamerunta has made you all welcome, that the monks have built a church and a house and settled in well. Why are you here now?’

Dominica looked at Keynae and wondered if she dare say what was really on her mind, if she dare tell her the whole truth. ‘When you ask that, do you mean the church ... or just me?’

‘Just you sister, I find it strange that the first people to come would be the leader of the monks - and a sister.’

‘Well, I am not just a sister, I am his sister by blood, and so he has known me all my life - and he knows how God guides me sometimes, so we came together.’

Keynae’s eyes widened, ‘God guided you here?’

Dominica nodded.

‘Why, what reason did God send you here?’

‘I do not know... yet. I only know it is important that I came.’ There was a silence. The fire hissed, the bubbles seethed quietly.

‘Then I welcome you, and will support you.’

‘Thank you.’

‘Cador is ... a strong warrior, and he is head man, but he isn’t the most clever or cunning man when it comes to running the territory - but we make a good pair.’

Suddenly it all made sense. Keynae, brought up in the home of the Big Man had absorbed more than her mother’s milk and how to run a household. She’d grasped the nitty-gritty of running a territory, its men and its livestock, its factions and its intrigues. In short, Cador wasn’t the power in this area, Keynae was - and Dominica thanked God for bringing them together.

‘Tell me about the area you lead.’

Keynae smiled and settled back, using her hands and arms expansively to illustrate directions, she began. ‘Tamerkam’s territory stretches from the banks of the Tamer here, up river to the big stream running in, the Cut, down river to the big stream that way, the Pil. Then you follow those as our boundary. There is another stream that cuts across from near the Pil to the Cut and separates us from Ventonpemps's territory - with their stronghold, Kerbanal, across the valley from our other stronghold, Pensinys, beside Bo Barr.'

Dominica translated the place names as she heard them. Tamerkam, that was 'bend of the Tamer'. She could understand that name as that is what it looked like when she'd looked at the river from the height of the stronghold. Ventonpemps, was 'Springs-five' - perhaps the settlement was based where five springs surfaced? Kerbanal, 'stronghold in the gorse' was easy to imagine but Pensinys 'headland of the signal' might need seeing to understand - and the home of the Big Man, Keynae's father, Kellyventon, 'Woodland-spring' suggested a significant spring – one that didn't fail, if it supported the largest settlement in the area.

Keynae continued, 'Within our territory, up river and high above the Cut, is the Bo of Etherick's family, been there generations, but they look to this stronghold in times of trouble. Then there's another large Bo over on the Pensinys border - and that's mostly Barr's family and they man that stronghold – and of course there's here, Tamerkam – there's many more people than you'll see in this stronghold – now most only come here for market day or if there is trouble. There's not been much of that lately, which means that people have set up their homesteads outside – working land further away from the stronghold. It is good land and with good people.' It was obvious that she loved and was proud of their territory and its people. 'And you? Tell me of your plans, or God's plans, now you are here?'

Dominica paused a moment whilst she sent a silent 'arrow' prayer, *'Lord, give me the right words, for I am here at your will, Lord, speak through me.'* She smiled, 'When we stepped ashore, so recently, I didn't know. But now I say, I hope we'll be able to build a religious settlement here,' her voice became stronger as her confidence suddenly rose within her, 'where we can have an infirmary to help bring healing to those who need it, where we will study and teach the bible to all, where we can teach, to those who want to learn, how to read and write, and establish Christ as the centre of this place, and this place as a centre of Christ's grace.'

Keynae was staring, fascinated – Dominica's eyes were shining, she seemed lit from within. 'Well,' she said softly, 'I, for one, believe you.'

They both looked to the door as they heard shouts and running. The door flap was thrown open, Cador, glanced at them, his face a picture of fury, 'You!' he snarled, pointing at Dominica, 'Get out!' As she jumped up Dominica glanced at Keynae for a clue. Keynae made a 'stay' sign with her hand, though Dominica still found herself stepping back under Cador's glower.

'Cador, husband? What is it?' she said calmly.

'They, *they* want to *rule over everything here!*' He swept his hand around fiercely, bringing it back as a fist to thump into his other hand, 'And I won't have it!'

Opposite: Map 3 - Tamerkam and Beyond

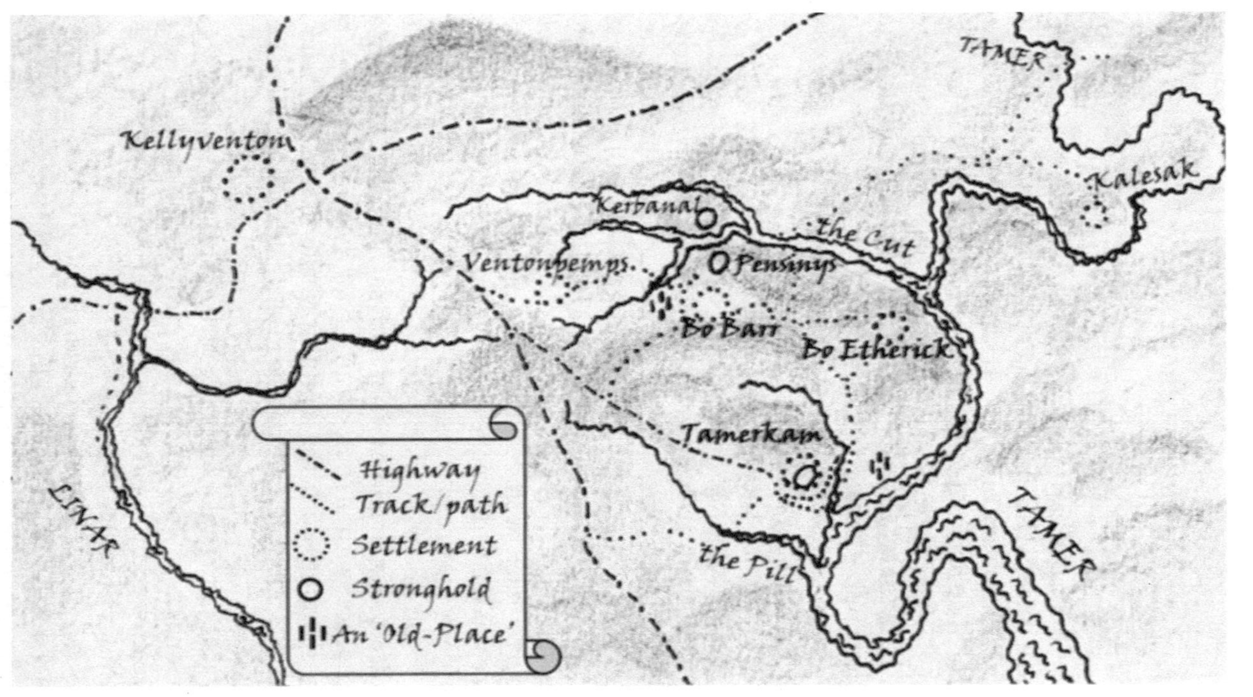
TAMER
Kellyventon
Kalesak
Kerbanal
the Cut
Ventonpemps
Pensinys
Bo Barr
Bo Etherick
Tamerkam
TAMER
LINAR
the Pill
Highway
Track/path
Settlement
Stronghold
An 'Old-Place'

Chapter 21

***The Covenant** - circa AD 689*

Keynae stepped up-close to her husband and said in a low voice. 'What did he *actually* say?'

'They want to set up a stronghold and rule here!'

'A stronghold – or a monastery?'

'*His* words were clear – a strong place of ruling! I know what I know! I asked him straight out - is everyone under your rule – he said, yes, everyone!'

Keynae looked back at Dominica, 'How good is your brother in our tongue?'

Dominica shook her head a little, 'Not as good as he thinks he is.'

'But you are very good in our tongue!' Keynae turned back to Cador, rested a hand on his arm, 'Husband, I think we need to question the brother again, with Sister Dominica here as a translator.' The flap was snatched open and there stood Indract, his face red, looking a little dishevelled, surrounded by three huge armed men. At a nod from Cador he was hustled into the house and manhandled to the other side of the fire pit.

'Sit there!' Cador pointed at the bench, 'And you!' directed at Dominica. They both sat, Dominica glancing at Indract with a quick raising of her eyebrows – he responding with the slightest shake of his head and a minuscule shrug. He had no idea what had gone wrong.

It didn't take long to get the correct translation of a monastery, where all the people in it were under a strict rule of godly behaviour - and then Keynae added in the things that Dominica had said - a place of healing, a place of learning and a place for worshipping God. The two men got to the point of laughing at their mistakes, the two women smiling as they brought out more cakes and ale.

At dusk the main meal was taken in the meeting house, alongside the off-duty guards and some of the other people who lived and worked inside the stronghold, but there was also a whole group of older men who ranged around the space.

Cador told everyone assembled who their guests were, and their proposed plan. A few questions were asked and answers given, often with Dominica making sure they would be understood correctly before Indract spoke them aloud.

It did not escape Dominica that Cador fixed his eyes on certain older men in turn, and from some she noticed the slightest nod, while others looked up a touch, as if undecided. There seemed to be no shakes of the head - which, Dominica prayed, boded well.

This formal part of the evening was followed by the storyteller, telling of an heroic leader of Tamerkam in the past, and then music and song from a bard, joined in with at the chorus by those who raised their horn cups and sang along.

At the end of the evening Indract was invited to sleep in the meeting house, alongside the guards, and Dominica was offered a space in their own house by Keynae, and so went with her. Cador, however, came into the house much later, by which time Dominica was wrapped in a blanket and tucked away on a small platform in a usually open alcove, but with another blanket hooked up to provide a little privacy.

In the morning Dominica rose very early and went outside to a higher point to spend time in prayer as the sun rose across the river and blessed the landscape. It was truly beautiful, the river turning liquid gold as the sun touched it, the expanse of view uplifting.

Dominica returned to be welcomed by Keynae and offered some barley-meal porridge to eat. Indract was also brought in from the meeting house and was similarly fed.

Cador arrived from somewhere, looking very pleased with himself. 'Good morning Brother Indract, Sister Dominica. If you are ready I have something to show you,' he glanced at Keynae, and Dominica caught the smile she gave him in return.

They all set out together, Cador leading the way. They crossed the stronghold, heading for the gateway they had come in by the afternoon before, but instead of turning downhill towards the river they turned up hill following a pathway that rose then, at a junction, turned off to the left. A little way down this path they stopped and Cador turned into a sparse woodland. He led the way along a narrow track winding through the undergrowth until they came to a much clearer area, where the river could be glimpsed way below.

'We have decided that we will offer your mission this land, from the track beside the stronghold to the Pil stream, and from the top track down to the river. With this you should be self-sufficient given a year, even with the due share on the lower part. In return for this holding you can build the places you told us of here - a place of healing, a place of learning and a place of prayer to serve our community. You may hold this land for as long as the monastery serves this community.'

It looked a huge area, with a lot of potential and larger than that provided by the people at Tamerunta. Indract smiled and clasped his hands together in prayer. 'May the Lord bless and keep you Cador, and all those who you lead, for this is a pleasing gift to the Lord. Amen!'

Dominica had been caught up in wondering why she had been led to the other area when they landed. She had felt sure that would be the place they would set up their religious settlement when the time came, so she had to hastily clasp her hands as Indract called on the Lord, responding to the Amen just in time.

They were then shown the land in detail - there was a good strong spring nearby that could be used to provide the main water supply for all that the monastery should need. There were a number of patches of woodland, enough to provide timber for construction, and some land that was scrub, which they thought could be could be cultivated, and which, they could see, reached right down to the edge of the river. Then Cador led them across towards the Pil. As they walked they could see relatively flattish land in the angle between the Tamer and the Pil already under cultivation.

Cador took Indract and Dominica further down towards where the Pil spilled into the Tamer. A man stood there beside a coracle and, as they approached, Cador said, 'Riol has this land from me, and it pays a due share, but he has no family left to take it over from him - he would make a good land steward for you.'

Dominica saw a very old man, his clothes had tears that could be easily mended, his skin looked grey and his hair wild. It was obvious he had no-one to care for him and, as he turned his face to meet these usurpers of his land, she could see the tell-tale whiteness that told her he was blind in one eye.

Indract too had made his own conclusions and said in a low voice, 'How?'

Cador slapped Indract on the back and said in a hearty voice, 'No one knows this river or this land as well as old Riol. Isn't that right, Riol?'

Riol grinned a near toothless smile. 'Ay, it speaks to me - it does.'

'Riol is older than any man or woman in Tamerkam! He tells the other elders *he's forgotten more than they know!*' There was a warmth in Cador's voice, and Dominica could imagine Riol telling Cador this from a young age.

Indract smiled at this and turned to Riol, 'Your guidance will be welcome as the brothers are not farmers by rearing or calling, but are willing to learn.'

'And this will give you a position and a living, Riol. Stronger backs to do the work and a place of comfort for you to live in and be cared for,' Cador said looking at the old man.

'Aye, as you say chief,' Riol said, with a nod and something that could pass for a smile.

Dominica and Indract spent a further night at Tamerkam, to be ready to catch the falling tide the next morning. They said their formal farewells and, with a promise to be back soon, left Cador and Keynae at the door to the meeting house.

Mist wreathed the river banks when it came into view as they walked down with Drustan, Cador and Keynae's son - the 'lookout man' at their arrival. Dominica was sad to find that they had helpfully brought their coracle over to the nearest place to push off from, not far from where she had first seen Drustan standing when they came up-river – she had really wanted to go and stand in the clearing again, to check the feelings she'd experienced when they had landed.

Dominica could see that the river was running fast towards the sea as she stepped into the coracle. She checked she had her scrip safely held and looked back at Indract. He was talking to Drustan but soon joined her, pushing the coracle out a little more, then jumping in, ready to draw the coracle into the swirling current. Drustan stepped into the water and gave them a push, with a shout of, 'see you soon!' And they were away. Indract drew them into the main current and they were soon swooping around the tight bend of the river that gave their new mission place its name. As the coracle turned with the flow of the water Dominica could glance back, see the tops of the buildings in the stronghold high above the river, see the figure of Drustan looking their way, watching them leave.

Chapter 22

***The Mission Plan** - circa AD 689*

Only the settlement lookout saw them arrive back at the same place they left Tameruntajust a few days before, and he ran down to help them pull up the coracle and get out without wetting their habits too much. Yet, because of his whistled messages, by the time they were up on the higher ground, a few other men had arrived too.

Leaving the lookout boy behind they all set off on the walk alongside the creek back to the village, with a few questions aimed at Indract. He deflected most of them, just saying that the people at Tamerkam had been very hospitable. Back at the monastery they were greeted fulsomely, yet the brothers, for all they wanted to know, kept their peace and went about their work.

Later that day, after their meal, the brothers and Dominica met to discuss the events at Tamerkam.

'Brothers, sister,' Indract began, 'God had prepared the way for us - the people were expecting our mission and welcomed it. Brothers, praise the Lord, for they have already offered us a large and fertile area of land to plant our mission and grow the Lord's harvest.'

Murmurs of 'Amen' spontaneously came from many lips.

'I propose that we leave but a few here to grow this mission. We already have postulants and lay members growing this place, so we can plant a new mission with some of our core missionaries.'

'And who do you propose leads this mission – here in Tamerunta?' put in Cormag.

Indract turned a smiling face towards Cormag, 'Brother, it is not for me to propose, as you know. It is by prayerful assent of all of us. We may all propose, we may all choose, as is the correct way.'

'And the same goes for the new mission then – both will need a priested monk.'

'Indeed brother, and these are both for prayer and discussion. Right now we must pray for guidance as to who should go and who should stay. There is great work to be done for the Lord in both places. God has gifted us not one, but two mission bases and we must not fail Him. Pray well brothers and we will discern tomorrow who shall go, who shall stay, who shall lead and who shall follow – to the Glory of our Father who reigns in heaven, Amen'

'Amen,' echoed the brothers and, even as she also did so, Dominica couldn't help thinking how gifted her brother was in his speech when using his own tongue and talking to his own people. Yet she wondered how the discernment would go - she felt so certain in her very soul that she was intended to be at Tamerkam. It seemed impossible that she should stay – but under the rule the choice was not entirely hers to make. It would have to be by consensus.

The following evening they met again, where prayers were said and the matter was raised again.

Firstly they listened to inspirations received in prayer about the mission to Tamerkam. Among other positive responses in prayer, Teagan spoke of seeing a golden glow flowing up-river and settling on Tamerkam. All were in accordance that the mission was God-led. With this agreed they then moved on to who would stay and who would go.

Durragh spoke up quickly, 'Brothers, what is obvious is that each place needs a priest, as each place would benefit from having someone to celebrate the Eucharist, not only for the brothers but for the community. On our peregrination God had the foresight to place two among us. Surely this means that one should be in each.' There were general murmurs of assent. Dominica, having noted in the past Durragh and Cormag's relationship, wondered if this was as simple a statement as it seemed, but a quick glance at Cormag showed him looking piously blank-faced.

Dairmut spoke next, 'I think we vote on this first. Should the two priests, Indract and Cormag, be the only ones to be considered as leaders of the two missions? We shall take a vote - you each have a black pebble and a white pebble. If you agree that these two only should be considered as leaders for these two missions, drop in the pot a white pebble.

There was a shuffling of pebbles in hands and then each took it in turn to go and drop a pebble into the narrow-necked pot. When each had settled back, Dairmut tipped the contents out on the bench before him. Out rolled eleven pebbles, eight white, three black.

'Carried,' Dairmut said. 'The next question then is who leads which mission?'

'Don't you want to ask if either of us has had a calling from God to lead this mission to Tamerkam?' Cormag asked.

Dairmut looked taken aback. Like most he probably assumed that the trip to Tamerkam had been Indract following his own vision to set up a mission there – in which case it seemed an odd question for Cormag to be asking.

Dominica was suddenly very alert – what was Cormag up to? Surely no one else knew that it was really her that had the call to go up the river – except Indract of course. Had Indract inadvertently said something? Whatever, she knew, Indract would find it hard to tell a lie and say that God had spoken directly to him – Cormag was another case altogether - she chided herself on her suspicions about him, but the thought remained.

Dairmut looked from one to the other, 'I see no reason why not. Brother Indract, were you led to go and seek out the people at Tamerkam for God?

'I was. A vision was vouchsafed to me of a place on the river where the river made the shape of a hook and a place above it where He, Jesus, stood waiting.' This was greeted with a murmur of whispered alleluias and amens, blended together. Dominica saw how he had spoken without lying, re-telling her vision as she'd told it to him - and thanked God for the wording Dairmut used.

'Brother Cormag,' Dairmut continued, 'did God lead you to seek out the people at Tamerkam?'

Cormag smiled, 'Of course! I had a vision of a golden glow running up the river and shining on a hilltop at Tamerkam. Confirmed by Teagan in our discernment just now,' he smiled at Teagan who stared back, eyes narrowed. But a few murmured, 'amen'.

'Brother Cormag, why then did you not seek to go up-river before Brother Indract, or indeed, with Brother Indract?' Dairmut asked.

All eyes turned towards Cormag, who seemed to grow in their gaze, 'I did, but Brother Indract chose to take his sister.'

Indract instantly stood. 'Brother, you will withdraw that falsehood!'

'Falsehood?' Cormag said softly, 'I distinctly remember telling you that I should be the one to go with you, and you saying I could not.'

'Agreed, that was said!' There was a gasped intake of breath from the brothers. 'But you said nothing of a vision to me, and my reasons were two-fold. I knew not what the terrain or the meeting would be like and your ... injury could make both tricky. And secondly, for both of us to leave together on an uncertain journey would be unwise and possibly detrimental to the home mission.'

Dairmut stood now, and Indract took the hint and sat down. 'It seems to me, brothers and sister, that we know sufficient to take a vote now on who is to lead the mission to Tamerkam. The proposal is that brother Indract will lead the mission to Tamerkam.'

The same procedure was followed, when all were seated again, the pot was tipped out. Nine white and two black. It wasn't hard to guess who had put in the black pebbles, but the reason why was not so clear to Dominica.

'Then, as the other priest, Cormag will surely lead the mission here,' Durragh said before the subject of Tamerunta could be raised.

Whether it was because everyone felt bad for Cormag it couldn't be told, but no objections were raised and so this didn't even go to the vote.

Brother Indract, as the leader of the new mission, was entitled to name those he felt most suitable for the work ahead. First naming Finn for the teaching, Dairmut, Fergus, and Kellagh for the building, and Dominica with Brannon's assistance for the healing and the victuals.

Dominica acknowledged his discretion - Finn had worked with Niall on the teaching, so Niall should be equipped to carry on that part of mission. Most of the building work was done, and some of the new postulants were well versed in such tasks already. She knew he'd liked to have named more, Teagan was well liked by both of them as was Niall, but he had to leave some choice for Cormag.

Cormag looked around, 'Brother Durragh, certainly, not sure what use I'll have for a bard but brother Niall can do such teaching as is needed, I'm sure.' He paused and looked slowly around the assembly. 'However, I would claim we have need of Sister Dominica here. You could take Erbin - he must have learnt some cooking by now.'

Dominica's heart felt as if it had stopped, and then as if it raced to catch-up with itself - this couldn't be happening, couldn't be God's will. She looked at Indract. Indract was still looking at Cormag, as if waiting for him to say more. When he said no more, he turned and looked at each in turn. 'Sister Dominica doesn't just cook, Sister Dominica heals, knows the herbs and the poultices and has a wonderful ministry among the households and families she visits, both of which we need at the new mission. Here, Liaden is skilled in healing,'

Cormag interjected a 'pffft' sound and a sneered, 'Huh!'

'*Liaden, the wife of the chief here* **is** skilled in healing - without her knowledge you could have *died* Brother

Cormag. However, if you do not wish for Teagan to help at Tamerunta I will gladly have him with us.'

'Leaving me with but two brothers!'

'And all six of the postulants and lay brothers, which makes there nine here and but eight to set up the new mission.'

Dominica smiled to herself, Indract had somehow made it so that any quibbling by Cormag would now just look greedy. She felt for Niall, with his hesitant speech he could be a target for Cormag's acerbic tongue. Hopefully, by keeping himself engaged in the teaching wherein his confidence grew and his speech cleared, he'd not be undermined too much. She could argue that Indract should have taken Niall and left Finn, but she knew Finn was the one who Indract confided and trusted in the most, and so needed the most too.

And so it was agreed and the preparations began. A message that they would be arriving at Pentecost was to be sent with a river-man to Tamerkam. The tools, that could be spared, were gathered together, the materials for teaching and learning folded away into scrips. The supplies of herbs, seeds, pots and a mortar and pestle carefully packed in reed baskets. It wasn't long before they were ready, coracles bought or borrowed, supplies stashed ready to load, excitement amongst the brothers.

On the day of Pentecost they held their leaving service attended by most of the people - so many that some had to stand outside the church. Blessings for the journey were called for and made, the Holy Spirit was invoked to accompany them in their mission and, it being Pentecost, the expectancy was high.

After the service everyone set off down the creek-side path to see them off – it was a beautiful late May morning for a change, the persistent rain having eased at last. The banks were strewn with pink, blue and white flowers brightening up the way, the water sparkled where it was glimpsed through the trees which lined the creek - it looked and sounded like a festival as people chattered excitedly as they followed them.

The coracles were soon loaded and with a prayer, led by brother Cormag as the new leader within the Tamerunta mission, they were pushed off. Four larger coracles, seven brothers, one sister, all also loaded with the carefully gathered and selected goods to begin their new mission - plus one local river-man, who would bring back the two borrowed coracles.

As the coracles were taken up by the rising tide Dominica glanced back; only a few people remained at the shore looking out after them, eyes shaded by hands against the glare from the water. She blessed them all and prayed the mission there would be safe.

Chapter 23

***The Building Up** - circa AD 689 - 690*

The journey seemed so much faster to Dominica this time, but she could see the interest that the others took in the surroundings, and the way the river swept them from side to side, revealing more river as it twisted and turned.

Then there it was! She could see the stronghold and suddenly wondered whether they would stop at Tamerkam's landing spot or run on to where they'd landed the first time. The lead coracle was steered by the local who'd come with them - he headed straight for the landing place and so all the others followed. After Dominica had stepped out of the coracle she stared across to where they had landed before – and told herself she would have plenty of opportunities to visit that small clearing whilst she was here, for she suddenly felt so grounded - as if her body knew the earth beneath her feet - that she felt she would never leave.

Before they were fully unloaded, Keynae had arrived at the landing place and called to Dominica, 'Welcome Sister Dominica! I have brought helpers to carry your things.'

'Blessings on you,' called back Dominica, her heart light at seeing Keynae again.

When they were unloaded Keynae added, 'You will stay with us until a suitable building has been made for you in the new monastery - shelter has been made for the brothers already.' They walked up to the stronghold together, sharing news as if they had been friends forever, and Dominica's sense of being at home increased.

Indract had all their tools and goods taken to the land allotted them, where he was surprised, but pleased, to see Riol waiting for him beside a new building. Riol had taken the weeks between their visit and their return to have a smallish hut built near the spot where Cador had stopped to show Indract the area he was offering. It was right on the edge of the clearing, carefully not taking up any of the best building positions. It looked a tight fit to sleep seven but would do, and would store some of their tools and materials until other provision was made.

'Good day, Riol, the Lord's blessing upon you.'

'Good day father. With Cador's instruction I had this built, it's small and out of the way so it can have other uses later. Cador said you have plans for a church and places of learning and healing.'

'We do indeed, and this is a blessing indeed - a roof over our heads to begin our work from.'

Riol tilted his head and nodded a little, but seemed pleased with what he heard.

Thus started a time of intense work. They knew a lot better what it was that they needed to do this time. There was much prayer and discussion over the size and siting of the Church, of the monks quarters, of the position for a place of learning where people not committed to the monastic life could still come and learn without intruding upon the core of the monastery too much, and the same for a place of healing.

It was decided that these two in particular would be just inside but either side of the entrance, the food preparation and laundry behind them to the side and the Church straight ahead from the entrance, as usual. Whereas the buildings for the monks and nuns and for ablutions would be either side of the church and lower, behind.

They set aside the straightest and stoutest trunks and limbs for the building of the church, wanting to make it as vast as possible - so at the services for the major feast days many people could fit inside - and to make it a great and noble building, to reflect the glory of God.

Very early on the spring was captured in a deep stone-lined basin, covered with a little roof and a door to prevent debris or animals fouling it, and then channelled off in different directions from that point, as required. There was discussion about also making a place for baptisms, as they had back at Tamerunta, but this was put on hold until they had those wanting to be baptised – there was enough work to do already.

Cador was generous. Though the brothers set time aside to work the land that had been Riol's alone, under his guidance, as the supplies they had brought with them diminished, Cador found sufficient grain to help keep them going until their first harvest. In return he merely asked that the brothers be available to help with the Tamerkam harvest when it next came. Riol was also a wonder as a hunter. He not only caught fish in his traps he laid in the Pil but was also skilled at trapping birds for the table too, for the rare days when the brothers ate flesh or fish.

Each day Dominica and the brothers met for prayers five times; at dawn, at noon, mid afternoon – the service called 'Nones' - at sunset and at the end of their day. After the prayers at nones they shared a simple meal which was followed by reviewing the works achieved and planning the next day or week.

By the time the crops were ready to harvest their monastery had a visible form. The church was begun, the first of two houses planned for the monks was built as was one for nuns - though there was only Dominica to occupy it as yet. The refectory and kitchen buildings were complete too. There was a start to the infirmary - or healer's hut as it was named to the locals - and the school, the holes dug and the wood being cut and made ready.

In the meantime Dominica made use of the original hut as her herbarium and makeshift infirmary, as she soon found that her skills in healing were in great need in the community. The Tamerkam settlement had been relying on the wise-woman from the settlement at Bo Barr - but she was so old now that it was hard for her to visit outside her own area.

Quite early on Keynae took Dominica to visit a sick woman at Bo Etherick. 'It's a fair walk uphill,' she warned Dominica, 'but not too steep.' It reminded Dominica of the walk from her home with Nuala, by the stream's ford, up to the court on the ridge overlooking the river, long and steady.

The homestead was surrounded by a low wall of loose rock, nothing that would keep out a determined man or beast but enough to mark a boundary. Inside were half a dozen houses and some other shelters for livestock or processes.

The woman lay on a low platform in one of the huts and was covered in a fur yet, despite the heat of the day, she was still shivering. She had an open sore on her leg where she'd been bitten by a 'gwybesen', she said, and it had swelled and opened up. The smell was unpleasantly sweet and instantly recognisable to Dominica who had helped Nuala treat a wound that had suppurated and spread down a man's leg, as if it was eating away the skin the ooze spread to.

'What is a ... gwybesen?' Dominica asked Keynae – it wasn't a word she recognised.

'Like a small fine gwiban that sucks blood.'

Ah! Gwiban – a fly, she knew that one – so maybe a 'cuil' from the bogs, or 'gnaet' as Guda called them. Whichever, she knew how to treat this and soon had the woman's leg cleaned - bathed in boiled and cooled mint water and the pus and rotting edges of flesh cleaned off. She then covered the open wound with a layer of the thin green skin peeled from navel-wort leaves, gathered by the woman's daughter from a shady place nearby. Finally she sealed it with honey and wrapped it with a boiled cloth from her scrip and tied it on. She said a prayer over the woman in Latin and gave her a tisane of herbs and willow bark, to help reduce her temperature and promised to be back each day until the leg began to heal.

Over the weeks the woman's daughter, Eiliwedd, became so useful in helping Dominica, that she wondered if she might be a suitable apprentice. It was obvious that she was quick witted and eager to learn, going and collecting more navel-wort leaves from the second day even without being asked to. She suggested this idea to Keynae, explaining that Eiliwedd didn't have to want to be a nun; she could be a lay-sister who lived and worked in the monastery. Keynae said she would speak with the family, though to be aware, it may not be as simple as it seemed.

*

As time went on Dominica worked with the brothers for the first part of each day, hard physical work preparing the land or helping with building. After noon prayers, she took her scrip and went visiting those that she was told needed advice or care, and upon return, using her skills to make their simple fare others had prepared for their meal a little tastier with the additions of herbs she'd brought or found.

After much negotiation Eiliwedd came to stay with Dominica at the nuns' house, and began her herb and healing education working with Dominica on a daily basis. She also helped with the other tasks in the monastery and the food preparation, whenever Dominica did.

The negotiation had been necessary as Eiliwedd, their eldest, was much doted on by her father and already very useful in the house, particularly while her mother was ailing. This was sorted out by Keynae, by apprenticing a girl from Tamerkam to the family. On the face of it to learn housewifery with the Bo Etherick family – in reality also to help that girl's family, who had too many mouths to feed – and all those, bar the last, girls – so the second eldest wouldn't be too missed. It helped that the wound had healed well and that Eiliwedd's mother was back on her feet and had the sense to see that Eiliwedd really wanted to take up this learning.

By the end of that summer, Dominica had become a welcome and frequent sight striding around the Tamerkam homesteads and along the path up to Bo Etherick, always with a spring in her step.

One day, in early autumn, a message came from Bo Barr - the elderly wise-woman there, herself, was ill.

Chapter 24

Mother Barr - circa AD 690

Keynae said she'd accompany Dominica up to Bo Barr, to pay her respects to the wise-woman, Mother Barr, as well as showing her the way.

They set off, Dominica carrying her scrip of medicinal supplies and some treats, a piece of honey-comb and a small pot of mead.

They were taking a different route. The path this way was wider than the Bo Etherick path as it was a highway, a main route to and from the main settlements, following the ridges and hill tops as much as it could, trying to maintain height without excessive climbs, except when they came up from river levels, as did this one.

'How is it that Mother Barr has no one to take over from her?' Dominica asked well into their walk.

'Ah!' Keynae said, taking the opportunity to stop and take an extra breath or two on the steeper part of their journey.

The views where they paused were spectacular - deep below the river twinkled, but to one side across a wide and sweeping set of valleys they could see an expanse of purplish hills far in the distance.

'She had trained up her daughter but sadly she died in child-birth, her second babe - a girl, who Mother Barr managed to save. Mother Barr took up the care of both children and when the babe was old enough she began to train her in the lore and tried, it is said, to persuade her not to marry. She had become quite clever in healing, but regardless, the girl fell ill with the plague that came through here not ten years since and passed away no matter how carefully Mother Barr looked after her. No one would become her apprentice after that. I suspect if there had been anyone else to help them they'd have shunned

Mother Barr too – but by then we all depended on her as that sickness also took our wise-woman.'

Dominica considered what she had heard as they crested a hill and then turned off onto a narrower path. Dominica glanced back, looking in the direction the wide path went on.

'The highway goes on that way - joins the one coming from Kellyventon,' Keynae said. They followed the small path and soon it began to head steeply down the hill. Far off ahead she could see smoke rising from a clearing, and then, off to the right more smoke.

Keynae paused to point at the first – that's Pensinys. I'll show you that if we have time after we've seen Mother Barr. She'll be at Bo Barr – that's just over there,' pointing right.

Downhill was easier and faster but there was a point, shortly after they'd passed above a spring rising and flowing away down hill, when Dominica felt something odd, like a tugging sensation in her head. She glanced around, but they were walking fast and the feeling left as quickly as it came. Within moments Keynae led Dominica off the downward path, turning right onto one leading towards a collection of homes gathered within a slightly flatter area scooped out between the hilltops, yet above the steep valley.

Keynae greeted people as they passed various round-houses while heading towards the far side of this settlement. She paused at one particular house with the door open and called, 'Anyone home?' There was no reply and no one came out of the house. 'Very odd,' she said and lifted the door flap, calling, 'Mother Barr?' Still no one spoke.

As Keynae hooked back the door flap, Dominica stepped inside. She closed her eyes tight, then re-opened them. In the poor light she could see a bundle on a platform bed over to one side. The hearth, as she passed it, appeared dead. She heard Keynae following her across the space.

'Fire's out,' Keynae said in a disgusted tone, but then she paused to stir it with a stick, the glow of an ember showed it had not been out long, at least.

At the bedside, Dominica said gently, 'Mother Barr? I am Sister Dominica from the monastery.' A wheezing sound came from the heap on the bed. Dominica's head swam with memories that threatened to overwhelm her, *Nuala!* Her heart squeezed. She leant closer; Mother Barr was ancient, her skin wrinkled in deep ravines, her hair white and thin. 'Mother Barr, I have brought herbs. I can make a tisane that may ease your breathing. Can you speak?'

'Can't help me!' she croaked.

'Mother, do you have a sickness?'

'Death,' she said and almost chuckled, it turning into a cough.

'I can't understand why there's no one here – at least to sit with her,' Keynae said sharply.

'Scared,' Mother Barr husked, 'idiots,' and that chuckle again - and the cough.

Turning to Keynae Dominica said, 'Let's get the fire going, I will make a tisane to ease the cough and add something that can help with some kinds of pain.'

Keynae turned and went straight out the door – which wasn't what Dominica had expected. There were some sticks near the embers so Dominica pushed the finest ones in and blew on them, the white ash flurried up but the embers caught the ends of the twigs. She laid a few thicker twigs across the fine ones and then turned away and began to empty her bag.

A commotion made her look up, and then she heard Keynae's voice and it wasn't holding back, she was telling someone, or some people, that they were a disgrace – leaving their wise-woman, their relative, to die alone and without care. A couple hastened into the hut, filling it with their clumsy apologies and an armful of sticks. Mother Barr coughed loudly. Whether she had laughed first Dominica couldn't tell.

'Don't just stand there! Get the fire going, we need hot water – you – go and get fresh water.' The woman hurried off and the man added to Dominica's work and blew to get the flames working harder.

It wasn't long before Dominica was able to bring a brewed, cooled and strained tisane to the old woman's lips. As she tasted it she smiled, and nodded, a glint in her eye,

'It has bittersweet in it for the pain,' she said, glad that she'd collected and saved some of the fluffy white-headed plants when she'd found them blooming earlier in the year, 'with honey and mint to take away any bitterness,' Dominica said clearly but gently. The old woman nodded and smiled. She drank it all and sighed.

Dominica poured the rest of the concoction into a narrow mouthed pot and blocked it with a screw of soft leaves as a plug. She turned to the woman and said, 'Give Mother Barr a cup of this, morning, noon and sunset, but warm it first! If she will eat, give her well boiled barley porridge, with milk added and an egg beaten in, if there's one to be got.' The woman nodded. 'And I will be back tomorrow to see how she is getting on,' Dominica added in a meaningful way, before turning to the man, 'and I'll expect you to make sure she has a fire here, enough to keep off the chill in the day and warm the house overnight.' The man nodded and cast an eye to Keynae who stood haughtily regarding them from the doorway.

As they ducked out of the small house Keynae glanced at the sky, 'We will go home, but via Pensinys, just so you'll have the lie of the land for other times that you come here – it looks like your skills will be needed here as well, in the future.'

They turned their back on the hut and walked quickly past other houses before leaving by a wide but unkempt path. Dominica could see a singular higher hill in front of her, way off. Keynae noticed her looking into the distance.

'Kellyventon lies near the foot of The Hill, the one you see there, not down in the valley but aside from the highway where it sweeps round it.'

Dominica nodded, indeed, that hill seemed higher than any she had seen since arriving in the area. As they walked the path dipped a little, but she could already see the ramparts of a defensible rath, the earthen banks and the stakes buried in it to make it hard to overcome. She could also see that it sat on the edge of the valley, a deep curving tree-filled valley, but up here there was a cleared, scoured area surrounding the stronghold so that no one could creep up on it.

'Pensinys,' Keynae said, unnecessarily.

'And is there a signalling point there too?'

Keynae looked at Dominica, 'You really are good at our tongue. There is a signal, but it is actually further along – as it is at a point where it can be seen by more of *our* outlying homesteaders. We use it to call people in as well as a warning. We won't go that way today – I'll just introduce you to the leader here. He's of the Barr family I'm sure you won't be surprised to hear. I'll have some words for him if he knew how Mother Barr was being shunned.'

As they continued towards their stronghold Dominica saw across the valley another, 'Is that Kerbanal?' she asked pointing.

'Indeed it is, well remembered,' began Keynae, then waved and called, 'Tudwal! Cador sends greetings.' The man who turned to her call was squat and muscular – he didn't seemed at all surprised to see Keynae, so he must have been pre-warned, though Dominica hadn't seen any lookouts.

'Who's this then?' he said.

'Have you any idea of how your wise-woman is?'

'Sick, I'm told. I sent word to Tamerkam.'

'And we came - only to find she was unattended, her fire all but out – abandoned in the heart of her family.' Dominica saw the flash of annoyance on his face, but was unable to judge whether he was annoyed the wise-woman had been left so – or that Keynae had raised it. She soon knew.

'What? I ordered those two who live beside her to care for her until you came!' Then he shouted, 'Ger! Get here!' at one of the young warrior-dressed men. 'Go and see to that worthless pair of idiots beside Mother Barr's - see why they are ignoring my word!'

'I've sorted them out already!' Keynae said. Ger stopped and looked between them - Tudwal stood him down with a dismissive gesture.

'I'll still have words!' Turning towards Dominica he added, 'And is this your new healer I have heard so much about?'

'Sister Dominica – she is with the new mission.'

'Welcome sister. Hopefully we won't need you up here too often,' Tudwal said, his tone and face much more pleasant now he was calming down.

'It is as well I get to know the area – I will be coming here for the next few days at least to minister to Mother Barr.'

Tudwal just nodded thoughtfully then looked at Keynae again. 'Tell Cador that I've done the improvements he wanted to the fortifications - just in case.'

'I will tell him. Anything else?'

'I have some ideas for the low way up from the rhyd, to make that more defensible.'

'I will pass that on, but I am sure he'll be this way soon.'

Tudwal nodded and smiled.

'And we must be on our way back now. Sister Dominica will be back tomorrow.'

'Sister.' Tudwal said and nodded again. Dominica replied with a smile and a signed cross in his direction.

As they started to walk away Dominica asked what the 'rhyd' was, to be told it was the name of the place where the water ran wide and so was shallow enough to walk through easily. 'We will be cutting across the path to the rhyd,' Keynae said, as they took a narrow path away from Pensinys, 'it is the weakest point between us and Ventonpemps, but when times are peaceful it is a handy trade route without having to climb up to the highway. See, here it is to the right, see how the path curls down and at the bottom is the rhyd. We'll go uphill here now though.'

They started walking up a steep incline with scrub on one side and trees on the other. They had just passed the fine stand of trees when the feeling came again – as if something like a trickle of ice-water or a thread of fire ran swiftly through Dominica and, as they were stepping slowly she felt it – and this time recognised it – the same welcoming feeling that drew her to tell Indract to miss the landing spot for Tamerkam and to go on to the other below the hidden clearing.

She paused as the feeling left her. Keynae stopped too, catching her breath, 'It *is* a bit steep,' she laughed.

Dominica gazed around and said, 'That's a fine stand of trees, it's a wonder it hasn't been used up so close to the homesteads and the stronghold.'

'Ah! No, they won't touch it – it's around one of the old places – like where Drustan found you and Indract that first day.'

'Oh, I see, and no one goes there? I mean, to take wood.'

'No. No one would dare cut wood from there - people are afraid of the ghosts of the old folk, and collecting the fallen has always been gifted to the wise-woman – so same there. Other people *may go* there though, I suppose, but I think most wouldn't.'

'Hmm!' Dominica mused – being scared was the opposite of the feelings it gave her. She was glad she had a reason to be coming back to Bo Barr again soon.

Chapter 25
The Old Place - circa AD 690

The next afternoon Dominica left Eiliwedd collecting, and hanging to dry, herbs she knew they needed stored before winter overtook them, and headed up to Bo Barr on her own. The walk was hard but she took her time at various points to look at the surroundings, watching out for herbs, for the lie of the land, and to praise God for the beauty in this landscape.

She remembered where to turn off onto the small path towards Pensinys and Bo Barr, and took it. However, this time, as she came down the hill she slowed to a stop as she felt the pull, the line, running like a fine stream through her head. She stood still, closed her eyes then turned herself to feel where it went. When she opened her eyes she was looking straight at the stand of trees. With a sigh she turned again and headed down toward Mother Barr's house. The 'old place' could wait until she had treated Mother Barr.

The door flap was hooked up as she approached, a good sign, and inside the space was warm. The woman sat by the fire warming some pottage and looked up as Dominica ducked in the doorway.

'Blessing on this house,' Dominica said, then, 'Mother Barr, how are you feeling today?' as she went to crouch beside the old woman.

'You're a clever one,' she husked, 'slept better than for a month.'

'That'll be the honey and the bittersweet. You know that.'

Mother Barr nodded with a small smile on her face. 'Still dying though, I know it,' she wheezed, 'A growing lump of pain, here,' she placed a hand on her chest.

Dominica heard the description, then placed her hand upon the old woman's chest, where she had shown her – and then she also knew. She'd only known one person cured from that type of pain, dear Dugan, and that before she even knew what healing herbs could, or could not, do or what canker was.

'Is there great pain?'

'Ha! Only when I breathe,' she coughed again, her face screwed up, her hand holding her chest.

'Maybe I can ease your pain though, Mother. Do you have in your herbals any of the special hemp?'

Mother Barr coughed, 'No. I wish!'

'Then I will use more of the bittersweet in the drink today,' *Not as strong as the willow bark, but at least it won't cause stomach gripe on top of everything else.* She smiled, then spoke to the woman, 'Please, fetch some fresh water to boil.'

As the woman left the hut, Mother Barr husked, 'Just make it with the foxglove, there's some powdered in my store,' pointing to her pots by the wall.

'Mother! I cannot - God forbids it.'

'Mercy, child – didn't your Jesus always have mercy?' Her speaking triggering another bout of painful coughing. The woman returned to the hut and put the water in a pot on the edge of the fire, feeding it, around where the pot sat, with small twigs.

Dominica felt torn, Mother Barr was right, and many a wise-woman eased someone suffering into the next world with the ultimate pain-relief – but she stood between the old ways and God's ways, and the commandment not to kill was high on the list.

After Dominica had made her concoction and given the woman the same instructions for the new brew she said her farewells with a promise to return the next day, and left. She walked out through the gathering of homes and headed for the point where, the day before, they had turned towards the path that would lead to the rhyd. As she came to the way Keynae had pointed out, she decided to go down a little – to see the rhyd. The path curved steeply through the wood and scrub until there, below, she saw a wide shining expanse of water, like a small lake. Yet, as she drew nearer, she could see the stony bottom under the hands-span of clear sparkling water.

'Where do you think you're going?' a rough voice shouted at her. She jumped, her pulse racing, looking around sharply, trying to see who shouted. He stepped out from beside an oak tree that stood close to where a spring streamed out from the hillside – a smile on his handsome young face. It was the warrior Ger, obviously on guard at this vulnerable spot.

'Oh, you! Ger?'

He broke into a smile, 'Yes, sister. Not sure why you're here though?'

'Simple,' she said as her heart steadied, 'Keynae told me of the rhyd, and I wanted to see it for myself – to understand it. Your tongue is new to me, I now know what it is. In my home land we have another word for it altogether.'

Ger sauntered towards her, 'Where are you from then? We heard you came up from Tamerunta?'

'Oh, recently, yes, but before that, across the sea from *Eriu.*'

'Ha! Someone said you'd been shipwrecked, but we thought that was a fire-side tale.' His eyes twinkled mischievously.

Dominica judged him to be of a similar age as herself, or maybe Indract and couldn't resist smiling back at him, 'No, absolutely true! We were supposed to take a short day-long crossing to San Dyfed's but we met a fierce storm, broke our mast, broke our steering oar, sent us on a much longer journey to, praise be, a place the currach master knew and into safety at Tamerunta.'

'Praise be!' he laughed, 'That you met with a shipwreck?' He chuckled, 'Most would curse it!'

'Ah, I can see that, but we always look for God's hand and His plan.'

'Fine, sister, may your God be with you,' his smile faded, 'and I'm sure you have to get back to Tamerkam,' he said, his voice firm and raised. Dominica was surprised by his change in attitude and tone, until she turned to go - and noticed another warrior coming down the path. She looked back at Ger, nodded and smiled at him. He returned a small nod and she headed up the path, the other warrior stepping aside for her to pass.

She continued up the path and turned onto the steep incline, but when she felt the tug of the line in her head she turned off the path and made her way into the stand of trees.

It was as if the world was suddenly cut off. The air itself seemed fresher, no taints of smoke or cooking smells. The air was also stilled amongst the trunks, the undergrowth sparse and easy to pass through. Using the feeling in her head to guide her way forward she came to a clearing and, as she stepped near the edge of it, she stopped still, holding her breath.

The grass grew long and bleached against them but the sun that filtered though the surrounding autumnal trees lit up the standing stones so that they glowed. *White stones?* Quietly, as if they were listening, she crept up to them.

She reached the first stone and put her hand out to touch it where it was smooth - a tingle spread around her whole being. This smooth surface glistened and shone in the light, but patchy moss and lichen had dulled much of its surface elsewhere. She rubbed at some of the moss and it peeled off to reveal rougher stone that held angles, crystals, that flashed sunlight at her. They were like nothing she had seen on this scale before. The stones were not tall like in some stone circles back home, these were all less than her own height, some only the height of a young child, and even the ones that seemed not to be of the crystalline stone were so pale a shade of grey as to look white.

She realised she'd been breathing shallowly and took a deep breath and sighed. At some level this place spoke to her. She stepped into the centre of the circle. The grass was greener here, but no trees grew inside the circle and the ground here had a harder feeling, rather than just woodland soil beneath her feet. Though, looking down, she couldn't see any difference. She looked around, wondering if there was a centre stone and soon saw what she was looking for, a low flat stone, more grey than white, but smooth. She'd expected it to be raised but it was only just above the earth level and half hidden in the grass. *But maybe the earth has built up around it?* She brushed the grasses back from it with her hand and stood up straight again.

And then - the peace settled upon her. All God's creation around her seemed enhanced, colours and scents heightened. She looked up to the sky and her spirit soared. She closed her eyes as she felt embraced by the peace. Her arms raised in adoration, her mind filled with sunlight and a sensation of great love - and into this light came the words: *'Tell the people of my love - here'.*

She did not know how long she stood like that, enraptured, but when, with a sigh, she lowered her arms and opened her eyes, the shadows had moved and the centre now stood in the shade of one of the taller trees.

And she knew what to do about the conundrum Mother Barr presented.

Dominica turned and went back out of the trees the way she came. Reaching the path she turned straight off it, back to Mother Barr's. Ducking into the hut she was relieved to see the woman was absent.

'Back already?'

'Back, Mother,' Dominica said. 'Can you tell me anything of the 'old place' in the stand of trees?'

Mother Barr barked a laugh, and coughed, holding her thin chest to try to stop the hurt. 'Been there have you? Well, it's sacred that's right, and it has power. Folks are scared, but I don't mind that. Do you know the blessing for a wise-woman's passing?'

Dominica was taken aback by the turn in conversation, but answered in truth, 'Mother Nuala taught me, in my language, but I have it – and the blessing of God too,' she added swiftly.

'You've decided to help me, haven't you? I would have the blessing – both if you must.'

'I was – praying, in the clearing with the – white stones?'

'Yes?'

'And – God wants the message preached there – and showed me how to have mercy.'

'Bless him.'

Dominica shook herself as if casting off a chill, 'Which pot is your powder in?'

'Small one with two strings of red,' the cough threatened to cut off her words. She swallowed, 'red thread tied on it.'

Dominica found the pot, taking it to the light to check the colour of the two strings, just to be sure, she then returned to place it in Mother Barr's hand, looking into the woman's rheumy old eyes. Mother Barr nodded and tucked the pot into the folds of the bed covers.

'Do you need anything else?'

'No, my dear sister, nothing, I will make do when I am ready.' The two women stared at each other for a long moment. Dominica stood tall and reached out her hand to hover it above the supine woman, 'May the wise women of all ages be with you, the powers of earth, water, air and fire fill you, and mother earth welcome you home – and may the Lord bless you and keep you ever safe in his arms, may he make his face to shine upon you and welcome you into his joy, forgiving all things in his great mercy. Amen.'

'Amen, sister.'

'Amen,' the woman said from the doorway, making Dominica turn sharply.

'Oh, you startled me,' Dominica said, and turned back to look at Mother Barr, who winked at her. 'She only just come in,' she whispered, then a little louder, 'Asked sister for a blessing before she left, I feel my time is close,' the effort to speak with volume visible in her face, the cough coming as a punctuation and explanation.

Chapter 26

The Trader *- circa AD 690 - 694*

Dominica returned each day to Mother Barr's, each day greeting her as if she had not been expecting to find her gone, and making up the potion of mint, bittersweet and honey to leave with the woman to ease the pain. Mother Barr said nothing of her pot, which she must have secreted in a safer place than just under the covers, considering how much the woman had to support and help her.

Each day Dominica would spend a little time in the clearing of the white stones. She took with her a piece of rough, cured animal skin and rubbed at the mosses and lichens so that they peeled or crumbled away from the stones. She'd taken a small sharp blade she usually used to cut woody herbs and pulled or cut the long grasses from around their bases - which made them stand out more than they had before. Whilst doing this she realised that there *were* stones beneath the surface inside the edge of the circle. For as she pulled up some plants their roots dragged away a chunk of the soil revealing the tops of white rocks beneath - fist-sized and larger, from what she could see. Moreover, she found these rocks were also further inside the circle as, when pulling the odd tussocks of stiff grass that were dotted across the space, she found the rocks beneath the earth there too. It was as if wherever she stood inside the circle there was this layer of smaller white rocks buried beneath the soil under the grass.

*

One sunny but windy day at the end of the greater harvest, when the yellow and brown leaves whirled in eddies and the last of them shook free from the trees, Dominica arrived to find the woman standing outside

Mother Barr's, stock still, head bowed. As she approached the woman looked up and relief flowed over her features.

'Sister! Mother Barr!'

'What?' Dominica said, though she knew, she ducked inside, but the woman stayed outside. 'Come in!' Dominica called - she wanted her there at the point she pronounced her dead. 'Was she like this when you came this morning?' The woman nodded. 'But you've not told anyone yet?'

'I was scared to – without you here – they might blame me.'

'Come here.' As the woman slowly approached Dominica felt for the life-thump in Mother Barr's neck. There was none, and the old woman's flesh was cold. 'Mother Barr has been taken into God's care,' she said, 'go and tell her nearest kin.' The woman nearly ran from the house. Dominica rummaged around and found the pot wedged under the frame – the seal still firmly pressed down, it looked as if it had not been opened after all, and she felt a little relieved at that. She took it and placed it back in the row of pots.

Tudwal himself came, 'Sister!' he said, his voice raw, 'It is true then, Mother Barr has gone?'

'She has. She had a growth that was stealing her breath away, day by day. All I could do was ease her pain, she knew it would claim her. I am sorry for your loss.'

'We will all mourn her. Most have not known another healer their whole lives,' he paused then added, 'And she has no one to follow her here.'

'I understand this, and I am training one new healer already. I can train others who are of quick wit and caring mind as time goes on – you will have another healer in time.'

'And in the meantime?'

'In the meantime you will find I will be here often, Bo Barr will be cared for as part of Tamerkam.'

**

The seasons changed. The winter being mild; spring seemed to come early. Dominica went each week to Bo Etherick and to Bo Barr on regular days, often wrapped in her mother's blue brat against the cold or wet.

At Bo Barr the healer's house was kept for her to use for healing and keeping her things. Some mornings she'd find two or three people waiting for her when she arrived. Quite naturally she'd taken over Mother Barr's store of herbs, and more than once she wished she'd asked after the names and thread-code that Mother Barr used. As it was, some unidentified powders had to be thrown away, so their pot could be used again, rather than mistreat someone with something guessed at.

She also had, as she had said she would, taken on another trainee. This child, for she was much younger than Eiliwedd, hung around the hut whenever she was not about her chores, her mother often scolding her when she found her there *instead* of doing her chores. However, the child watched intently and asked questions intelligently and said she wanted to learn to be a healer.

It hadn't taken much encouragement from Tudwal for the mother to let her go to learn to be a healer, and so Avandreg, called Avan by all, joined Eiliwedd and Dominica at the mission. Together they formed a little family, both like daughters with Eiliwedd taking the role of older sister. Dominica taught them as she worked, how and when to gather the herbs, how to preserve them, and always what to use them for, how much, when and how. She taught them both how to read, little Avan taking to reading and writing so quickly it astonished Dominica. Sometimes they accompanied her on her healing trips, sometimes she left them with studies or work to do back at the mission.

Dominica also took Indract up to the, now tidied, 'old place' in Bo Barr and asked if she could pray with the people there. She watched him keenly as he stood in the space, closed his eyes and prayed. She wanted to say how much she felt it was right, even though it was an 'old place', but held her tongue so he could discern for himself, all the while praying his discernment would be the same as her call.

Eventually he opened his eyes and smiled at her. 'It has the true feeling of a thin place, sister - one of those special places where God and heaven feel so close!'

Dominica nodded, 'Brother, it is how I felt it from the first time He led me here. I prayed and felt a such a peace come upon me here.'

'We will bring a cross to set up here,' he looked round, 'and, if we can, raise up this stone to stand on,' indicating the flat stone.

**** AD 694 ****

After a few years the mission was strong and self-sustaining. All the buildings were made, and a baptism pool had been built at a spot a little closer to the river, where a small spring had been found in the scrub land. This spring had been captured, a pool created, and then allowed to flow on to a set of fish pools built beneath it, as at Tamerunta.

The rectangular church, the only building this shape in the whole area, was used by the monks five times a day but was packed with people from the whole of Tamerkam on a Holy Day, including Dominica's flock from Bo Barr, nearly all of whom had been baptised in the new pool. God seemed to have blessed the mission and, as they took in more lay brothers and sisters and postulant brothers and one postulant sister, it seemed a good time to send some of the original monks back to help out at Tamerunta for a while.

Though there was always a coming and going, visiting and sharing, between the two mission sites, reports suggested tension back at Tamerunta – the people weren't happy, and it seemed they weren't happy with the mission there.

Indract was loath to return himself as he thought Cormag would see it as interference. After all, it had been decided that Cormag should lead that mission. Yet Indract still had a feeling that *he* should be there, even if Dominica had led them to Tamerkam and that was so fruitful for the Lord.

*

One late summer day, having heard of a beating given as a punishment by Cormag to a lay brother, that had upset his family, Indract decided he had to go back, even just for a visit. He took with him Finn, as ever, and they caught the earliest tide down river. Dominica asked him to give greetings to Liaden and a letter she had written to her, and to read it to her. In it she'd asked if Liaden knew where to get the female buds of the healer's hemp, as she had none and thought the special potion made using it would be important to have in her inventory of medicines.

A few days later, when Indract and Finn returned, they brought Liaden's reply. She had told them to say that she had none, but she knew there was a trader coming soon - he always came at this time of year bringing things that were hard to find locally, sometimes fine needles, often silver cloak-pins, sometimes furs, frequently beautiful cloth and braids from overseas, but always some hard to get herbs, and she would tell him what Dominica was looking for.

Indract had also sorted the problem with the family, though it had been hard and the business had done the mission no good. Cormag had beaten the young man, Colan, so badly that he'd had to spend time in the healer's hut. Liaden, still the only healer in the community, had complained to Cormag of the severity of the punishment, but he had told her it was none of her business and was justified because of the severity of the sin.

When it came to it, the boy had been found with a girl - the girl he was betrothed to. The families on both sides had no problem with this, and the mission should have been lenient as he was not destined for tonsure. Though, as he had promised celibacy while he worked as a lay-brother to receive teaching in reading and writing in return for his manual labours, dismissal should have been the only discipline needed. But Cormag had 'gone mad' as it was described by one of the other lay-brothers and beaten him with his staff until the boy lay bloodied on the ground.

Niall described to Indract the tight rein that Cormag kept on everything, saying that even the joy in the Lord was frowned upon, and anyone who tried to disagree was met with threats from brother Durragh – described as whispered words asking, 'Are you a heretic? Do you know what happens to heretics?'

Indract decided to send back the senior and steadfast Dairmut, and with him the bardic Teagan, the cheerful Brannon, now a tonsured monk and, though he wished to keep him at Tamerkam, Finn – for his diplomacy skills and his worldly rank, as the latter seemed to affect how Cormag responded to advice. They were to build up the trust in the mission again, to bring a little light and beauty to the services and friendship to their dealings with the people of Tameruntа – to repair the damage Cormag had wrought with his austere ways and harsh dealings with the people and the lay brothers. They set off the next day.

Around noon a few days later the stranger was spotted by the lookout up in the stronghold as soon as his coracle entered the far loop of the river's hook. Everyone had heard that the trader had been at Tamerunta and, for the first time ever, had chosen to come up river with his goods - so he was met by an excited party of men and women at the landing place. In her heart Dominica wanted to join them but she had work to do and so remained in the herb garden with the girls, harvesting.

Later in the afternoon Keynae sent word to Dominica to come to the stronghold as the trader had asked for her, saying he had the herbs she had asked for. She left the girls bundling and hanging the fresh herbs and went to find Indract as she knew she would need silver to buy this exotic herb, only to find he'd been asked to visit the stronghold too.

The trader had set out a cloth and arranged his goods on it - people stood at a respectful distance, just looking and chatting excitedly amongst themselves. Most people here had little enough to spare and not much actual silver as such, as almost all trade was by barter, but looking was fun anyway. The group parted as Keynae led Dominica to the trader, Indract staying back behind everyone.

The trader bowed low to Keynae and Dominica, 'I am Joseph the Trader,' he said, and when he stood up straight again Dominica found herself looking at a man like no one she'd seen, his eyes were of the brightest blue, his skin tanned darker than she'd ever seen before and his hair such a glossy black it looked as if it were oiled, yet the breeze moved it lightly.

He smiled and nodded a small bow towards Dominica, 'Sister, your healing work goes before you - mistress Liaden speaks highly of you. I have brought the herbs you need, and I have another very special one to show you.'

Dominica smiled back, now also fascinated by the way he spoke, his words lifting in unusual ways, musically. 'Thank you, Joseph the Trader,' she said and glanced round to see where Indract was. 'Can we do our exchange later, when the excitement here has died down?'

'Most certainly sister, the chief has offered me space in the meeting house for the night – I will not be going back down river today.' At which there was a commotion as a runner from the lookout came to tell Cador that a party from Kellyventon were coming down the highway – it seemed that others had heard of the trader's visit.

Cador nodded to Keynae and they headed back to their own place, re-emerging a little later with fine two-colour cloaks thrown over their shoulders, pinned in place with elaborate brooches. They returned to the place where the trader had spread his goods, and spoke with him. Keynae choose a length of smooth linen in an unusual colour and a band woven with colourful threads and Cador offered a number of old coins, which the trader checked carefully, but accepted. She was standing there holding the cloth and band when the Kellyventon party arrived.

'Brother! Sister!' called Cynan as they approached on their ponies.

Keynae went to meet him, 'Dear brother! And sister!' She called, welcoming Cynan her brother, and his wife Rannoeu, 'Welcome – news of our father?' she looked from face to face.

'Still alive, fear not.'

'We come to see the goods this trader has brought,' cut in Rannoeu, eyeing the bundle over Keynae's arm.

'She insisted,' Cynan said as he slipped from the pony's back and clasped hands and arms with Cador.

The trader looked pleased to see others arrive who obviously had the silver to buy with, and spent time showing off his wares to Rannoeu, drawing out and unfolding lengths of fine material, flashing bright woven bands and cloak pins. She gathered a number of pieces to herself, then the trader turned to a bundle he'd not unpacked. He loosened the strips tying it and out rolled some beautiful fur pelts, not large, but shining and pretty and delicate; white, white with patterns like shadows of leaves, glossy black like his own hair, russet red like autumn berries. Perfect to edge a hood or collar of a cloak. Rannoeu clapped her hands – and picked them up one by one, stroking them and trying them for length. Eventually she turned to Cynan and showed him one she had chosen, which he came and duly paid for along with her other pieces.

Later, when a few of the people had also parted with some of their hard-won silver for a cloak-pin or a woven braid, the trader packed his goods and then sought out Dominica.

'Here sister, a packet of the buds of the healer's hemp, five pennies to you,' he said, then looked at her carefully, 'Have you knowledge of the recipe for dwale? A potion to make men so fast asleep they cannot feel even a cut. It is a potion used when surgery must be performed?'

'I have never heard of it, but then, like you I am a stranger in this country.'

He smiled warmly, 'Maybe you know it by another name? I have the recipe and I have the one herb it asks for that can only be found half way across the world, beyond Rome. Are you interested, sister?'

'I would like to see the recipe first, so that I may see if I recognise it.'

He smiled again, this time his smile was unreadable as he reached into a pouch and produced a fold of paper. Dominica turned the paper to the dwindling light and read.

Many of the herbs were dangerous in quantity, but as she read she recognised the lowering of the dose as it was diluted with much wine, and the final dose was not all of the quantity, but just enough to induce sleep. He had been right, though some may be difficult to get, all the ingredients were available locally, except one which she did not know, *'pape'*. 'What is this one?' she asked pointing to the word.

'Pappy,' he said, 'the dried juice from a special colour of the flower. This is what I have for you.'

Dominica prayed silently, 'And how much is this herb?'

'It grieves me my lady, but I must ask for sixty pennies,' he said, a look of sadness on his face, 'for enough for that recipe.'

'A fortune, Joseph.'

'It it a hard thing to harvest and has come from so far away, through so many hands,' he said quietly, 'and it is quite miraculous in effect.'

'I'll ask,' she said and went to speak with Indract.

Indract was taken aback by the price, but Dominica persevered, reminding him of the agony Cormag endured that could have been wiped out with such a potion. He said they must put it to everyone for a vote, as the sum was so great.

Dominica returned with some old silver coins, each with the face of a man wearing a crown of leaves on, sufficient to cover the five pennies for the healers' hemp buds and a further six for two fine needles.

To her fascination, the trader brought out a tiny balance, placed a weight on it, checked it against the weight of her various old coins, until they made it balance - and then gave her the extra one back.

She gave Indract's message to the trader, who bowed and said he'd wait to hear from them. She promised he would hear from her the next morning and bade him sleep well before walking back down to the monastery with Indract.

Chapter 27

The Old Evil - *circa AD 694*

The discussion was quick – as there were so few of them now that the others had gone to support Tamerunta. Neither Brother Fergus or Kellagh raised any objections, especially when Indract described Cormag's agony that could be eased by such herbs.

As leader, Indract had been given the care of a sum of silver – the old foreign coin and hack-silver which his father had given to the monastery at Drom-Mhor years ago - to support their peregrination and ministry. He knew they could afford the pape, as they had spent very little through the generosity of the peoples in the two missions, but it wouldn't last forever if they were not careful.

'I will still try to haggle sister,' he said as they headed up to the stronghold, 'The trader may be taking advantage of your kind spirit.'

Before they reached the meeting house they saw Drustan hurrying down towards them, 'Just the person!' he shouted, 'I was coming for you! The trader is ill – come and see if you can help him.' He turned and strode back up with them.

'What is wrong with him?' Dominica asked. *Perhaps he's had too much ale after retiring to the meeting house – it has been known.*

'Sweating, his head aching fit to split - and his joints in pain, he says.'

Still sounds like too much ale. 'Did he drink much ale last night?' she ventured.

'No sister, maybe a cup. He asked if we had wine instead, hah!'

Dominica knew that there was wine to be had, but very little of it and that kept for important guests. She thought of the transaction they were about to make, and how very much wine was required – that would be another expense unless she could use a substitute, but she left that thought for another day - for now had more immediate concerns. If it was not a hang-over then what was making the trader so ill? They stepped into the meeting house. Only a few people were in there at this time, and the trader was propped up over on one side, fortunately where some light from the doorway shone on him. Immediately she could see a sickly sheen to his face.

'Set up something for him to sit on outside, I need more light,' she said quickly to those around. To the trader she said, 'Is this come all of a sudden or has it come on slowly?'

'Felt a little achy yesterday, but nothing too bad,' he shook his head, 'but now, today, I've never felt like this before and ...'

Dominica tipped her head at him questioningly.

'It's ready for him,' Drustan said sticking his head in the doorway.

'Can you walk? Enough to get yourself outside to sit there?' The trader nodded and leant his whole body forward to pull himself from the wall of the building then pushed on the bench to raise himself, staggering like a drunk out of the door. He flung his hand up at the light, but turned and sat heavily on the bench set just to the side of the doorway.

Dominica could hear him breathing heavily as she came to look at him, but she kept back a little thinking of the contagion that Nuala had and how it could be spread by the breath. In the light she could see how his colour looked grey under his tan. 'You were saying you'd never felt like this before?'

'No. I'm hot and I'm cold,' as if to illustrate he visibly shivered, 'my head - splitting, as if I'd drunk an amphora of bad wine, thirsty too - and my joints are sore.'

'All your joints?'

'Hmm?'

‘Are all your joints sore or just some? Are your shoulders sore? Are your elbows?’

He managed to crack something like a smile, ‘Shoulders always sore – heavy packs to load, unload.’

‘But this is different you said?’

He paused and moved his arm, ‘Shoulder joints sore, elbows not.’

‘Where? Show me where it hurts?’

He raised one hand as if to touch the other shoulder, then, just as Dominica was breathing a sigh of relief, he moved his other arm, reached across his body and barely touched the exposed armpit, yet winced.

‘Loosen your shirt, let me see your armpit,’ she said quickly.

Fumbling he loosened the ties and the sleeve dropped away. He lifted his arm again, wincing. Dominica took an involuntary step back as she saw the angry red bulge under his skin.

‘Wait!’ he said, staring at her, ‘No? Oh, no! God protect me!’

‘I don’t know! It is a possibility. We can care for you, keep others away from any contagion, but look after you.’

‘Shut me away and pray?’

‘I will care for you myself,’ Dominica said, already planning how to keep everyone else safe. She had not met the plague before, but Sister Ciar had, and had told her of the symptoms, the dangers and of the only ways that were, sometimes, known to save the person. Yet, the main thing was to keep that person away from everyone else - to isolate the contagion as much as humanly possible – without abandoning them.

Dominica asked Drustan to tell the girls, Eiliwedd and Avan, that they were to both go to Bo Barr to stay at the healer’s hut there until they were asked to return. She also asked him to arrange an escort for them and the postulant nun, Sister Aylwyn, too. Also for someone to help them to carry their bundles - food, clothing, bedding, cups, bowls and a pot for food cooking.

She asked another to find Keynae and ask her to come to the meeting house. She met her away from the trader – he still slumped against the outer wall of the house.

'I have worrying news. I fear the trader may have a spreading disease. It might be,' she spoke the next words softly, 'might be plague – I have only the description to go by, but I think it may be. Tell me, when there was the sickness here before – those that suffered, did they have bulging sores in their armpits or in their groins?' Keynae's hand flew to her mouth, her eyes wide - she nodded.

Dominica nodded back resignedly, 'In that case – first we must make sure he is kept away from everyone else. I want to take him to my healer's hut, but he may need help to get there. Was there anyone who suffered the plague but recovered?'

'There were just two, one is no longer with us – he had an accident a few years since and died, but the other is still with us, why?'

'Sister Ciar told me that those who survive have some God given protection. She knew of a doctor in Rome who survived and had worked fearlessly with plague patients as it returned in waves each season. Who is it?'

Keynae pulled a face, 'Cador.' She shook her head, 'You'd better be right – we all thought it a miracle and a sign when it happened that way – it would be a terrible thing if you were wrong.'

No one had announced the plague, Keynae and Cador having been asked to say nothing – yet the rumour of it ran round the community – hissed from every mouth. How close had they been to the trader? Did they buy something? Touch the goods? Surely it was best for him to be cast out! Not one of them! Didn't he come to see the monks? Never come up to Tamerkam before! Now look!

Indract organised the emptying of the healer's hut as Dominica said to do. Everything was taken to the nuns' house - leaving only the bed platform with a layer of bracken and dried bedstraw and a cover. The fire was raised and a pot of water set to boil, then everyone was told to keep away from the hut.

Cador didn't argue when Dominica told him of Sister Ciar's experience – and explained it was to protect the village. She even made him wear one of her tie-on wild garlic and mint soaked masks, like they used back in the mother house, as he helped the trader down to the hut and brought him in. Once the trader was laid on the bed, Dominica got Cador out quickly

'Cador, bless you! Go now to the baptism pool, strip off your clothes and drop them into the bottom of the pool, then wash yourself. Use this,' she gave him a small piece of garlic infused soap tied in a rag, 'for your face and hands, any part of you that touched him, then rinse - go right under the water. I will send a message to Keynae to let her know to bring you fresh clothing to put on, the rest can be collected for washing the next day, but not before.'

Dominica told the trader she would be back soon and went to the nuns' house. She found her herbal and looked for the instructions and recipe that Sister Ciar had given her. She looked down the list and decided she would go and collect some of these now, using fresh herbs where she could to save her precious dried supply. Snatching up her basket and her sharp knife she went out to the herb garden. There she gathered yarrow, mint, fennel, rosemary – she was pleased with how well the tiny rooted split she'd brought with her had grown, and sage, which hadn't taken so well, but a few leaves were all that were needed. The ramsons' leaves had wasted away over in the shaded damp area, so she'd have to use more of the dried leaf powder, then she cut a willow wand from the edges of the patch and took this all back to the house. In a pot over the fire in the nuns' house she warmed a little sour wine, then steeped all her finely shredded fresh ingredients in it. She drew the pot out of the edge of the fire and added the other ingredients; a small spoon of bile and the ramsons' leaf-powder, leaving her copper spoon in the mix to stir it with - often, as directed.

It was only then that she thought about the trader's packs. Sister Ciar had explained that it was not known how the plague moved from one to another, but it could be through breath, like some other diseases, or touching - as surely those in close contact suffered the same way. She had heard that people who shared bedding, or took the clothes left by the dead, most often died of the plague too, and so she had wondered if the plague could be caught through sweat, for the sick sweated profusely.

If Sister Ciar was right, and if the man had the plague, then his sweat was on those packs – they had to be removed from the meeting house before people started handling them. Packs were easier to deal with than the man; they could be hooked up and carried on a pole without touching anyone – but where to put them? In the end she decided they would have to come into the healer's hut. She looked in on the trader and left him a simple drink of willow-bark and mint to try to help his fever and chills, then headed up towards the stronghold to get the packs removed and moved down.

Many eyes followed her - but not one person spoke to her.

That evening she was able to give the trader his first dose of the potion she had concocted to Sister Ciar's recipe, and some broth in a deep cup to sustain him. Always she was careful to keep back from him, placing the cup down for him to pick up, and always wearing her special mask .

He murmured, 'Thank you sister. You meant it.' And he was obviously cheered to see his packs when Dominica dragged them in with a long hooked stick, 'Bless you, sister!' he said, the old smile flickering on his face.

The next morning she was pleased to see he looked no worse when she took him the second dose of the potion, and another deep cup of broth. She was loath to spend much time inside the building – but left the door flap back to bring in fresh air.

And so it continued on the third day - each time she went to him no worse, but not noticeably better. On the morning of the fourth day he asked if he could try some bread. She fetched some and watched as he ate, dipping it in the cup of broth and closing his eyes as he put it in his mouth.

'How do you feel? How are the armpits?' she asked as he finished.

'Much less sore, still there, but much less.'

'Let me see.' He lifted his arm carefully, the swelling was much diminished - from fowl's egg buboes down to blackbird's - and the redness had gone. 'And the fevers? Chills?'

He looked up surprised, 'Long gone, just ... achy, but not so sick feeling.'

'The Lord be praised!'

'Indeed, sister, indeed,' he said with a small smile.

She couldn't wait to tell Indract. She sought him out after prayers. 'I think the trader will live. He seems much recovered, praise be!'

'Praise the Lord! Maybe it wasn't the plague after all?'

'That would be so very good if it is so!' she said and set off back with a joyful step.

It was the morning of the next day, the sun not yet high in the sky, when she suddenly heard Indract calling from outside somewhere. She dropped the copper spoon she was stirring the potion with back into the pot and headed out of the house. Running round the side of the Church she could see Indract shouting up by the healer's hut.

'I'm down here!'

Indract turned, 'Thank God!'

'What is it?'

'We have had bad news from Kellyventon!'

Chapter 28

Lord Save Us - circa AD 694

'What?' Dominica asked as they came close enough to talk.

'Rannoeu is sick. They think it is the plague - and they've heard we have it here.'

'No!' Fear ran through Dominica, 'I was thinking I was wrong. The trader seems to have recovered, didn't even get too sick. Maybe it is only what he had?'

'Keynae wants you to go and treat Rannoeu - Cynan is beside himself.'

'But!' Dominica began, then stopped. 'Don't they have a healer there? Who will care for the trader if I go?'

'Yes, they have a healer, but Keynae knows the trader lives and would have her brother's wife live too. Call back one of your healers to look after the trader - you said he is so much better.'

'No, if it is the plague I won't endanger them! No, I'll go and come back today. If Cador can let me have a pony - then I can do both.'

Cador provided both pony and escort to show her the way. That afternoon Dominica put a day's worth of potion in a narrow mouthed pot and stoppered it. She also took with her herbs to make a brew there if they were not to be had.

The journey wasn't as long as she had imagined. She realised she could probably walk it if she had to and had the time, but riding made light work of it. They began to descend the long gentle hill towards Kellyventon, it showing itself from this direction as a smear of smoke above the surrounding trees. As the highway began to curve away right towards the great hill, they took a turn off to the left, shortly after which the settlement could be seen - much larger than Tamerkam. They rode steadily in towards what seemed to be a meeting house, as it was so large, but it turned out to be the home of Cynan and Rannoeu.

Cynan came out as he'd been alerted to their arrival. 'Sister, thank God you have come!'

'Blessings, Cynan, where is Rannoeu?'

'At the healer's house. I would have kept her here but Meduyl said she must be with her.'

Dominica nodded, 'A wise lady, please tell me where to find her.' Cynan's reply was to lead them there himself, calling out for the wise-woman as they approached. Meduyl came out of her house, a strikingly tall dark-haired woman with an angular face, one of the few women Dominica had met who was taller than herself.

'Cynan. I see you've brought her here anyway!'

'It's not as it seems, Meduyl. My sister sent her here – the trader she treats is recovered!'

'Recovering,' amended Dominica, realising that she was not really welcome. 'Sister,' she said, addressing Meduyl, 'I am glad to meet a fellow healer who will understand everything. I have brought some of the potion that my teacher showed me how to make, and the recipe she brought back from far across the seas, as far as Rome, many years ago. I can show it to you then leave Rannoeu in your care and return to Tamerkam.'

Meduyl regarded Dominica with a long stare, '*Show* me the recipe?'

Dominica took from her bag her herbal and opening the book beckoned Meduyl over. Standing so the slanting sunlight fell on the page she pointed to the recipe. 'And I have brought some of everything needed except the wine, as I do not know what you have in your stores.'

There was silence as Meduyl looked at the page and then looked at Dominica. 'You read it out to me!' she snapped. Suddenly realising that Meduyl, like so many wise-women in villages, would not have ever had the opportunity to learn to read and write, but instead had an amazing recall and committed recipes to memory, Dominica said, 'Of course,' and read.

Meduyl nodded, 'I can make this!' she said, chin raised and looking at Cynan.

Cynan nodded, 'I'll leave Sister Dominica with you then. Come and find me afterwards, sister. I will be at home.'

In a prickly atmosphere Dominica explained about trying to keep the sick person away from all the others, including family. She explained how she tried not to not even touch the cup where the patient had drunk from it, washing everything in boiling water. She poured a dose of the potion, and Meduyl took it to Rannoeu - but wouldn't let Dominica go in to see her. Then together they began the preparation and steeping of the batch of potion to take over from when the pot ran out. As they worked together Dominica spoke of her thoughts about how the contagion spread - maybe by breath, maybe by sweat - and suggested the masks she and Sister Ciar wore.

It was only then Meduyl broke her silence, 'You have strange ideas, sister.'

'But ideas that do no harm and seem to protect – at least a bit. I have been the only one to treat the trader, and it has not claimed me,' she said, sending an arrow prayer for her own safety in the next thought.

It was full dark, though with a half moon, by the time they had finished. 'If you can show me back to Cynan's house, I'll leave you. May God be with you and your work here,' Dominica said. Meduyl set off and Dominica followed. The settlement was vast compared to Tamerkam and she was glad to be shown the way in the dark.

'Here,' Meduyl said, indicating the huge house.

'Do send word if you need anything,' Dominica said.

Meduyl looked down and was silent a moment, 'I will, thank you,' she said – and that, for Dominica, felt like a break-through.

Cynan roused Dominica's escort and the pair set off back to Tamerkam. As soon as she returned she fetched a lit rush and returned to her healer's hut to give the trader his potion. The flap was down which was odd, but then she couldn't remember if she'd left it down or up. She lifted it and fastened it up, stepping inside the torch gave its small light to the space but it was not until she had placed it in a holder that she could properly see – and that showed her that the trader's bed was empty!

She snatched the torch from its stand again and went outside again, going right around the hut, looking to see if the trader had gone outside to relieve himself or something. There was no one. 'Joseph? Trader?' she hissed, not wanting to wake the whole monastery. There was no answer, and the only sounds small rustles of leaves and tiny creatures she disturbed in the undergrowth.

She returned to the hut and held the torch high, she could see shapes against the wall at the back – the trader's packs. Would he have gone and left them? Would he have gone at all? She left the hut again but this time walked to a spot where she could see the river shining in the moonlight, sparkling as it ran from left to right, a falling tide. He couldn't? Could he? She ducked back into the hut. This time she took the torch to the back of the hut and set it on a short stand there. Yes, there were two packs, the bundle tied with strips and the bag that held the linens – but his smaller pack with brooches, woven bands, herbs and his silver - had gone.

Without thinking Dominica raced from the healer's hut and straight round to the path that led to the landing place – of course, she thought, as she went, he could be long gone. As she slowed her pace reaching the river she saw a man standing there. It had to be the trader! She called out,

'Joseph? Trader!' the man turned and, even by moonlight, she realised it wasn't the trader, but the night lookout, and felt foolish. 'Lookout – have you seen the trader here?'

'No sister,' he said. 'No one here this night.'

Dominica thanked him and turned her steps back up the hill. *Where could the trader have gone?*

As she returned to the healer's hut she saw the flap was closed. She was certain this time she had not closed it as she ran out. She approached quietly and carefully, considered if she ought to rouse Indract first, but then decided not to and lifted the flap and fastened it back in place. The torch still burned where she had left it, the trader was on his bed. Suddenly angry she strode into the room, 'Where were you?' she snapped, 'I have been looking for you everywhere? You took your pack!'

'Sister, I am sorry, I went to get a drink from the spring. The water had all gone.'

And that was my fault, I should have left more. 'But, I didn't see you, I ran right past the spring?'

'And I took a quiet walk in the moonlight. It feels so long since I felt the breeze on my face and I thought it safe enough for others if I walked alone by night,' his voice sounding plaintive.

'But your small pack?'

'It has been hidden the last two days, here,' he said, indicating the side of the bed platform.

Dominica subsided into an exasperated sigh. 'Of course!' she said, 'and I am here with your night potion, late - but I have been at the home of the lady from Kellyventon, the one who bought the silver dappled fur. She is ailing too.'

'But sister, she will be well, won't she? I am recovered, stronger day by day.'

'I hope that is the case for her too,' Dominica sighed, carefully taking back the cup from the trader.

The next day Indract sought out Dominica again, ‘How did it go sister?’

‘The wise-woman wasn’t happy, but she will make and serve the potion. She wouldn’t let me see Rannoeu – but there was little point in forcing that issue. When we were making the potion together I could tell she was good at her trade. If the potion really helps, it should help Rannoeu.’

‘Of course it helps! Look how you’ve healed the trader.’

Dominica smiled. It was true in that he seemed to have got his strength back and his interest in life. She wondered how long she should insist he stayed inside.

However, by sunset she had to turn him out – as one after another, seven people from Tamerkam area came down to the monastery, feeling achy and sore – and some of them, to Dominica’s dismay, were carried by their friends or family.

Chapter 29

***The Monks' Field** - circa AD 694 - 695*

She tried to tell the first pair of men who'd carried down a very sick woman to go and bathe in the baptismal pool, but they were having none of it, so Dominica sent a message to Cador. When he came he was like thunder, and the men went shaking to the pool, accompanied at a distance by one of the warriors. There was no problem from anyone after that.

Brushwood and dried bracken bed platforms were hastily made up and covered, with each patient given as much space as possible from the next, women one side, men the other. The two women Dominica recognised as the wife of the blacksmith and the wife of one of Cador's warriors, both wealthier households who may have been able to buy goods. Most of the men, though, were those who habitually stayed in the meeting house of an evening, except one, a lad who had helped carry the trader's bundles up the hill. Dominica prayed that these were the only ones affected as she had no idea how she was going to care for them all alone as it was.

After noon day prayers Fergus and Kellagh asked to speak. Indract agreed.

'So, Brother Indract and Sister Dominica, we think that you will be needing more help in the healer's hut,' began Kellagh.

'And we felt called, last night!' interrupted Fergus.

'I know! Last night! Both of us.'

'To heal the sick,' 'Yes, both, to heal the sick,' they said in almost unison.

There was a silence, into which Fergus added, 'In a dream.'

Dominica looked at Indract. Indract looked at the two men. Could it really be, they seemed an odd choice for the Lord. He himself had been thinking to recall Dairmut and Niall, steady and careful men.

'We ... I could do with the help,' began Dominica.

'We will pray and ask for discernment.' Indract said firmly, 'After the next prayers we will talk again.'

Dominica headed back to the nuns' house and began making up a larger batch of potion. She also tore and tied some more old linen to make masks for the monks. She barely needed to pray about it. Her heart had leapt at their news as if it knew what they were going to say. And so it was, Indract had spent time praying for discernment whilst he worked in the gardens with the postulant brothers and at their meeting after nones the brothers' conviction had not changed, and Dominica and Indract confirmed it.

So began a seriously challenging time, Dominica teaching Fergus and Kellagh the basics of safe practice around the patients, if they were to avoid catching it themselves. Plague or no plague it seemed debilitating judging by some of the older men as they lay, sweated and whimpered with the pain in their armpits and groins. The swellings were large, about the size of a small fowl's egg, but they were not discoloured, which gave Dominica hope - as Sister Ciar had said that if they burst or if they mortify then there was only prayers left to help them.

They fixed up some wicker hurdles between the women and the men for some semblance of decency. Fergus and Kellagh then worked with the men, and Dominica with the women.

A day later, two more were added to their number - there was now no room left in the hut. News also came from Kellyventon to say that though Rannoeu was improving, Cynan, one of the house guards, and their servant had also started showing signs and were being treated with Rannoeu.

The first death was one of the old men. He had been in much pain before he was brought in, having been insistent on being left alone. That he died shook Dominica, as others were showing signs of the condition steadying.

Cador was told and seemed unmoved, 'He was old already. Maybe it was his time?' he said.

'Maybe,' agreed Indract, 'but it would be best if any who may have died from the plague - if it is the plague - are buried somewhere separate, somewhere where the ground won't be accidentally dug again.'

'We have a burial place, on the hill beyond the stronghold.'

'But graves are always being dug there are they not?'

Cador thought a while then said, 'You have a piece of land between your monastery and the track - that can be cleared of scrub and made into your special burial place, if that's what you want? You can write it down - that it is the monks' field and must never be dug up.'

'It will be a holy place,' Indract agreed, thinking quickly, 'and a separate part will be set aside just for our brothers and sisters as they depart this life.'

Indract set the lay brothers to clearing the lower part of the field, where the scrub was thinnest and then set them to digging the first grave.

The second death came the next day, at daybreak. The body was found cold - the blacksmith's wife. Dominica did her duties, then purged herself clean, water as hot as she could bear, using garlic and mint wash, and went to prayers and to tell Indract the bad news. Her confidence was shaken as yesterday the woman had seemed no worse than the day before. Indract comforted her by saying it must have been God's will, and sent others to dig a new grave beside the first. At prayers, they all prayed it would be the last from this affliction.

The trader came to Dominica to bid his farewell. 'Sister, I am sorry that this – ailment seemed to have come with me. I did not bring it knowingly, but I suffer with having to travel far and wide and meeting so many people. I'd only arrived from Britannie, at the harbour of Porthkudh, a few days before coming here. What news from Tamerunta? Did they escape it?'

'All seem well back there, thanks be to God.'

'Sister, I am leaving this afternoon on the falling tide. Here, this is for you,' and he held out a small pot with a stopper tight in it. She lifted her hand and he placed it in her palm. 'It is a gift for you, the pappy I told you of, and here,' he passed her the slip of paper, 'the recipe for Dwale. No silver can thank you for my life – and I did fear for it. I know of such disease and know how it can take the strong with the weak. I know your potion helped, I felt it ease my head, cool my brow and take the swelling from my joints – what else it did to cure I can only guess at, but here I am, strong enough to go on.'

'Thank you, Joseph. One day this will ease some other person's agony, and I will remember you in my prayers.'

He gave his warm smile, 'Thank you sister, I am ever in need of your prayers.'

Dominica smiled, 'May God go with you. He obviously has work for you to do.'

Fortunately the others in their care steadied in their decline and began to revive. The young monks, Fergus and Kellagh, worked hard, carefully and with a kind or encouraging word for the men they cared for. Dominica was impressed and wondered if they would be willing to learn to be fully trained healers for the men of the monastery too, when this time was all over.

News from Kellyventon was fair. Cynan was doing well, as was his house guard. The servant girl, however, young as she was, appeared to be getting weaker. Dominica was loath to interfere but suggested a broth made from a boiled fowl given four times a day or as often as she would take it, with bread if she could eat. Sometimes recovery needed sustenance greater than was usual in the patient's normal foodstuffs, whereas other times it needed a fast.

A week later all the patients who were left had recovered, and no new ones came down with the same or similar symptoms. Keynae had said it was a miracle, compared to the last time the plague had come their way, when more than twenty had caught it but only two had survived.

Gradually the healer's hut emptied and eventually order was restored and the girls and the postulant nun returned. It had only been a few weeks, a month at the most. It was hard to recall with all the pressure and anxiety, but Eiliwedd seemed to have grown into a woman and her confidence shone in her face.

The postulant nun, sister Aylwyn, told Dominica how Eiliwedd had been treating people who came to the healer's hut, and how the people were happy to listen to her. She also, very quietly, said that some had asked for herself to say prayers with them at Sister Dominica's cross, to be delivered from the plague, and that she was surprised to find it in the 'old place'. She hoped it was all right, as she wasn't a nun yet, but she only led the ones who came in the set prayers for the time of day, adding a prayer to preserve them from the affliction.

Aylwyn then told her of another girl, Esselt, who had come to pray with them each time, and who had said she wanted to be a nun too, and that she had told her to ask God and then, when Sister Dominica came next, to ask her. Dominica rejoiced and told her it was just as God would have wanted, which she could see pleased sister Aylwyn, and it wasn't long before Esselt joined them as a postulant at the monastery, her parents being more than willing for her to go.

**** AD 695 ****

Indract called a meeting of the two missions and, as fewer of the full brothers were at Tamerkam than at Tameruntа, it was decided that they would meet at Tamerunta. Accordingly they chose a day when the tide would be falling early in the day to allow a return in daylight.

They took their two coracles and set out after the second set of morning prayers. The journey was swift this way, the flow of the river and the draw of the falling tide speeding them towards their destination. The only difficulty was crossing the flow of the other river to make it into the mouth of the creek. The tide was still high enough to take them up to the landing stage part way up the creek leading up to Tamerunta itself. Lookouts saw them and by the time they reached the landing place there were plenty of hands to pull them in so they didn't have to soak themselves. Once the coracles were stashed higher than the highest tide and weighted against the wind carrying them away, they set off up to the monastery.

Indract had kept his reason for this meeting very close to his chest, not even telling Dominica. After they had heard prayers and broken bread together Indract looked around this group of brothers, and his very own sister, and said, 'My brothers and sister, the Lord has seen fit to bless the missions, both here and in Tamerkam. We have also been delivered of the plague. We all know that this has been a miracle in itself. Sister Dominica and Brothers Kellagh and Fergus worked tirelessly with those who suffered the boils, fevers and sweating of this terrible disease that carries many away and infects many who are close in any way, yet the Lord preserved them.' He drew a breath and looked around. 'All seems settled and well with our missions now. And now, the Lord has laid it on my heart that we had promised a pilgrimage to Rome, and that we should now complete this. I come to suggest we pray for three hours, seeking discernment on this matter.'

'When would you have us go?' Dairmut asked.

'First, brother, we ask God if this is a true guidance from the Lord, and if it is so, we will plan.' And that was agreed, so they all took to the church to pray.

Dominica knelt near the back, alone. She glanced forward. They were all here, all still here. The Lord be praised. She would pray, she would clear her mind and try to listen to God – as her mind was torn between longings and certainties. She longed to see Rome, Sister Ciar had seen Rome and what she described was still painted on Dominica's mind's eye, but Dominica also had that knowledge of her call to Tamerkam, and that kept echoing through her whole being.

Her knees had gone through the numb and the pain and back to the numb stage, but her mind was now completely clear. God wanted her at Tamerkam. He did not want or need her to travel to Rome, for He would be with her in Tamerkam.

When they reconvened each had their say. Most brothers were in favour, and wanted to join the pilgrimage, even Durragh, who usually chose to be at Cormag's side. Cormag had already spoken bitterly of being forced to stay behind as his old injury would not allow him to travel. Looking at the way he had crabbed up, his injured leg somehow worse than when it had completed healing, Dominica could see his point and she wondered if he was now in pain all the time too.

She glanced around the group as it came to her beloved Brannon's turn to speak at last. Eyes sparkling, he said he prayed he could go to Rome, as it would be the most wonderful thing to stand where Saint Peter had stood. Her heart filled with joy for him as she thought of the boy who fell from the tree - going to Rome!

And then it was her turn. 'Brothers, I have prayed and much as my wish would be to visit Rome for myself, I am to stay where I am at Tamerkam. God wanted me there and it is there He wants me to stay.'

'But sister, we need a healer on the journey,' piped-up Brannon.

Dominica smiled, she thought she understood him. He wanted her to come, to share the experience. 'Brother Brannon, you are right in one way, a healer is useful on such a journey, but I know God wants *me* to stay. So I shall train one of you - or two?' she said looking at Kellagh and Fergus, 'after all Brothers Fergus and Kellagh showed they had the dedication to do the caring during the plague - what do you say brothers? Surely there will be time, before you go, to learn the basics?'

The brothers looked at each other and then turned back to her, 'I think we will, sister, with everyone's blessing?' Kellagh said, speaking for both of them, without need of discussion.

And so it was decided, Brothers Indract, Finnachta, Dairmut, Durragh, Niall, Teagan, Fergus, Kellagh and Brannon were going to Rome.

There still being a little time before they could catch the rising tide to head back to Tamerkam, a few more things were discussed. The main point being that which Dairmut raised - when would they go? After Pentecost, was Indract's suggestion, and one which pleased and was agreed by all - with a good clear seven months to go, any other planning could wait.

Before they left Dominica took a chance and asked Brother Cormag if he was in pain with his leg. His eyes glinted, 'Sister, how kind of you to ask. Yes, indeed, it does pain me, but I have decided that it is my cross to bear, much as Saint Paul had his affliction to remind him he was human and had human frailties – when we know how close God was to him and how wonderfully he worked through him - then my pain becomes an inspiration.'

'Yet brother, that doesn't mean we have to suffer if God has given us herbs to alleviate such pain.'

'What would you know? Your concoctions come from heathen sources like as not. Maybe they are the problem, not my pain.'

'I only seek to help ease your pain, brother.'

'Do not lure me with such things. Get you behind me, temptress!' he snarled. Dominica stepped back, looked at him her head half-averted, then turned and left. There was definitely something wrong with Brother Cormag, and it might be more than just the pain from his leg – she would speak with Indract, so at least he knew.

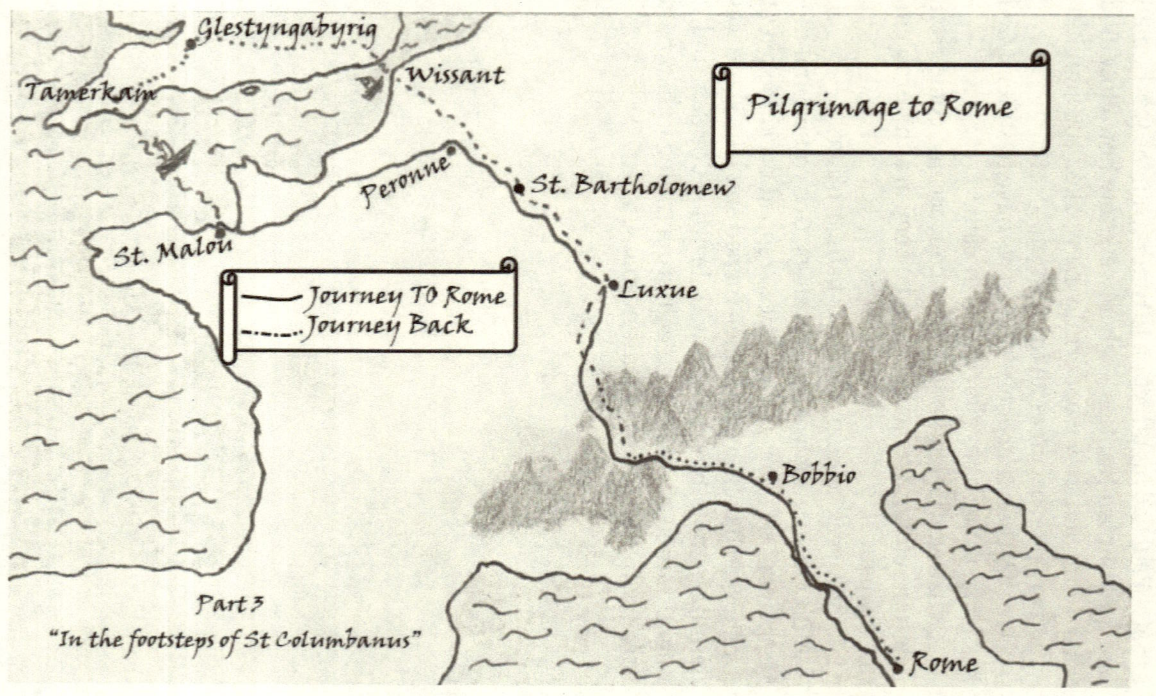
Pilgrimage to Rome
Glestyngabyrig
Tamerkain
Wissant
Peronne
St. Bartholomew
St. Malou
Journey TO Rome
Journey Back
Luxue
Bobbio
Rome
Part 3
"In the footsteps of St Columbanus"

PART THREE

'In the footsteps of St Columbanus'
- the pilgrimage to Rome and back

Chapter 30

To Rome - *circa AD 696*

Seven months passed quickly. Indract had heard of the route taken by Saint Columbanus which crossed Kernow, leaving for Britannie from a place called Fawi, and this was the way he was determined they should go – to follow in the footsteps of Saint Columbanus. However, the river-men he spoke with encouraged them to cross straight to Britannie, not to travel so far west to a different port. They said, the trade routes from Porthkudh on the other side of the bay which their rivers spilled into, were well known. Indract wanted to know where the trade routes went to, and after a while he was told, and when he heard one trade route landed nearby Saint Malou he agreed, for he understood that was the same landing place of Columbanus, and felt sure of a monastic welcome there.

The closer the time for their leaving came, the more foreboding Dominica felt, but she put this down to fearing for anyone leaving on a long journey, even to the sense of missing out, even though it had been her choice.

She had been delighted with the seriousness and effort that brothers Kellagh and Fergus had put into learning healing and wondered at their transformation from boisterous careless young men into careful and caring monks. They were not as quick to know by their senses what was needed. That seemed to be only gained by many years working with people or by some kind of intuition, but when the recipes and their uses were written down they were meticulous in the making and the dosing of patients. And they had done that - copied out their own herbal for the journey, and crafted a bag to keep it safe from water. They had collected the essentials, strips of linen, small parchment folds or small pots of basic herbs, a bowl for grinding with a pestle, a copper spoon for measuring and stirring potions that stipulated a copper spoon, and pots for steeping and boiling. Then they made strong leather scrips to carry it all in.

Pentecost came - but the brothers didn't go. The weather was thunderous and there were storms at sea. The very thought made Dominica shiver and she could sense the anxiety in the pilgrims. However, the ship they had bought space on said it would not sail until the weather was better anyway and there was relief all round - and so it was not until mid to late May that they set out, the day bright, still and warm. The river-men of Tamerunta had agreed to take them - in many coracles - down-river to, and across, the great bay to the port of Porthkudh, as they had said it was a far easier journey than across the land.

Dominica had already said her fond farewells to her brother but now sought out Brannon, as much like a brother as Indract, if not more, being of an age.

'Brother Brannon, I would say farewell?' Dominica said, coming near where the brothers were gathered making sure they had their needs packed in their scrips. All limits on talking had been lifted on this, their leaving day, and so Brannon, all smiles, came over to Dominica. 'Brother, dear Brannon. Look at you! Ready for your adventure? Look at your staff! The bronze ferrules are shining like gold!'

'Oh yes Domca! So much!' He looked at his staff, 'They are to stop the staff splitting on the journey, and everyone has polished them, not just me. But have you seen Indract's staff? He has carved and fixed a cross piece on his, with ferrules to mark the ends of each part, so that wherever we go we have our Lord's sign before us!'

'I will look out for it! You must remember everything you see, hear - or even smell,' she laughed lightly, 'and tell me when you come back. Tell me *so* much – so it will be as if I had been there with you!'

'I will, Domca! I wish you were coming too!'

'I really do believe I need to stay – and you can ask Teagan to write some wonderful words to tell of your journey and the wonders of Rome for the people here to listen to. Indract will tell me of all the serious parts and saintly people, I'm sure.'

Brannon laughed, 'I will tell him that you insist!'

'And,' Dominica added quietly, 'please say to Brother Finn to take care, and to look after Indract, for me, please.'

He nodded, 'I will Domca, I will.'

Cormag led the blessing for the pilgrims at Tamerunta and everyone said farewell as the coracles streamed off in the falling tide.

Dominica, along with a few of the people, hastened down to the point to see the coracles join the flow of the rivers leading down towards the sea. Dominica remembered so clearly when they had come the other way, when she first saw the tree-lined mouth of the creek that was their salvation, and now her brother, Indract, Brannon and all their dear friends were going back out into the unknown and the wildness of the sea. She shivered, despite the warmth of the sun upon her face.

After they were completely lost to sight she wandered slowly back to Tamerunta. She knew she had to wait for the turn of the tide to be taken back to Tamerkam by Cador and Drustan, who had taken the opportunity to also visit with Eudaf whilst saying farewell to the pilgrims, so she decided to see if Liaden was free to talk.

As she wandered thoughtfully back towards the meeting house she saw Liaden coming out looking pensive but, as she looked up and saw Dominica, her face cleared and she broke into a smile, 'Sister!' she called, opening her arms wide and hurrying her way. Dominica sped up too, feeling a smile spread across her own face, and they embraced.

'So good to see you again. Come! The men have their feast, let us have ours.'

With food and drink before them they relaxed and chatted freely. Then Liaden looked solemn again, 'You know,' she said, 'that Father Cormag was - harsh, until the other brothers came and changed things?'

'I did hear,' Dominica said slowly.

'Now the older brothers are gone I fear he will return to his old ways.'

'Does this affect your people, or only the monks?'

'It affects our people, in that all the monks and the lay brothers who remain - who still remain after what happened - are all from our people. Is there anything you can do?'

Dominica thought about Cormag and the last time they had conversed, 'I am sorry sister. I think he will not listen to me - he will not even listen when I wanted to help *him!* I think he hurts badly still.'

Liaden nodded, 'I agree, but he will have nothing to do with me, as you say, even when I offer something for the pain I can see in him.'

As if conjured by their talk they heard Cormag's voice outside, 'Sister Dominica? A word before you leave!' Dominica looked at Liaden then towards the door.

'Well, it seems I am summoned - what now? I'd best go,' she said standing and opening her arms to embrace, 'Liaden - until we see each other again, may God be with you,'

'And with you, sister, and with you!' Liaden replied, returning the hug.

Dominica stepped from the house just as Cormag started to call her name again. 'Brother Cormag?' she said quietly.

'*Father* Cormag, sister! Listen! I am now the only one left here able to celebrate the Eucharist. Therefore you will be under my rule and answerable to me. Is that understood?'

'Certainly you are the only one left to give Holy Communion. I presume you will come to Tamerkam for the great Holy Days?'

'*I* will decide when I come, when it suits me – I cannot be both here and there on the same day.'

'As you will,' Dominica said, trying to sound as if she hadn't just won something.

Brother Brannon

I have decided to commit to memory as much as I can of our journey, everyday, so to be able to let my sister Domca know what the journey was like and what wonders we saw, as she asked me to do. So each day I will recount it to myself before I sleep, starting with this day, the day we left Tamerunta.

We left on the ebb tide, the river pushing and the tide falling, swiftly taken down the river, through the narrow pinch and suddenly into the great bay. I had forgotten how big the sea is! As the coracles skimmed around the edge of the bay the blueness and the vastness came back to me, and I was a little afraid.

The coracles had to work hard to cross the mouth of the river on the other side of the bay, to reach the port tucked in a nook behind a towering block of land that protects this landing place from the might of the storms, and from being noticed by sea. It's name means hidden port, and we're told only those ships who know the way find it easily.

The ship we are to be sailing in is so much bigger, wider and stronger-looking than the one we came from Eriu in, thanks be to God. It isn't hide-covered either but seems to be of flat lengths of wood which, by some miracle, do not let water in. And now it is time to sleep - for we leave on the early tide.

Chapter 31
To be a Pilgrim - *circa AD 696*

Life returned to its usual pace in Tamerkam. There was one difference. Indract had nominated - and the monastery agreed on - an older local-born tonsured brother, Talan, to lead their monastery in his stead. He told Dominica that by this he hoped to prevent too much interference from Cormag. Many still looked to Dominica, as the only one of the original group of missionaries, and some, maybe, couldn't forget that Talan had been one of them, not so long ago, but it was agreed.

Dominica continued to go up to Bo Barr to say prayers and sing the simple call-and-repeat songs of praise that Teagan had composed in their language. As time passed, some from the Tamerkam stronghold would follow her up there and stand with the Bo Barr people at Dominica's cross among the stones and join in.

Brother Brannon

The crossing began well. We left on the first tide in the morning as planned, the ship rocking so gently to begin with that I thought this a marvellous improvement. The ship itself smells like sour half-burnt wood, like is found in an open fire when it has rained. After a short time, I didn't notice the smell any more as the fresh salt air seemed to wash it away.

As the day heated up, dark clouds appeared all around us, as if converging on our ship alone. Sister, I do not have to tell you the fear that beat upon us at that time, but the sail was down long before the storm found us.

The waves came higher and rougher, but the oarsmen, many more than in the currach, kept steady pace, though the ship rolled mightily. Many of us were sick. We prayed, and I thanked God you hadn't come after all, as there were times I feared the waves would wash right over us, fill the ship and take us to the bottom of the sea.

As if in answer to prayer the sun returned and with it a good following wind. They were able to set the sail again and the oarsmen were able to rest a little, taking it in turns to speed us on our way. I admit that I slept. The journey was long, and when I awoke the sky was already darkening, but with the sun hiding below low clouds.

The sun had still not quite slipped away when the sail was dropped and tied and the oarsmen brought us carefully around a headland and into the pocket of a bay where the water lay calm and they could bring us alongside a jetty, where others caught ropes and pulled the ship in.

Brother Indract was heartened to hear the people speaking a similar language to Tamerkam and sought the way to the mission of Saint Malou. We were directed out along a long thin spit of land where, in the dark, we found a welcome despite the lateness of the hour.

The next day we broke fast on a thin porridge and then the brothers at St. Malou sent us on our way with some bread and cheese and directions to travel. We are heading for a place called Peronne, near where the monastery begun by Saint Fursey is placed and where that blessed saint is laid to rest, but this will be at least eight or nine days walking, though there are places to rest, they say, in churches or monasteries, on our journey.

We soon got into a rhythm in our walking, single file, the tap of our staffs and the slap of our feet making a beat, each of us lost in our own worlds of prayer and wonder. We scarcely stopped that first day, except for prayers and water, eating about the middle of the afternoon and, from then on, asking those we met for news of a monastery or a church to rest our heads that night. There being none, and that night being blessedly fine, we slept under the stars, tucked tightly under a tree whose leaves were pale green and abundant.

The second day was much like the first, except we had no breakfast and we carried no bread and cheese for the day. Water was not a problem - there are plentiful springs here. We came upon a small place that held a market of sorts, and there Brother Indract bought bread and a small sack of barley. Later we made a fire and used the potions-pot that brother Kellagh carried to make a barley soup with herbs that Fergus found sprouting nearby. Along with the bread, we felt we ate well. I must remember to tell you this, for I thought how fortunate that you taught these brothers all your herb-lore, not just the medicines.

On our third day I confess my legs ached and the soles of my feet were sore. I could see that brother Dairmut was walking with a bit of a limp but when I asked after him, he merely said it would pass. As he has been on the pilgrimage before I suppose I believe him. Thank God for an old abandoned hut to sleep in and a kind woman who brought us a pottage of some kind to eat.

Our fourth day of walking, I will admit I wished it over and done! My feet are beyond sore now, even my hand where I hold my staff feels sore. I was praying that we would sight this Peronne when it began to rain. The steady drizzle wet everything thoroughly, each step seemed to drag on my tired legs as my habit stuck to my shins and my feet slipped inside my shoes. We tried to walk on the edges of the way, as what had been a dusty road the day before was all turned to slippery mud, but the sides were laced with brambles and nettles. Brother Fergus gathered some of the latter and stuffed the fresh shoots into his scrip. Not long after a traveller told us that we were not too far from Lisieux, where there is a monastery! This put a spring in our step as we looked forward to a bed for the night, no matter how simple.

As it darkened we did not know if we had missed this place – or whether the traveller had misdirected us, or we had misunderstood – they speak a different tongue here. Eventually we slowed and began to look for anywhere dry to spend the night. It was not to be, and we had to huddle close around a fire we made beneath a wide-spreading oak, the fire smoky as much of the wood was damp. Our nettle and barley soup did little to fill us, only to warm us, but our Sunday devotions still filled the air.

The next day, out of curiosity, we enquired of anyone we met as to the location of a monastery. Eventually we gathered that there is a Holy Man, a hermit, living in a cave in the forest nearby, but not a monastery as such. We walked on, the mud drying and falling in flakes from our habits, hoping to find another market to replenish our barley and to buy some bread.

We did not find a market, but as the day lengthened Indract and Finn approached a fine looking house, in a larger settlement we were passing by, and offered to buy some provisions from them, using a mixture of the tongue and a little Latin which the man seemed to understand.

The man of the house was welcoming and insisted we stay and eat with them, chasing his servants to fetch this, fetch that, and sweeping us towards a large table set under a roof - but also in the open air having just one solid wall, the sides and ends of the roof supported by, what seemed to be, whole tree trunks. We sat. Strange how feet, tired as they have been all the time, only complained more when we rested them.

The servants returned with bread and pitchers, along with a well-dressed woman who I assumed was the lady of the house. She was certainly looking sternly at the man. The servants left and returned with cheeses and butter! They left and returned with large bowls of green herbs. The man and the woman stood at the end of the table and made it clear we were to eat; we took out our bowls and drinking cups.

Indract stood, and lifted his hands and prayed to God, praising the man and the woman, and thanking God for them and their bounty. They looked well pleased. We were well pleased! Such riches, butter and cheese. The pitchers contained, not water, as I had expected, but a heady amber liquid full of flavour. It was quite strong and made my head swim, but maybe that was the tiredness and the previous lack of food.

The man asked Indract if he was able to give the Eucharist and baptise. As far as we could tell they were a Christian family who could find no priest in the area. Indract, of course, was able to do both these offices and so it was arranged that the next morning both would be done. We slept well in the open sided barn that night, tucked in against the protective solid wall.

The next morning a great deal was made of making the barn like a church, the table set against the wall with the benches facing it. A piece of white cloth was place in the middle of the table then a bowl was brought, placed on one side of this and water poured into it. On the other side a platter of fresh bread was laid. As for us, we made ourselves as clean as we could, brushing our habits free of the last mud, washing ourselves well.

People came. Not just the householder and his servants, but others, too many to sit so most stood. We sang chants and one of Teagan's songs of praise. It was a great blessing. Twelve children and one adult came to be baptised. Without flowing water, Indract could only pour cupfuls of the blessed water over them - but that seemed to be their way to baptise. Many took the Eucharist, some with tears in their eyes. Indract preached a short sermon in Latin, not sure how many could understand anything outside the words of the service, but all were attentive as he spoke.

We were determined to continue our pilgrimage, and so by the noon we left with provisions and many thanks and farewells - our spirits uplifted so much that we sang hymns of praise even as we walked along, Teagan leading with his mellifluous voice. The day had been dry and so we were not too disappointed to find the woodland as our shelter once again.

Trust in the Lord. That was part of our morning reading. Trust in the Lord – and he will make your paths straight. It was as if they were words spoken to me, as I need to trust more in the Lord. This pilgrimage seemed all light and excitement – but we are only a week or so in and already I find the disappointments and drudgery can overwhelm my sense of purpose, of service, of loving the Lord. I'm not sure I'll tell you this, sister, as you always seem so sure of God's purpose for your life.

We kept a steady rhythm this day, maybe not as fast as that first day, but we made good time, even Brother Dairmut - who is still limping. At last we met someone who knew of Peronne – and could tell us it was a day away! Oh, how my heart leapt! But we did not come to Peronne before darkness threatened to engulf us. Indract managed to get a man to let us stay in an animal shelter, empty of animals now that the spring grass was up and they were out, but by no means cleaned. Fergus made a nettle and barley mash which was warming to the stomach. At least there was a spring diverted nearby where the next morning we could wash the dust from our hands and faces and drink our fill.

I think the man who said Peronne was a day away must have travelled there on horseback. Still no sign of the place even as darkness drew in again. Another night under the stars - thanks be to God that it is dry. And praise God for Kellagh and Fergus – they are treating more than one of us for sores and eruptions on the skin.

Praise be to God! We reached Peronne! The monks bade us welcome and treated us royally – there was good food to eat, a place to wash and treat our sore feet, and dry beds for the night! In the morning we went to the church where the blessed Saint Fursey is buried and said prayers there. Later we joined with the brothers in all the offices, and slept again comfortably, ready to make an early start in the morning. Our next proper stop is said to be a great town called Reims, three day's journey from here.

We made good time. The walking was easy for the most part of the day, and we were fortified by good food and a proper rest and care. As evening came we began to labour up steep hills or seemed to wander in semi-circles of paths to go round these hills. Eventually we settled ourselves amongst trees and huge rocks that seemed older than time, and rested for the night, our evening prayers drifting over the plains below.

This morning we were woken by a fine rain and set off swiftly, saying our morning prayers as we walked. The hill walking continued, but it was getting harder, sometimes we dropped into a valley only to have to climb up again and even higher, the paths narrow as goat tracks! As dusk approached we were on a long upward trek, and I was praying it did not just herald another drop, as I had heard Laon church described as being on a hill top. The Lord be praised! Laon church was indeed on this hill top and it was that building that we repaired to for the night.

This day saw us taking the high ground for much of the way, the path well used but much drier and dustier than any I have trodden before. The glorious views across hill tops and valleys were full of God's beauty. We crossed the side of a mountain, but still quite high, and as we came over the side we could see Reims below in the wide valley. Dairmut says that a great church is there, made of stone, and a large monastery and a nunnery on the outskirts.

The journey down seemed to take forever. We had been walking for many hours and were exhausted when we came to a small monastery dedicated to Saint Bartholomew the Apostle, on a small hill top just outside the city. It was very late in the day and so we were grateful for the welcome we had there. It is a small monastery, with fewer than thirty monks, but they made us very welcome, saying most pilgrims did not stop there but went straight into the city. In the time allowed for talking together they were agog to hear of our travels from Eriu to Britannia to here. We shall stay at the monastery here for two nights.

On our first day of rest we went on into the city - let me tell you about the cathedral! It is built in stone! That said, I am told that much of it was from stone from Rome. I cannot understand this as I know we are a long way still from Rome. Yet it is grand and impressive! Kings are crowned here – it is such an important star in the Lord's sky.

On the four sides of the town stand huge, vast - like as to touch the sky - stone gateways, made up of large arches. I now understand, these were left by the Romans who in antiquity built much in this place. These are the 'stones of Rome', the remains of Roman buildings, that were used for much of the building of the cathedral.

Tomorrow we set off again. I have spoken to some pilgrims we met at the cathedral, who are on their return journey, having left Rome itself a few weeks ago. They say the next stretch we take, over high mountains, is a penance to be endured for the glory of seeing Rome.

**

We have been walking for thirteen long days now. We are headed for a place named Luxue where Saint Columbanus founded another great monastery. The way has been very steep, both up and down, but we are also constantly on our guard. The forest is evergreen here, dark, letting little sunlight in, and the roots wind amongst the rocks ready to trip us if we are unwary. My admiration for Saint Columbanus, however, grows - he had no knowledge of where he was going or what he would find - just a burning presence in his heart for the mission the Lord had given him.

We were warned about outlaws, hiding in the forest and preying on travellers crossing the mountains, so our ears and eyes are strained for the least strange sound or movement. We now sleep with our staffs lying beside our hands, the only things we have to protect ourselves with. Brother Dairmut took a little time in Reims to teach us how to make a circle to fight off outlaws as a team, and how to fight, back to back, with a partner each moving to cover their right.

Praise the Lord, for we arrived this evening at a monastery we knew nothing of, Fontaines, which was also founded by Saint Columbanus. Here they put us up for the night and we slept better than we had since Reims.

The next day we pressed on for Luxue, less than half a day away - it is a wonderful place, a school for so many followers that Saint Columbanus had to create Fontaines - yet even this was his second school here. The first school was at Annegray, a little off our route and higher in the mountains, where an old Roman fort used to be. The Romans built in stone wherever they went, and it seems they went everywhere.

We stayed here for two blissful days, cleansing ourselves and reviving our spirits in the hot springs, which are part of the grounds of the monastery now, blessedly reclaimed from pagan practices by the saint himself.

The second day was spent in celebration of the birth of Saint John the Baptist, much revered in these places as an example of the simplest life and the highest calling. The service was followed by a full meal to which anyone was welcome, and come they did from all around to share in the feast, and we and the monks living and studying here, served everyone.

*

At Tamerkam, midsummer and the holy celebration of Saint John the Baptist's birthday, came and went – without sign or word from Cormag, for which Dominica was prayerfully grateful.

The church at Tamerkam was full - with brother Talan leading the service with grace and authority, confirming Indract's choice – and the following feast plentiful and welcomed by all.

A month or so already since the others left for Rome, Dominica thought, and prayed for them and their journey - as she did every day - wondering where they were, what wonders they were seeing.

Chapter 32
Across the border - circa AD 696

They say the devil arrives when you least expect it, muttered Dominica to herself, then chided herself for being uncharitable, and sent a prayer for Cormag, and for healing for his spirit and his leg.

It was the day after Saint John the Baptist's feast day and he'd arrived on the early tide, him and a scurrying young monk – and the lookout had sent a boy to run to the monastery.

The message came to her as she was preparing herself and the healers' hut for the day. She hesitated, wondering if she should rush to meet him – or be found working at her God given tasks. Too much second guessing was not good, she thought as she removed her coarse apron.

'Eiliwedd!' she called towards their herbarium. Eiliwedd looked out. 'I must go and meet brother Cormag. Please see to those coming for help this morning,' and left, walking swiftly.

Cormag was stumping up the track towards the monastery when she met him, his young aide fluttering round behind him, unable to walk beside him where the track narrowed as his ungainly gait caused him to lurch sideways.

'Welcome Brother Cormag!' she called brightly.

His face clouded. '*Father* Cormag – and more decorum, sister, we do not shout and gallop about. It is not seemly.'

Dominica determined not to be sour and dipped her head, 'Of course, father. I was only hastening to greet you. Brother Talan is out in the fields at this time, as are the majority of the other monks, and I was at the monastery as this is the time the people come for healing care.'

His face clouded again, his dark eyebrows pulling together, but he said nothing. They entered the monastery and headed for the refectory as a suitable place to receive visitors.

'I will send Avan to call brother Talan here to meet you. She is fast,' Dominica said, starting to leave.

'Call her here,' Cormag ordered.

'It won't take her long.'

'I said, call her in here. I want to speak to her.'

'As you will,' Dominica started for the healer's hut but, seeing Avan outside before she got there, called her to follow. When they returned to the refectory the young monk was standing outside the entrance looking nervous. They stepped inside and Cormag addressed Avan immediately.

'Sister Avan, do you know who I am?' asked Cormag.

Avan looked at him hard, 'Might you be the monk at Tamerunta that beat our Colan half to death?' Cormag's face suffused a deep red, and he stared at Avan and then at Dominica, who was as astounded and as dismayed by Avan's words as he seemed to be. But Avan went on, oblivious, 'I heard all about it from my mam. Colan is her cousin's son. She said it was the black-haired devil with a gammy leg.'

'Avan! You should not speak to Father Cormag like ...'

'He asked!' snapped Avan.

'Father Cormag, forgive her. Avandreg is but a child...'

'A child of the church and as such she must learn to obey, to be meek. She will take a penance ...'

'No, you cannot ... she is only a ...'

'Then she will be dismissed at once!'

Dominica turned to Avan, 'Go and stand outside.' She went. Dominica said softly to Cormag, 'Father Cormag? Was it actually Aylwyn, our newest nun you wished to speak with?'

He looked at her blankly.

'Avan is a lay worker, helping with the growing and harvesting of plants for the herbarium. I can call Aylwyn, if you like, she is in the church cleaning.'

'You will still dismiss that hellion.'

Dominica came closer and knelt before Cormag, 'No one heard what she said, Father Cormag. We were alone in here. She is no hellion - she merely repeats what her family said. She is a good worker, and the Lord gave her to this mission - in a way attested by prayer and discernment by this monastery. *He* may have plans for her we know nothing of.'

Cormag stared at Dominica for a long time, but his mind wasn't on the problem of the girl. Seeing her on her knees before him had stirred and turned his mind to his old fantasies - Dominica his to do with as he willed ... she would be grateful to him if he relented. Inside he smiled, but his features remained passive. 'Let it be so,' he said. 'Bring Sister Aylwyn that I may speak with her.'

Dominica stood, said, 'Thank you, father,' and left the refectory. Avan, with a face like thunder, stood rigidly beside the novitiate monk.

'Avan, run and tell brother Talan that Father Cormag is here. And do not worry, you are still with me.' Her face cleared in an instant and she dashed away. The monk looked at Dominica and raised his eyebrows. She smiled at him and walked off to the church to find Aylwyn – on their way back telling Aylwyn who it was she was about to meet so she could present the perfect picture of herself – a serious and prayerful novitiate nun – as she was.

Dominica was torn between meeting Talan as he came up, to fill him in on what had happened, and being with Aylwyn as she met Cormag. She went with her duty to be with Aylwyn, but chided herself for her caution when Cormag was so kind and gentle with Aylwyn - though it must have helped that she was prepared for his questions, that she looked so meek, that she was dedicated to the church.

Brother Talan arrived, looking hot and sweaty despite it still being early in the day, his easy smile a breath of fresh air. 'Father Cormag. Welcome!'

'Brother Talan, I come to hear confession and give Communion to all here. I am sure that you can arrange this so that I may leave on the second falling tide of the day.'

'I am sure we can. Sister, would you and sister Aylwyn begin and I shall arrange for all of the brothers to come in order of age. Work can continue until time for the service, which, with your permission father, we shall have at nones, before we eat.'

'That seems in order, Brother Talan,' Cormag said, 'I shall hear confession in the Church.'

As Brother Talan left Dominica asked Cormag if he would have some refreshment before the confessions, but he rebuffed her, saying he was able to wait until after nones, like everyone else.

It took very little time for Cormag to set himself up in the church to hear confessions. He moved a bench so that the angle meant the penitent, sitting beside him, would see the altar and cross just behind him. He settled himself into a pious attitude of prayer and waited for his first penitent.

Aylwyn came in and stood before him. He looked at the slight girl and thought she was too young and naive to have much in the way of sins or sinful thoughts.

'Come sister, sit, let us begin.'

Aylwyn sat on the other end of the bench from Cormag. 'Forgive me father,' she began, 'for I have sinned.'

'Confess your sins, sister, and the Lord will be merciful and forgive you,' Cormag replied.

'Father I confess to the sin of greed. I took an extra portion of bread whilst carrying it to the refectory.'

'Sister, you know what you did was also theft from others ...'

'And I confess to the sin of envy,' Aylwyn pressed on, 'And I confess to the sin of anger,' she drew breath and Cormag cut in.

'Sister Aylwyn, your penance for greed is to take two days with just the single portion of bread and water, no other food. For anger, was it in your head only, or did you express it?'

'In my head, father.'

'Then say ten psalms a day for two weeks, and another day of bread and water. And for envy, who are you envious of?'

'Eiliwedd.'

'Eiliwedd? Is she not sister Dominica's apprentice herbalist?'

'Yes.'

'Why are you envious of her?'

'Because Sister Dominica loves her.'

'Hmm, for envy, you are to say an extra twenty psalms. Complete these your penances and your sins are forgiven – go now and sin no more.'

Cormag watched her go, and wondered what she had meant by love, as he edged his way along the bench a little more towards the middle.

Dominica entered, Cormag straightened his spine but remained in his pious stance, hands folded in his lap.

'Come sit down, sister,' he said, his voice low.

Dominica sat as far away as she was able, but it was still close enough to smell Cormag's breath when he spoke. 'Forgive me, father for I have sinned,' she began, wondering what she should confess to, there were so many small things for which she'd already asked God's forgiveness.

Cormag gave the response and Dominica took a deep breath. 'I confess to the sin of anger,' she said. This was true, she had been so angry sometimes at the stupidity of, mostly, men and rarely asked God's forgiveness when she felt in the right. She waited to hear the penance but instead

Cormag asked her if she had expressed her anger or held it in her head.

'Um, mostly in my head. Sometimes I have spoken it, but only when it was to correct an ... injustice.'

'The penance for this is to say ten psalms a day upon rising for two weeks, and to take only bread and water for two days.' He paused and then said in an earnest tone, 'What other sins do you have to confess?'

Dominica recalled her unkind thoughts about Cormag himself, but could not put that under a specific sin, but he was waiting, as if he knew she harboured something. The longer there was silence, the more she felt a pressure to say something.

At last he murmured, 'Gluttony?' then, leaving a long gap between each of his words, 'Envy? Luxury? Pride? Lust?'

Dominica reflected on each. Most she had no problem with, but was she prideful? Maybe, she had pride in her abilities, but always gave God the glory for healing. No, then. Lust? Huh, lust, she had no problem with lust, certainly not since Indract had sent Finn away. There had been a time when she might have had to confess her longing to be held by Finnachta, though she never saw anything in his eyes but brotherly love. 'No, father, nothing since my last confession.' Not that she'd even contemplated confessing this feeling before she'd been pushed into dwelling on sins as Cormag had made her do. She wondered about what Liaden had said so long ago when they had been tending to Cormag's leg. Maybe Cormag was projecting his own sins on to her?

Cormag released a breath he'd been holding, 'Complete your penance, sister, and your sins are forgiven – go now and sin no more,' he recited.

'Amen,' Dominica replied and stood, glad to be able to move away from Cormag's side.

Cormag watched her go and moved uneasily in his seat, adjusting his habit to accommodate and disguise his arousal, and sliding back along the bench again before the next penitent arrived.

Brother Brannon

They say that we are best to engage a guide for the next stretch of the journey – it takes us through the mountains. A harsh landscape, they say, easy to take the wrong route. Indract has found and engaged a guide, an older man, wizened, but still looking about fit enough to walk the distance. He has told us all we need to carry for the journey, and what we may hope to get on our way. We now carry a sack-pack each on our backs as well as our scrips over our shoulders.

The first few days we made good progress, the walking being in hills rather than mountains. On the third day the hills were noticeably higher but as we didn't dip too much between them it was only as we saw, through a break in the trees, how much further below us the landscape was that we realised just how high we climbed. The guide knows of good places to stop for the night. This is a blessing.

This day was hard. The path very stony, and steep. The guide, weighted with as much of a pack as we, makes light work of it.

The views from the top of the mountain were magnificent. We had to stop and give praise for the wonders of God's world. Our guide was not so impressed and urged us to keep moving. With good reason we found - as our descent to the next suitable place to sleep was long, with the last hour in failing light. And all on dangerous scree that meant an unwary step could take you sliding over the edge of a precipice. Truly scary!

Today we continued descending, the scree behind us. The path here is more compacted and we are back amongst the trees. It is all downhill - all day. As dusk came we could see the bottom of a valley not far away.

Most of this day we walked though the valley bottom. We bought some fresh bread and felt rested despite walking all day. Tomorrow the guide says we shall see Camberiaco.

Another hill today, steep to climb, flatter across the top so that it seemed never ending – and then, there below, we saw what the guide told us was Camberiaco, a place where the great journeys across the mountains and borders meet. We were to make that distance before dusk, he said, as the mountain trail hereabouts was not safe after dark, neither to walk nor to camp. This news pushed us on and we arrived at Camberiaco in time and were taken to an inn, there being no monastery here. Indract was not best pleased as this cost us dear. Our guide will go back, maybe with a returning group, if there is one to be had, he says. Though he says he will find us another guide for the next part of our journey through the mountains – he laughed when we looked shocked, told us we had only gone half-way through the mountains and that the highest part was yet to come.

He was as good as his word, and brought us a man the next afternoon who had just brought a group thus far the other way. A good exchange for the guides. We stayed this night at a church, staying on after the service at the invitation of the priest here. There are no comforts, bar the roof over our heads, but we are grateful. Tomorrow morning, we fill our sack-packs and set off again. We are heading for Taurin. Indract and Finn have both heard of this place, and somehow that makes me feel better. Dairmut says it is in Lombardia, and Rome is just beyond, and now it feels as if we are really getting somewhere!

We left Camberiaco early having been woken at daybreak. We ate simply and left swiftly, saying our prayers on the way as before. We know we have many days journey before us, but the thought of getting close to Rome bears us along. The way was easy, compared to the previous days, and so far a blind man could find the way – we walk within earshot of, or actually beside, a river. All day.

Reluctant to use an inn again, we were shown to a shelter made for pilgrims for the night, but warned to keep anything of value close to our bodies, for some pilgrims have been robbed in such a place.

The next day, we were told, we would make our way to a place named after the blessed John the Baptist where a relic is kept there of his fingers, having been brought there many, many years before by Saint Thècle from Egypt. I think the guide has our mark, and knows what will make us walk faster. I am curious to see the relics though.

As before, we left early, so we arrived with enough light to see, and we were fortunate as we will leave here tomorrow too early to visit the cathedral then. Lights were brought so we could pray at the shrine to John the Baptist. The relict is in a gleaming casket, pierced with many ornate windows so you can just see the remains lying on a cushion within. There is an awe and stillness in this place. We all knelt in silence and the Lord alone heard our prayers.

On the next stretch, even wood and water needs to be carried as we cannot be sure of springs, and we will have little enough fuel to keep us warm, let alone to melt the ice for water. A pile of wood was presented to us before we left and we were told that we each must carry our share. We divided it amongst our sack-packs, Dairmut being excepted for he is still limping, adding considerable weight and bulk in addition to the food supplies, the water and our personal needs.

We left the place named after Saint John the Baptist early, again, having been woken at daybreak, breakfasted swiftly and said morning prayers as a chant to speed our steps. We are right in the mountains now, for the most part walking along trails that go neither along the river valley nor over the top, but are just thin ledges along the face of the mountain, and so precipitous on one side.

Even when we break for a drink we stand, or just lean, against the rock-face as there is no room to sit. The plants here still make a purchase and grow quite thickly, except in patches, where the scars show the thin soil has given way and taken all with it to the river bed.

Looking carefully, whilst stopped - it is too dangerous to try to look anywhere except at the ground you are about to step on while moving - I can see why we walk here part way up a sheer mountainside. Below the river carves precisely, so the banks differ not from the mountains side, save they are scoured clean of plants by the rushing water, and drop vertically into it.

I did wonder where we would sleep. This is why we have a guide – and why we left early. He led us to a scoop in the mountain side that was not only flattish but sheltered from the wind. We arrived none too soon before dusk, which came early and swiftly in this cleft amongst mountains, and made our fire for cooking and warmth, each adding a measured portion of our carried wood.

The next day we were up early and on our way again, the guide harrying us to keep up. Dairmut is still limping, but says not a word about it. Finn has dropped to the back of the line with him and keeps him cheerful. I wish I was not just ahead of Durragh - he keeps up a litany of complaints which dull the soul of the hearer.

We had just got used to edging ourselves and our packs round the rock outcrops that reduce the trail to a slim man, when we met a different kind of obstacle – a group of pilgrims coming towards us! Our guide said something, sharp and loud. The man leading the other group responded in kind. I am not sure what was said, but no one wanted to go back. The solution was scary enough. The other party squeezed themselves against the mountain, finding the widest part or a niche to tuck into, and we had to treat them as a rock outcrop, though not hugging them as we did the mountain side, or grasping them as we did the plants gripping onto an outcrop. Sister, I did not know whether to laugh or weep! It was strangely funny, but also very scary – an untoward movement from one of them could easily send one of us skidding off the path to fall to a watery death.

Another day of walking this trail and all we see are

mountainside and the path. It is getting colder, and the wind has teeth of ice. Sister, do you really want to hear of new blisters, dry tongues, peeling skin and the rags we wrap our fingers with to be able to hold our staffs? Thank God the guide knows the places where we can rest. He says that tomorrow we have a surprise. I cannot think what it is, but do not lose sleep wondering.

The surprise is a lake, crystal clear and reflecting the sky. We walk beside it for part of the day. The land around it is flatter and covered with grasses and wildflowers and there are even goats grazing here! We camped near the far end where it has a small beach and I even dared to put my tired feet in it – momentarily, for it is freezing!

From here we seem to be looking straight at mountains wherever we look, some with snow on them in shady places. The guide says this is the start of the pass – though we still have to climb to get to this pass - the only way out of these mountains. We were warned to keep a portion of our carried wood for tomorrow night, no matter what a burden it was or how cold it felt now, as it would be worse then.

Today, the guide has said, will be our hardest day. If we do not want to spend a night in the freezing pass we much press on all day. There is, he says, shelter once we are through the pass. We believe him. Every night it has got noticeable colder - last night there was a rime on my cloak when I woke and this at the end of June! We walked, and walked, and every so far we turned back on ourselves, but higher than we were, winding breathlessly up and up. Then the turnings got closer and closer, and breathing harder and tighter.

Then we were suddenly up! Up on another flatter area. We laughed - with what air we had! The guide permitted himself a smile and us a drink before pressing on. This place would be too exposed, he said, to spend a night. We must get through the pass and over down into a sheltered position, so we trudged on! Very soon we realised we could not be carefree, as our way shortly took us along a cliff edge path, one side plunging down to depths we could not see without getting far too close to the edge, and our path so narrow that we could not get far away from the edge either.

The walking is interminable and hard. I am not alone in just walking and watching my every step! We dare not gaze at the landscape and walk at the same time. The path is narrow and treacherous. On the left side is the drop, on the right a broken wall of rocky ridges. It is icy in places underfoot, and the wind is sneaky - trying to blast us off the path with icy gusts shooting round the ridges on our right - and the sun relentless when shining, and so little shade, except near our feet from the rocks. There are no trees on the exposed parts of these mountains.

The guide keeps urging us on.

Chapter 33
The Rome stretch - *circa AD 696*

Brother Brannon

The first sign of relief are the tops of scrub and small wind-sculpted trees. The path wound away from the drop and towards these, and the guide turned and told us, 'Well done, we will make shelter before nightfall'.

The shelter was crude, but welcome none the less, based between giant rocks and the mountainside which stopped the icy wind. We now understood why we each carried so much firewood - there was none to be had even here. The scrub is spitefully sharp, still growing and green so not fit to burn, and the land beneath mere rock. Any broken bits or dead wood has been taken by man or the wind. We huddled around the fire whilst a soup was made, and ate this with the bread we each carried. Durragh threw his wood down at the same moment as I did, otherwise I would not have noticed - his was but a handful, and he added no more. For warmth this night, we packed ourselves tightly in the shelter, only the guide choosing to remain a little away from us, by the entrance, wrapped in his furs.

The downhill continues, sometimes the path winding steeply in long zigzags, sometimes more gently down a straight ridge, but always down and always needing care whether because the path was tight and the stones easily rolled underfoot, or was narrow with little leeway to stepping over an edge. Another pilgrim shelter this night, but the wood is now plentiful so we keep warm, and the guide is more relaxed here - he says, 'They will have the Lombards to answer to if we are harmed,' and with that he touched his head.

The guide says we will reach Taurin by this evening. We passed through a number of small villages, buying bread in one and some cheese at another – there is a cheerful air about our pilgrim group now, and our step is lighter and the way is easier. And the guide was right - we reached another of those places where I can tell the Romans had been. Stone remains and stone buildings. We were taken to a refuge, a place for pilgrims to stay, behind the huge stone church, yet another dedicated to Saint John the Baptist, and there we paid our guide and said our farewells.

A discussion this evening about our next move. Indract said he had thought we might need to stay in Taurin for an extra day, and recuperate from crossing the mountains, but he wondered what we all thought. He and Finn had spoken with the guide at length and were assured the going was easy between here and Bobbio, where Columbanus had founded another monastery, and where we may like to stay the extra day instead. Our decision was to press on. The longer we journey, the more I am in awe of the blessed Columbanus!

The next few days went quite quickly, and walking on far more level ground felt a bit like walking on air. We also did not have to carry extra sacks for food, water and wood as all were readily available when we would need them.

Bobbio! And a warm welcome from our brothers here. We were right to press on and rest here. The opportunity to get clean, and to clean our clothing, is most welcome. Indract, Finn, Niall and Dairmut are admiring the library. There are so many books here! Kellagh and Fergus are at the herbarium and asking after remedies and herbs, Durragh has disappeared again without saying, to me at least, where he will be, leaving me and Teagan to wander and wonder at the countryside hereabouts.

We sourced food, that won't spoil, to carry and some fresh bread and cheese. Indract has been told that the path is well known and marked from here onwards towards Rome, and that we shouldn't need a guide. We bade a fond farewell to our brothers at Bobbio and set off in the morning, our face set towards what appears to be yet more mountains.

Sister, one by one we have fallen sick. We have vomiting and watery stools. Fergus and Kellagh are not sure what has caused this, but they are as sick as the rest of us. We cannot walk far, for one or other of us has to rush into the undergrowth to evacuate or vomit before we go more than a hundred steps. So much for getting ourselves and our clothes cleaned up. We have made a camp in the forest where we can rest, wash in the nearby stream and keep warm by the fire, there being an abundance of wood. This malady brings with it chills that chatter our teeth even though the temperatures are warmer now that we are out of the higher mountains. We barely have enough energy to say our Hours.

After two days rest and just boiled water, as Fergus said that should be all we take, we seem to have returned our bodies to stability. Except for Durragh, he is still wracked with cramps and still must rush away. God forgive me for doubting a brother, but I think he must have food in his scrip which he continues to eat. We broke our fast with a little plain bread this evening and plan to move on tomorrow, and hope Durragh is well enough. We go to sleep early this evening around a well-stoked fire.

We gathered and decided we could walk on in the morning. Durragh complained that he had not had sufficient rest, but Indract relieved him of his burdens, sharing all he carried between us. Dairmut excepted. Dairmut, protested that he can carry his own share at least. Indract told him he may, once we were on level ground again. I sometimes wonder where Indract gets his wisdom from.

This evening we came to the crest of a high part, to see in the distance the sun glinting off the sea. Indract and Finn were delighted. It seems once we meet the sea we are walking on almost flat land until Luca.

Such a blessing, sister - three days of easy walking, one down hill and the others alongside a shining sea, with fresh fish to buy to sustain us. The weather, if anything, is too warm, but welcome after our ordeals. We turned inland on the latter half of the last day, walking between mountains. Luca is a city, which I can tell you those Romans had a lot to do with! It has a grand stone church founded by a saint from Eriu, none the less, named Fridianus, and a hospice for pilgrims - which meant we slept under shelter, not that any of us would be concerned this night.

People here talk of people coming through from Rome everyday. Can it be we are so close? Today we left the city well provided and heading for a place called Siena.

The walking is all through valleys, one leading onto another. Occasionally we must go higher to cross a marshy area or to a little bridge over a wide stream entering a river, but it has been easy going for both days, the night spent outside the walls of a small town crammed on top of a small rocky hill. This morning we bought bread, hot from the night baking, and set off. To have more hours for walking we have taken to saying all offices as we move - God's wonderful creation, our chapel. The last stretch of the road was uphill all the way, and there at the top, Siena.

We found a pilgrimage lodging where we had a simple bed each, and bread dipped in oil for a breakfast - this is usual here - for a small sum which Indract was pleased with. Whilst visiting the church for prayers we were asked if we would be joining the church for the feast of the Assumption on the coming Sunday - just two days hence.

We were told we had four or six days to Rome, depending how fast we walked. We are joyful at this news, and determined to walk it in the shortest time - after all, the walking is so much easier here.

We left Siena and began well enough, but after noon our path began to ascend and it seemed we were to walk over the side of a mountain. This slowed us down, and then the descent to river level was not easy. At this point we ate and filled our water bottles as we could see another mountain ahead, and knew not if we were to walk around it or over it. We determined to keep walking until we found a suitable place to camp, or the next village, before dusk.

*

Dominica had taken to asking Eiliwedd to accompany her to Bo Barr when she went there for her weekly visits, as Eiliwedd had made such good relationships with people over the time of the plague, and it gave her time to speak with the older girl alone.

Eiliwedd had found some good sources of wild herbs in the area and showed these to Dominica, and between them they had revived and replanted the herb garden to the side of the hut.

Over the weeks they often saw Ger on their walk to the healer's hut. Sometimes he'd happen to join them as they walked in from the highway, or out, or would be passing the hut and stop for a few words. Dominica found him a pleasant young man, kind-hearted despite his warrior standing.

Dominica was wondering if Eiliwedd was ready to take over as the wise-woman for Bo Barr, with herself as back-up if some new ailment that Eiliwedd had not encountered or heard of arose. She suggested this to Eiliwedd as they walked back one day.

'You ... do you really think me ready?'

'Eiliwedd, daughter, I would not suggest it if not – did you not cope so well while here during the plague times?'

'Yes, I know, but they will see me in a different light, I think, as a proper wise-woman, and expect too much of me.'

'You are a proper wise-woman, and you know so much already – and I will always be ready to help if you find something that puzzles you.'

'And, may I still come down some days to learn more? I know there is much more to learn.'

Dominica hugged her! 'Of course! That would be the best of both worlds – and I will come here often anyway as I will still come for prayers with the people here.'

Dominica took herself along the path to Pensinys to speak with Tudwal and tell him Bo Barr could have a wise-woman again. He was delighted and they made plans for when Eiliwedd would be made wise-woman to Bo Barr and they decided on the feast day of the Nativity of Saint Mary.

The next Sunday, after prayers at the old place, Ger met Dominica on her walk back up to the highway and asked to speak with her.

Brother Brannon

We came to neither village nor suitable place to camp, and so ended up rolled in our cloaks under a shelf of rock on the mountain face. I think we may have lost our way – or is it the fact that the walking is over mountains again and we had got used to the valley so easily.

The next day saw more mountains but at least we had plenty of water. After a long while we saw a valley below us and prayed that this was our proper direction. We have seen no-one to ask or to reassure us we are on the right trail.

There is a lake shining in the distance. Indract says that a great lake, called Volsinii, is our destination. We take hope and walk on, keeping our eyes on the track as it is often loose with gritty stones as we head downhill all the way.

Volsinii - though some here call it by another name – Bolsena. Never have I been so glad to see a town! We made our way to the church, and found it had a refuge for pilgrims, for which we were grateful. The town has a pleasant aspect beside this lake, but the land seems quite poor. Nevertheless we are told that the way is clear from now on - the Roman Via Cassia runs straight to Rome they say. After our meanderings we are glad to hear this.

We set off fully prepared for our last part of the journey. We were told that there are places to rest on the way, as so many travel this route, merchants and pilgrims both. Indeed, as we left I noticed we were walking along a mostly stone faced road, the stone dark-grey and glassy where it is wet. We also had to make way for carts and strings of donkeys coming towards us, and this slowed our progress considerably.

Sister, it took us two days until we could see the Holy City. We came over a hill, and there below was what once must have been a mighty place, for now we could see many ruins of momentous size. As it was getting dark we took ourselves off the route, along a narrow but well beaten path, in order to make camp. Passing between rocks and a thicket there was suddenly a commotion. A man, a vagabond, had jumped out in front of Indract, and behind us two more appeared. They shouted at us with fearsome sounds and the one at the front waved a dagger. Finn, like lightning, dashed forward and swept his staff at the man, catching his arm. He did not drop the dagger but stepped back. Indract and Dairmut took up the same action, driving the man back. I turned again and saw that Fergus and Kellagh had turned and were swinging their staffs with intent to hit the other men, I immediately joined them whilst seeing, out the corner of my eye, Teagan, Durragh and Niall all raising their staffs ready to ward off any who might break through from the side, but it seemed there were but three. The vagabonds ran and disappeared into the growing dusk. I thank God for Dairmut's teaching. I am sure we presented a stronger party than they expected of us monks. Brother Finn made a joke of it saying, 'I guess we are no longer in the Lombard's kingdom,' and gave a wry smile, as he does.

We did not sleep well that night and were up early ready to find our way through Rome to the Holy Basilica of St. Peter. As the light strengthened we made our way down into Rome. I cannot describe adequately the size of the ruins here. Some pillars standing taller than ten men, others scattered in sections in a line across the land where they toppled. Massive boulder size pieces with carvings and straight edges tumbled together. So much under tangles of vines. Yet, looking at the hills all around, some of these extraordinary buildings still stood, to show what might have been everywhere – surely these Romans were some kind of giants?

As we got closer to the central area I could see where some stones had been reused – yet as we came to the occupied centre, the houses, though of stone and brick, were simple and modest in size by comparison. We found the market area, a huge paved square where it seemed almost anything was for sale. We needed only food, though Indract seemed to be looking for something else in particular.

Later, when we began to follow the directions we had to reach the Vatican and the Basilica of the blessed Saint Peter, he told us what it was. Sister, he had bought a paste to polish our ferrules with. This we did, merrily, until they shone, then we washed ourselves and brushed down our habits well before crossing the Tiber and walking towards the Vatican where the great basilica could be seen on the hill.

Chapter 34

Rome and Home - circa AD 696

'What is it Ger? You look worried.'

'I'm not worried, sister, it is just that I don't know what to say now I have stopped you.'

Dominica laughed, 'Go on, spit it out, a wise-woman hears almost as much as a confessor!' *Maybe he has got himself a pox of some kind?*

'I know you are a nun, so you won't be married, but do you know if it is usual for a wise-woman to marry?'

Oh! Oh? 'Yes, *they can*. But you must have known old Mother Barr was married and had children?'

'Yes, she did, it's true, but it is well known that she said a wise-woman should *not* marry and have children, and would not let her grand-daughter wed, despite some good suitors.'

'Ah!' Dominica suddenly recalled what she had been told before she first met Mother Barr, 'There is that, Mother Barr did not want to see all that learning lost if the healer dies in child-birth. It's a very dangerous time for women, you see. There's not more to it than that.'

'I see,' Ger said, a smile on his face.

'But I am not sure I do? Why are you asking me Ger?' *Though, I can guess now.*

'Sister, I only have eyes for Eiliwedd. I did not want to say more to Eiliwedd, or anyone, if it was forbidden.'

'Not forbidden by me, though I would hope she would stay as wise-woman here, and you'll have to ask Eiliwedd herself, of course ... and you know Eiliwedd has family in Bo Etherick?'

'I do, sister. Thank you.'

'God bless you, Ger,' Dominica said, smiling to herself.

*

The feast day of the Nativity of Mary was coming up soon, so Dominica arranged for everything that Eiliwedd would need to be taken up to the healer's hut at Bo Barr, and together they made everything clean, comfortable and tidy.

The day arrived when Eiliwedd would be presented as the wise-woman for Bo Barr. Dominica had been preparing for this day since she took on Eiliwedd as apprentice - she'd made Eiliwedd a special hooded cloak, using weld and woad dyed wool. It was woven in a pattern she knew from back home, one that Flanna would weave. Nuala had a cloak just like it - with yellow and blue bands and checks. She had also beaten it in that special way to make it shed water better - for there was one thing a wise-woman needed and that was to stay dry when she was called out in all weathers to visit the sick or those giving birth. She decided to present it at the prayers as a symbol of the position and of her confidence in Eiliwedd.

Tudwal had let it be known that there would be the prayers and then a feast for all who came. The whole of the people of Bo Barr came, even those so far away they were closer to Bo Etherick in distance than Bo Barr. Eiliwedd's family came and with them a good number from Bo Etherick too. Keynae came as well, with many who knew Eiliwedd from Tamerkam. The small clearing of the white stones was crowded, so much so that people were standing amongst the trees all around the edges.

Tudwal, Brother Talan, Dominica and Sister Aylwyn, the latter holding the cloak carefully over her arms, stood either side of the cross planted behind the preaching stone. Eiliwedd stood facing them her back to the standing stones - aligned with the front row of the congregation.

Brother Talan spoke a few words of welcome and prayers appropriate to the feast day of the nativity of Saint Mary and then Dominica led the people in the prayers they usually said at this place. A short hymn composed by Teagan was sung and then Brother Talan gave a blessing.

Tudwal stepped forward. 'Good people, we are most fortunate that, as from today, we will have a wise-woman in our settlement again. Many of you know her, as she has ministered here under Sister Dominica, but she will now live with us and be there for us. Eiliwedd, please step forward.' Eiliwedd stepped forward to stand before them. Dominica took the cloak from Aylwyn and held it before Eiliwedd, saying, 'This cloak is a symbol of the care you will bring to this community. Will you use your learning and your skill to care for the people here to your utmost ability.'

Eiliwedd said, as bidden, 'I will care for these people.'

'May God bless you in all you do!' Talan said, making the sign of the cross.

Dominica lifted the cloak and put it around Eiliwedd's shoulders, quickly fastening it with a simple pin. Then taking her hand she turned her round to face the people, and lifted Eiliwedd's hand up high in her own. The people cheered and clapped. Eiliwedd turned her face, wreathed in smiles to Dominica then back to the crowd - seeking out one special face.

Brother Brannon

Sister, we have been blessed in more ways than one. We presented ourselves at the entrance to the great basilica, and were welcomed into the 'atrium of paradise'! A large courtyard with a well at its heart, lined with beautiful plants and being a wonderful grand space. Indract petitioned for a blessing on our pilgrimage, and the cleric we spoke with was much taken by our story, saying he knew of someone we must meet, a fellow from our homeland, and we were not to leave the basilica until he came.

Before long a tall, thin monk came striding across to us; his name is Willibrord and, though really from Northumbria, he studied in Eriu! He has spent many years in mission and is now here to be commissioned Archbishop to the Frisians. I do not know who they are, sister, but I am told they are peoples in the north of this huge land. He, Finn and Indract had much to talk of – and he will show us the Vatican and Rome, firstly finding us a place to stay where we won't be robbed.

As much as there is a state of ruin about the greater Rome, this vast hilltop place of the Vatican is in good condition and there is an atmosphere of grandeur and yet piety. We were taken back down into Rome itself for somewhere to stay and we were advised to buy food and prepare to come early to the basilica the next day, where Father Willibrord would meet us at the fountain in time to say Terce.

This we did, and before time we waited to meet with him, and he came, leading us into the basilica – our first steps into that hallowed building where St Peter's bones are laid.

Sister, this building is so vast I have trouble finding words for you. There are a fine row of more than twenty towering pillars down each side within a breadth of open space maybe as wide as the river above Tamerkam. Beyond the pillars each side is a further covered space and a further row of pillars, leaving a space to walk or to pray at the many icons and prayer stations along them. We prayed with a congregation of other people, monks, clerics, lay, and then the majority of them left. We were then escorted forward to the very front and there, under the smaller curved end of the basilica – the holy tomb of St. Peter. Prayers were said, sister; everything here feels so holy and blessed.

Father Willibrord has said he has asked for an audience with the Pope for us. This is very helpful as we have been told by others it is hard to see the Pope at all as he is a busy man who has to travel often. Each day we wait for word from him.

We have been here in Rome for sixteen days now! It is expensive to stay so long, but today Willibrord told us that tomorrow we will see the Pope.

We made ourselves as presentable as possible, and arrived early. It was not long before we were brought and stood in a line with many others seeking a blessing. After what seemed an age, Pope Sergius appeared, with other clerics just behind him, all dressed in beautiful robes, and moved slowly along the line, pausing at each group. I felt I ought to have my head bowed but I couldn't help but watch him - he wasn't as tall as I expected, but held himself upright and looked imperious. His skin is tawny and he has the nose you see amongst many here, prominent and curved. When we were named to step forward, Pope Sergius himself blessed us as a whole group and prayed for our mission in Britannia - Willibrord must have told him all about us!

*

We are on our way home! After we were blessed by the Pope we set off as soon as we were prepared for the journey, back towards the mountains, retracing our steps. We could not tarry as we've been told that the mountain passes close for six months of the year – so we had to make haste for the first snow fall usually comes about two months before Christmas, sometimes earlier, and it is getting near that already.

As we walk I realise there will be little new to recall for you, for we are taking the same route back as we came. At least, most of the way. Indract has told us that he hopes that we can return via a special church, that of Saint Mary at Glestyngabyrig, where he has been told of the tomb of the blessed Saint Patrick by Willibrord. We all thought this a marvellous way to complete our pilgrimage – so there will be new journeys to recall, but for now dear sister, I will content myself with only remembering for you the momentous and extraordinary.

**

Sister, we were none too soon in leaving Rome. Already, as we start to climb up to the mountain pass from Taurin, the air freezes our breath. The guide we have employed keeps looking at the sky and tutting. He is fearful that the snows will come early this year.

When pressed he says we will be safe to cross, but he thinks he has not many more days to earn money this way, this year. He is to take us as far as Camberiaco and, as before, we find another guide for the next part.

***

Never have I been so glad to see the other side of a mountain. When I saw that 'surprise' lake again I was relieved beyond words. If I thought the wind cold the time we crossed in summer, then I was wrong. The wind cuts right through our habits, though we were wearing all we owned to try to keep some body-heat in. The guide wears furs, laced to his body the fur side in, and even laced around his legs, on top he is cloaked with a thick fur brat - and even he looked chilled. He says it is too cold for deep snow, so we should be glad of it.

****

I had forgotten how far we travelled through the mountains before we came to the pass. We are still very high. The air is cold and we pray there is no snowfall as the ledge-paths would be so treacherous if covered with snow - they are bad enough as it is.

I praised God when the path opened out and we started our descent into the valley and towards the place of the relics of John the Baptist ... and then it began to snow.

Chapter 35

After All Saints - circa AD 696

It was the day after All Saints. There had been a bonfire and merry making up at the stronghold, and prayers for the lives of the saints nearly all night in the monastery – and everyone was a bit tired this morning, and now, in the mid-afternoon, the tiredness was catching up with Dominica.

Dominica heard someone shouting her name and came out to the path to see. Some of the monks were carrying what looked like a person, and as they neared she could see something shining in a trail behind them. *Water?*

She ran towards them, closing the gap so she could see properly. It *was* a person – and had to be one of the monks and he was soaked through.

'Lie him down!' she commanded. 'Here! Now!' as they struggled with understanding. It was Talan! She knelt down quickly, he was already blue about the lips, his eyes were open, but there was no movement in them, Dominica's heart squeezed. *Oh no! Too late?* 'What happened?' said as she tipped his head and tried to feel a breath on her cheek while resting her hand very gently on his chest and looking for movement, any movement. She could feel no breath, see no movement.

'We were taking the path back beside the river with our arms full of cut reeds. We were just near the point and he turned to speak to ...' began brother Yowann, one of the older brothers.

She put one finger under Talan's jaw trying to feel the life thump - there was none and his skin was so cold already.

'To tell Brother Resmen off for chattering ...' cut in Matuid.

'Brother!' Yowann snapped, with a shake of his head, 'and he slipped, or caught his foot on a rock, and tumbled backwards into the river, head first. The river is running fast downstream, he went under, we dropped our bundles and chased after him...' Yowann continued.

'Help me tip him on his side. You two, lift his body so his head in lower than his chest,' Dominica ordered. A trickle of water left his mouth - but not much.

'He took a long time to surface, and was face down when he did. We were running beside the river and when we caught up with him we waded in - but we missed him. The younger ones ran ahead and waded in there.'

Now, at this angle, Dominica could see the back of his head. She looked carefully, there was a wound just behind his ear in the remaining hairline.

'We caught him and drew him ashore. Then we ran with him here, though with his habit so wet he was very heavy and the going slow,' Hedrek added.

The bang on the head, and the weight of the habit dragging him under, might explain why he didn't strike for the surface, or just try to stand. 'Rest him down again,' she said softly. 'Brothers, you did well to bring our brother back from the clutches of the river, but I think Brother Talan hit his head when he fell, was knocked out, and drowned very soon after. See, here,' she showed them where the skin was broken. The two older brothers nodded.

'God rest his soul,' Dominica said as she closed Brother Talan's staring eyes. The brothers, who had become silent whilst she spoke, murmured, 'Amen.'

Cador came down to the monastery as soon as he heard and, having checked that what he heard was true, he sent for those of Talan's extended family to come. The funeral would be arranged for three days hence - as was their custom in these parts, and one the monks had no quarrel with. Brother Talan's body was taken to be washed and covered with a shroud and laid on a bier in the church. At all times of the day and of the night two of the brothers stayed and prayed in the church with Talan's body. Family came, prayed, wept and left, others that knew him came to pay their respects.

News soon reached Tamerunta that Talan had drowned, and Cormag sent notice that he would preside at the funeral.

All this left Dominica both saddened and concerned. She did not understand why God would let a good man like Talan drown, when he was still full of life and was running the day to day works of their mission so well. She thought round the remaining full monks at Tamerkam. None of them has Talan's presence or learning. He had taken to the habit of a monk as if he had been waiting for their arrival from the start of his life.

Maybe Yowann - but though he was gentle and learned he had little organisational skill. Matuid was far too hasty and judgemental to make a good leader, though he obviously thought himself very suitable, and had already suggested himself as a possible successor. The others were too young yet, though some showed promise and in time might be ready. Dominica also feared what Cormag's plan would be, but she felt sure he would have one.

Solemnly the first monk's grave was dug at the top of 'The Monks' Field', as their cemetery was now known by all. Cormag arrived the evening before and immediately began to interfere with the plans made by Dominica and the brothers. Funeral fare had been prepared by the monastery, but would now have to be taken to the stronghold for the wake, as Father Cormag had decided it was unseemly to have 'all those common people' in the monastery grounds. Cormag also stated that only the brothers of the monastery should be in the church for the last overnight vigil, yet Dominica knew that Talan's blood brothers expected to be there.

Cador arrived at the monastery as the sun touched down on the hill behind the monastery with all Talan's family behind him. Cormag stood at the door of the church, stony faced.

'Father Cormag,' Cador opened warmly, 'Thank you for presiding at Talan's funeral. It is an honour.' Cormag inclined his head as if accepting homage. 'Here are all of Talan's family - it is their tradition for the senior men to keep a vigil on the night before the burying. His brothers are here and would come and sit with him.'

'Our dearly beloved Brother Talan renounced the world and his worldly family when he joined God's chosen family of this monastery. His heavenly brothers will stand vigil and their prayers will keep him company through the night - alone,' Cormag said evenly and in a tone that is learnt by all rulers at their father's knee – one that brooks no argument. A murmur started behind Cador - he turned a little and shushed them with a gesture.

Dominica stepped forward, her heart beating wildly. She wasn't sure if she should intervene or not, 'Father Cormag, please. You can see how his family suffer. Pray do not add to it.'

It had been a mistake. His dark eyes flashed on her, 'Sister, it is not your place to speak here! Hold your tongue!' he snapped.

Cador looked from one to the other quickly and stepped between them, bringing himself closer to Cormag. He leaned in, 'Father, may I speak with you quietly for a moment?'

Cormag eyed the large family group, 'Very well,' he said and stepped inside the door of the church. Cador followed him – indicating the family should stay put.

Dominica edged towards the door, partly to show a friendly face to the family, partly to try to hear what Cador said. She smiled in a sad way, and bowed her head. Listening, she heard only the odd word, but it sounded as if Cador was reminding Cormag of the generosity of Tamerkam to the monastery, and Cormag reminding Cador of the benefits that the monastery had brought to the area. There were words she could not catch and then the tone of Cador's voice changed. He was also used to giving orders that were obeyed. 'Cormag, if you do this, you will break the trust of the people with the monastery, as you did before over at Tamerunta – where Brother Indract had to go to sort out your mess. If you do not listen to me, he will have a much bigger problem to sort out on his return than you can imagine. I am still the ruler in this area!' There was silence for a moment. Maybe the reminder of Indract's return might change Cormag's mind? Dominica held her breath, waiting to hear what would be said.

'How many brothers has he?'

'Three.'

'Then one may wait vigil with our brothers for each of the hours. One from sunset to midnight, one from then until matins and one from then to daylight.' Silence again.

'That might work. I will speak with them,' Cador said in a conciliatory way, and emerged from the shadows to go and speak with Talan's brothers. The idea didn't go down well initially, judging by their stances, but they ended up nodding.

The next day the monks carried the body on a bier to the burial site, and Cormag led the formal service all in Latin, barely a word understandable to the people - the family, standing behind the cordon of brothers. Dominica spoke the responses in Latin, her heart so angry at Cormag she felt guilty that she wasn't giving Talan his due reverence at the very end.

After the burial service Cormag turned and began to lead the brothers, sisters and lay people back towards the monastery. The family followed but when they appeared to be about to turn into the monastery site itself Cador called out, 'Brothers, Father Cormag! Are you not coming up the hill with us? We thank you for sending the funeral feast to us, but we hoped you would also be joining us at the meeting house?'

'We are not.' Cormag replied, '*We* shall remember our brother Talan with prayers and fasting.'

Cador, who had by now caught up and was addressing Cormag face to face replied, 'Well, that is a poor way to celebrate a man's life on earth, even if he is in heaven.' As he turned to leave he caught Dominica's eye, and raised an eyebrow. She could only respond with a wry frown and a half-shake of the head, something caught halfway between an apology and heartfelt regret, and hoped he understood that Father Cormag's way was not in accord with her way.

The following day Dominica proposed that they hold the meeting to vote-in the new leader of their monastery, as was usual in the case of a leader dying. Father Cormag had other ideas.

'We cannot do that! We must have everyone in the whole monastery, both halves, for the vote.'

'But we are a separate monastery here!'

'Not at all, both are now under my care as prior and priest. Therefore you are part of one monastery. All brothers are eligible to vote and so all should be able to vote on this.'

'How can this be? Indract was the prior here, he nominated Talan, but we, only we here, voted him in.'

'Exactly. When Indract was present he was able to nominate and officiate – and I was happy for that to be the case. Until he returns you are under my rule – the vote shall be taken at Tamerunta in five days - three days after the Sunday. You may send your nominee from here to Tamerunta the day before to meet with the monks there, and bring everyone else on the fifth day for the vote.'

'Only one nominee? What if we have more than one to choose between?'

'You may vote on that here then, and send the chosen one the day earlier, and the final vote will be taken on the fifth day from today, is that understood?'

Dominica nodded, the vote would be in the middle of the week, and the tides should work for the travelling there and back - but she still wondered what Cormag was planning.

Chapter 36

***Vote** - circa AD 696*

The next day, after Cormag had left on the early morning down-tide, Dominica called a meeting to explain all that Cormag had demanded and to seek nominations. It was as she had expected; Yowann and Matuid were nominated.

When all had secretly dropped their chosen stones into the pot, white for Yowann, black for Matuid, the two nominees stood at her shoulder while she counted out the stones. Equal numbers - she'd been so keen to get this done she hadn't thought of that problem – and, of course, there was no one to cast the deciding vote.

When she announced that each had equal numbers supporting them and that she might have to allow Father Cormag to choose which should go forward, there was a murmur of disapproval.

Aylwyn raised her hand. 'Sisters, brothers, before he went on pilgrimage Brother Indract was telling me that in double monasteries, where monks and nuns share the same church and offices, like ours, they are often ruled by a prioress. Can I nominate Sister Dominica and we cast our votes again, our number will not divide equally between three.'

There was silence. Then Yowann said, 'She's right! I've heard him say that too, and we are fourteen, and it will not divide by three. At least *we* still choose who we want.' There was a murmur of approval, so Dominica asked for a simple hand raised assent to the idea. All agreed. Now they needed more stones. Usually things were black or white, but today they needed another colour. Dominica called for Avan.

'Avan, run to the riverside and see if you can find us fourteen brown stones, about this size,' she said, showing her those in her hand. Avan grinned and ran off.

Dominica realised that there would be a wait, so suggested they all go to the church and pray for guidance while Avan found the new stones. This was agreed by a general movement to the church. Dominica, Aylwyn and Esselt followed behind and stayed nearest the back as they usually did. There was a bit of shuffling as they all knelt and composed themselves for prayer, then a restful calm seemed to descend on the building and its occupants.

Dominica didn't know what to pray for, but sank deep into meditation, beyond words, just being, just listening. No word came to her at first, just a feeling of acceptance. And the feeling formed into a word, 'acceptance'. Acceptance. The word filled her so she no longer was concerned about what to pray for. All she had to do was accept what God had planned for her, whatever that was, whatever the vote. Just acceptance.

Avan tugged on Dominica's sleeve and showed her hand full of shining-wet brownish stones. Dominica stood and gently said, 'Brothers, sisters, Avan has returned with the stones. We may return to the refectory to complete our task.'

Each person was given a brown stone to add to their one white and one black. The voting began again, white for Yowann, black for Matuid and brown for Dominica.

This time Dominica called for Avan to come back in to tip out the stones and to sort them into colour groups while the rest looked on.

There were two white stones for Yowann, one black stone for Matuid and all the rest were the wet brown stones from the river.

Yowann said clearly, 'Our chosen one is Sister Dominica – by a good majority. Father Cormag cannot argue with that,' and there were smiles almost all round.

'Brothers and sisters, thank you for your confidence in me. I hope I can serve God in the way He and you would want.'

Later Dominica sought out Keynae and Cador. She was spotted by Keynae who stood watching her approach.

'Keynae, sister!' Dominica said as she reached her, 'I come to say my sorries for the way Brother Cormag treated you all yesterday.'

'Yet you did not stop him?'

'I tried! Ask Cador. I tried but I was silenced.'

'But you told me that you and Indract were equal in God's sight.'

'Well, yes, Indract always saw it that way, but I confess, it is not wholly that way in the church, and certainly not when it comes to Brother Cormag.'

'Don't you mean *Father* Cormag?'

'Argh! When did you hear Indract make everyone call him *Father* Indract, or Prior even, yet they are both of the same learning and position!'

'Come sister, I tease you,' she said with a genuine smile, 'come and have a drink with us, Cador has just come in from a jaunt along our border with Ventonpemps.'

They sat on a bench beside their home. Cador heard Dominica out, apologies and worries about Cormag's interference both. 'So, how many are nominated for leader of this monastery?' he asked.

Dominica couldn't help smiling, 'Three were, eventually. It is done - we have chosen.'

'Oh! And who do we call upon as your leader?'

'It is me!'

'Sister!' Keynae shouted joyfully, 'So what do we call you now then?'

'We still have to have a general vote with the other monastery at Tamerunta – but, if confirmed there, it could be Prioress, but its just a word that means first among equals, so I'm happy with sister – just as Indract is happy with brother, rather that father or prior.'

Thank the Lord, we reached the place of the relics of St. John before nightfall on the eve of All Saints, the snow making our last descent treacherous.

*

Our journey is slowed. Some days stopped. Walking in a habit is impossible in this snow. The ice clogs together in clumps along the hem and tangles together, wont to trip us – to say nothing of the perpetual freezing wet rising up the fabric and causing it to slap and scrape our legs. We need to do something to make it possible to make progress despite the weather, yet we would want to still be recognisable as monks and pilgrims. This afternoon the guide has brought us to a place which sells furs.

**

Our journey resumes, sister! We now have leg-wear like the guide, laced to our legs, and we kirtle our habits up through our belt, so it is folded and falls to just above the knee. This way we can walk, yet we wear our habit too. Our staffs are such a boon in this walking, slow though it is.

***

The guide is taking us by a different route – one he says is better as there are more places to stay on the way. He is right, there are more villes - but barely any churches and no monasteries so far. Some places they put us up for the night for the 'price' of a Eucharist. This is a blessing for us and for them. In other places it is only silver that will satisfy, and we must take care with what we have, though happy to purchase food where we go, for the people are not rich.

****

We are at a small city named Besantio, beside a river, we arrived in time to celebrate Mass with the brothers of a small monastery here. The guide says we must stay here until the weather improves - the snow is blowing sideways in the wind and we cannot even leave our pilgrims' rest at the monastery. The weather is harsh! Even indoors with a lit hearth, our breath plumes.

*

On the second day after the Sunday Dominica caught the tide down to Tamerunta in a coracle paddled by one of Tamerkam's fishermen. She left behind her a monastery ready to follow her there the next day. The lay members were instructed on their duties and Cador and Keynae would assist should there be any problems.

There was a monk sitting beside the lookout when they came into view of the setting down point. The lookout stood and pointed, and then the monk stood too. Dominica held still until the fisherman had drawn the coracle onto the silty sand and the lookout had come down to steady it. Only then did she hang her scrip over her shoulder, get up and step over the side, lifting her hem to avoid dragging it on the wet rock-strewn sand.

'Sister Dominica?' the monk said, peering behind her, across the river, 'we were expecting the nominated monk from Tamerkam.'

She smiled, 'And instead you have the nominated nun from Tamerkam. Come, let us go to the settlement,' then realising she recognised him from one of Cormag's visits to Tamerkam she asked, 'What is your name brother?'

'Brother Maban ...' he said, somehow still managing to sound confused.

She knew the way and led confidently, the young monk following in her footsteps along the path.

As they reached the edge of the settlement she said, 'Brother Maban, I will greet the chief and his wife first, and then follow on to the monastery. He bobbed his head and scurried off. *Gone to tell them the news.*

Someone had also got ahead of her to the settlement, for Liaden came and met her on her way in.

'Sister Dominica! What a lovely surprise to see you. Have you escorted the man for the vote?'

'Oh, you know about the vote?'

'Of course, it is the talk of Tamerunta – that both monasteries will be here tomorrow for the vote.'

'Oh, but it isn't such a big thing? We've chosen and surely the others will confirm our choice.'

'It's between your man and theirs though, isn't it?'

'Theirs?'

'Father Cormag has been preaching about the virtues required of the man to lead a monastery and has nominated his man to go against yours in the vote.'

'He's what?'

'Dominica, *who* is your man?'

'Not a *man!* Our people voted for me.'

'Oh my! That is wonderful! But I can't see our old friend liking it one bit.'

Dominica shook her head. 'I should have realised when he said it had to be a whole monastery vote that he'd have a plan, but we foolishly believed it was just to confirm our choice. He asked us to send only one, the one we'd voted for ourselves.'

'What will you do?'

'Do? There's nothing I can do, but I am glad to understand the lie of the land before I step into the lion's den. Maybe, like Daniel, I need to pray for our deliverance.'

'Amen to that,' Liaden said fervently.

Dominica strode on towards the monastery, her head high but her mind whirling. What could she do? What were the numbers here? Oh! Equal - Cormag had moved all the novitiates through to full monks quite soon after the others left on their pilgrimage. Equal if Cormag voted – and why wouldn't he? Hmm, maybe to hold the deciding vote?

'Sister!' a voice called to her. She turned, it was Brother Maban again.

'Yes, brother?' she said, waiting for him to catch up.

'Prior Cormag would have you go to meet with him in the church as soon as you arrive. I am to escort you.'

Oh, it's Prior Cormag now, is it? 'It's alright, I remember the way.'

'No, no, I must. The Prior said, I must and you were to go straight there.'

'Oh, really? Then that is what we will do,' she replied. *What is Cormag up to now?*

They entered the church, Brother Maban bowing out as soon as he had delivered Dominica there. Her eyes adjusted to the dim light and she saw Cormag on his knees in front of the Altar. He made no move, so she just stood inside the doorway and waited. After what seemed a totally unreasonable time he pushed himself up, using his stick to help him, and turned her way.

'Ah, Sister Dominica. Welcome. I am informed that you are the choice from Tamerkam. I admit to being surprised – did you nominate yourself?'

'No, father, I did not,' biting her tongue to stop herself adding what she thought of his accusation.

His eyebrows raised, 'Yet someone did.'

'There were three nominated - you may ask them when they arrive. The vote was in the majority for myself, so here I stand.'

'Indeed,' he gave a wry smile. 'You may meet the monks here after vespers. That will be the time for you to explain how it is that you are the Tamerkam nominee and why you would be best to lead rather than our nominee.'

'And who, may I ask, is your nominee?'

'Brother Godric. A pious man who understands the way that a monastery should be run,' he smiled and tipped his open palm towards Dominica, the merest suggestion that she didn't.

'Brother Godric? Is he from Tamerunta?' she couldn't remember him, but then she was here so rarely.

'No, not from here, he joined us from a monastery further inland, beyond the moors.'

No family ties to the other monks here then, at least that is something. Oh, joined as a full monk, they have a majority, if they all vote for Cormag's man.

‘And now sister, I am sure you will want to remain here, in the church, in prayer and preparation for later.’

It sounded more like an instruction than an invitation. ‘I will do that Br... Father Cormag, though I would take some water beforehand.’

‘Perhaps not, sister. We are all fasting and praying today until vespers.’

‘Not even water?’

He smiled, ‘Not even water – until after vespers. It is a great decision we must take tomorrow.’

The mere ruling made her thirstier. She had deliberately not drunk much before leaving on the coracle, and now wished she’d taken a drink with Liaden while she had the chance. There was nothing for it but to settle herself into prayer and banish the thoughts of water from her mind and body – she knew it could be done. As she settled herself into a comfortable kneeling position at the rear of the church she wondered where the monks were praying if not here in the church.

The hours passed and, judging by the beam of sunlight through the church door, evening was coming as it now slanted in the door, moving inexorably towards the centre and glowing gold as it looked for the horizon.

There was the sound of feet and the monks appeared and filed into the church. Dominica struggled to stand again, her lower legs completely numbed.

Cormag swept in last. He went to the front and began the service of Vespers, the monks chorused the replies, with Dominica joining in.

After the last Amen died away Cormag began speaking again. ‘Brothers,’ he began, ‘and sister. We shall hear Sister Dominica’s statement before we break our fast, then once we have eaten you have permission to discuss anything that has been raised. Sister, won’t you come to the front and speak to the brethren.’

Dominica wasn't ready for this. She had expected to hear from Brother Godric too, but then she realised, they all knew Brother Godric, it was only her that they didn't know. As she walked forward she wondered which monk he was, but was also trying to work-up some saliva to moisten her mouth.

'Brothers, for those of you who do not already know me, I am Sister Dominica. Just like Prior Cormag, I came with the mission from Eriu about eight years ago, along with my Brother Prior Indract. After this mission was set up here at Tamerunta we had a vision to take a mission to Tamerkam. The Lord was there before us, prepared the way, so that when we came we were welcomed. This mission, this double monastery, for we are two full nuns, a novitiate and female lay workers as well as those in the men's part of the monastery, has been doing God's work in peace and harmony with the settlement. That this great work may continue fruitfully whilst Prior Indract is on pilgrimage to Rome the brothers and sisters nominated me, as well as two others. At the final vote I was chosen by the majority, so here I stand, and I ask you brothers to honour the choice of those who labour for God's harvest in Tamerkam, and affirm me as the leader until my brother returns.'

There was silence. Dominica didn't like it, but they had been told, after all, that they could only ask questions after they had eaten. Cormag let the silence hang for longer than was comfortable, then announced they would go to the refectory to take their meal – this, of course would be in silence. Dominica followed them to the refectory. It would be a while before anyone could speak – even if they had a question to ask by then.

Only one monk came to speak with Dominica after they had broken their fast. For some reason Dominica had been expecting Brother Godric to be a tall imposing man, someone handsome like Finn maybe. In reality he was, if only slightly, shorter than she was. However, he had presence, she had to admit. He looked serious, stood straight and wore his sandy hair, surrounding his tonsure, cropped short.

'Sister Dominica, why do you think your people voted to send you here?' he opened.

His speech had an unusual rhythm that made you listen more carefully. She felt sure he'd come from much further away than just beyond the high moorland you could see from the hill on the way to Bo Barr.

'You will have to ask them that, but I hope it is because I always try to be fair, and take the word of the Lord seriously in everything I do, both inside the monastery and outside.'

His blue-grey eyes twinkled, as if he was amused, 'Very commendable. But do you not think they are swayed by your femininity?'

'No, I do not! I am a nun - I do not - flaunt - my femininity. I go about God's work in the community modestly, helping to heal. Besides, in our prayers women differ not from men.'

'Come now, even dressed as a nun it is obvious that you are a beautiful woman.'

'I *am* a nun, not *dressed* as a nun. And my looks are nothing - God sees only my heart and my deeds.'

'But not men - men are not Gods.'

'Indeed, and in my experience men are more likely to *not* choose a woman over a man, rather than the other way round.'

'Indeed? In your experience?' he repeated, with a glint in his eye.

The next day brought the rest of Tamerkam's monastery, they arrived with the tide, meaning it was already past noon before they landed. Dominica met them and filled them in on her news. Yowann was incensed that they could overturn the choice that had already been made.

Others seemed more worried they'd have someone they did not know rule over them.

The vote was set for nones, mid afternoon. They all met in the church for the service of Nones, after which both nominees were allowed to speak.

Dominica's was much the same as the previous day, she had prayed but no inspiration had come beyond that which she felt was right, so she asked again that they respect the choice of those who knew Tamerkam and her ministry best.

Brother Godric spoke well and passionately about the work of prayer, the brotherhood of monks and the strength gained through this brotherhood, diligent work and prayerful, celibate lives, and the fact that, as he was also an ordained monk he could provide the Eucharist for the monastery, relieving Prior Cormag of the journey and that duty to the Tamerkam mission.

Dominica reeled, no one had mentioned this to her, and yet even as she thought it she knew she had no counter to it. The only question was whether it would make any difference to her monastery's voting.

After Godric's speech they were issued with their stones for the vote. Stones were drawn by the candidates, and the voting was announced as white for Dominica and black for Godric.

One by one the monks and nuns entered the refectory and dropped their stones into the narrow-necked pot. After everyone, except Cormag, had voted the pot was brought into the sunlight and tipped out carefully onto a table top. It was obvious from the start that it was close. Cormag pushed the stones into piles, and then grouped them into fives - plus the remainders.

Chapter 37

***Curtailed** - circa AD 696*

'Fifteen black and thirteen white!' Cormag smiled, 'Brother Godric will be the Prior of Tamerkam.'

'Until Indract returns!' Dominica snapped.

'This is not right,' Yowann grumbled.

Cormag addressed Yowann, 'It is right! And if it had not been I still had my vote to cast – and it would still have been right. As for you, sister, yes, when your brother comes back he shall return as Prior, but by then the mess that is your monastery will have been straightened out!'

Prior Godric accompanied them back to Tamerkam, declaring that there was no time to waste. It suggested that he was packed already.

Dominica begged leave to say farewell to Liaden and Eudaf, but it was denied, almost simultaneously by Godric and Cormag. She turned to look at her party of brothers and sisters, her distress clear in her face. Aylwyn came to her, rested her hand on Dominica's arm and spoke softly, 'Sister, come.' Dominica smiled wearily and went with her, the whole group walking solemnly down the long path beside the creek ready to go home.

When they settled themselves into the coracles and had pushed off Yowann was just behind Dominica. He leant forward and spoke quietly to her. 'We are so sorry this has happened. Just know we are with you,' he hesitated, 'most, nearly all.'

'Thank you, brother,' Dominica whispered back, but it raised the question she'd been trying to ignore, who amongst them had voted for Godric?

*

Prior Godric took over Indract's place, slotting into his bed space in the dormitory, his space on the benches in the refectory, his role at the front of the church. And it was in church that he made his first move.

It seemed it wasn't enough that the sisters arrived last, sat at the back and left first. He installed a wattle screen and now they were to arrive first, go to the far left, beyond the screen, be quiet in prayer before the brothers arrived, then remain heads bowed in prayer while the brothers left. There was no discussion beforehand, and no questioning was expected but Dominica couldn't leave it.

Dominica tried to explain that sometimes, as they were often involved in the work of caring, that they may not always be on time. That you could not leave a poultice half laid, or a burn half treated.

'Tardiness in attending to services is precisely one of the aspects of slovenly behaviour in this monastery that Prior Cormag sees as symptomatic of the disreputable state of this place. You and the other sisters will be on time for the most important part of our service to the Lord!' he said, his voice rising in volume but remaining deadly low in tone.

'Most important? Most important?' she could hear her own voice rising and becoming stretched in her anger, 'Go heal the sick and the lame - in my name! This! Our Lord told us to do this, as if we were ministering to Jesus himself. He did not say go and sing nones or matins at a set time!'

'Sister, you forget yourself. Go and tell the others what is required of them. You can be sure that your insubordination has been noted as will any absence or slothful attendance.'

Dominica spoke to the sisters but they decided that they should not upset Prior Godric too much, and to acquiesce to his demands with regard to the church services. When it came to it, they were mostly involved in other aspects of the monastery life. It was only Dominica who was hands-on with healing, with young Avan hanging on her every word but not expected to be in church for all the offices as she was only a lay sister.

Time passed, uncomfortably, but Dominica tried very hard not to exacerbate the friction between her and Prior Godric. There were one or two times that she only just made it into the church before the file of monks arrived.

That was a change too. Before they'd hear the clank of the bell and arrive at the church from wherever their work had been, as a working party or as a single man. Now they had a warning bell, that also told the sisters to be in church fast, and the brothers to congregate outside their dormitory to process to the church together.

She kept reminding herself that her word was 'Acceptance', and though she had thought it meant acceptance of the place of first amongst equals, now she thought it meant of the trouble she was experiencing.

After about a month Prior Godric called Dominica to see him after vespers. When she arrived he told her that he believed that the sisters should take their repast at a separate time to the monks as it wasn't seemly for them to be together for this time. Dominica thought back to the monastery she came from. Most certainly this was the way there, yet it made sense as there were almost as many nuns and monks and the refectory would have had to be twice the size if they ate together in the same space. Here there were so few nuns that it made no difference.

The fuss and amount of extra time this meant for those whose turn it was to prepare and clear the meals did not seem to occur to Prior Godric, nor did he care when Dominica mentioned it, merely smiling and saying that all service for the Lord's work was blessed. In the end she agreed, but it felt like she had no choice. Then it was decided by Prior Godric that the men would eat first and the nuns were to wait until after all the monks had left and were well away before entering the refectory.

Dominica comforted herself with the thought that all this would only be for a while, only until Indract and the other brothers returned. It felt so long since they left, and now winter was upon them she wondered how long it would be before they came back. In their talk before leaving of the days of travel needed to reach Rome and to return it sounded like they thought they might be back in the early spring, and so Dominica held onto that thought.

Brother Brannon

Sister we have been stuck in this benighted place, Besantio, for more than two sabbaths! I begin to lose track as each day is too similar.

I call it benighted as we have been here so long that we have spoken a lot about our journey - and so we were told that the blessed Saint Columbanus had been here too and was famous. As you can imagine sister, we were interested to know more. So, laughing, they told us his legend here. It seems he, in righteousness, made an enemy of a rich and powerful woman, by the name of Queen Brunhilda and she had him captured and held here - awaiting execution upon the King's order! They told us, praise the Lord, that he then made an escape and was not executed - but exiled back to Eriu.

*

The guide, a man in as much hurry as we, tells us today we can go forward. The wind has dropped, the snow stopped, the air cold enough to keep the snow crisp. We are bundled off with a few provisions and wrapped as well as we can be. Our aim is Luxue, and the guide says we can make it in as few as five days if we will. We have the will; our memories of Columbanus' Luxue are amongst our most cherished.

**

Sister, the days are short, the snow deep in places, making the going slow, and we have had to make camp at some places where we have not much more shelter than a lean-to roof. Just as when we went over the pass, we carry our own wood now too, and so make even this as warm as we can, heating water, or sometimes snow, to make a warming gruel. Five days have passed; we are not there yet.

***

Luxue! A total of eight days journey, who knows if the guide fooled us, but for certain he took his pay and left early the next morning. It is like an island of mildness here, with the most amazing icicles decorating every overhanging ridge and branch where the steaming water cools and freezes. It is nearly the Nativity of Christ, and so we will remain here with our brothers at least until Epiphany.

*

It was a week before Christmas and Dominica was taking the service in the 'old place' at Bo Barr when a cowled figure stepped into the back row behind the trees. Dominica saw him and almost lost her place in the recitation of the words.

It had to be Prior Godric from the shape of him, though she couldn't see his face. She thought of the hymn they would sing next, one of Teagan's that this congregation loved and sang with gusto! Would he disapprove as he wouldn't know it – none of Teagan's hymns had been sung at the monastery church since he'd arrived.

She finished the service by telling the people of her plans for their Christmas day service, to welcome the new-born Christ. She planned a special service to tell the nativity story with a play and had been schooling a few willing people from the settlements, as the previous year more had come to this service than usually came on a Sunday - and then they had come ever since.

She was quite surprised that Godric did not stay after the service and speak with her, and she allowed her heart to hope he approved of what he'd seen and heard. So it was on the following day she was not too perturbed when he sent one of the lay brothers to find her in the herbarium and ask her to attend upon him in the church.

Quickly removing her apron she washed her hands and set off for the church. Seeing him kneeling at prayer at the front gave her a flash-back to Cormag doing the same. She wasn't going to stand waiting at the back for Godric to recognise her though. She went to the front and knelt in the nuns' space, so he could not avoid knowing she was there. After a bare moment he crossed himself and turned to her. She did the same and stood.

'You wished to see me Prior?'

'Indeed, I do,' he began, 'I was in attendance at the,' he hesitated, 'the service you presided over up at Bo Barr.'

'I saw you, Prior. I hope you saw how much the people enjoy the service there.'

'On what authority do you take a service, sister?'

'On ... on the authority of Prior Indract,' she said, already fearing where this was going.

'I do not think it proper for a nun to take a service alone. In future this service must be taken by one of the brothers. You may be present.'

'But this was approved. I have grown this church ...'

'God has grown this church! Not you! You are too full of yourself and your reaction proves that I am right. I withdraw my permission for you to be present!'

A wash of loss threatened to swamp Dominica, 'Prior Godric, forgive me my, my foolish pride. Only let me stay with these good people, especially for the Christmas service, we have planned ...'

'You will obey me completely! And, maybe, I shall review the matter after Epiphany.' He looked Dominica in the eye and must have seen her rising objections and continued, 'This is my final word. Any more from you and I will not think to reconsider at all.'

'I understand,' she said - yet praying in her heart for the return of Indract as soon as possible.

Chapter 38
Epiphany - *circa AD 696 - 697*

Christmas came, and Dominica stayed in Tamerkam feeling wretched, though she knew Eiliwedd had told the people there that Dominica was so very sorry, but she had to obey the new Prior.

Epiphany came and went, and Dominica was reluctant to push the matter of returning to Bo Barr with Godric. She was sure he was waiting for her to ask, just so he could chide her for impatience and use that to deny her.

In the meantime she made sure she found cause to visit each week anyway - to take dried herbs to Eiliwedd, to teach her some new method or to visit with someone Eiliwedd was concerned about. *That part* of her ministry Godric had no control over, and while there she was able to quietly reassure people she had not abandoned them.

They still had a service - Prior Godric sent Brother Matuid - but word was that is was all in Latin, dull and dry, and some had given up going. This saddened Dominica greatly, but she didn't speak ill of Godric or Matuid, just said she hoped one day to return to the services in Bo Barr.

As for herself, she had remembered the feeling she had when she and Indract first arrived and stepped into the clearing near the river, so, deprived of the 'old place' at Bo Barr, she returned there now. It was like walking into an embrace, light and joyful, and it soon became her place of refuge and solitary prayer - another true thin place.

Brother Brannon

Snow still covers everything, and we have been advised sternly to remain longer. It is hard not to agree. Indract has said we will stay but consider moving on as soon as there is a let up. We have learnt some beautiful chants here, and Teagan's music is appreciated too, and some of his hymns in Latin also.

*

We celebrated the feast of the Presentation of Christ here, and within a few days the weather cleared and the snow was melting rapidly. So Indract decided we would move on. It is true we had been with the brothers a long time, about six weeks – and we feel indebted to them for their hospitality – so we have an obligation to move on when we are able.

**

The going is difficult, many small streams are rushing torrents, and we have to divert from our path often. The days are still short and shelter and food not easy to find – but we are making progress. There are places now where the snow has gone, but the ice remains treacherous, and the wind is biting

***

We are descending each day, true sometimes we must ascend, but generally we are coming out of the mountains, now out of the hills, and today, a bright clear day, we saw in the distance, Reims.

****

Today we rest, for it is Ash Wednesday and a day of prayer. We remembered our brethren in the small monastery outside Reims in our prayers, and decided to stay with them again overnight if they are willing to host us, which means we will cross the city tomorrow to reach them.

*

Dominica felt weary all the time, even the possibility of a new apprentice to learn to be a wise-woman for Bo Etherick did not seem to lift her spirits as it would normally. She trudged up the hill toward the smaller settlement and prayed on her way for guidance. It was Eiliwedd's mother that had suggested the girl, so she would visit with her first.

Eiliwedd's mother was outside her home, draping some washing to dry in the frosty sunlight. She smiled readily when she saw Dominica heading her way and swept the tunic she was holding smoothly to rest over a nearby bush.

'Sister Dominica,' she said, with a small bow of the head, 'it is a pleasure to see you. Will you take a drink before we visit the family?'

'Thank you, yes. The hill is always longer than I expect.' The woman ducked into her house and returned with a small cup of warm liquid.

'A herb drink our Eiliwedd has us make,' she smiled. 'You will have heard that our Eiliwedd is betrothed to her Geraint?

Dominica took a sip of the drink, 'Lovely!' she said with a smile, 'Yes, I had heard, and I am pleased for them. He seems both a brave and gentle soul and they do seem to be in love. Now, tell me about this girl?'

'Ah! She is a strange one, but she has a mind like a trap. She's only about twelve summers, but she'll tell you things about plants, animals or birds that you didn't know, and anything you can tell her about them she will remember word for word. Her parents ...' she hesitated, 'well, they don't seem to know what to do with her, sad to say, and they don't seem to care much for her either.'

'And you think she will want to be a wise-woman?'

'Not honestly sure. She doesn't talk to anyone much, but talks to herself a lot though, huh? I do think she is interested in such things, plants, herbs, you know. We could ask her.'

'And what would her parents think?'

'They wouldn't care either way, her mother as good as told me so. They have other children who are ... more normal. She is strange, even the way she looks, or rather doesn't look, at you.' She gave a little huff, 'I feel sorry for her, but I hope you will find her suitable, I really do, if not for a wise-woman, then maybe a helper in your herb house, as a lay sister?'

'Come, take me to her, we will see.'

Their home was on the other side of the settlement. As they approached, Dominica saw a woman also hanging washing on the bushes. She was aided by a girl of about twelve, both were neat and clean. The woman spotted them and tossed the item she had in her hand to the girl who caught it deftly, flicked it out straight and spread it in a fluid movement to rest over a bush. If this was the girl then she seemed capable already.

'Good day, sister,' the woman said. 'You'd like to talk to Merewin?'

'Thank you,' Dominica said, glancing towards the girl, but the woman walked round the house and started yelling, 'Merewin! MEREWIN! You get here girl, the sister has come to see you!' There was a further commotion and the woman reappeared tugging a girl of about the same age as the other, but this one was unkempt, her face streaked, her clothes grass-stained. She was tugged to a spot just before Dominica. 'Say good morning to the sister!'

The girl sort of looked at Dominica. To Dominica it felt as if Merewin was somehow hiding, though right in front of her. Merewin's gaze focused somewhere a little over and behind Dominica's shoulder, as if one of the two of them wasn't actually there. It was a little unsettling.

'Good morning, Merewin,' Dominica said softly. *Did the eyes flick briefly to her own?*

'Sorry she's such a mess, I put her in clean clothes on the Sunday, but she rolls down the hill most days,' her mother interrupted.

Dominica's heart opened for the child. 'No matter. Can we talk quietly ...' Dominica glanced around, there was a bench beneath a pair of trees a little away, 'over there?'

'Yes, yes. Good idea, I'll finish up here,' the mother said nodding to the washing, where the other girl had almost finished.

'Merewin, please come and sit with me,' Dominica said and led the way to the bench, sitting herself at one side of it. Merewin, after a glance back at her mother, now chatting with Eiliwedd's mother, followed. She sat about as far away as she could from Dominica, but sit she did, her eyes cast down.

'Merewin, I am Sister Dominica, from the monastery, have you heard of me?'

Merewin nodded, but didn't look up or speak.

'Tell me some of the things you know about plants and herbs.'

Merewin looked up, almost startled. After an agonising pause she said, 'What about? There are so many.'

Dominica smiled, 'Tell me about ... nettles.'

Merewin looked up but gazed off into the distance, 'There are different types of nettle, their leaves and flowers are similar, but flower colour is sometimes different, some are soft and do not sting, but are not as useful as those that do. You can eat all of them, raw, cooked simply in water, cooked in fat is best though. But the stinging ones, you can make cloth from them, do I need to tell you the way to do this? I do know it all.'

She took what seemed to be her first breath and flicked a look at Dominica, Dominica shook her head.

Merewin continued, 'The best nettles grow where it is a little damp, and in a little shade, the tall nettle stands are best for making cloth and cord, but the best for eating are the smaller spring plants.'

'And who told you all this?'

'About the cloth, I have helped once. About the nettles, no one. I just know,' said defiantly.

'Very good.' Dominica said and saw Merewin relax a fraction. 'Can you tell me about rolling down hills?'

Merewin tensed up again and a flash of panic showed in her eyes, 'What?'

'Your mother said you rolled down the hill most days.'

The look flashed to anger, then the eyes went blank. 'Yes.'

'I just wondered what she meant? What do you do? Why?'

A pause, as if she hadn't heard, then speaking quickly, 'I like it. I lie down and push myself off and roll. There's one place that is good to do this, it is my special place. The grass breathes for me. It makes me feel right inside when I am not. She doesn't like me doing it ... at all.'

Dominica smiled, 'I can see it is important to you though,' she paused. 'It has been suggested that you might like to come and learn about plants, herbs and healing with me in the monastery. Has anyone asked you if you would like to do this?'

'No.'

'Would you like to?'

A very long pause. 'Can I come to see it?'

'Of course, you could come back down with me today.'

'No! No,' the panic back, 'um, um, tomorrow?'

'Tomorrow will be fine. Shall I come here and walk down with you?'

Definitely a look straight at Dominica, as if she'd just noticed her, 'Yes.'

'Come, we will speak to your mother,' Dominica said, standing.

Brother Brannon

Sister, I am scared and also feel we must trust in God. We went down to Reims - there is plague here! We bought food where we could and hastened out the other side of the city heading for the little monastery of St. Bartholomew. We rang the bell, heard it clatter, then waited and waited. After a long time the little speaking hatch opened and we saw, standing well back, one of the brothers. This is how it went:

'God be with you, brother,' Indract began.

'We have the plague here,' the brother said wearily. 'You are best to pass us by.'

'How many are ill?' Fergus spoke out of turn.

'And how many to care for them?' Kellagh added quickly.

'Four have died, twenty are sick, there are just three of us left standing.'

The two brothers turned to Indract, 'We can help, can't we? We were trained in a plague house.'

Indract stood a while and then withdrew our group and asked us what we wanted to do. There was a lot of heart searching, but regardless of what the rest of us thought Fergus and Kellagh were determined to help, saying they would stay even if we all went on. We wouldn't leave them.

We stay, not inside the monastery, but have set up camp outside, except for Fergus and Kellagh who go and help care for the sick. The rest of us are asked to pray to discern if we should also care, with training from those two brothers.

Fergus and Kellagh asked if any of us knew of certain herbs and where to look for them. I knew, of course - we could not help but know growing up as we did. I am the man to find the mint and the garlic, if it is to be had so early in the season. Luckily they have a good collection of dried herbs in the monastery it seems, but no-one left to say what to use, as their herbalist was one of the first to die.

Chapter 39
St. Bartholomew's - circa AD 697

The next day Dominica set off for Bo Etherick in a more positive mood. She already thought that Merewin was probably not a candidate for a wise-woman - but as a herbalist - she had real potential. Besides, Dominica knew she had another reason for wanting to help the girl. She could see how alone she felt, just as Dominica herself had felt in the monastery, and she wanted to reach out, just as Sister Ciar had done to her, to give her a purpose and a place to belong. This, she thought, she could offer - if Merewin felt able to trust her.

Merewin was waiting. Dominica had the feeling she had been put into her clean clothes then held in place, not allowed to go to the hillside, until Dominica arrived. The mother had a sack of her few belongings ready, a very unsubtle hint. Her father was there too, but said not a word, nor even offered Merewin a hug.

'We can take it,' Dominica said, indicating the sack, 'but if Merewin does not want to stay we will bring her back with it, you understand?'

'Of course, sister, only she has been looking forward to it. We are sure she will want to stay. That's right, isn't it Merewin?'

Merewin nodded. Her mother gave her a quick pat on the shoulder and briefly kissed to top of her head. Seeing Dominica watching, she said, 'She doesn't like fuss.'

Dominica took the bag and let Merewin walk unencumbered beside her. After a short time Merewin began a litany, scarcely more than a whisper, nodding towards and naming all the plants as they passed them, not just the obvious ones, but each different plant she saw first on the journey down. Dominica, realising what she was hearing asked her to speak louder. Merewin gave her the first smile she'd seen from the girl, and then spoke louder, almost singing. 'Plantain, coltsfoot, little thumb, pilewort, purple vetch, cow parsley...' Then suddenly lifting her head, 'Fox's been here,' and back to the plant names. Dominica couldn't help but be impressed. Pilewort, with its bright yellow star flower and heart shaped leaves, was one of the obvious ones, but it being early in March barely any of the others had flowers, and some were very small with only a few leaves to show they were growing there.

Only as they made the turn and dropped down into the lane, the way that meant they didn't have to cross the stepping stones as this path bridged the stream where it was narrower, did Merewin cease her naming. They walked up and round to the monastery in silence.

Dominica took Merewin straight to her herbarium, thinking this would give her the best idea of the work.

Merewin stood in the hut and turned very slowly, Dominica could see her looking at everything. The drying herbs, the labelled pots, the work bench with pestles and mortars on it, knives, baskets, the fire with its range of steeping and boiling pots nearby. She tried to see it through the girl's eyes then she said, 'This is where we make up our tinctures, tissanes, oils and potions.'

'Yes.' Merewin said. 'Can I see the monastery too?'

Dominica smiled, 'Of course! Come, but note, we are always quiet when about in the monastery, I will show you round.' She left the girl's bag in the herbarium and they walked out, first to the healer's hut, then to the nuns' house, which she explained was shared by the lay women too.

Then to the church, which they went in and out of quite quickly, as Merewin turned and left it after only a few steps inside. Past the refectory, Dominica naming it, and pointing to the monks' dormitory beyond, but had to hurry to keep up with Merewin who was heading out of the enclosure, her head turning this way and that, walking quickly. It seemed as if Merewin was looking for something.

'What is it Merewin? Are you looking for someone? Or something?'

'Is there a hill inside the monastery?'

'Ah!' Dominica thought quickly, wishing she'd got Merewin to show her the hill she loved, 'How about over here,' she said leading her out of the enclosure, round and down to the baptism pool with the fish ponds stepped below it, and the slope beside them that led down to the river. This grassy slope was kept clear of tall plants and bramble so that the ponds could be tended easily.

Merewin ran forward and, quick as a hare, lay down and pushed herself off, flip, flip, flip – she rolled, gaining speed and stopping just short of the lowest pond. She sat up, looking back at Dominica with a huge smile on her face. 'Yes!' she called, 'Yes!'

And Dominica knew that Merewin would be staying with her after all.

Brother Brannon

Sister, you would be so proud of your students. They set about making the masks you used, and teaching those monks left healthy enough how to use them, how to keep themselves properly clean and, as far as possible, from the contagion. Dairmut and Finn have joined our brothers in their work within the monastery, to give the St. Bartholomew's brothers who were doing the caring a little rest, as they are worn out and frail with the strain.

*

I was amazed to be able to find early wild garlic and even some leaves of water mint in a sheltered valley, and the brothers were well pleased, the willow bark was easy as the same stream was lined with them. They brewed the concoction you made adding the dried herbs and it is delivered to the sick with great care.

As for the rest of our group, they are to find sustenance. 'Lent or no Lent,' Fergus said, 'some meat and eggs were needed to restore the strength of those who were sick.' This was both easier and harder to do.

Reims itself is not a good place to go, so we sought out homesteads out in the country to buy food. Sad to say in one place all we found were the dead. A whole family, some buried, others lying where they died. Their livestock disappeared, taken by wolves, or other farmers, most likely, but a few hens must have escaped notice as we found plenty of eggs. We buried the dead with great care, took with us the hens we later found and made use of the uncollected eggs.

At others homesteads, with great difficulty as they had no wish to have us come anywhere near them, we bought bread, oatmeal or meat, as was available.

**

A whole week has passed since we came here, and we have only lost two of the St. Bartholomew's brothers who were sick when we arrived. The others are not recovered, but do not get worse. The hens are laying well.

***

Today another of St. Bartholemow's brothers died, but worse, Kellagh has fallen sick. Fergus is caring for him and will let no one else near him. Finn has proved a fast learner and has taken over the potions making, following instructions with care.

*

Within a few weeks Merewin had settled herself with the others. They were quiet and kind around her as Dominica had asked them to be. Esselt, a quiet one always, befriended Merewin, making sure to be the one to sit with her or to walk with her to church on a Sunday.

Dominica was delighted to find she had been right in her assessment of Merewin's ability to remember anything to do with plants that she cared to teach her, from how to grow, to what recipe to make and how much of each ingredient to use. Prodigious though her memory was Dominica thought she would be best to still learn to read and write, and so it was that she joined with Esselt for her lessons. However, Merewin was reluctant to apply herself to this.

When almost a whole month had gone by, Prior Godric sent Matuid to find Dominica to tell her to meet him in the Church. Dominica suppressed a sigh and, smiling, said, 'Of course,' to Matuid and headed off to the church.

This time Prior Godric was waiting for her at the door, as if she had kept him waiting.

'Sister, I need a word with you.'

'Prior?'

'You have accepted a new lay woman into the monastery and yet she has not been presented to me, your Prior, to see if she is of good character and acceptable to the monastery as a whole.'

'Ah, I understand! I have not, yet, because she is young and is just in initiation, to see if she is suited to the lay task. Once we are sure this is a suitable path for her I will, of course, bring her to you for the blessing of the monastery.'

'This is not what I hear. I hear you are teaching her to read and write. This is not necessary for a lay woman.'

'With respect, Prior, it is if they are to be a herbalist, especially one in a monastery, where all look to for the teaching of healing. I must be sure she has this ability too.'

He screwed his mouth a little, then said, 'And I hear she is strange, and has ungodly practices.'

Oh, no! He has heard of her hill-rolling, or even seen it! 'Prior, she is ... a little different, and in need of the safe care of a monastery. She has a very clever mind, but sometimes she plays like a small child and rolls herself down the hill beside the ponds. Even our Lord encouraged us all to be as little children. It is harmless - she is harmless.'

Godric was silent for what felt like far too long. 'Bring her to see me two days before Good Friday,' he said at last, 'you will have had long enough to discern her qualities by then.'

Dominica left sending arrow prayers of thanks to God. She had been careless not to involve Prior Godric at least a bit in the choosing of lay women. She should have known he would be offended.

Brother Brannon

Praise the Lord, Fergus says that Kellagh does not suffer from the plague, but exhaustion and some other affliction that has stolen his vigour and given him a shortness of breath. All the other patients continue to improve, and no-one else has fallen sick.

*

It looks like we will leave this place and our dear brothers at St. Bartholomew's as most are returned to health enough to do without our help. The ones who had been caring when we arrived are now well trained by Fergus and Kellagh in the ways you taught them, sister, and they have the recipes written down too. We leave in the morning and head towards Laon, a short distance - which we pray is a place safe from the plague.

**

The Lord be praised, Laon is clear of plague, but that helped us not, as the whole hilltop town is sealed and so the church could not offer us shelter. We walked on a little and found an abandoned shed to shelter ourselves.

***

Now, sister we are beginning to take a different route. We are to head for a place called Wissant on the coast, but we first must walk three days to Aras, where, we are told, there is a great Benedictine monastery dedicated to Saint Vaast.

****

We stayed over an extra day at the monastery of Saint Vaast to recover ourselves a little. They are most hospitable, and seem to live in more comfort than we are used to experiencing ourselves. The next day we have but two days journey to a place named Terwann, where we are told we should find shelter at the monastery nearby the cathedral built by Saint Audomar, of which great things are told. After Rome, what can be so marvellous?

*****

The Cathedral is all but new - and is immense, by far the greatest we have seen since crossing the mountains. We are impressed - even after Rome.

We have also learned of a connection to our pilgrimage from the monks here. We are told that when Saint Audomar began his missions in this area, so great was the challenge that a goodly party of monks came from Columbanus' Luxue to help, and stayed to form the monasteries here. We feel blessed to have come this path.

Onward now to Wissant, sister. Not long before we are home and I can tell you all I am remembering for you.

Chapter 40
St. Patrick's tomb - *circa AD 697*

Brother Brannon

We are at the coast again, alleluia! They say that on a clear day you can see to the coast of Britannia from here, or at least from the cliff nearby. This harbour is called Wissant and the boats travel back and forth regularly, so we do not have so long to wait to take a passage.

*

Sister, the passage was short and smooth compared to that we have known. It is clear why this is a crossing more often made even this early in the season, not yet mid April – when you think how we were cautioned not to seek to cross from Porthkudh until nearing the end of May for fear of the dangerous swells on that route.

It is auspicious too that we have come home safely just before the Holy time of Pascha. We stay here, not far from the port, to celebrate this most holy time with thanksgiving, beginning today with the Good Friday vigil. We prayed for the missions at home - I think of Tamerkam as home now, and long to be back.

* *

Dominica had tried to use the time wisely with Merewin, to prepare her so that Prior Godric would not reject her. She couldn't allow that. She had talked to Merewin about Prior Godric and how he would most likely ask her some questions, and how to behave, how to keep her eyes cast down and answer simply. Dominica prayed he would not goad the girl, for some things could trip her into her odd behaviours and, she feared, Prior Godric would see her reaction as disrespecting him, or worse, as a sign of a demon.

As for her rolling down the hill, it was less frequent the longer she was with them, but it happened. She wasn't sure how she could explain it more to Godric than she had done, but she had thought of a way to take away the accusation that it was indecent. She had made for Merewin a pair of hose, as men wore beneath their tunics, to wear beneath her clothes, so that even if she rolled and her dress rode up, her legs would remain covered. It wasn't easy to convince Merewin to wear them, she complained they were too rough and too stiff, but Dominica had them washed and pounded until the fibres were softer and the objections faded.

Dominica took Merewin along to see Prior Godric as appointed. Merewin had been rolling that morning, but now appeared calm, clean and as ready as she could be.

'Prior,' Dominica said with a smile, 'May I present Merewin, of good family in Bo Etherick, who has shown to be very quick of mind in relation to herbs and the recipes for the making of healing tinctures, poultices and potions. She had also proved to be capable of learning the written word as is required of a herbalist. I, therefore, ask your blessing on her entering this monastery as a lay sister,' A quick glance at Merewin showed her to be standing perfectly still, hands clasped before her, eyes cast down.

Godric pulled a taut smile, 'And you, child. What do you say? Do you want a life in the monastery?'

Merewin did not look up, 'Yes.'

'Yes, Prior!'

Merewin looked up at Dominica, her puzzlement clear on here face, one hand beginning to pat the other, and Dominica smiled at her to reassure. 'Yes, Merewin, we say, 'Yes, Prior', don't we?'

Merewin bit her lip, looked at the floor again but said, 'Yes, Prior.'

'Are you sure she is of sound mind? She seems a bit simple to me!'

'Prior Godric, as I tried to explain, Merewin is very talented in herb lore, but in life she is child-like.'

'And the ungodly behaviour?'

'It is but childish play, it is innocent, and decent.'

Godric was silent for a long pause watching them both. Merewin continued to pat her own hand rapidly but lightly, Dominica rested her hand on Merewin's shoulder, but she shrugged it off.

'This – child will be your responsibility sister, totally. Take care that she does not disrupt the peace and sanctity of the monastery in any way – or you will return her to her family - regardless of how long she has been here – she is here on sufferance – you understand?'

'I do, Prior. Thank you,' taking Merewin by the hand, with a little squeeze of comfort, and leading her away. 'Well done, Merewin, you are to be a lay sister,' and Merewin, much to Dominica's surprise and delight, gave her hand a squeeze back!

Brother Brannon

We are looking forward to visiting the tomb of the blessed Saint Patrick at Glestyngabyrig and we are going straight there by means of the old ways. I am glad. It will bring us quicker home, and I have so much stored in my mind to tell you.

***

Pascha feels long past, yet we still travel in the hungry gap and so can't find much to supplement the porridge we eat most days - except nettle tops, ramsons and hawthorn leaves. At least now we can buy eggs when we are at a market.

This last week the weather has also been against us, coming in wet and windy, more like March than the end April, all muddy and slippery underfoot. We kirtle our habits again now and wear our leggings as we did in the mountains. It is easier to walk and yet easy to loosen our habits to be presentable when we reach a town.

Walking back all this way, after all we have seen, has been tiresome. I know I should be more glad of the experience, but day, after day, after day of walking, and nothing so wild as the mountains, nothing so cold, nothing so grand as Rome, nothing so hot, nothing to awe us beyond what we have already seen – this makes the days long.

****

A week into May and at last we have reached the church of St. Mary at the place called Glestyngabyrig. The last part of our journey was made following a guide. It isn't wise to travel across to here without one it seems. It made me smile to think that we had walked across mountains without a guide, sometimes, yet here, on this flatland we needed a guide. It has been wet lately and the land here is boggy at the best of times, we are told. The firmer built-up causeways are not always easy to see when it is this wet and, though they are said to be marked with withies, it seems it is not beyond villains to move them and then pounce once the unwary traveller is mired.

Glestyngabyrig is on a higher piece of land in this marshland, with a pointed steep hill to one side and a ridge on the other. The church is of a substantial size set inside a small rath, though after all the grand stone buildings with tiled roofs we have seen it looks poor, being mostly made with wooden frames filled by wattle and with a thatched roof. The priest welcomed us, hastening out of his small abode to one side of the church. He is a small rotund man who looks well in his position here.

He led us into the church with great solemnity and to the very point where a tall, slender, stone pyramid stood to the right of the altar. This was the resting place of the bones of the blessed Saint Patrick he told us. He led us in a prayer and then said we were welcome to stay as long as we liked in prayer ourselves, and retired to the far corner of the church where he sat, his eyes closed.

After our prayers we gathered at the back of the church with the priest. I ventured to ask why Saint Patrick was entombed here, when he was a saint from Eriu. The priest said he was not from Eriu, but originally from a place near the coast here, and when he had converted all the Irish he retired here to live as a monk, amongst other monks living as hermits, some of whom were also from Eriu. He explained the church was part of a monastery really, and that there were still monks living as hermits in the monastic area behind the church. He said that they came to mass in the church together, but lived solitary lives each to their own small hut and prayers, outside of that time.

Much blessed by our time in prayer so close to the holy relics of Saint Patrick, we began to leave the church, Indract pausing to hand a small bag with a number of coins in it, for alms for the poor, to the priest.

Outside, as our eyes got used to the dazzle of sunlight, I noticed a group of four men with horses standing to the side of the church. As the priest came out last with Indract, thanking him loudly for his generosity he suddenly stopped half way through his words. Glancing back at him I saw him pale, and tuck his hand with the bag in behind himself. In Latin he muttered, 'Take care, brothers!' before moving to the front of our group.

'Greetings, Husa. News from the King perhaps?' he spoke to them in Anglisc, and I felt for the meanings as your lessons came back to me.

Husa turned out to be the tallest and stockiest of the four. He took a step or two towards the priest, who shrank within himself. Husa was dressed in expensive-looking warriors clothing, with worked leather protection across his breast, his sword slung at his hip, but it was his face that I found remarkable – it did not look like it belonged to the body beneath it. It was handsome and fine-boned, marred only by a livid scar that ran from beneath his eye to his jaw.

'Time to pay your tithe, priest,' he said with a quick grin that showed his teeth - his voice didn't belong to the face either, grating and gravelly.

'Ah! Ah! Let me, let me see these good brothers on their way, and I shall find the ... the...'

Husa laughed, looked at his men, who also laughed - the laughter cut abruptly as he looked back, 'Go on then, see them on their way,' and, as if seeing us properly for the first time they all ran their eyes over us, with small glances to each other, an eyebrow raised, a silent language between them. Instinctively I felt my grip tighten on my staff and scrip and wondered if I was the only one who felt it.

We walked with the priest to the outer edge of the church boundary wall, the priest walking slowly. 'Will you be alright?' Indract asked him.

Speaking to us in Latin again he replied, 'I will, but I regret to say that not all your donation will reach the poor though. I will have to give them something, but not all. They are the king's men - but a law unto themselves.' He kicked at a stone on the outer edge of the rath, it dislodged easily, and he poured some of the coin in the gap and heeled the stone back in place. Then he turned and said he would bless us for our journey, and we bowed our heads and received his blessing.

Our guide took us off the 'island' which supported Glestyngabyrig and through the marsh until a point when he said we didn't need him from there on as the track to Hywsic, where another church would be found to shelter in, was clearly and safely marked. From there, he told us, it was but short way to Lindinis and 'the fosse', which is an old straight way to Excancastre.

We continued south, keeping to the high ground as we had been told to, looking for a turning towards the west. The track was marked though narrow at times, well trodden by both men and horses and we soon fell into our usual pace. The hours passed and we began to wish we had sought some bread at Glestyngabyrig before we left, but had to make do with water, of which we had plenty.

I can only think that we may have taken a wrong turn somewhere, or missed the one we needed. There were options along the way but none had seemed to be well trodden or marked as a turn. Eventually the time came when it grew dark and we could barely see where we were heading. We had crossed a small plank bridge and felt sure that it must indicate a settlement, yet we saw no light anywhere and there was no lookout at the bridge. The path then offered two directions; both seemed as well travelled as the other, and we took the right hand turning.

Shortly before the last light left the sky it was decided to take ourselves off the path to find somewhere dry to sleep. At least there were enough dead shrubs to gather to make a fire, though many were sharp with thorns. We found a clearing of wiry grass near to the edge of the marsh, signalled by the great stands of reeds, and made our fire. Our poor supper was warmed water flavoured by a few of the precious seeds and herbs that we had brought back with us – we said the set prayers and settled for the night, rolled-up in our cloaks.

At some time I woke, maybe out of habit for the services, but I felt the need to go and lose some of the water we had drunk in the day. The sky was just lightening to the east, and I could see the reeds dark against it so went towards them so as not to disturb the brothers, treading carefully as I neared the edge of the marsh. I was settled in my stance gazing at the unfolding pre-dawn and relieving myself when I heard a noise over the constant sighing of the reeds - but assumed it just another brother on the same mission. A creak, however, made me turn my head. There stood Husa a few paces back, sword in hand, and in that eye-blink his empty hand made a short chopping motion. My head exploded in pain and the reeds rushed towards me.

Chapter 41

***Silence** - circa AD 697*

Brother Brannon

I came to - drawn out of the blackness by shouts - angry shouts and screams. My face was half sunk in the mud but the reeds had saved me from drowning. Everything hurt, even the light in my eyes, misty as it was. I closed them and tried to stand. My arms pushed but my legs would not lift, knees would not bend, just pain jarring through me. Raised on my arms I could turn my head to peer back through the reeds; what I saw filled me with fear. I closed my eyes and opened them again.

My brothers were fighting for their lives, using their staffs to sweep around them. I recognised Kellagh and Fergus back to back, sweeping wildly, screaming, 'You'll go to hell! You'll go to hell!' In our tongue, so it made no difference to the men trying to get to them. The one facing Fergus kept ducking and moving forward, suddenly he grabbed at the staff, caught it and dragged Fergus towards him. Fergus struggled against him holding tight to the staff. The warrior had drawn him in and the sword struck deep into his guts. As he shook the dying Fergus off his sword, Kellagh turned and began beating the man about the head with his staff - until Kellagh was hacked down by the man behind him. The men snatched the staffs and threw them to the ground, clattering together as they fell.

It was then I saw Indract. He wasn't fighting with his staff, our cross, but with another, maybe mine. I wondered where his was but not for long as I saw another join his foe, two against one. When one managed to snatch the staff Indract wielded, Indract was clever and pulled, but then pushed it back so the man pulling fell back. In that fraction of a moment Indract snatched up the cross-staff from the ground and began to run from them. I am not sure where Husa was before, but suddenly he was there behind Indract, he thrust and the sword plunged into him. I saw Indract's back arch, but he ran on. Clasping the cross staff to him he staggered into the marsh, his steps slowing as the marsh and his wound took hold, then he fell - and I could see him no more.

Husa sent one man after him into the marsh, while the other disappeared from my view. I saw the man struggling to move forward in the marsh, and soon he turned back shaking his head. A touch on his arm and he and Husa headed out of my view.

I could still hear the sounds of fighting. I tried to raise myself more to see, but could see no-one, only hear shouts, screams. And then there was silence.

But not for long, the warriors came back into view, one pair dragging a body, right up to the reed edge. They then hefted the body and threw it into the marsh. It looked like Finn. One of the others carried a staff and dropped it with a hollow sound of wood on wood. They stood together in the clearing.

I saw one walk in my direction and sank myself down, peering back at root level. Then I saw him swaggering back, carrying our scrips, he put them at the feet of Husa. He nodded and the man picked one up and opened it. He tipped out our carefully collected and purchased seeds. Husa shouted something - it sounded like an oath! The next scrip was opened. It must have been Fergus' or Kellagh's as pots and packets fell out. More swearing, words I didn't know, yet I recognised the tone of them. Frantically they tipped out each scrip.

Husa screamed at his men, 'Nothing, not even one stinking gold coin!'

One man dashed aside and came back with a staff. He rubbed it with his sleeve, and they all looked at it in the misty sunlight.

'It's not gold you turds! It's bronze! Bronze, fools, not gold!' he shouted at them, then turned in a circle looking up to the sky. 'Are they all dead?' he snapped as he came to a stand still.

They stood and looked round, one seemed to be counting off on his fingers. They then looked all round again pointing and muttering. I could barely breathe.

'What do you mean? Two missing? Are you sure?'

'Lord, there were nine at the church, not counting the priest,' the man pointed around the area, 'the big bastard there, two

beside the fire, two over there, one too far into the marsh, and that one we just brought in.'

'And the one that was pissing when we arrived,' added Husa. 'Still leaves one!' He shook his head, 'There cannot be any witnesses! Not matter how much King Ina depends on us, he'll not forgive this. You want-wits – how did one get away?'

'There are eight staffs here,' said one slowly.

'And their leader ran off into the marsh with the crossed staff - and a mortal wound,' Husa said, 'Which means the missing one just ran. Just ran ... and hid somewhere. Find him!'

Am I a coward sister? I lay down again, what could I do. I seemed stuck where I was, just waiting for them to find me and kill me off - but they all went in different directions and not one my way.

I decided to try to work my way further into the reeds. I found I could pull myself forwards with my elbows, my legs dragging behind me. I knew I left a trail through the reeds but I hoped to take a turn to make it not so clear a path. Lying down meant I did not sink easily where it became much wetter. I dragged and breathed, and dragged again, it seemed lighter ahead and I realised there was a break in the reeds. I held back until I realised it was a channel, a small stream. If I could pull myself up or down the stream I could re-enter the reeds where they would see no trail. I dragged myself forward and slid down the bank into the stream, gasping at the cold.

My legs screamed at me, but the cold water also took away the worst of the pain, and for the first time I felt like they might not be broken. I watched as globs of mud slid off of my robe and dissolved in the running water and my legs began to feel freed of the weight that was in them.

I pulled myself upstream, looking for a place to push back into the reeds, clambered up, finding my legs actually helping, not dead as I had thought. By going up stream I had placed myself closer to the clearing, and through the reed stems I could see a bulky lump - which slowly resolved itself into a body and, nearest to me, the top of a tonsured head. Indract, face down in the mud.

I said a prayer for him, certain he was already at Jesus' side. It was then I heard the men again. I dared not look as the sun was well up and the mist beginning to lift and I could not risk being seen now.

Sounds filtered through to me. A bird crying out – or a man? Cut off quickly. Then the rustle and footfall of the returning men.

I know what the sounds I heard next were - now. The men were grunting and throwing something large and weighty to land in the marsh - the flump made the marsh quiver each time. I counted. Six. Then I heard Husa's unmistakable voice again, 'Use their staffs to poke them right down into the marsh! Make sure nothing shows! You, take one and go back and do the same to the shit-coward we found back there. Then you can chuck their worthless staffs where no-one can find them.'

I panicked, started shoving myself back away from Indract. If they were coming to submerge him, they couldn't help but see me. Two body-lengths back and then I turned and dragged myself between the reeds. I kept my face low and listened, silent prayers rolling out of my mouth

The men were grunting with effort, cursing the mud and how they kept sinking themselves. The stench of the marsh leaked across the surface of to me, suffocatingly putrid, stinking like long dead carrion.

Would they realise I wasn't where they'd left me and know I was still alive? I prayed like I have never prayed before. There was a whoosh sound and a staff stuck itself into the mud just to the side of my head. I wrapped an arm over my head and prayed again as all around I heard the thump of the staffs raining down.

I thought I heard them leave. Had they forgotten to find my body? I lay there a long while to be sure that they really had gone. Then used the staff that had landed beside me to help pull myself up a little, so I could actually see. Thanks be to God - the clearing was empty! I also realised I would have to drag myself further forward before I could try standing, the mud gave under me with too much weight. I threw the staff forward and then dragged myself after it, passing the place where Indract's body had been, now just a patch of black oozing mud. I threw the staff forward twice before the ground could bear my weight even on my knees. Nearer the edge I managed to stand and used the staff to support myself and help my agonised legs to move.

Once in the clearing I neared our fireplace and sank to the ground once more, my robe a case of mud about me. The fire was kicked about, two pools of congealed blood beside it – I wondered who were the two killed before they even knew what was happening. I thought the placing meant Teagan and Niall, I murmured a prayer as I thought of them. Further over, seeds and broken shards of pot scattered far and wide. No sign of the scrips. I felt sure I would know this spot again but decided I needed a marker. I could use the staff I held but I needed that, so I stood and looked into the reeds to see if any others were close enough to retrieve. I saw one! It was standing up amongst the reeds, like a thicker reed, and not too far in. I stepped carefully, keeping my feet near the stems of the biggest clumps of reed. Using the other staff I knocked it towards me, just enough to pull on the end. It was so hard to grip tightly enough to pull the other end out of the sucking mud, but it came, slowly, slowly, and then suddenly free so that I tipped back and landed in the mud. I laughed. I laughed! Madness or what? Then threw one staff out of the reeds and limped back onto the solid ground with the other.

I found a spot firm enough for the staff to stand, but soft enough for me to push it in, right by the edge of the reeds - in line with where Indract had gone in. Then I turned and stumbled my way back towards the bridge.

It seemed so far that I wasn't sure I was going the right way, though I followed a track made by both feet and horses between shrubby trees and bushes. A gap ahead showed me a clearing. I headed towards it and, there off to the left, saw the simple bridge. I staggered towards it, my head spinning as I drew level. It was then I thought I heard horses' hooves beating a hollow sound from the ground behind me, turned and plunged again into darkness.

*

Dominica strode swiftly towards the church. It seemed impossible that Godric had a problem with Esselt. She wondered if he'd confused the quiet Esselt with Avan. It wouldn't be the first time Avan's brash ways had got her in trouble with the monks, and they were of a height.

As soon as she was in sight of the church door she realised it wasn't a confusion. Esselt stood there looking downcast, Prior Godric looking angry and Matuid looking smug. *Matuid! Everywhere there is discontent there seems to be Brother Matuid.*

'Prior, you wished to see me - urgently?' Dominica opened.

'This, novice of yours, has been interfering with the duties of our monks.'

'Sister Esselt?' She turned to Esselt, 'Sister, can you tell me what has happened?'

'She stopped us from working!' Matuid snapped. Dominica ignored him and continued to look expectantly at Esselt.

'Sister, I was only keeping the monks from going to the ponds,' she looked hard at Dominica, 'for just a few moments.'

'Time we were meant to be working!' grumbled Matuid.

Dominica understood. 'How did you stop them sister? You are but one, very young, and not that strong,' she had to control her face so as not to smile.

'I only stood on the path and asked them to wait for a few moments to listen for the strange bird I had heard. I wanted to know what it was and I thought they might know.'

'And did they hear the bird?'

'No. I think Brother Matuid shouting at me frightened it away.'

'So they were not detained long?'

'Not really.'

'Yes we were!'

Dominica rounded on Matuid, 'And how much more time have you wasted with this matter? Not only yours, but the Prior's, mine and Sister Esselt's?'

'I find Brother Matuid's zeal commendable, to listen for a bird call is a distraction to our life and calling. Sister Esselt shall take a penance ...'

'She will not!' Dominica snapped.

'She will! I will not have the life of this monastery disrupted on the whim of a girl – and you, sister, forget yourself. You too shall take a penance, both of you, two days fast, with prayer in church when you would have been at table. You will forfeit the blessing of communal services. I do not wish to see either of you for those until two days hence.'

'As you will,' Dominica said tightly, took Esselt's hand and walked away. *Two days without having to look at Godric or Matuid – a blessing - but foolish to have allowed myself to get angry. Oh! I can't wait for Indract to come home! This is not how our gentle mission should be run.*

'Where is Merewin now?' Dominica asked quietly, as soon as they were well away from the men.

'Back in the herbarium - I hope.'

'Thank you, Esselt. You have been brave and kind. And, if you had truly heard a strange bird, then they should have listened for it, for birds are part of the creator's world and can teach us much.'

'I did hear a bird. It said chee-ow. I didn't know it.'

'Hmm, neither do I, but never mind. Let's go and see if Merewin is all good.'

Brother Brannon

At first I could only smell. Peat burning smoky-sweetly, it reminded me of home. I wondered for a moment if this was Heaven? Was it like this - going home and back to your childhood where your mother cared for you and you had few concerns in the world?

But then I heard voices - at home they didn't speak like this – this was not my mother tongue – so I began to listen and try to understand what was said. I peered through half closed eyes. I was in a house, a simple place, one room, the fire central – all usual – except the walls were not curved, but straight. The only light came through the open door, though I could see some kind of covering on a side wall, perhaps a wind-hole. I stirred. On the periphery of my vision a woman stood and came towards me.

'You are wakened?' she also spoke in the Anglisc tongue that you taught us, but thickly.

'Mmm,' I nodded slightly, the movement causing pain. She moved away again, and then returned, this time bearing a shallow bowl.

'Drink!'

I raised myself painfully to my elbows. My body felt clammy and my head felt heavy. She held the bowl to my lips and I drank – it could have been nectar from heaven, it tasted so good – I recognised mint-water sweetened with honey. 'Bless you,' I murmured. 'Thank you.'

Later, I awoke again. I do not remember going back to sleep. Now there was more noise in the small house, men's voices, with an urgency to them. I lay listening. Their accents were broad but I could recognise many of the words you had taught me. They seemed to be wondering what to do with me. One was scared and seemed to be saying they should turn me out – the other that they should take me to the churchmen. I lay a little longer trying to recall enough words to get them to take me back to the church at Glestyngabyrig. My line of words fixed in my head, I stirred. The men fell silent. I lifted myself onto my elbows, I tried to swing my legs around but my muscles screamed at me to lie still – yet I knew I needed to sit up properly, I lifted one leg with my hands and then the other and sat upright as the men edged closer and stared down at me.

'Who are you?' one asked.

The other snapped at him, 'You can see he's a monk, idiot!'

I answered both, 'Brothers, I am a monk, a holy brother from Dumnonia. We were on pilgrimage and were attacked, I must get back to Glestyngabyrig.'

'See,' the first said, 'we just take him there – no longer our problem.'

'Depends who attacked him.'

'Just return me to the church at Glestyngabyrig, please,' I said, then added, 'as secretly as possible.'

'See! See! He's trouble!'

'Then get me out of your home and away from your land as soon as you can,' I said, trying to keep my voice firm and gentle, though I wanted to cry and scream. In inspiration I added, 'And surely God will bless you for your mercy.'

'Glestyngabyrig's a half day walking away – and he's not fit – I say we take him to the church here – let him deal with it.'

'I'd not leave my worst enemy with that priest. He's in Husa's hand!'

'Well, if Husa has anything to do with this – I'm not having anything to do with this man, monk or not.'

'I never said that! I just said why I wouldn't trust that priest.' I shivered at the name, and prayed they'd not choose that option.

'Can you walk?' the first man suddenly asked me.

I tried to stand, cast around for my staff. 'Maybe with my staff.' He brought it to me, I dragged myself up, pulling hard and leaning heavily on the staff.

'Barely,' he said, then turned to the other man, 'but we could tie him over a pony and cover him with hides, it wouldn't be comfortable, but might get him there quickest?'

The other man stood and stared at me, as though not seeing a person, just a problem. I sank back onto the makeshift bed. I couldn't walk, that I was sure about.

'How about, later on, before dark? I'll bring my pony laden with hides – and we'll set of at dusk,' he offered.

'Agreed.'

'Just keep him out of sight and swear your household to silence.'

'Good man, I'll see you this evening.'

I praised God under my breath, and aloud said, 'Bless you, bless you both!'

Chapter 42
Hiding - *circa AD 697*

Brother Brannon

I had been given some watery stew, mostly roots I think, but warming and I felt a little more human, and able to sit up, at least. The woman looked at me with worried and tired eyes, but helped me brush much of the dried mud from my habit.

Then the men came. They hustled me to my feet and half dragged me out of the hut into the dark. There was a short-legged pony waiting nearby, and a stack of hides beside it. With scarcely a word they hoicked me over the back of the pony, just an old blanket between me and its hair. Then they began layering hides over me, suffocating in their noxious stink and in their weight.

'That's enough - he's well covered,' one said. I thanked God.

'Listen-up.' A voice close to my head. 'You keep quiet, not a sound - no matter what! And no movements! You are not here!' I made not a sound.

'Did you hear me? Not a sound!' Realising he needed an answer I gave a grunt of assent. The pony moved off, the motion making me feel queasy beneath the hides.

We hadn't been travelling long, just enough for me to have settled into a trance-like state of not knowing where I was or what was happening outside the stink and weight of the hides and the constant motion of the pony's muscles beneath my gut, when I recognised the hollow-sound of hooves on wood. Almost as soon as this crept into my consciousness I was startled by a cry of alarm from the men.

'Aiee! What is that?'

Almost forgetting that I must not move, must not betray my presence beneath the hides, I tried to turn towards their voices.

'I, I don't know? Devils work?' Awe and fright in his voice.

I was prodded through the hides. I held still as I could. Had someone stopped them and was investigating the pile of hides.

'You!' the voice was beside my head again, 'You, monk!' the pony was shifted around in a half-circle, I felt the hides pulled aside from my head. As my face was uncovered my eyes saw what they could see. 'What is that? What - is - that?' the fear in his voice trickling ice through me.

I knew where we were even in the half dark, the small bridge not far from where we had camped – and what I could see were like pillars of light glowing in the dark. God had sent markers of my brothers bodies, crying out for all to see the evil that had been visited on them.

'That, brothers, is a holy sign from God! That is where my brothers in God were slain.' I was gratified to see them cross themselves.

'Let's get you to Glestyngabyrig,' the man said and flapped the hides back over my face.

Much later, so much that I think I may have dozed despite my discomfort, I was aware that the pony had stopped. I heard a knocking noise, repeated. And eventually words called loudly but low asking the 'father' to open his door to an injured man. He must have done so, as very shortly after the village men slipped the hides off of me and tugged me to standing.

The priest held a candle to my face. 'Brother?'

'Father, we, company of monks were with you just a few days ago, on our way home from Rome.'

'I remember.'

'We were set upon and all but myself, saved by the grace of God, were slaughtered by ...'

'There's poles of fire in the dark, big as men, just where they died!' one said in an awe-stricken voice, 'We saw them!'

'Come in, come in!'

The men helped me over the threshold of the priest home. 'We will not stay father. Please do not tell anyone who brought this man back to you.' One leant my staff against the wall, then they turned and were gone.

'Scared men,' the priest murmured. 'Do they know who did this sacrilege?' he asked as he helped me further in and had me sit myself down.

'I know who, but I do not know who they think did it - but maybe they guess? They are truly scared, that, I do know.'

'If you know who – then I will guess it was our friend Husa who you saw the other day. You would know no other in this place who could overwhelm so many monks. And the poles of fire?'

'That is true, pillars of light - quite bright in the dark, gathered like sentinels where they were buried - well, thrust into the mire.'

'A sign! You are sure?'

'I am, as God is my witness, I am. It was not far from the wooden bridge leading to their settlement that we were set upon, and it was from that bridge that we could see the lights.'

The priest smiled a little, then solemnly clasped his hands and prayed for guidance and the deliverance of the wrongdoers into the hands of justice. I said the Amen to that, but had no idea what he was thinking.

I slept deeply and the priest woke me with a bowl of porridge.

'We cannot let this iniquity pass,' he said, though he looked as if he held a secret and was pleased with it. 'I must leave you today for a while. Stay in here and do not answer to anyone. Indeed, if you hear someone knock, hide. Do you understand? Your life may depend upon it.'

'I do, I will. Where will you be?'

'Telling the King of the miracle - he will want to see it,' he flashed a small smile.

I had eaten the piece of bread and cheese that the priest had left me, and all but drunk the jug of water. I could tell it was getting dark, and he had not returned. I feared that he had been spotted by Husa and his men, or that the King had called them in to be confronted and then they had waylaid him on the way back.

When he returned, not knowing it was him, I cowered in my hiding place between his bed and the wall, as he rattled his door open.

'Brother, here, I have brought some food from the King's own table.' I emerged from my hiding place. He was tired but looked cheerful as he saw me and said, 'The King is coming soon and I must lead him to the miracle. Pray that the pillars of light are still there to be seen! Remind me, how many were you all?'

'Brother Indract and eight of us monks.'

'Why do you name Brother Indract?'

'He was the brother who led us on our pilgrimage to Rome, he was our Prior at our monasteries on the banks of the Tamer in Dumnonia.'

'I see. How many pillars of light?'

'I, I didn't count them, I couldn't count them - I was slung over the pony, and they were a little way off, some crowded together.'

'But there should be eight altogether, no?'

'Yes, for I am here.'

'Good.'

'If Husa finds out I am alive – I won't be for long.'

'Do not worry, I have a plan,' he said and laid the food on the board.

I was hiding again, behind the rough cloth curtain that separated the priest's simple bed from the main room, when the knock came on the door. The priest wrapped his cloak around him and hastened out. I shivered and settled myself on the bed.

I must have been asleep when he returned, as the first I knew was him shaking my shoulder, 'Come, now!' I struggled up. He pulled back the curtain to reveal a man sitting at the board. I stiffened as I knew instantly that this was the king. He reminded me of King Conall, your father - he had the bearing. His clothing was of exceptional fine quality of a heavy material and richly coloured. Everything you'd expect of a king – except he was the only person there, no guards with him.

'This is the monk who survived, lord King,' the priest said quietly.

King Ina regarded me calmly. I wondered what he saw; a dishevelled and filthy monk of none too great a stature. Would he believe me?

'Tell me who you are, and about those who were killed,' he began then, after a momentary pause, he added, 'and how it is that you are alive?'

I told him about Indract, and you, Sister Dominica, even his vision that took us from Eriu in the first place, how God had sent us instead to the banks of the Tamer, of our two monasteries there, of our deliverance from the plague and our pilgrimage to Rome. Like a spring unblocked I could barely stop talking until it came to the time we met with Husa outside this very church. Only then did my throat dry and my words get stuck.

'You came out of the church and saw?' he prompted.

'Some warriors.'

'And?'

'And.' I looked to the priest in desperation, he nodded. 'And they demanded a tithe from the father here, and they stared at us a long time.'

'A tithe? And stared? Do you know who the men were?'

'Sire, the father here said their leader was named Husa.' I noticed the King's eyes flicker.

'What did he look like?'

'He was – he seemed, like two persons in one body. His face looked like it was meant for fine things, music and poetry, all bar the scar running down his cheek, but his body and voice were full of fight and gravel.'

The King barked a laugh and leant forward, 'The best description I've ever heard of the man!' he said in a harsh whisper, 'And you told the father here that it was Husa and his band who – committed this atrocity?'

'It was. I recognised him, voice and face.'

'Yet you lived?'

'Luck! Or God's answer to prayer - they thought me dead, I am sure. I was the first struck, but I came to, thought my legs broken, but dragged myself further into the mire, away from the slaughter.' My tongue had grown quick and bold but a gesture

from the priest reminded me to keep it low, 'Husa was the one who stuck his sword into Indract's back as he tried to save the cross staff - I saw that,' swallowing hard to stop the cry escaping from my throat. 'And I heard them. They expected our scrips to be stuffed with treasure – but sire, we only carried herbs and seeds. They had even thought we had gold tips on our staffs. All this I heard as Husa was so angered that there was nothing of worth. Then he was determined that no one should find the bodies, he had them pushed under the mud - with their own staffs.'

I swallowed, my mouth feeling full of bitterness. 'After they had gone, when I struggled out of the mire, I left one staff stuck in the ground in line with Indract's body, as best I knew where it was. He had the cross staff with him. No need it seems, as God has intervened and made them a light in the darkness, crying out for justice.'

The King was silent for a moment. The only sound the hiss and crackle of the fire. 'I believe all you have said, and I have just witnessed those very lights in the darkness. This is what will happen. Your brothers' bodies will be retrieved and buried in this church as martyrs. Your Prior will be honoured. I shall deal with Husa and his men - they will be tried for this ungodly crime.'

'And this brother?' the priest said.

'Will disappear, will never have been here, for your sake Father, as well as his. Give him your pony and some coin and set him on the road in the morning. Make sure he is away before full light – I will send you another pony and recompense.'

The King stood. The Father bowed, so I did too. 'Go back,' the priest said with a tip of his head towards the bed area. I hid.

The door was opened and the King said clearly, 'Thank you, Father, for bringing me to witness the miraculous pillars of light, and for your ministry and prayers with me this evening.'

'As ever in your service, my Lord,' he replied.

Chapter 43
Welcome Stranger *- circa AD 697*

Dominica headed toward the Church; called again by the Prior, and they had only just returned to the table that day! One thing after another. Oh! Indract - hurry back! Prior Godric was standing at the corner of the church, his face turned towards the warm sun when Dominica saw him. She walked towards him - he didn't appear to hear her.

'Prior? You sent for me?'

'Sister, yes, come and sit with me in the Church,' he said and swept past her to enter the building. He sat on the end of a bench at the front. After a second's hesitation she sat on the end of the bench across the aisle from him. He didn't look pleased.

'We have held a meeting, and we have a proposal. If you agree then we will make plans. If you do not agree we will just have to have a formal vote on the matter,' he stopped and looked at her.

Bewildered, she shrugged and asked, 'Agree to what?'

'To you and your sisters and lay women setting up a separate nunnery outside of this monastery.'

'What? That's not how this was arranged! This is a double monastery under one prior – Indract!'

'I didn't say you would not be under the auspices of this monastery or its prior. It would be a daughter nunnery, just totally separate in location.'

'No! This is – this still excludes us!'

'No, sister,' he shook his head once and pulled a little regretful smile, 'I realise you have very limited experience. However, in many, no, most monasteries the women and the men are in completely different settlements, often a long way apart.'

'I may have little direct experience, but I can read, so I know this is the case in some parts, but not usually in Eriu, and not hereabouts. Besides, it doesn't change the fact that this place was set up for harmony and a sharing of strengths as a double monastery, in the Lord's cause and for the people of this place.'

'We would, of course, do the building work as a whole monastery, we would not just cast you out.'

'To what point? Why? I can tell you now Indract will not see it this way - I know my brother. Then all your effort in building a new place will have been wasted.'

'So you make us take a vote?'

'I'm not *making* you take a vote – I am saying it is an unnecessary, wasteful and foolish idea,' the words out faster than thought.

Godric reddened, 'So be it. We will take a vote after nones in seven days time – Prior Cormag will be here that day,' he stood and marched himself from the building.

Dominica sat very still and closed her eyes, her hand pressed to her chest where it suddenly ached as if she'd been hit. Why couldn't she keep her tongue still? She'd only made it worse.

Brother Brannon

I've been riding for two days, the first as fast as I, and the pony, could take it, with much turning and looking back, scanning for horse-riders, and darting off of the track to try to hide if I saw any, heart thumping the whole time until the rider passed.

The second steadily and with many rests, where there was good grazing and water - for both of us. I slept beneath trees or even shrubs, with the pony hitched to the trunk, and wrapped only in a cloak. I've eaten nothing since the bread and cheese the priest gave me as he set me off in the grey of dawn.

This day I came to face to face with the high moor and, following directions I'd been given by travellers coming the other way, turned to follow the track with the moor at my left. Gradually the track turned sun-wards, so by noon it was full on my face.

I rode steadily, wearily, aching all over, almost in a daze, letting the pony find his way. The track is well used and I met trades people on their way along it and asked about Tamerkam, but none had heard of it, nor Kellyventon, but some could tell me that the sea was the way I was headed, so we plodded on.

A well-dressed woman, with two armed men escorting her, took pity on me, recognising me as a monk despite my dirty and unkempt condition, told me there was a small monastery founded by Saint Rumon, on a bluff overlooking a shallow river called Tafvi, not too far along the way. She said I couldn't miss it as the track passed behind it. I recognised the name of the river and wondered if it could be the same river which joins the Tamer near Tamerunta.

I hope to find this monastery, and food and rest this night, as all the energy from fleeing death has left me feeling hollow and witless.

After a while the track led me to a river. I hoped it was the Tafvi, and we plodded alongside it until the track was driven inland, to cross where the water from a tributary stream was shallow enough, before continuing towards a hill. Ahead of me the land rose and then there, on the bluff over looking the river, as she had said, I could see houses and what looked like a church. My spirits rose and I found myself sitting a little straighter and hoping for a warm welcome.

And so it was, sister, as I arrived I was met by a monk at the entrance, 'Welcome stranger, or, maybe, are you a brother?' he asked, looking unsure.

'Brother, Brother Brannon, of Tamerkam, on my way home from a pilgrimage to Rome,' I replied.

'Welcome! Come in. Come, you look weary and I think in need of a good rest, which we can surely offer.'

I dismounted and was led through into the central area. The church looked bigger than the one at Tamerkam even, and there were more round houses too. By now a few other monks arrived. One came and offered to take the pony and see to its care, which I gladly accepted and another, with an air of authority, spoke hurriedly with the first monk, then beamed and came over to me.

'Brother... Brannon?'

I nodded.

'Welcome, we can offer you fresh clothes. It looks like you have need of them. The laundry will care for yours and return them. In the meantime you can wash and rest.' He walked me towards a hospice hut into which a young monk brought a pitcher of water and a bowl.

'You said you were on your way home from Rome. Maybe the Abbot will permit us to hear of your pilgrimage after vespers, if you will tell it?' he said quietly.

I could do little more than nod and raise a small smile. Now I was safe I felt fit to drop. I washed and changed, was fed a hot potage and left to sleep, with a promise of being woken for Vespers. The hot food was delicious on my tongue and the bed felt like it must be made of feathers it was so comfortable and warm, though I knew in reality both to be the usual available in a small monastery. I slept.

Clean, fed and rested I was ready to do as I had been asked. The Abbot had given permission for me to tell of our pilgrimage – I only wondered whether to say anything about what happened at Glestyngabyrig.

Sister, I didn't want to tell. Not that our brother's lives and deaths shouldn't be known, but that I feared others may come seeking me, even here, and the fewer who knew what I had witnessed the better. I told of our journey, glad I had committed so much to memory for you, and spun enough tales of Rome I thought to satisfy the brothers, the odd one or two asking questions that told me they, too, had been.

Then the Abbot himself asked me a question. Brother Brannon, he said, all through you have said you were part of a pilgrim group from your monastery, yet here you are on your way back there, looking weary and beaten, and all alone. How is that?

What could I do? I had to relate what had happened at Glestyngabyrig, and why I was scared to mention it until asked. When I had finished there was a deep silence, and I knew tears ran down my face unbidden and unstoppable. Abbot Kenver then led a prayer of remembrance for our brothers, put his hand upon my head and blessed me.

I awoke feeling hot, my head painful, my body soaked in sweat. I pushed off the blanket, but shortly was shuddering. I dragged the blanket back, wiped my face with it and hugged it to me. I heard a sound and whirled around – the hut continued moving even as I froze in place – there was a light, and there was a ball of light, it said, 'Brother, are you all right? You don't look well.'

*

Dominica tried to have a quiet word with a brother or two when she happened across them, always glancing round to check that Godric or Matuid were not to be seen. From her hurried talks it seemed that a few would vote against the proposal, but the preaching for the separation was making many feel it would be easiest and best.

Just three days before the vote Yowann came to the healer's hut, with a cut that was festering.

'Yowann, did you not clean this?' Dominica said in surprise as she released the grubby strip of linen he had wrapped around it.

'No, I didn't,' he said, looking her in the eye, 'took four days to get this bad,' he smiled.

'Oh?'

'Matuid sent me to you when I showed it to him. He can't abide anything like this.'

'Let me get it cleaned and see if I can put a stop to the infection. It wasn't wise to let it get like this – but, thank you. You can talk while I work.'

'Sister, for some reason Godric and Matuid are determined to set you and the sisters up in a different place. I cannot fathom why at the moment, but I wanted you to know that there are some of us who will vote to stay as we are.'

'Thank you, Yowann, I did try to point out that it was a waste of time. It has been almost a year since the brothers left, and a year is considered a reasonable time to be able to go to Rome and come back. So when they arrive, well, I can't see Indract being happy, and he would make sure we reverted to a dual monastery again, I am sure.'

'I am sure too, sister. Thank you. That feels so much better already.'

'See who else will listen. Maybe we can at least split the vote so there is no mandate - or we could have a counter proposal to wait and put this idea before the monastery only when Indract and the other brothers return.'

'That sounds a good idea, we could try that.'

'Thank you, Yowann. God bless you!'

All too soon the day arrived, heralded by the arrival of Cormag. A delaying tactic still seemed to be the best option. Dominica was determined to get an agreement for this divisive proposal to be raised only when Indract was back. That also seemed to be the best way to encourage more, than just the brothers who favoured a dual monastery, to vote with her - as it was only to put the decision off.

They gathered in the refectory after Nones and their repast. Cormag presided. And that was another thing - he would insist on his being the deciding vote if there was a draw.

'Brothers and sisters of Tamerkam. Brother Godric has raised the problem of distraction from our labour for the Lord, from prayer, from teaching and learning, from study. All of these aspects of the life of a man dedicated to God require a clear head, without distractions or unnecessary temptations. It is for this reason we separate ourselves from the world, that we keep ourselves pure in thought and deed. Monasteries can be that place of seclusion and sanctity. However, here, we also have a healing mission. Though this applies to our own brethren too, it is also for the people of the area. Because of this, those ailing come here – into our sanctified areas, men, children ... and women.' He paused and looked towards Dominica.

Dominica could see how he was being so careful not to make this about the nuns themselves, but about the ordinary people who came to the healer's hut – women in particular. It made it seem so much more reasonable.

'The solution, to move the healing part of our mission to a new location, away from the main monastery, seems to me to make perfect sense.'

'So not the nuns then, just the healer's hut?' Dominica blurted.

'Patience, sister. I have not finished speaking.' He looked back at the men and drew a breath. 'It would not be – practical for the nuns to live away from the healer's hut. It would not do, nor be safe, for the holy sisters to wander around from place to place at all times of day and night, as I know they would have to do to care properly for the sick. It follows that their living quarters need to be where the healer's hut is. Prior Godric.'

Godric stood and came to stand beside Cormag. 'Of course, we brothers will do all the building required for the sisters, but after that only they will come into this monastery, no other females, and then only for the Sunday services and the great holy days in the Church.'

Dominica jumped to her feet. 'So you would separate us from the building of the church all through the week too?'

'Sit down sister! You will have your chance to speak when called on!' Cormag snapped. Dominica stood a moment or two, wavering, wanting to protest, but knowing it would not help their cause at all. She sat.

Godric continued, 'We will ask for land at a distance from here - to set up the healer's hut – and also the nunnery, which will remain part of this monastery and still under its rule.'

‘Now, Sister Dominica,’ Cormag said, ‘You may speak to the brethren, and then we will vote.’

Dominica stood and started to come towards Cormag and Godric.

‘You may speak from there, sister, no need to come to the front,’ Cormag said in a deep warning voice.

She stopped and turned; at least she was far enough forward to be able to scan most faces. ‘Brothers and sisters, it all sounds very reasonable doesn’t it? However, this is a fundamental change to the way that this monastery was formed. Between us, Indract and I were called in a vision to this place – called as two, male and female, to share the burden, to share the joy of spreading the word of God, of caring for his people. A dual monastery to use the strengths that we each have for the benefit of all and to the Glory of God.’ She noticed a smirk on Matuid’s face and glanced back at Godric and Cormag to catch them gazing up at the rafters.

She inhaled and continued, ‘Indract and the rest of the original brothers who came on this mission are sure to return soon. It has been a year, almost, and that is considered the span of time for such a pilgrimage. I propose we vote *only* when they have returned.’ She was pleased to see quite a few nodding their heads.

‘Very well, but we don’t need a formal vote for this,’ Cormag said quickly. ‘Those in favour of waiting until the pilgrim brothers return before we vote – raise your hands.’

The brothers began raising their hands, some quite quickly, some hesitantly, Dominica began to smile, then noticed the hesitant monks dropping their hands. She spun round, the glare Cormag and Godric levelled at the gathered monks was fierce, and spoke volumes.

When she looked back, only the sisters and the few monks that had raised their hands quickly, remained with hands aloft.

‘Thank you brothers, we shall ...’

'Brother Brannon! Brother Brannon!!' shouted Avan as she raced into the refectory.

'Get out!' roared Godric.

'No! No!' Dominica shouted back at him. 'Avan! Say it again!'

'Sister – Brother Brannon has just ridden into the monastery!' She glanced back through the doorway, 'Look, here he comes!'

'Thank the Lord!' Dominica said and darted for the doorway - and it was true! There he was walking towards them - her spirit soared.

Chapter 44

New beginnings - circa AD 698

The rest surged through the doorway behind her. Dominica got to him first, but she couldn't help glancing beyond him, looking for Indract, Finn and the others. She could see instantly that he was tired, and maybe not fully well, but the tears in his eyes? Were they of relief, joy or sorrow? She stood close and took his hand, 'Dearest Brannon, I am *so* happy to see you! *So happy* to see you!'

Brannon was shaking his head and couldn't look her in the eye. He swallowed.

'What is it? Where are the others?' she said, squeezing his hand. The rest of the monks and nuns had caught up with her now but had stopped just a pace or two behind. She could feel them close and drew in a deep breath. 'Come brother, come in and take some drink after your journey,' she dropped his hand and turned to lead Brannon back to the refectory. As they approached Cormag, Godric and Matuid stepped away from the doorway, back into the building.

As Brannon and Dominica went to the front where the trio waited, everyone else followed into the refectory, even Avan, who stood by the door.

'Welcome home, Brother Brannon,' Cormag said, 'But where are our brothers who went with you?'

Brannon shook his head, glanced at Dominica, then looked at the floor. He took a deep breath, 'They are never coming home.'

'What?' Dominica gasped, turning to look him full in the face, 'What? They stayed?' Her only hope was that she was confused.

'They are - with the Lord.'

‘Dead?’ Cormag asked, his voice actually carrying a note of disbelief. ‘Killed? There was an audible gasp from the assembly.

‘Martyred!’ Brannon said, hearing again King Ina say they would be buried and honoured as martyrs.

‘No! *No! All of them?* How?’ Dominica felt sick.

‘I will tell you - just not now. I cannot just now,’ his voice cracked.

‘Indeed, not now, we were about to have a vote on ...’ began Godric.

‘No we won’t! How *dare* you!’ Dominica spat, distress pushing her, ‘What we need to do now is go and pray, to remember our dear brothers in Christ before God, not play petty games! *We* are going to the church – come sisters, come all you who would honour and remember our brothers ... martyred,’ and she strode from the refectory the tears already streaming down her face.

Immediately all who had known the pilgrim brothers followed her, and eventually all came into the church. Cormag, seeming chastened, opened with a simple prayer of thanksgiving for their lives, then joined the rest on their knees to pray in silence.

Time passed, the shuffling of monks preparing to stand brought Dominica back from the trance she had slipped into.

She had begun her prayers by holding each of the pilgrim brothers up before God, remembering all the good and joyous things she could about each of them, even Durragh. She found herself returning to those she knew best, her surprise apprentices in the ways of healing, Fergus and Kellagh. Teagan with his music and song-writing. Finn - oh! Finn. And Indract, her brother, the one person who knew about her vision and the healing she couldn’t explain, and in that – her protector. None of it made sense, martyred or not, surely their work wasn’t done?

Then she had just rested in prayer, rested in God, and into that space came an answer, of sorts - she was shown the same vision she had before they left Tamerunta, the hook in the river, the raised place shining - with Jesus standing there, the place she now knew as the 'old place' in the clearing by the river where they first landed, and she felt His command suffuse her mind, '*Make a place* ***here*** *for my brothers and sisters to do my work*'.

It seemed so right to her that she had to question herself whether this came from God or from her own wishes.

When she opened her eyes Prior Cormag was standing at the front again. As he led the closing prayer Dominica knew what she needed to do, but knew she must seek discernment from others before she made plans.

As it happened, Brother Brannon came to her, after he'd had something to eat and drink, saying he was in need of treatment. It was true he had some sores that needed treating - there were wounds on his legs that had not healed. Whilst she worked on his legs, cleaning the wounds of pus, washing them well and binding them with a honeyed poultice to draw out the infection, he quietly told her what had happened at Glestyngabyrig. He seemed to be able to speak about it as long as she didn't look at him or interrupt.

'Domca, I feel so bad. I crawled away into the marshland and did nothing to try to stop those devils killing my brothers,' he added finally.

'What could you have done? You were injured, you were but one, and the attackers,' she closed her eyes and swallowed, 'they were armed and trained. No, God wanted you alive to come and tell us what had happened. And maybe to tell King Ina. He must be a God-fearing king if he does as you say.'

'The pillars of light were God sent, and he saw them. He was the one who said they would all be found and buried as martyrs at the church at Glestyngabyrig. He took note, sister, of Indract's name as our leader.'

Brannon was about to leave, to go back to the monks' area when Dominica stopped him. 'Brannon, if I said I had a vision given to me, that we should set up another monastery close to here, a dual monastery, what would you think?'

'When you say a vision, do you mean like Indract had to come here?'

'Please, believe me now, Indract said that vision was his, with my blessing, as it made it easier. Yet, that was *my* vision shared with him. Earlier, just as you arrived, our monastery here was on the brink of banishing our nuns to a distant part of Tamerkam - a vote had just been called for.'

'Oh? So that was what that new brother was on about? Surely not?'

'Indeed, yes, and that *new brother* is in Indract's place as prior here! But, tell me, what do you think about this vision? No!' She closed her eyes momentarily, 'No - not what do *you* think. Please, pray overnight to see if the Lord affirms this with you - or not. And, if you are able, share this vision with those monks you know well and are true to the mission here as we set it up - and ask them to pray for discernment too. Go, rest now, dear Brannon, and please come back to me to have your dressing changed tomorrow morning.'

Later that evening she called Aylwyn and Esselt together, led the prayers for Compline and then explained her vision, explained even how it was that she and Indract came to Tamerkam in the first place, where exactly she'd felt drawn to actually set foot upon the ground first. She set them to pray for the gift of discernment, to see if she was being led astray or being guided by the Lord, and they all retired for the night.

The next day Dominica was anxious to see Brannon and hear his answer. As for herself, she knew the same vision had run through her dreams that night.

The sisters gathered for morning prayers, and both believed that the Lord was calling them to follow the vision. Dominica was so elated she could hardly bear to wait for Brannon to come at midday.

After prayers, she saw the few who were waiting at the healer's hut and then she told Avan that she would be back soon if anyone was needing her and set off for the clearing by the river.

Nodding to the lookout she went across the stepping stones, glad the tide was low, and up the shallow hill that would lead her through the woodland and over to the clearing. Once there she turned in the sunlight, holding her hands up to the Lord. She prayed and cried, for Indract and all the pilgrim brothers. With no one to hear her she howled at God, questioned, doubted, let the pain run through her ... and ultimately accepted that what had happened could never be changed. Exhausted at last she slumped to the ground - and felt - reached out - for the vision again. And it was there, she could feel the energy in this place, this holy place. Yet, it was so close to the original mission, could it be done?

Midday came, and went, the sun definitely past its highest point. She was beginning to feel concerned - and then Brannon came. He was solemn as he walked towards the healer's hut where she had been waiting. He saw her and gave a small wave, 'Sister,' he called, 'I have come as you said, to renew my bandage.'

'Come in, brother.'

She began to remove the dressing and poultice but couldn't wait, 'How went your answers to prayer about the vision?'

'Mine, sister, was that God speaks to you, and you should be guided by that.'

'And others?'

'Mixed. Yowann, certainly, and the few he pointed me to, but I spoke with some I knew here while they were still novitiates, and they have been much swayed by preaching from Prior Godric and do think that even nuns are a distraction.'

Dominica was silent - and still - for a moment of two, holding the poultice poised on her hand, staring at it. 'Yet Yowann and those he named, do they believe it is a vision from God.'

'Yes, they saw it as a way God would work.'

'Thank you Brannon. It was the same with us all.' She turned the poultice onto his leg and began to wrap it into place.

'Then the Lord be praised!'

'Amen, to that! Yet there is a long way to go. If only we could find an abbot or abbess who would be our sponsor, send us an ordained monk for the Eucharist and the great holy days, then we needn't be dependent on Cormag or Godric.'

'Hmm! I didn't say so before, too much else to say, but on my way here I stayed at a monastery just a day's ride away. It is more than twice the size of ours, on the edge of the moorland and overlooking the Tafvi where it is younger and shallower than it is by Tamerunta. It has an abbot and is similar to our monastery in its practices. It was set up by Saint Rumon who, they say, studied in Eriu around the time of Columbanus. Maybe they would help?'

'Oh! Brannon! Thank you! I see God has been making the way smooth before us! When you are recovered, and if we know a new mission is a possibility, would you return to them and ask for us?'

'Certainly, sister,' he said with a smile.

'And now brother, come every two days to have the dressing changed, and in the meantime pray that our kind benefactors in this place will be moved to supply our new mission too. I must go and tell them the news about Indract and the pilgrim brothers, pray it does not shake their faith, as well it might.'

That evening Dominica spent time in prayer and then headed up the hill towards Tamerkam's stronghold to find Cador and Keynae. Cador was crossing the space as she crested the slope and the meeting house came into view. He swerved to meet her. 'Sister Dominica - we hear rumours?'

Suddenly she found it hard to form a word in her mouth. Instead she felt her face crumple and tears start up, 'Indract and ...' she began, her voice giving over to sobs.

Cador drew her into his arms. 'Shhushh ... come, come to Keynae,' turning her and helping her move towards their home. Keynae appeared, saw them and rushed to Dominica's side, sliding her arm around Dominica's waist as they entered the house.

A cup of mead was placed in Dominica's hand, and she sipped it, glad of something to give her time to restore her equilibrium.

'We heard only Brother Brannon has come back? That the others, all of them, were killed?' Cador said.

Keynae glared at him, 'Give her a chance!' He looked abashed.

'Martyred.' Dominica said, 'Brannon says the King in Wessex says they will be buried at a church there as martyrs.'

'It's unbelievable that they went all the way to Rome and then were murdered back on this isle.'

Dominica nodded, she had no words.

'What about your mission? What will happen there now?' Cador mused.

'Prior Godric will most probably stay in place.'

'That man!' Keynae spat.

'That doesn't seem right. Won't it need another vote?' Cador sounded aggrieved.

'No, it was until Indract came back. He won't be coming back now! I'm sure Prior Cormag will ensure that nothing changes.'

'That man!' Keynae said again.

'Cador, I have a question for you? Just before Brother Brannon returned the mission was about to vote to send the nuns and the healer's hut to a different area in Tamerkam, to move us out of the mission and well away from the monks.'

'Where to? No one has spoken to me!'

'I supposed they would once they had voted to put us out.'

'Oh really? Who do they think they are?' Cador rose to his feet, turned right round and looked back at Dominica, 'We made a huge donation of land already to your mission - and now they want more?'

Dominica's heart sank, she wondered if she dare ask for the 'old place' by the river now.

Chapter 45

A Holy Place - circa AD 698

Sending an arrow prayer Dominica drew a deep breath. 'I know and I understand. I remember how blessed we were by your welcome and your generosity. I fear that those that rule the mission now do not understand, indeed, do not even understand that we are part of the Tamerkam community, and they would see themselves cut off and separated. Cador, I have a huge request to make of you.'

Cador sat again and looked at Dominica closely.

'What is it?' Keynae said quietly.

'I received a vision. I have spoken only with the nuns, Brother Brannon and a few of the older monks, and they have seen God's hand in this,' she paused. Cador and Keynae looked at her, Cador tipped both hands up, a question in itself. 'In this vision I am in a coracle arriving here, as if for the first time, and Jesus is standing in a space of shining light on a raised bank, right where Drustan found us that first time.'

'In the old people's place?' Keynae asked.

Dominica nodded, 'In the old people's place, yes. This vision is almost the same as the one I, we, had before we came from Tamerunta that very first time - but with this difference - this time Jesus spoke, saying - make a place *here* for my brothers and sisters to do my work - and this time - I was alone in the coracle.'

Silence. Cador looked at Keynae, who looked back at him. 'Here? At Tamerkam or at the old people place?' Keynae asked looking back to Dominica.

'The old people's place, I am sure.'

'Who would rule this new monastery?'

'It is always the rule that the brothers and sisters choose their own prior, by a secret vote, so I cannot say.'

'Yet it *could* be you? They voted for you before,' Cador said.

'It could.'

'Huh! But they'd overrule again, put their man in place instead,' Keynae sniped.

'Unless, unless we could be under the care of a different monastery, one which would not interfere,' Dominica suggested.

'You have an idea!' Keynae said with a smile.

'God granted Brother Brannon a stay in a larger monastery a day's ride from here which may be amenable - we do not know but I pray Brother Brannon will find it so - he has promised to return there.'

'Sister Dominica, you have never failed us, and your healing skills and teaching are welcome,' Cador said, then looked hard at her, 'Do those leading the monastery now, know what conditions were set when the land was granted? For as long as they served the community, in healing, teaching and prayer?'

'I don't know. I don't know if Prior Cormag recalls or if he told Prior Godric about that at all,' wondering what Cador was thinking.

He smiled, 'Let us know if they try to have this vote to remove the nuns and the healer's hut from the monastery again and I will speak to our elders. I cannot grant land without their backing. Leave it with me.'

Dominica returned to her healer's hut and continued with her work, yet all the time she held both an ache of loss, and a prayer for the future in her heart, each ready to surface whenever her mind was not working on some problem or other.

*

Within a few days it was announced that another meeting to discuss the removal of the healer's hut from the monastery was set for the following Monday, the tides being right for Prior Cormag to be with them again at nones. Dominica had not yet heard anything from Cador, nor had Brannon been able to ride out to Saint Rumon's monastery.

On her way out to visit Bo Barr Dominica sought out Keynae to see if she had any news and to tell her of the meeting coming up. Keynae welcomed her, and said that the news she brought was just what Cador was waiting to know, and she did so with a smile, but would say no more.

**

The days until Monday passed both slowly and swiftly, and there they all were again. Cormag and Godric at the front, Dominica and the sisters at the far left and the brothers central and right.

Cormag concluded the prayer then said, 'Brothers, we are met again to decide the way forward for our monastery. Alas we now know that our pilgrim brothers are with the Lord, and yet this means we are those who will make this decision today, for once, and for all.'

Dominica caught a flicker of something out of the corner of her eye, a shadow by the door. She turned her head slowly a fraction and realised it was Cador, just outside the doorway, hidden to any but those on the far left. He saw her and stepped further away around the curve.

She focused back on Cormag. He was outlining the proposal again; the healer's hut should be well away from the monastery, so there was no need for outsiders, especially women, to come into the sacred area set aside for prayer and solitude. And to keep the nuns safe, their part of the monastery would re-locate to the same place as the healer's hut.

'For the vote, in favour of the proposal you will use the white stone, against this proposal will be the black stone,' he concluded

'Prior, may I ask a question before we put this to the vote?'

'Only if it is pertinent!'

'I believe it is, Prior. Where will you move the nuns to? Sorry, I mean the healer's hut - and the nuns?'

'That has yet to be decided.'

'So can we presume it will be close, situated on the land we have here?'

Cormag looked annoyed. Godric stepped in, 'That would be too close sister. We thought at Bo Barr or Bo Etherick, you already spend a good deal of time at both.'

'So this will mean we could no longer be a dual monastery, we would be separate entities.'

'Indeed, but under our rule. You would need to have communion sister, you would not want to be without,' Godric added.

'Enough! White for the proposal, black against. Everyone outside,' Cormag ordered.

As they left Dominica cast round looking for Cador. She had expected him to step in and tell them they were going against the agreement - or maybe stop the voting.

One by one they stepped back through the door to drop their stone into the narrow-necked pot. When the last had done so the pot was brought out and carefully tipped out into a wide flat bowl. That there were more white than black could be seen in an instant. Yet Godric had Matuid count out the number of each. Six were black stones, that meant at least four men were with them, Brannon, Yowann and two others, yet they had lost the vote.

Cormag and Godric looked pleased. 'The vote is for the proposal,' Cormag announced, 'we shall make the preparations. Return to your labours, and may God go with you.'

Dominica could not respond with the Amen, just turned and went towards the healer's hut, with Aylwyn and Esselt following her. Avan met them at the door, her face questioning.

'We lost the vote,' Dominica said.

‘It is unfair that that I could not have a vote too,’ Esselt added, ‘I will be a nun in this place so soon.’

‘Sweet Esselt, until your final vows no-one can be sure of that, no matter how certain you are. They took the vote by the rules.’ Dominica turned to Avan, ‘If anyone comes needing healing you are unable to provide, come for me, I will be in the church. Sisters, continue to do God's work as has been set for this day. We will meet again at vespers.’

***

Days passed. Dominica followed her usual pattern of visiting Bo Barr and Bo Etherick, teaching Aylwyn and Esselt in bible studies and writing, as well as their religious observances, and Avan and Merewin in healing, herbs, reading and writing,.

About seven days after the vote Dominica heard from Brannon, who ostensibly came to have his sores checked for the last time as they were just about healed, that Godric was going to go to see Cador that day. Dominica sent an arrow prayer that Cador had a plan.

Later that day Keynae came to the healer’s hut. Dominica, Avan and Merewin were stringing herbs to dry.

‘Keynae! How good to see you - I hope you are well and not in need of healing?’

‘I am well sister, thank God, but I would speak with you,’ she raised her eyebrows and looked towards the two girls.

‘Avan, Merewin, please take the herb basket and see if you can find some navel-wort leaves of the right size to tie over a newborn’s birth cord, then set them out to dry.’

As the girls went off Dominica looked at Keynae.

Keynae smiled, ‘I have news for you!’

‘Then maybe we should walk too. Who knows what someone just outside the healer's hut could overhear?’ Dominica said with a smile.

‘Good idea - let’s head up to Bo Etherick.’

Once they were away from the monastery, Keynae began to tell Dominica what had happened when Godric had gone to see Cador.

'That man is arrogant! He seemed to think that Cador could be summoned to see him when he arrived - with no notice! I told him that Cador was away from the stronghold. Unfortunately Cador came home just after he arrived and so the man wasn't kept waiting as long as I would have liked,' she laughed, 'but Cador was all calm and pleasant. Sister, we had discussed and made a plan, but even I was surprised by Cador's hospitality. He offered drink and my honey-cakes, sat the man down in the sunshine and waited to hear why he had come - as if we didn't know already! Having served them I sat myself inside the hut where I could hear everything.'

'What was his plan, for we know nothing more than he would have us at one of the Bos.'

'It seems Godric had been walking the area and had decided a good place would be part way *between* the two Bos. He told Cador - There is a flattish area on top of the hill between the two settlements. It has a spring not far from the track and it is only grazed, as far as I can see - and so he saw no reason why Cador would not grant it to them for the healer's hut and nunnery beside it.'

'So, not *near any* of your settlements and a great distance from the main settlement at Tamerkam itself?'

'Far away from the monks! Oh sister, what on earth do you do to trouble these men so?' Keynae laughed, then turned serious again, 'Cador thought exactly as you did - we would be losing our healing centre - and they would be breaking their condition on having the land.'

'So? What did he tell Godric?'

They stopped speaking for a while as they passed a couple walking down towards Tamerkam.

'He said, as he understood it the monks wished to become more secluded, to concentrate on prayer without any contact with the community, was this so? Godric said, yes, that was the purpose of a monastery and that this one had gone astray. So Cador asked about the teaching to read and write that had been offered the community, which some have had up to now. Godric said that was to be reserved only for those training to be monks, but that any called could take that path. So Cador asked what about those who were sick? And he said, the healer's hut would still be available for them, and the nuns would run it, but now the sick would not have to come into the monastery grounds. So Cador asked about the services in the church, and he said that only the monks, and the nuns on holy days, would use the church in the future, as this would keep the monastery apart.'

'I am not surprised. I do not know where Godric came from, but I think it nothing like the monastery we left in Eriu.'

'It was then Cador said in such a serious voice, I see. You do know that this will break the agreement, and that this will mean the monastery shall have to go, leave Tamerkam altogether? Godric asked, What agreement? and Cador replied, Perhaps you should ask Prior Cormag, or maybe he has forgotten? In any case, I shall tell you. The land is forfeit if the monastery does not bring to the community of Tamerkam teaching to read and write for those *we* think need it, teaching of the Lord, prayer and communion with the church, and healing to those who are sick. You have just told me you are to break all of these. At which Godric stammered out, Not true! If there are sick, the nuns will look after them. Then Cador added quietly - but they would not be here - where the land for that was granted. If the nuns move they will have to be separated from you. I would not accept them set up in a new place if they were still part of a monastery that broke an agreement with me. And *if* they move *I* will choose their place and *I* will grant them their living, for this land is Tamerkam. He must have been planning what to say since we worked out the plan as he kept himself so serious and calm, more like my father used to be. But your Godric he...'

'Not *my* Godric!' Dominica said with a sharp laugh.

Keynae laughed back, 'Well *that man* added - And, and, if men want to become monks, they will learn to read and write as novices - whereupon Cador said, Not good enough! My son has no vocation, yet he has learnt to read and write here, not even as a lay brother as they insist at Tamerunta. Brother Finnachta taught him and two others together. This is what was agreed. Godric didn't give up. You know what he said next? You won't credit it! He said, There is still a place of prayer - and communion can be arranged. Cador was silent, and I also wondered what the prior meant, then Cador says, What church is that in? And that man had to say it wasn't *in* a church, as such, and that he meant the place at Bo Barr, where Brother Matuid takes a service of a Sunday. Cador laughed in his face at that - more like the Cador I know - he says, Do you mean where Sister Dominica used to lead a service with many people joining her, and now your Matuid speaks to but three. This does not count. As far as I am concerned, if you do as you plan you will forfeit the land the monastery is founded on by breaking the agreement made before God.'

'Did he leave then?'

'No, I think he must have stood up, because Cador told him to sit down and listen. He said, I will grant land at the old people's place by the river, but it is not more land for the monastery - this is for a new monastery, the healer's hut and those who would work to serve the community of Tamerkam. If the monastery wanted to stay but did not want the community within its boundary, it would have to give recompense to cover the services it was not providing to the community. That would be a share of all produce, set by me, and my steward there will be the one who arranges the payment. Take that idea and see if your brothers like what you have brought them to. Then Godric did go, without saying another word. I caught sight of him stomping off as he crossed the open doorway.'

'It sounds very clever - well planned. I hope it works, that we are able to become a dual monastery of our own. Either that or we return to normal.'

'Which would you prefer sister?'

'Truth be told, one of our own. Now Indract is gone I see the way of life in this monastery as changing so much from what was intended, from an active life serving God and those we live amongst, to a cloistered life of praise and prayer. I understand the Lord's command as to go and help, not just to pray and praise, to be his hands in this world until he comes again.'

'Amen to that,' Keynae said, wondering at the light in Dominica's eyes when she spoke of their work this way. 'And you think that there is the possibility that an abbot at another monastery would take yours under its wing?'

'I pray it would be so, I do.'

Chapter 46
The Fruit of Defiance - *circa AD 698*

The next day Dominica learnt that Godric had taken the first tide down to Tamerunta. She had a good idea why. While out collecting herbs she managed to find herself walking close to where Yowann was working. 'Brother Yowann, has the Prior said anything about a meeting with Cador?' she asked, almost in passing.

Yowann, not looking at her, replied, 'Nothing, but I can tell you our Prior is not a happy man,' he looked up and smiled briefly. Dominica continued on her way. So Godric has not spoken to the other monks yet then. It all rests on Cormag, and even now I do not understand his mind.

She also managed a word or two with Brannon about the possibility of getting to the other monastery.

'Domca, I'm sorry. I doubt there is any way I can go there now. When I promised I had no idea how things have changed here. There is no way I'd be given permission to leave the monastery, let alone the area of Tamerkam,' he gave a short laugh, 'especially on the monastery's pony! Have you not noticed that we monks are rarely seen outside our perimeter now? We are admonished to stay close and not to speak with, or even look at, the common folk - even the men.'

It was only when he mentioned it she realised that what he said was true. The monks rarely left the rath or the fields that surrounded the monastery, and those were all bordered by track. banks or water. Whereas before they could be seen helping in the Tamerkam fields at harvest, or gathering tall rushes from beyond the old people's place up river. Subtle, but quite a change in such a short time. *Yet I felt sure that Brannon's contact with the other monastery was God's work - was I mistaken?*

*

Two days later Godric returned, and with him came Cormag. It wasn't long before they summoned Dominica to meet with them in the church. Dominica found them standing before the Altar, waiting for her. As she walked towards them she thought how their great church was so rarely full any more, no-one except the monks to share the glory of God. Today the dimness in the church seemed to create an atmosphere of foreboding, rather than quiet and calm, the two of them, standing with their cowls up and their hands clasped, seemed threatening already.

'Prior Cormag,' she nodded a bow towards Cormag, 'Prior Godric,' she nodded towards Godric. *I'll give them nothing for free to beat me with.* 'How may I be of service?'

'Sister, I am told you have been of great disservice to our Lord and to this monastery,' Cormag began.

'Prior, I have no idea what you are talking about.'

'You poured tales into the ears of the local chief about our mission here and turned him against this holy monastery,' accused Godric.

'When you should not even be talking to men, especially those outside of holy orders,' Cormag added.

'I am obliged by my calling as healer to speak with men, while there are no male healers at our mission, for this place was first made as a mission as much as a monastery, and I have *not* told chief Cador anything of your plans - *you did.* His wife told me he came to speak with someone at the monastery but finding us all in the refectory he waited outside for our meeting to finish. He could not but overhear what you both said.'

'You must have said something to him - he seems to want to give you a monastery of your own!' Godric's pale eyes were bulging.

'No, I spoke with his wife *when she asked me,* and I said, as I have said to you,' looking at Godric, 'this monastery was set up as a dual monastery, to use the strengths of all to the good of all, and as an active monastery, bringing God, education and healing to the community we are part of. This is how we were meant to be here in Tamerkam. This was the vision that God gave, that Indract and I shared,' she finished more breathless than she expected to be.

'See!' Godric said to Cormag, 'She foments the locals against us.'

Cormag was studying Dominica, she was - vibrant? Ecstatic? 'So you didn't ask to be set up as head of your own monastery?'

'No! On the contrary, I told her, that is a position voted for by the members of a monastery.'

'Tell me, sister, would you have all those who follow you in this folly be cut off from the sacrament and from God? Will you have them all excommunicated with you?' Godric snapped.

Dominica sighed, 'Will you send a messenger to Drom-Mhor to have this excommunication declared? If you do, be sure to tell our great uncle the Abbot that Indract is martyred, that I still survive, so he may tell his nephew, our father, the King. And tell him that I would raise a new monastery in the way of Drom-Mhor, in Indract's name.' *Oh! Where did that come from? Ah! Is that it Lord? A monastery in Indract's name?*

Godric looked at Cormag, his face a picture of puzzlement.

Cormag snorted, 'She speaks the truth. We are under the rule of the abbey at Drom-Mhor - in Eriu.'

'Then never mind the excommunication. No one would join a monastery without the blessing of the Eucharist, and who would give you that? Eh? Not us, not if you leave our monastery,' Godric blustered on.

Cormag glared at him, then looked back at Dominica. 'Sister, Prior Godric has a point.'

'If this is what the Lord has ordained, the Lord will provide,' Dominica said, barely knowing where the words came from even as they came out of her mouth.

Dominica left the meeting both shaken and heartened. She had been surprised by the vehemence shown by Godric, more maybe by the fact he let it show so much, when usually he presented as a model of contained certainty in his dealings with the brothers. His certainty, his assumed knowledge of all things monastic, swayed many of the brothers who had known no other place than Tamerkam or Tamerunta - the suggestion being they knew nothing, yet he had experience and so knew much.

She was heartened by the word of the Lord speaking through her, without her will, without her knowing before the words emerged. Surely the new mission would be blessed if the Lord had named it for Indract, as a martyr. She also thought that maybe the idea to separate the nuns and the healer's hut from the monastery may have been dealt a mortal wound. She could tell Cormag was not as wedded to the idea as Godric, and it would take both of them to make it happen. Maybe Cador's conditions for the separation and the loss of the education and services was too high a price for them to push forward. She didn't know what to pray for most, her vision, or the monastery and community relationship restored. The first seemed almost unattainable, the second desirable.

**

All went quiet. There was no talk of sending the healer's hut or the nuns away. Yet there was also no talk of admitting any to learn to read or write, but that may have been because the few who were thought suited to it had already had their lessons. The next test of the community relationship would not come until after harvest, when in previous years the church had welcomed in many to thank the Lord for a good harvest.

When harvest came Dominica noticed that the monks were all working their own fields, and none left to help with the community harvest. As this had not been a commitment, beyond the first few years as they became self-sufficient, it seemed to go without comment from Keynae or Cador.

Prior Godric was clever. He sent word to Cador early that he would bring a service of thanksgiving to the community up at the stronghold of Tamerkam, himself. Cador welcomed this, saying everyone from the wider community would be invited.

On the appointed day in late September Prior Godric set off up the hill, accompanied only by Matuid. No other monks were permitted to accompany him, and certainly no nuns.

***

Early in the following week Keynae happened to be at Bo Barr when Dominica took some herbs to Eiliwedd, and met her at the healer's hut there.

'Keynae, how lovely to see you, I didn't expect to see you here.'

'It is no coincidence. Eiliwedd told me that you were expected.'

Dominica looked at her quizzically, 'And?'

'And I feel that I would be both unwelcome coming into your healer's hut when not actually sick, and that if I did it could cause a problem for you, that the Prior would hear of it and want to know why I was there - talking to you alone.'

'Why? Why do you think this is a problem?'

'Oh! Prior Godric stayed just long enough after his dour harvest service to lay down some strict lines. One, only if a person was really sick, ill enough to need special care, should they go to the healer's hut. No more for minor things. Aches, pains and superficial wounds should be dealt with at home, they were not something to trouble the monastery with.'

'That's ridiculous!'

'That's not all he said, two!' she held up two fingers, 'That no women were to come for healing without a senior male family member, preferably the head of the house, accompanying them.'

'What is the man playing at?'

'I do not know! He says this is so that the women would be kept under control and would not wander where they might lead monks astray.'

'I see! So he is trying to split us up again? What does Cador say?'

'So far he doesn't see it as a breach of the agreement. He says, it is annoying, that a man must leave his work to accompany his wife or daughter, but the healing is still available and the healer's hut has not moved.'

'But - not coming unless it is serious. Those are the words of someone who does not understand healing - you know that aches, pains and small wounds can be just the start of things that can be too serious to cure by the time the person is deemed really ill!'

'I do! So you see why I came to you here.'

'Bless you for coming to let me know this Keynae. I knew nothing of this. I had hoped he'd given up. After the two priors confronted me, back shortly after Cador had told them his conditions for the monastery to remain, they have gone very quiet.'

****

About two weeks later Drustan arrived at the healer's hut, apparently in a hurry.

'Sister,' he said, ducking in and looking round. Seeming satisfied, he added, 'I have a message for you,' and flashed a quick smile.

'What is it? Is someone hurt?' she asked, though not understanding his smile or his looking round.

'Ma just said to come quickly. There is a visitor who needs to speak with you.' *So he was checking that no-one else was in here.*

'So no-one is hurt? I don't need my healers' scrip?'

'Not unless you think it will look like a good excuse to suddenly go up the hill?' he said, with another flashed grin.

Within a few moments they were heading out and up towards the stronghold, Drustan walking fast, the scrip over Dominica's shoulder.

As they came near the chief's house Drustan said, 'They are indoors. Ma is with them,' and he veered off. Dominica walked the last piece to the hut, the door flap was hooked back open.

She called, 'A blessing on this house,' as she arrived, and Keynae came to greet her.

It took a moment to accustom herself to the gloom, but she soon saw a mature man dressed in monastic garb sitting with Cador. He stood.

'Sister Dominica, I understand? I am Abbot Kenver of Saint Rumon's on Tafvi. I have heard of you.'

Dominica, for a moment, opened her mouth but found no words to fill it, then shook herself, 'I *am* Sister Dominica and, from Brother Brannon, I have heard of you too, Father.'

Chapter 47

***St. Rumon's** - circa AD 698*

'Sister, as you will know Brother Brannon was sick with a fever for a few days when he came to us. What had happened to him, to his brothers, and his journey had exhausted him. Simply rest, sustenance and time healed him. So it was that he spoke with those in the infirmary while there, and told us much about your healing experience and how God works through you.'

'Father, he may have exaggerated my skills.'

'He told us he had known you since you were a child, learning herb lore with a wise-woman and that afterwards you were trained at the monastery in healing. He told us of the healing of your own brother when all had given up on him. Were these exaggerations?'

'Brother Brannon was my milk-brother after my mother died, so yes, we have known each other forever. And yes, my brother was healed. I was told that the monks in the infirmary had said they knew he would die, and so I tried to help.'

'Then what he said is true. He also told us of the plague here and how so many survived. Chiefman Cador has confirmed this for me already. I have come myself to ask for your help, as when I called for one of our monks to be my emissary, God told me to go myself. So here I am. We have need of your healing skills at our monastery - right now.'

Alarmed Dominica glanced at Cador, then addressed the Abbot, 'Father, are you sure you have not brought the plague with you?'

'Sister, we do not think it the plague, but some other ailment that attacks our people. It oppresses their breathing, fills them with green bile and has claimed three brothers already. And, through aforethought by my infirmarer, I have been excluded from the presence of anyone who has the signs. Maybe another reason God sent me.'

'I am not sure I recognise this ailment, Father, but if God has sent you, who am I to refuse?' praying it wasn't the same condition that had taken Nuala from her, 'If I am given permission to leave with you, I will come. Come down to the monastery with me and make your request to our Prior.'

As they entered the monastery Dominica saw Matuid, 'Brother Matuid! Can you tell us where we might find the Prior?'

Matuid stared a moment at the two of them then pointed to the newly built Prior's house.

The door was hooked open and Dominica called softly, 'Prior Godric?'

The Prior's voice preceded him, 'What now?' He appeared at the door scowling into the light.

'Prior, Abbot Kenver has come and wishes to speak with you.'

'Abbot Kenver?' Godric frowned, and turned towards him, 'Ah, we meet again.'

'And you a Prior now?' Kenver left a small silence, 'We, at Saint Rumon's, have a request, that you allow your healer to come to help us - for a time.'

'Ah! I do not know if I can do that,' Godric said with a quick glance at Dominica. 'We are in need of Sister Dominica's services here. She is the only one hereabouts that can minister healing to our monks. You understand, the other healers are women, but not nuns. There were other more suitable healers, monks, but they, unfortunately, died whilst on pilgrimage.'

'I know all about them. Brother Brannon told us when *we cared for him.*' Kenver said, '*Prior* Godric, brothers are dying now - and it maybe that your Sister Dominica can help - I know no other reason why God should have instructed me, me - myself, to come here to find her.'

Godric looked at the ground. Dominica wondered what it was that he was hiding. He looked up, 'I will grant it. Sister, prepare Sister Aylwyn to preside in the women's house, and then you may leave. Do not stay longer than absolutely necessary and take care not to bring this ailment back with you.'

They set off the next morning. The Abbot had brought with him a second pony for Dominica to ride and to carry her bags of herbs and potions. *Faith in action*, Dominica thought.

They took the way towards Saint Rumon's with the ponies at an amble, as fast as was sensible on this track. At one point they came to a stretch where it was wide enough to give them the chance to ride side by side, so Dominica hurried her pony forward.

'Father, may we speak?'

'Yes, sister.'

'I gather you already knew our Prior?'

'Ah! I thought you would speak more of the ailment?'

'No, you told me as much as would help me be prepared yesterday afternoon. I confess to being curious.' Abbot Kenver was silent, and Dominica worried she had overstepped the mark, that this question, just to sate her curiosity, broke the rules.

'Huh!' Kenver then drew breath, 'Brother Godric came to our monastery on his journeying. He said he was an ordained monk authorised by his Abbey to preach wherever he went. His preaching was not to our taste.'

'I see.

'Do you sister? He comes from the east of this isle, from an area called Cent. The monasteries there are different, secluded places for men who would not engage with the world at all. That they have sent him out into the world is extraordinary. From what I understand, from your Brother

Brannon, you come from a monastery that engaged in good works with the people, alongside the prayer and praise due our loving Father in heaven.'

'Indeed, father. And, though we nuns only hear his holy-days preaching, which is dictated by the day, I understand his preaching to the brothers each and every day is of seclusion.' *Should I tell him of my vision? Should I ask?*

'I am not surprised. I *am* surprised he has been elected as prior where you are though. How did this come to be? He had to be voted in I presume?'

'I can tell you, father. Though please do not think the worse of me for telling what happened, for you asked how he came to be our prior.'

Dominica told Abbot Kenver of how the vote had been made at Tamerkam, and how it had been overturned. He listened and only once asked a question.

'This Prior Cormag? He supports Prior Godric?'

'He does, though I think he alone would not go for the total seclusion.'

'And you wish to start your own monastery, dual monastery, in Tamerkam?'

Dominica found herself pulling her pony up, it stopped, Kenver's ambled on, then he too stopped. He turned to look back at her, 'Come on! Cador told me of this while his son went to get you. It seems you had even thought of asking me if our monastery would sponsor your new one and oblige with the sacrament when necessary.'

Dominica urged her pony forward, 'Abbot Kenver,' she bit her lip and took a deep breath. 'Yes, you see I received a vision earlier this year. Not the first I have had. My brother had a vision to go on a peregrination and that I should be with him. Yet even before we had arrived where God had sent us, Tamerunta, I received a vision to set up a second monastery - at Tamerkam. And the Lord went before us making our path easy there. Of late I have had another vision, similar to the first, but this new vision set the place of the monastery somewhere aside from the monastery now. It is to be a dual monastery, an active monastery and, now I know it is also to be in Indract's name as Martyr. She smiled, 'And what you say is true, I had hoped at first that Brother Brannon would be able to go back and speak with you - but the monks are barely allowed to leave the monastery now, let alone the area.'

'And so God, instead, sent me to you,' Kenver said in hushed tones. They resumed riding, the path narrowed and they were both left to their own thoughts.

They arrived in the late afternoon, and as soon as they arrived were brought drinks and food in the refectory. The infirmarer was called to speak with Dominica, and she asked that they meet outside. Kenver agreed and the three of them stood in the shade of a tree.

'Brother Tethion, as the Lord pleases, Sister Dominica has come to help us,' Kenver said.

'The Lord be praised. Sister, Brother Brannon told us of your skills. I am at a loss. I have met many ailments, but do not know this one and nothing I do seems to help.'

'Brother, I may not know it either, but together we can work for the best for the brothers. Come let us visit with them. Tell me, how do you think it passes between the brothers?'

'I am not sure. I thought it bad air as all those who suffer are from one dormitory, yet, of the monks who were helping me - both have taken sick too.'

'But not you brother?'

'The Lord be praised.'

Dominica wondered at the difference between his healthy helpers who had succumbed and the infirmarer. 'Have others replaced your helpers?'

'Indeed, for one cannot lift them alone. It takes both helpers to do that.'

They arrived at the infirmary, which was much like the one back in Drom-Mhor. The infirmarer went to open the door, but Dominica stopped and set her bags down.

'I have my ways with treating the sick, they are the ways that I learnt at Drom-Mhor, and that I used when the plague came to Tamerkam. May we have a large pot of hot water set up to boil out here, and also in the infirmary? I also would need a bowl to wash our hands in, out here.'

'I can arrange that,' he said and called into the hut. Two monks came out. Dominica looked at them, looking for signs of sickness. He gave his instructions.

When the water was boiling Dominica took out quantities of water mint, crushed it in her hands, dropped it in the boiling pot and added some ramsons powder and gave it a stir. She had a bench brought to act as a table and she dipped a small jug into the pot for some water to wash her hands when cool enough. Then she removed from her bag two masks and her apron, the one she had fashioned from nettle-linen to cover both her arms and the front of her habit, and deftly tied it on. She dipped a mask in the water and drew it out to drain over a stick, and then a second. When they cooled a little she gave them a squeeze and turned to the infirmarer. 'Do you have your own mask, brother?'

He shook his head. 'I - I. Sometimes I hold a cloth to my face if the stench is strong, to stop me breathing in the foul humours.'

'At Drom-Mhor I was taught to think it is more than just when you can smell the sickness, we think that sometimes the sickness is carried on the breath of the sick person, and so can be breathed in, or even on their sweat so we must cleanse our hands if we touch them or anything near them. These masks we tie on to leave our hands free, they're soaked in mint and garlic water, which seems to help, even more so if there is a stench as they are pleasant to the nose.'

The infirmarer washed his hands as Dominica had done and copied the way she tied the mask on. She thanked God for his willingness to listen.

'Follow me,' he said and led the way into the hut. It was dark inside and the coughing that she had heard from outside sounded so much worse. They came to the first bed. The infirmarer lit up the monk's face with his candle. The monk seemed quite young, the hair dark and thick, but his skin was so grey looking, his lips a little blue even and, as he lay on his side on the bed he hugged his chest as he convulsed in pain with each cough. A patch of greenish sputum was splattered across the sheet before his face. Dominica felt his brow with the back of her hand. It was clammy but burning hot.

They moved on. The next was obviously much older, and his condition seemed a lot worse too. The splatters of sputum here were streaked with dark red that were, Dominica thought, most likely blood. As they came to the next, Brother Tethion whispered, 'This brother was helping me until two days ago.' This man's breath came as gurgles, sending a shiver down Dominica's spine. 'As was the brother here,' he added as they stepped across the space to another bed and another brother struggling to breathe between wet coughs.

'Are there any more?'

'There were five more. Two seem to have recovered - mostly - they are over the other side. Three have gone to be with the Lord.'

'Thank you, let us go outside to speak.' As soon as they left Dominica went and dropped her mask into the boiling water and then washed her hands, and after a couple of minutes she drew the mask out to drain. She asked the infirmarer to do the same with his mask, noting he washed his hands after, as she had.

'Brother, I will make up a potion which, if the Lord pleases, may ease their condition. I think that steaming, with cleansing herbs in the water, may also aid their breathing and, maybe, make the coughing less painful. We may need larger pots or more of them in such a large space. This is the easy part. I will look to my herbals for something that will loosen the sputum, for by the noise of their breathing and the skin colour, those blue lips, I think it is drowning them, from the inside.'

'Sister,' he nodded,'I will get the new helpers to set up the fires and pots.'

'And, for the sake of the new helpers, send them to me first. I will give them masks too, and explain how it may help save them,' she gave a little smile to take the edge of her words. 'Oh, and Brother, the potion I shall make needs a cup of soured wine, if that can be found?'

Brother Tethion nodded and went without further comment, and Dominica felt relieved that here was a man who seemed to care more for those he treated than for his own importance.

She began to lay out ingredients for the potion she had used to counter the plague. Trader Joseph had said that it took away the fever and pain in his head and the aches of the body, so it would be good if it did that again here. When Brother Tethion's helpers arrived Dominica explained to them about the masks and the hand washing, and they just did as they were told, for which she was again grateful.

She next sought her herbal and discovered she needed a quantity of self-heal and of honey, the former she had, but only a little dried, and the latter she had not carried with her. When Brother Tethion returned, with a youngish boy carrying a stoppered jug of soured wine, she asked about some honey and, as she had expected, the monastery had plenty of that. She asked about the wild herb self-heal and whether he knew of somewhere close that it grew.

He looked a little puzzled and said he didn't know the plant - nor did he recognise it even when she described it. Dominica asked if the nearby village had a wise-woman, as she may know it. The infirmarer wrinkled his nose a little, but said there was a wise-woman, and he called a boy and sent him immediately to bring her to Dominica.

It was then she realised, here was a man who had learned from manuscripts, his talk of humours and bad air made more sense now. She knew of this teaching, from the ancients far away but, but having been taught by a wise-woman first and a learned woman next, she had a very different understanding in herb-lore and healing.

The boy brought the wise-woman to where Dominica had set up her bench.

'Sister,' Dominica said, 'Thank you for coming. I am Sister Dominica, from another monastery just a day's ride from here.'

'They call me Mother Cole, sister.'

'Please Mother, I have need of a herb. It grows wild around the monastery I am from, so I hope you can tell me where I may find it here? We call it self-heal. It grows low and spreading with many purple flower heads set tight around a square shaped stalk, and is good for healing wounds and bringing up the phlegm.'

Mother Cole was already nodding. 'Come with me sister, I can show you. Flowers will all be brown by now, mind.'

Chapter 48

Restored - *AD 698*

Once Dominica had collected the self-heal, with many thanks to Mother Cole, she boiled a new brew. This time with self-heal seeds and roots first crushed in a mortar with a little hot oil, then stirred into hot water and steeped for a spell, with the honey added and stirred in well as it was taken from the fire. She strained some off into a cup and as soon as it was cool enough to drink without scalding, she took it to the youngest monk first. The infirmary was warm and the air felt damp with the pots of mint and ramsons water boiling merrily.

One helper lifted the young monk and, as the other helper sat on the end of the bed, propped him up against the helper's back The cup was brought to his lips and he was encouraged to drink. The young monk's eyes closed as he swallowed. Then opened wide, he tipped his head up and opened his mouth for more. A couple more swallows and a paroxysm of coughing overtook him, Dominica bringing a cloth to his face to catch the sputum. Dominica noted the cough didn't look as painful as before, as he didn't clutch at his ribs.

'Does it feel good? A little easier to cough?' The monk nodded and looked to the cup again. When it was gone they laid the monk down again, and moved onto the next bed while Dominica brought in a different cup that had been cooling.

When she returned she noticed the young monk clutching at his ribs again as a new cough wracked his frame, though it sounded less harsh than before. Whilst they ministered to the old monk she thought about the idea that they were drowning from inside, and wondered if lying down flat was best or not. After they had helped all the others to take some of the honey and self-heal drink she went to the young monk again.

'Brother, can you tell me, is it easier to breathe sitting up or lying down?' He lay a moment without answering. 'Up, I think sister?' said as if he thought there was a right answer and he was hoping he knew it.

'Thank you, brother.'

The potion, which she called in her mind the plague potion but to others named it 'Sister Ciar's potion', was brewing. She gave it good long stir with its copper spoon yet again, leaving it standing in the pot, and wished it didn't take so long to brew. 'At least it will be ready to give them the first dose just after compline,' she said aloud to herself.

The helpers came again at that time, and they performed their trick of supporting the sick monks whilst Dominica gave each a dose of Sister Ciar's potion, and then the honeyed self-heal drink. It was very late by the time they left to go to their beds. Dominica had been given a place in the hospice house, but before she went to bed she put all the cloths they had used in a pot of hot water and fed the fire with small sticks until it boiled, then washed herself well and made her prayers before sleep.

By the morning an idea had formed. Maybe they could find a way to support the sick so they were sitting up more of the time? It would save the helpers from having such long close contact too. Maybe they could try it with the young monk, as he was strong enough to hold himself, and one of the two more recent sick to compare how they fared. She lay there in the creeping dawn wondering how it could be achieved. She recalled the frame of sticks that Brother Tighe had made for a cloth-tent to hold the steam in when Indract was so ill. Could a shape be made to hold a bag full of bedstraw upright, strong enough that they could lean back into, but be more upright? Was there a simpler way?

She shook herself and got up, determined to go and visit her charges first thing.

Brother Tethion was already there with the helpers. Dominica wished she'd not laid abed thinking so long.

'Good morning, brothers,' she said as she came to them.

Brother Tethion looked at her sombrely. 'Brother Finn died in the night.'

Dominica felt as if she had been struck. Her eyes closed, her hand flew to her chest. *Finn!* Eyes open, 'Oh no! But, brother you did not tell me who was who? Which monk was this?'

'The second from the door, our oldest monk here.'

And the sickest, 'It grieves me that he has died, though I fear his suffering had been too long and too great already.'

'You think that your treatment had nothing to do with it?'

'No, it could not! There is nothing in my treatment that could kill a man, even one so weakened.'

'What about the stuff that wise-woman showed you?'

'Mother Cole is a good wise-woman. She recognises the simple herbs that heal and how to apply them - it was definitely the one I asked for. She also told me she had never been called into the monastery before, that you have never spoken to her, ever.'

'She is a woman - and I have had no need to. I am an infirmarer with a higher learning. Why would I speak to her?'

'Yet you listen to me?'

'Sister, you are a nun, properly trained at a monastery.'

'Indeed.' Dominica understood now, 'Yet much of my most helpful training is the herb-lore that Mother Cole also knows,' she sighed. 'Brother Tethion, I have a thought, that if we can help those who remain to sit up, they may breathe easier. Can we bind something like a wicker hurdle to the end of the bed? Prop it up so it will not fall, and rest on it a palliasse filled with herbal bedstraw that they may lean back on?'

Brother Tethion looked at her a moment, then shrugged, 'You can try it. I'll find the lay brother than does this sort of thing for you.'

'Thank you, brother. And we will take the brothers their potions and drinks,' she smiled, and gave a little nod. He responded with a nod and turned away.

All of the remaining monks seemed to be, at least, no worse. The young monk accepted the potion and the cup of hot sweet liquid eagerly. The next two seemed to be bringing up sputum now. Dominica thought this both a good sign and a sign of the ailment's progression. She was glad the sputum was without blood spots, yet its thickness and green colour was repulsive. She explained to the helpers that each patient needed a cloth to cough into, one that may be taken away, washed and boiled before re-use, for she felt instinctively that the greenish globs could spread the contagion themselves.

The two on the other side of the infirmary, who were most recovered, looked a lot better. They were able to tell her that the steamy air was easier to breathe and the drinks soothed their coughs, and that, though their ribs still ached, the sharp pain was eased. Dominica thanked the willow-bark in the plague potion for dulling that pain.

The lay brother came, and Dominica tried to explain what she wanted. He left and returned quite quickly with other lay brothers carrying hurdles, already made for use in the fields, and some stout sticks and strips of hide. The hurdles were a bit big, but would do the job.

Dominica made them wear masks whilst they adapted the first bed, the young monk having been moved to the, now empty and stripped, bed beside him.

A palliasse, like a thin mattress, stuffed with herbal bedstraw, was folded and laid on the steeply sloping hurdle.

One of the lay brothers hopped on the bed and lay back on it, forcefully moving to make sure of its strength. Then the young monk was brought back to the bed and laid in it, leaning up, the cover pulled up to his shoulders. He smiled a little and nodded.

Dominica smiled too, 'Thank you brothers, can we do the same to these other beds now?'

The work did not take long once they set to, and after instructing them to wash in her bowl of boiled mint and garlic water, she thanked them - and it was time to give out the potion dose and the self-heal and honey drinks again.

Dominica also asked Brother Tethion to arrange for them to have a meat broth to take at least three times a day, as she was sure their strength needed building up. This was granted by Abbot Kenver immediately, but he still stayed away from the infirmary.

The night came and went, Dominica rose early and went to the infirmary. The monk on night duty was asleep on a bench just outside the infirmary. His task was to maintain the steaming pots overnight, and, whilst doing so, check all was well. Taking a rush light she lit it from the glowing embers under her wash-pot and stepped inside. The air was moist, but the fires had burnt down very low. She fed some small sticks into the embers and flames soon began to lick up the outside of the pot. She did the same to the others.

The movement must have woken the young monk as he was looking at her. 'How are you feeling today?' she asked, noticing that, though a little slumped to one side, he was still sitting up.

He took a breath with his hand on his chest, 'It does not feel like I have a demon sitting on my chest any more. That is a blessing.'

'You did not lie down?' she said, raising her rush-light to look across at the others, one of whom was half sat up, the other one having slipped down prone on the bed.

He wriggled himself more upright, 'No, sister. I slept like this. It was easier to breathe.' Dominica looked closely at him, went back and tied the door flap open and returned. She hadn't imagined it - his lips had lost the blue tinge. She hurried to the others, both of whom had wakened, hearing voices no doubt. The prone man struggled to pull himself up, but was caught by a wracking cough that had him pinned to the bed for as long as it took to subside, and a few moments longer to recover. The other just straightened himself on the palliasse.

'How did you sleep brother?' she asked him.

'Well enough. I woke and coughed many times, but I didn't feel so bad I couldn't sleep again.'

'And you brother?' she said, helping the monk move himself up the bed to rest on the palliasse and hurdle again.

'I don't know, I couldn't turn to be on my side,' he stopped and took a wheezing breath, 'ended up flat on the bed,' he shook his head, wheezed. 'Can't catch my breath,' he added, shaking his head.

'Thank you, I'll be back soon with the doses and the drink,' she said and went to the other side of the hut to see the nearly recovered monks, both of whom were doing well, though both still with a cough and an ache.

Each day they followed the same pattern. Inside the infirmary - doses, drinks, hot broth, the pots kept steaming, the sputum cloths changed, and the brothers moved each day, but supported up whenever possible, or walking around when able. Outside, the wash-pot always on the boil, the potions being made up, more herbs to be collected.

On the fourth day she had a chance to talk with Brother Tethion alone. It had been as if he'd been avoiding her since the death of Brother Finn. She needed to know something about the brothers who had died before; she wondered if they had all coughed up blood? Brother Tethion told her this was so, and they weakened as it increased - and that they had died shortly after.

She also talked Brother Tethion into coming with her to gather some of the herbs on the next day. While they were collecting she told him of her days as a child with Nuala, the wise-woman, as well as her time with Sister Ciar in the monastery herbarium at Drom-Mhor.

She showed him the herbs he could use easily and safely to relieve pain in the head or the limb, to treat upsets of the bowel or of the liver, to staunch bleeding, to bind onto sores, or wounds to draw out the pus and to help heal them. She promised him a copy of her herbal, as recipes written down obviously would carry more weight with him. She gently encouraged him to ask the wise-woman if he needed to know what any herb looked like or where it could be found near the monastery. She was excited to find great areas with the wound-moss growing, and collected a great quantity to dry for use back at Tamerkam, her enthusiasm sparking a kind of fervour in the infirmarer as he helped her gather it.

On the sixth day the young monk met her as she came in. He was up and walking around. His colour was good and his chest, when she put her ear to it, had no wheeze she could hear, and he said there was no tightness or pain.

She went to the other two men, one was sitting up on the edge of his bed, but seemed brighter than even the day before. The other lay up his hurdle, but spoke clearly and the talking did not trigger the cough. Dominica smiled. Whatever this ailment was, if the treatment was given early enough, before the bloody sputum, it looked like it really helped heal.

On the seventh day Abbot Kenver came to the infirmary to hear how well the patients were doing. Brother Tethion brought out the young monk, the first helper and the two who were already recovering before Dominica arrived, and explained that it was hard to know the difference between them, that the potions and methods that sister Dominica had used had made the more recently sick better so much faster. The only one left inside the infirmary was not far behind but, because he still had the cough, they felt it better to keep him away from the Abbot as yet. Abbot Kenver thanked him, smiled and nodded a bow at Sister Dominica and, aloud, thanked God for their recoveries.

Abbot Kenver led a service of thanksgiving and afterwards told Dominica that he, himself, would be her escort back to Tamerkam the next day. Dominica made her farewells to Brother Tethion, 'And I promise you a copy of the herbal as soon as I can have made,' she said, sure she would have to arrange for that herself with the nuns, as she doubted Prior Godric would allow his monks to copy anything but the holy word.

'Thank you sister, and be sure I have learnt much of healing through this time of trouble. The Lord has given you wisdom beyond your years, and we do well to learn from it.'

'Thank you, brother,' Dominica smiled back.

With Brother Tethion's thanks in her ears they left Saint Rumon's monastery and headed back towards Tamerkam, her future still unknown.

Chapter 49

The Blessing - *circa AD 698*

They rode into Tamerkam and went straight to Cador's stronghold. Keynae saw them arrive and came out joyfully to welcome Dominica back.

'Sister! And Abbot Kenver!' she called, then turned to say something to her house servant. One of Cador's horse men came and took the ponies to be watered, and Keynae led them indoors. The girl had set out beakers and a honeyed drink.

'Cador will be here soon,' she said, as they all sat down, 'What news? Are they all cured?'

'All,' smiled the Abbot.

'Not quite,' Dominica said, 'an elderly monk, Brother Finn, passed away the day after we got there.'

'Now, sister. Brother Tethion says he was very sick already, that he was coughing blood, and that is the sign of death.'

'Well, that's true. We do think that if it gets to coughing blood it has gone too far to be cured, except by God's own intervention.'

Keynae looked from one to the other, perplexed.

'Your sister here is hard on herself, maybe if we had her potions a few days earlier ... but it was not so. All the rest were healed and, the Lord be praised, no more took the sickness on. She is very careful.'

Cador arrived, bringing in with him the scent of the woodland when the leaves fall.

'Welcome Abbot, welcome back sister!'

'Chiefman Cador,' Abbot Kenver said, standing, 'I would have a word with you in private.' Cador nodded and the two men left.

'What is it?' Keynae asked.

‘I do not know, but I pray the Abbot will be saying he will take our new monastery under his charge, but he has said nothing to me on the journey back. Tell me, how has it been here while I was away - it seems far more than just eight days.’

‘Nothing of any note sister. We see nothing of the men in the monastery, but I hear your Avan did well in the healer’s hut dealing with a nasty cut from a skinning knife.’

Dominica smiled with pleasure at this, ‘She is a good girl, learns quickly. I have promised Brother Tethion, the infirmarer there, a copy of my herbal, so our nuns will be busy with that for St. Rumon's soon too!’

The men reappeared. ‘Sister Dominica,’ Abbot Kenver said in a commanding way. Dominica jumped to her feet, not even sure why she did so. ‘We are agreed. Chiefman Cador has granted the land near here known as the ‘old people’s place’ to you for a monastery, a dual monastery, an active monastery. The living will be extracted from the lands that the other monastery holds, in forfeit of breaking their covenant, the terms of which will be honoured by your new monastery. To teach reading and writing and the word of the Lord, to care for and heal those in the community that you can - and we, at St. Rumon’s, will provide you with our protection and all the people with communion on those days required.’

A wave of delight and relief ran through Dominica, ‘Praise the Lord!’ she said, and knew she had never meant the words as much in her life.

As Abbot Kenver wished to return the next day to St. Rumon’s he suggested that Cador send for Prior Godric, and his scribe, to meet with them all as soon as possible, and that Dominica bring her best scribe to take notes. Cador immediately sent Drustan to find the Prior and invite him to a meeting that very evening, at sunset. ‘If he quibbles, tell him it concerns the future of the monastery in

Tamerkam,' Cador said, then added, 'and come straight back with his answer.'

The monastery already lay in shadow when Prior Godric was spotted coming up the rise towards the meeting house, accompanied by another brother. The vantage point of the stronghold was still lit by the sun so, as they neared and came into the light, Dominica recognised the other monk as Matuid, armed with writing materials.

The Abbot took control of the meeting. He formerly introduced himself, though all knew who he was, and named Cador, giving him the title of Chiefman of the territory of Tamerkam, then he named Godric, Prior of the Tamerkam monastery and finally Sister Dominica. He asked for, and had added to the list, the names of Brother Matuid, and Sister Aylwyn to be noted as recorders.

He then outlined the problem caused by the monks withdrawal from the community, to become a secluded sect. He explained how this broke the agreement, the covenant, between monastery and benefactor. He then set out the terms that Cador had asked for, and the solution that he had planned to meet it.

Most of this went smoothly, until Abbot Kenver said, 'Any monk who wishes to leave the Tamerkam monastery to join the new monastery must be permitted to do so.'

Godric stood sharply, 'No! That is not right! They are sworn to *this* monastery.'

'Do not write that!' Abbot Kenver said quickly to the recorders - or this. 'Not as I understand it. I believe that your monastery is under the benefaction of the monastery in Drom-Mhor - yet you would make this one unlike the monastery which they have provided for and pray for. As an Abbot I would consider this an abrogation of the arrangement and blessing given, therefore those who would leave this new and *strange* monastery which *you* have created, for one that meets the standards expected by

Drom-Mhor, break no oaths. I repeat, for the record. Any monk who wishes to leave the Tamerkam monastery to join the new monastery must be permitted to do so.'

Godric closed his eyes and his fists, but said no more. Matuid sat looking at him, with quill poised as if unsure what to record, while Sister Aylwyn wrote fluidly and with a small smile on her lips.

'Write it!' Kenver snapped. Matuid jumped and hastily set his quill to scratching down the words.

Abbot Kenver went on to check with Cador his terms for the monastery remaining; that, as they were to keep all the land meant to support an active monastery, they must forfeit a proportion of their produce, in relation to the numbers within each monastery, to support the other monastery. It was agreed that those at the new monastery would be expected to help to work these fields as before. Then Prior Godric had it added that they would have no women in their area, even to work the fields - this was accepted.

Finally Abbot Kenver explained how St. Rumon's would hold a protective hand over the new monastery and support the community and the new monastery in Holy Communion when required.

The two records were read to check they were the same in all the relevant details. Then all were called to sign or make their mark at the end of the documents.

When it came to his turn Godric shook his head and said, 'I do not know what Prior Cormag will say, he may turn all this over.'

'Are you not the Prior here at Tamerkam?' Abbot Kenver said softly.

'I am. Yes, I am but he ...'

'Prior Cormag is merely the prior of another monastery. Surely you are the one in authority here, are you not?'

'I *am* the Prior here.'

'Then sign, as the man in authority here - or pass that authority to Sister Dominica, now.'

Godric took up the quill and wrote his name, flinging the quill down where it splattered ink on parchment and board. The Abbot took it up carefully, dipped and dated and signed the document.

'Here, Cador, your copy, and here Dominica the copy for the new monastery. It will be part of your founding documents.'

'What about our copy?' Godric demanded.

'You may make a copy of the one held by Chiefman Cador if you need it, but I do not see why you need a copy unless to explain what you did to break the covenant in the first place. Shall we go down to share the news with the brothers? I would be glad to tell them the terms and give them my blessing,' the Abbot smiled.

A meeting of the brothers was called immediately as the Abbot insisted, and he had his say about the whole arrangement, making sure to say that any brother that wished to join the new monastery would be given leave to do so with no hindrance. He asked that any who would join the new monastery right away come to him when the talk was finished.

When they gathered to the Abbot afterwards there were four brothers; Brannon, Yowann, Resmen and Hedrek.

'Brother Brannon I know, but I would ask you all your names and your reason for moving to the new monastery.' He pointed to Yowann. 'You first.'

'Brother Yowann, Father. Sister Dominica was one of the first that came here. She is led by the Lord and does His work humbly. This is the way this life was told to me, to be the hands of the Lord here on earth.'

'You are not concerned that the vote for Prior here went to her and not you?'

Yowann smiled, 'I voted *for* her, Father.'

'And now you, Brother Brannon.'

'We are called to be the Lord's hands here, and Sister Dominica has held firmly to this always.'

Abbot Kenver smiled and looked at the next in line.

'I'm Brother Resmen,' he began, shifting from foot to foot, 'Sister Dominica is kindness itself. It was she who told me that prayers and praise can be said by hands and feet if they are doing God's work. I am better with my hands than I am with my mouth; my mouth needs a bridle, it runs away with me, to my ever lasting regret. I do say my prayers and praises though too, but when I am working it is better.'

Abbot Kenver nodded. 'And you brother?'

'Brother Hedrek,' the big framed monk answered him, 'The Lord called me to work with people, to speak with them alongside to tell of his blessings. What am I to do among only those who already know Him?'

'Amen, brother,' Resmen murmured.

'Indeed,' Abbot Kenver said. 'May the blessing of the Lord be with you all, brothers of the monastery of Indract the Martyr, may He keep you safe and lead you to do His work here on earth until such time as he will call you home. In the name of the Father, Son and Holy Spirit,' he made the cross over them, 'Amen.'

'Amen,' they responded, then glanced round at each other smiling.

*

Dominica, Keynae and Cador stood in the clearing of the 'old people's place', where she and Indract had first landed. Dominica showed Cador her plan for the monastery, saying, 'I am thinking we must need to be quite crowded together, but we will fit in somehow.'

Cador smiled, 'Well, let's see. What if I say you have the use of this too,' he waved his hand at the woodland surrounding the old people's clearing, 'for we give you the old people's place as far as this side of the path to Bo Etherick, and over the rise here down to where the land flattens out the other side and,' turning himself to look uphill, 'up to the level where the path which drops below our stronghold turns off. Later I'll have it marked out for you, but for now, know that you have more than you might have thought - and you might want to re-draw your plan,' he added with a grin.

'Cador, Keynae, bless you, this is more than I expected, and may God thank and bless you and your people.'

'He has already,' Keynae said, 'He sent you to us.'

Part Four

A fresh start, a new monastery in an old place – named for Indract

Chapter 50

Saint Indract's *- circa AD 699 - 701*

They were blessed - the weather was dry and perfect for building work. The harvest was in, but the slaughter, salting and smoking was yet to come. Cador was generous with his men's time so that, alongside the men from both monasteries, the cutting of timber, the digging and the weaving of walls, all went faster than could have been dreamt of. Soon there were four large reed-roofed round-houses in the area, one for the healers with space to use as an infirmary, one for the refectory with space as a hospice for guests, one for the monks' dormitory, and across the other side, one for the nuns' dormitory - each of the latter with space for twelve bays. Along with these were five smaller huts, the herbarium, one for cooking, one for laundry, both near the spring, and two for sanitation, behind the dormitories and hard by the river.

As soon as they could, the monks, nuns and healers of the new monastery left their old quarters and took up residence in the new monastery. The first thing they did was hold their meeting to name their new leader. Only one name was put forward, yet even-so they voted, and Dominica was unanimously named Prioress - though she insisted that within their monastery she was still to be Sister Dominica, and only when others, outsiders, needed to know, would they call her by Prioress.

*

When the last leaves had shaken loose from the trees and the wind began to bite, the only place not built was the church - and that was Brannon's fault.

Brannon had come back from Rome with a fixation for a church built of stone. He told them of the amazing buildings he had seen, of the grandeur, of the honour to God of a church made of stone. He said he knew that they could not make anything quite like the ones he had seen, but maybe they could still build a church in stone.

He spoke so well about the idea, to all of the monastery of St. Indract the Martyr, that they set their hearts on it. However, it meant the church was not the first building made.

**

Come the spring they found a place where raw rock could be seen, where the land had fallen away, undercut by a stream. It was like that stone which they had used at Tamerunta, breaking into thick flattish grey slabs easily enough, and they decided it would be easy to build up and so the gathering of stone commenced. When not ploughing, sowing, weeding or praying the men worked on getting out the blocks.

They began their build by marking out a rectangle in the usual orientation for a church, then levelled off the ground. Having dug a shallow trench all round they laid in the largest stones as a foundation and set in the door posts topped with a great solid beam. From there they layered up the stones, sticking the blocks together with a sticky clay dug from a pit near Bo Barr, letting it dry a bit before adding another layer and, after a few weeks, there were walls.

The roof was to be made of poles of wood, with wattle frames lashed between to take the thatch. Brannon had spoken, wistfully, of roofs in Rome with tiles of a reddish hue, however, water-reed grew abundantly nearby and they understood how to use that.

The finished church wasn't large, it was more like a chapel really. It would be hard-put to hold the two times twelve they hoped would fill their dual monastery, but it was in stone and had a solid look to it.

By now it was late in the year, yet still unaccustomedly dry and without the usual frosts expected in early December. However, the day of consecration and dedication was set for the following May, for the day that Indract and the others were martyred, so they couldn't yet use it as their church for the mass, only for the daily services.

***

When the day came for the consecration and dedication everyone was invited, Cador, Keynae and as many of the community as wished to come. The invitation also went out to both the monastery at Tamerkam and at Tamerunta, of which Prior Cormag came, but Prior Godric did not.

Abbot Kenver, as a consecrated bishop under the rule, presided. The whole company, led by him, circled the church building three times, and then he and the nuns and monks entered. He blessed each wall and the altar with Holy Water. He then dedicated the church to the name of Saint Indract the Martyr, and blessed all who would use it for prayer and praise. Brannon and Dominica said a few words about each of the brothers and a song of praise, created by Teagan, was sung in memory of him.

Dominica sang with tears in her eyes, and vowed to God she'd go to say prayers at the graves in which her brother, and her brothers-in-God, were laid.

The copy of the herbal had been finished at last and, complete with Merewin's drawings of the plants in fine detail, it was exquisite. So after the dedication Dominica was delighted to present it to Brother Tethion and Abbot Kenver.

Cador had arranged for a small feast and, with May being a difficult time of the year to provide food for so many, Dominica was overwhelmed by his generosity.

At one point in the afternoon Prior Cormag came and stood beside Dominica. 'Prioress,' he said looking round, 'you have done well here, a fitting place to remember our brothers.'

Dominica glanced at him. There was no of sign of the pain or cynicism she often saw in his face, 'It is all God's work really,' she said, 'and you? How are you?'

He pulled something like a smile, 'The leg still pains me, but I have accepted the humiliation I fought so bitterly against now, so it is only pain, not anger too.'

'And we can give you something to help ease the pain, a potion made here in our herbarium, if you will take it?'

Cormag looked down at the ground, 'Maybe I will. I will pray on it and let you know sister - Prioress.'

'Sister will do just fine, brother. There are so few of us left from the eleven that set out, we are like family, are we not?'

Cormag brought his head up and looked at Dominica, to her great surprise there were tears in his eyes. 'Sister,' he said nodding and, turning, limped away.

****

Life in the monastery settled into a good pattern. People came to the healer's house, now named the infirmary, whenever they were sick or injured, and Dominica, Avan and even Merewin went out to people when needed.

Eiliwedd was expecting her first baby, and Dominica was the one to safely deliver the child, a boy, who Geraint and Eiliwedd named Dominik - after Dominica.

Avan went to help Eiliwedd in the healer's house at Bo Barr when needed and Merewin took on more responsibilities in St. Indract's, though still dealing mostly with the herbs and potions in the herbarium, rather than the people. Merewin had a new place to roll down the hill in the new monastery, but she seemed to use it less often than before, yet still appeared happy.

Dominica resumed services at the 'old place' in Bo Barr, and the people came back to join her, though she sorely missed Teagan's musical abilities, she had them sing all she and they knew of his songs of praise.

Winter came and again it was mild and drier than usual, the grass barely stopped growing and the wildflowers showed their colours earlier than expected. Dominica began planning with Brannon their short pilgrimage to Glestyngabyrig. It was decided that they should take Esselt with them as a companion to Dominica, and she asked Cador if it was possible to borrow a couple of ponies for the journey, intending to share her ride with Esselt as the girl had never learnt to ride. He was happy with that and offered to send one of his warriors to guard them too. After consultation with Brannon this was also accepted. The date to leave was set, and preparations made for leaving the monastery in the good hands of Brother Yowann whilst she was away.

***

They left right after the bright-fire and green-man celebration of spring was held at the stronghold, and were accompanied by Drustan who had begged his father to let him be the warrior to go with them. The journey took them five days, unused as most of them were to riding, and with taking great care of the borrowed ponies. The first evening they stayed with the monks at St. Rumon's, but thereafter they had to find shelter as they could. Dominica was glad she had brought her blue brat with her as, though it was beginning to fade, it still kept her warm and cosy at night.

**

On the fifth day, as they plodded carefully through a marshy area, Brannon sighted the tor at Glestyngabyrig and was sure that they were getting close enough to arrive before evening.

As they neared the settlement Brannon called back, 'They are building something big here! This was not here before, and I cannot see the church!'

They drew nearer, watching the men working on the huge construction, and then, as the path turned Brannon shouted back to the others, 'Oh! There it is! The old church is still here, beyond this new building!'

They rode around the building site until they came to the gateway of the old church boundary where they stopped. Brannon rode on a little way and dismounted nearer the priest's house. He knocked at the door, wondering if anyone would be there and, if so, whether it would be the same priest.

The man who came to the door looked a deal older, but it was the same man.

'Father, it is good to see you again,' Brannon opened, wondering if he would be recognised, and concerned to hear the fate or fortune of thegn Husa and his men.

The priest looked at him, squinting, 'Have we met before brother?'

'Perhaps, maybe when pillars of light were seen in the marshland?'

The priest stepped back a pace, 'God save you! You are well?'

'I am father, please tell me what happened after I left?'

The priest beckoned him into his house, 'Come, come, I'll tell you inside.'

'I have companions waiting by the church door.'

'No matter, it will not take me long - then we can go to them.'

Once inside the dim room, the priest turned to Brannon, 'The King was true to his word. He took those men and held them to trial, and all were put to the sword. We are safe from them, but I would still not boast of who you are, for they had friends in the King's service who saw it a harsh sentence, and could easily come to hear of you being here.'

'I understand. I shall be an anonymous monk. And what of our brothers' bodies?'

'True to his word, the King had them found and drawn out of the mire and buried again under the floor of the church, martyrs all, yet he has made a tomb the same as Saint Patrick's for your prior, Indract.'

'The same as Saint Patrick's? What an honour! And I am glad to hear this, for I accompany his sister, both in blood and in Christ, to say prayers at his grave and that of our other brothers in God. Indract and Dominica were the son and daughter of our king in Eriu, at Drom-Eanaigh, before joining the monastery of St. Declan and St. Brigid at Drom-Mhor.'

Dominica, introduced as Prioress of the monastery of Saint Indract the Martyr, and Sister Esselt were taken into the church to the tomb, and they and Brannon were left in peace to pray, with Drustan left guarding the ponies.

When they had finished the priest asked how long they would stay, as there would be a special mass said for the sainted martyrs in two day's time, on their day of translation. It was agreed that they would stay for that time at least.

'King Ina's determined to make this holy place a great abbey - he has his own Abbot in place here already and has given lands to support it,' the priest added, 'and, as he is nearby at Pedred again, will most likely come here soon to see how the works on the new Abbey church he is having built are going.'

'I would so like to meet such a holy King and thank him for what he has done for our brothers,' Dominica sighed.

'Well, he may even come for the martyrs' mass,' the priest said with a little nod. 'Maybe, if I remind him,' he added with a small smile.

Accommodation was found for them in the village nearby and, after they had recuperated from their ride, the next day they took themselves up to the top of the tor nearby to survey the surrounding area in the warm sunshine, a very different landscape to that they were used to around Tamerkam.

*

On the eighth of May they entered the church to say the prayers at Terce, glad to go into the cool as it was already warming up outside. The priest came in a little before noon and told them a rider had come earlier to say the King would be with them for the martyrs' mass, set for nones.

There was a bit of a commotion at the door and it was pushed wide. Two men carried something large into the church, and brought it to the front. 'For the King,' they said in Anglisc.

'Of course,' replied the priest in the same tongue, 'set it up here,' he indicated a space just below the altar step on the right, not far from the tomb of St. Patrick.

They set it down, pulled at it and it opened up to become a great chair. Another man had arrived by now carrying heavy cloths in King Ina's royal colours, gold and red, which he arranged on the chair, transforming it into something more like a throne. Someone else came bearing a footstool or kneeler in the same colours and set it before the chair.

Dominica and the others left the church as it became busy with arrangements and took a look at the work being done on the new church.

Brannon was fascinated to watch the men working the stone so the blocks were squared off and fitted tightly. He talked to the men and found that not all stone was good to build with, and then he learnt that even with the right blocks made, mortar was needed to bind together the stones in such a way as it would harden and hold the stones tight.

He asked more questions, and had himself laughed at for asking if daub would hold rock together, and so he wrote down the recipes for this mortar that would hold even when it rained for days on end, or was frozen hard for weeks.

'I feel a fool! All our hard work may be undone by wet weather, by deep-frost or strong winds,' he told Dominica. 'We have just been lucky that the winters have been dry and mild.'

'You are not a builder, and we had no-one who knew such things since brother Dairmut. Do not blame yourself Brannon. If it falls we will know how to build it better next time. If we had built in wattle it would need rebuilding in a short time anyway, there is not much difference.'

As the time moved towards nones they returned to the church. The priest spotted them and drew them towards a group of monks who stood near the front.

'Brothers, here is the Prioress I spoke of, sister to Indract, and in God, to the other martyrs.' He turned to Dominica, 'May I introduce the Abbot Beorhtwald, of the monastery behind this church, the brotherhood of this place begun by Saint Patrick.'

'Prioress, I am told you and Indract were from Eriu?' Abbot Beorhtwald said.

'We were. In fact all the brothers martyred here were from Eriu, all from the monastery of Saint Declan and Saint Brigid at Drom-Mhor.' *But you are of Saxon stock by your name, I doubt you know Eiru.*

'We have a few of our number from Eriu and though, through their vows, they seldom talk to each other let alone any others, we shall make an exception, if you will it.'

'Brother Brannon, and I would be blessed to speak with any who would.'

'After the service then, sister.'

Just then the arrival of King Ina was announced, and those few already waiting in the church bowed as he entered. Completely surrounded by six shining warriors, he processed slowly to where the chair was set. After the King was seated, they stepped away and stood behind him against the wall, a watchful row of matched flaxen warriors and all armed, one even held an impressive axe.

The priest had followed the royal party in and now took his place before the altar. He nodded, and other people were allowed to enter the church, the flow cut off when the standing room before the chancel step was filled.

The mass for the martyrs began, but Dominica struggled to hear what was said, her head was pierced by a pain that seemed to be emanating from where the King sat. She tried to divert herself by staring at Indract's tomb, and then by staring at the host on the altar, but it was as if there were a thread, tied painfully tight and pulled taut, between her head and the King - and it could not be ignored.

Chapter 51
After the Martyr's Mass - circa AD 701

The mass finished and the common people were shooed outside. The King beckoned to the Abbot. He went forward, bowed and was offered the King's hand, whereupon he kissed the ring upon it.

The King had a few words for the Abbot, who nodded vigorously. He then bowed again and took a few steps backwards before turning and rejoining his monks. They then all left the church, Abbot Beorhtwald giving a small smile and nod to Dominica as he passed her. Dominica wondered if they too should exit the church now, but a small cough from the priest drew her attention back to the King, who beckoned her.

The painful thread seemed to wind in as she approached him. She bowed and he held out his hand. She leaned to kiss the ring but as she did so it was as if a bolt of lightning shot through her, she almost lost her balance, and she suddenly knew - *he has such a pain, not in his head but in his foot.*

'Are you well, Prioress?' he asked sharply.

'I am, Sire,' spoken clearly. She drew a breath and added softly, 'but, maybe you are not? I am a healer in our monastery and I believe you have a great pain in your foot?'

His eyes widened, he glanced round at his men, all stony faced, and beckoned her closer. 'You saw when I walked in?'

'No, Sire, your men surrounded you. I, I felt it, your pain. I am sister to Indract, God gave us both gifts, mine is in healing.'

'And you think you could heal this?'

'God willing. And as He has shown me your pain, I believe He is willing.'

'Clear the church, I would speak with the Prioress!' Ina commanded, and as the priest and Dominica's party left, he turned to his men and told them to guard the outside of the door.

'Tell me, what you will do?'

Dominica felt a little scared now, but she sent a prayer for the right words and the right action, 'Sire, I feel the pain, but I would that you tell me more about it first.'

'It is damnable! I feel like an old man, forced to hobble along. The pain is almost unbearable. The toes, especially the large one and my heel are red, swollen and like needle spiked. My healers have bled me, and given me purgatives to drink, foul stuff that had my guts spewing - both ends. But it has done nothing for the pain - or the swelling, and overnight, oh, overnight, it is as if all the devils of hell are tweaking my feet with burning tongs, even a fine cover rasps at the skin like mail.'

'Sire, may I see the foot where it is affected?' King Ina rested his leg upon the kneeler and Dominica unlaced his fine-leather shoe and eased it off. The marks of the seams were impressed on the reddened skin of the area around his big toe and his heel. Both were shiny, swollen and almost glowing with the heat. She nodded, she had seen this before, back in Drom-Eanaigh.

'Sire, I will pray for healing, but I also know a treatment from my herbals, which I brought with me from our monastery in Eriu.'

'Do it! Nothing can be worse than it is now - or what I have endured from my own healers.'

'Please, Sire, pray yourself too, for forgiveness,' adding hastily, 'for we all fail our Lord in some way, and pray for healing too.' She clasped her own hands, paused, waited until he clasped his hands and dipped his head, then she began. 'Lord God, look upon your servant Ina, and have mercy. Pray send the Holy Spirit with healing for his pain. Remove this affliction from him.' She knew that she was the one praying, that she wasn't being overtaken by the Spirit, and it made her anxious. *It didn't work for Nuala on her death-bed, no matter how much you wanted it - why would it work now? Yet the Lord has sent me knowledge of Ina's pain!* She persevered. 'Lord, forgive me my sins, those that are so hidden that I do not know I transgress,' a small silence, into which slid the word *pride*, 'Forgive me for my pride in gifts that are yours alone, and not of my making.'

The spirit feeling began to grow, it filled her chest, making it hard to breathe. She dragged in a deeper breath, the heat spread all across her body, her clasped hands separated and rose without her bidding, the heat pooling in the uplifted palms, her voice strengthening. 'Bring your healing, Lord - in the name of the Father, Son and Holy Spirit!'

She sighed deeply, all the breath leaving her as she felt her hands tip over to palms down.

She heard the King sigh deeply, and came to herself, lowering her hands as she did so. The King was still in an attitude of prayer. 'Amen,' Dominica said softly,

'Amen,' repeated the King, then opened his eyes and looked up, then down at his foot, then back to Dominica. She could see the redness had subsided, and the swelling - a little at least.

Ina shook his head, 'Sister, the pain seems to have gone! Maybe it is you who should be made a saint, not your brother.'

'No, sire, I am just the vessel for the Holy Spirit, and it is only when God wills it.' She looked hard at Ina to be sure he was listening, 'The Lord God may have taken the pain from you for now, but I will say to you what you must do to help stop this condition returning. We must never wilfully test the Lord. Sire, you must abstain from rich meats and dark meats, rich shellfish too, and take very little ale or wine, but plenty of water from springs where they issue from the rock, each and everyday, to flush out these needles. I also know of a purgative that seems to help more than most, but I have none with me, and you seem to have had enough of purgatives already.' She smiled at the rueful face he pulled.

'I have heard you, sister. I shall not tempt the Lord,' and he smiled, and bent to replace his shoe. 'Thank you, and I am in your debt. If there is anything you want that is in my gift, I will hear you and do whatever I am able,' he added, as she assisted him in fastening the shoe.

Dominica wondered about asking for masons to build the chapel at their monastery, but something stopped her from saying this, so she merely smiled and said, 'Thank you, sire, I do not know what to ask for just now, but it may well be that we will have a need of your goodness one day,' though still thinking of the church as she said it.

The King and Dominica left the church together, the king's men glancing at him walking out alone, at each other, but not saying a word as they stepped in around him.

'Remember,' Ina said from the back of his mount, 'I owe you, and God, a debt.'

'Sire. Oh! Sire, I almost forgot, I wanted to say a thank you, for honouring our brothers in God,' then she added with a smile, 'and, so as not to vex the Lord, please to remember the instructions given.' The King nodded, before he turned his horse and led his men away.

The Abbot was waiting nearby with a few of the monks. Dominica swiftly explained to Brannon that they were to speak with some of the monks from Eriu, though she knew not the reason, only that it was unusual for this to happen. They crossed over to where the Abbot stood. He looked quizzically at her, but asked nothing about the King.

'Sister, Prioress, here are the brothers from Eriu, they have something to tell you.'

'Thank you Father Beorhtwald,' she said. Turning to the brothers she said in Goidelic, 'We are pleased to meet brothers in God from our home land. What is it you wish to say? We will help if we can,'

‘I hear you have not lost the tongue, how long have you been here?’ one asked.

‘Not long enough to have forgotten my mother tongue, it must be twelve or thirteen years now.’

‘Ah! Not half the time I have then.’

‘Forgive my brother. This is no time for chatter, we need to tell you of a vision,’ the other continued in Goidelic.

A tingle ran around Dominica’s frame. ‘A vision?'

‘We, that is us two brothers here ...’

‘Both from Eriu.’

‘Had a vision, both, but separately, yet the vision, or dream, was almost identical.’

‘It was the night after the day the King ordered the bodies found and drawn from the mire.’

‘I saw this King leading a great army, cross over a river by a ford, and sweep everyone before them in slaughter - to a great victory.’

‘And I saw the same, and then the vision swooped down following the river’s edge to where there was a rath with a gateway draped in the King's own colours. As I watched the flag grew so large that it covered every hut, every field, every tree within that place.’

‘And the slaughter did not see it hidden beneath the flag, and passed by,’ the second brother finished, nodding his head.

Brannon and Dominica looked at each other and back at the brothers. ‘Thank you, brothers.’ Dominica said, shivering at the images, ‘I cannot say what the vision means.’

‘Though our monastery is hard by the river,’ cut in Brannon. Dominica glanced at him. Had he felt the same as her?

‘Thank you for listening. Neither of us spoke of it at first, but, you must understand, this - dream, vision, returned night after night, so in the end I told the Abbot of it, and he told me I wasn't alone. When we realised we had both had the same dream we still did not know what it was about.'

‘Until the Abbot told of us your presence at this martyr’s mass - and then we knew. We were sure that this vision was for you, and we begged leave to tell you.’

‘Thank you, brothers. Time will tell what this vision is for. Thank you for telling it to us,’ Brannon said.

‘Bless you, brothers,’ Dominica added, ‘and it was good to speak in our home tongue for a while.’

The next day they bid farewell to the priest, and the four of them set off on the long journey back to Tamerkam - and their monastery hard by the river.

Chapter 52
The Calm *- circa AD 701 - 710*

There followed a time, years even, when everything seemed to go smoothly for the new monastery. The years of cold and wet seemed to fade in memory as the weather improved year on year. Light rains, in their due season, warm winds and sun to ripen and dry the crops. And gentle winters, some frost but not the bone aching cold of it day after day, and no snow, except on the tops of those distant moors.

Babies were born - more than expected survived, the people suffered less from the sicknesses of poor food or the cold and damp. More came to baptism, more came to services held at Dominica's cross at Bo Barr, under the great oak tree in Bo Etherick and beside the meeting house at the Tamerkam stronghold.

Their stone church, had held up well so far, despite Brannon's worry every time it rained, or when the wind whipped up the river. Yet it was so small it really only served for the monastery. Indeed, many called it 'the chapel' because of its small size. Dominica thought often of the greater church in the other monastery, echoing to the few who remained - and whose number had not grown, except by one, said to have been sent from Tamerunta.

St. Indract's had grown. People had come forward to join the monastery over this time, both men and women. Two were widows, ready to join the monastery, they said, but not to do all that learning, so they joined as lay women, but four were younger women professing to want to become nuns.

Joining the four monks already there came three older men to be lay brothers, and three younger wishing to be monks, one of the latter of a gentle and studious nature, reminding Dominica of Indract at a similar age. One had a voice so sweet Dominica wished they still had Teagan to teach him to sing and play an instrument, and suggested that maybe Tamerkam's bard, who played a seven-stringed lyre well enough, could teach the young man.

They'd built a further hut to be a schoolroom, both for the teaching of reading and writing to the monks and nuns, but also to the few young people in the area whose parents now wanted them to learn. As all reading and writing was in Latin, it required them to also learn a new language, something Dominica thought was useful, for she was convinced that learning Latin from Sister Magda and Anglisc from Guda while so young helped her pick up other tongues more easily. Aylwyn taught the writing to the postulant and novitiate nuns, and Esselt, the reading, alongside Dominica.

A new and larger herb garden was created, and two of the younger novices took to working with the herbs well enough to be taught their uses and preparations. Dominica felt this knowledge was in safe hands as they applied themselves earnestly - listening to Merewin with respect when she lectured them on the finer details of identification.

The creation of another copy of the herbal was also undertaken, with the written word worked mostly by Aylwyn as she had a beautiful written hand. When Dominica had asked Merewin to do her drawings again, the girl had fairly burst with joy.

Esselt, a full nun now, also read bible stories to the young people of Tamerkam. She'd go to the meeting house at a suitably agreed time and, gathering the children, tell them a story from the bible and say a prayer with them afterwards. She was a firm favourite with the youngsters, and it was a good way for them to be grounded in the word of the Lord, even when so young.

The monastery of St. Rumon's, as promised, sent an ordained monk to offer the Eucharist for their great Holy days. Each time they were asked if all was well, if there was anything that they needed. On occasion the Abbot came, and always took time out to visit the other monastery too. They could hardly turn him away as they did everyone else. Even Cormag came rarely to Tamerkam any more. Dominica wondered what was said, but had never asked, yet was somehow reassured that someone was at least visiting them.

She hadn't seen Cormag at Tamerkam for almost two years. He'd come back once since the dedication of their church, and had accepted the potion that Dominica had offered to ease the pain when it was too much. She'd also given him the recipe for it, to pass on to Liaden, so she could make more. She prayed it helped him.

*

It was about nine years since Dominica and Brannon had returned from Glestyngabyrig when, one late spring morning, Keynae came to Dominica looking distraught.

'What is it? What's happened?' Dominica asked.

'Our men have been called!' she cried, 'Cynan has told Cador to gather his warriors and all fit men of fighting age and meet at Kellyventon.'

'What for?'

'King Geraint has called all men to arms - to defend us all. He claims your Saxon King Ina is gathering his men at a fort he has on the river Tone and is preparing to invade Dumnonia.'

Dominica shook her head, 'Where is this? I only know of Glestyngabyrig in Ina's land, is it near there?'

'No, Cador says it is nearer than that, right on our borders. I had hoped we had seen the last of wars - King Geraint has kept us safe so far.'

'We will pray that it does not come to war.'

'Pray hard sister! I have only known our local feuds and they are bad enough, young men lost over old grievances, but in the past I have heard tell of the burning of homes and the raping of women, even children, by these Saxon beasts.'

'The King I met was a good Christian. Surely his men are more controlled,' she began, yet as the words left her mouth she thought of Indract, Finn and the rest, slaughtered like sheep by Ina's men, 'but we must pray that it does not come to war.'

**

Within a month Cador and all the fit men had left. Word was that Geraint had swept up through Kernow gathering his men as he went, so when they crossed the Tamer they were a mighty force, and hoped to double in number as they marched through Dewnen towards the old border with Somersaetus. It sounded as if they were such a huge army, none could stand against them.

***

St. Rumon's sent Brother Michael with a message for Prioress Dominica. He arrived mid afternoon and handed her a letter.

'What is it?' she asked, even as she opened the seal.

'News, the Abbot said, of the war.'

Dominica opened it and read it. Then re-read it. Abbot Kenver had it from a monastery near Escancastre that King Ina's army had swept forwards towards Escancastre and had met in battle with King Geraint's men. Ina's forces had pushed them right back, taking Escancastre. This town was now in King Ina's hand. Churches and monasteries were being sacked, along with the town.

‘This cannot be right? King Ina is a Christian King! Surely his army will leave churches and monasteries alone?’

‘It seems that we are all excommunicated from the Roman Church, as too many in Geraint’s kingdom refuse to accept the Pope's rule.’

‘How close to St. Rumon’s is Escancastre?’

‘Two days ride, if that. But for an army it would be more I think.’

‘Two days! *Two days?*’

‘Maybe they will stop there, at Escancastre.’

‘Thank Abbot Kenver for me. Do you know his plans?’

‘Probably to pray! We are a little out of the way, not in a great town, not rich – hopefully they’ll miss us.’

‘Pray! Of course. Pray.’

Chapter 53
***The Storm** - circa AD 710*

Dominica did pray. After they had eaten and found a bed for Brother Michael, Dominica went to their small church and prayed. She knew there wasn't anything she could do to help the fighting men, but maybe she could protect the women and children, the old and the weak? Her mind was working so hard to think of a plan, she forgot to pray properly, to let go, to let God in.

Eventually, tired of her thoughts going around in circles she sighed and laughed silently to herself. *Just let go, just rest in the Lord.* And almost at once, as she did so, a picture of a flag, at the gate of a monastery came into her mind, a pennant of red and gold, that grew to cover the whole area, that hid it from 'the slaughter'. She gasped as she recognised the brothers' vision.

None of it had made any sense before, but now, now it seemed clear what the their vision had been about! She would go to King Ina and ask him for ... something, a pennant perhaps, something his men would know meant their place was under the King's protection. Almost immediately the doubts crept in. *To go across country when it is at war - madness surely? To ask to speak to the King when he is planning war? He wouldn't listen, probably didn't even remember his promise; it has been years and years. And if he did, would he honour it, if he believes us excommunicated? Yet, if God had sent a dream, a vision, so long before - then surely she had to go, had to try.*

The next morning, as soon as Brother Michael was up and about, Dominica quickly told him of her plan, and said she hoped to follow him later. Once she had explained where she was going, he said that they may be able to help when she got to St. Rumon's, that he would explain it all to the Abbot and, soon after he had broken his fast, he set off back to his monastery.

Dominica called a meeting of all the monks, nuns, lay brothers and sisters. She told them of the news and she told them she would go to King Ina and ask for a sign to protect them. She had, by that time, thought how they might help to protect *all* the people of Tamerkam. If the King's pennant covered the whole of the monastery - then the monastery had to contain all of the people.

She explained, 'While I travel to see the King to ask for his protection, under the promise he gave me at our martyred brothers' mass, the boundary of our monastery land must be built up, where ever it isn't already, to make the wider monastery edges obvious. Use anything,' she said, 'be it proper staves, or cut and heaped furze, or earthen bank, or piles of rock - it doesn't have to look pretty - it just has to mark out and surround the whole of the cleared monastery land. Thank God Cador gave us so much, for now a greater number will be able to create make-shift homes within our grounds - and so be under the protection of the King - if he grants it.' *If it worked. If the King remembered. If the vision of protection was fulfilled.*

Next she spoke to Keynae, ruling in her husband's stead, and told her of the plan, of the vision. Keynae was grateful for the plan, and if she was doubtful she hid it well. They agreed that as many fit and able people as possible would help with marking out the monastery enclosure, and then begin to build shelters within it. However, she was shocked that Dominica might try to get to Escancastre alone, but was assured that Dominica would be taking Brother Brannon with her too.

'All but an old pack-pony have been taken to war, sister,' Keynae said, 'but you are welcome to her, though she can only carry your pack, she cannot be ridden.'

'Thank you, that would be very helpful. I am hoping our other monastery will lend us their pony too, at least then we could take turns.'

But they wouldn't, even though they had received the same message from St. Rumon's, nor would they join with St. Indract's and come within the rath, convinced that their robes and Godric's Centish origins and good Anglisc would protect them from any trouble Saxons might bring if they came to Tamerkam.

Taking blankets, food, drink, her healing scrip and a clean robe each, they wrapped them well and set them on the pack-pony and set off for St. Rumon's. By the time they arrived it was nearly dark, and Dominica was glad she knew where they were going.

The Abbot called for them to meet with him in the Abbot's house when they arrived and greeted them both warmly.

'Brother Michael tells me you intend to go to Escancastre? Are you sure? The news suggests you would not be safe.'

'I must. I have business with the King and it would seem he is there. Hopefully he is there and remembers his promise to me,' she said, and went on to quickly explain the vision the two hermits told her when they were at Glestyngabyrig so many years before.

The Abbot sat back and regarded Dominica for a long moment. 'May the Lord go with you - and I can help. We can send a guide with you, not a brother, but a trader I trust who takes the shorter way across the Moor. This time of year it will not be too cold, but you must follow him closely – it is a dangerous place to leave the track – and for the most part the track is scarcely visible to any but those who know it. If you leave early it will get you to within sight of Escancastre by the end of one day, and you are far less likely to come across desperate people fleeing, or any war-bands scouting. Leave your pack-pony here, I can lend you two strong moor ponies. Ride them all day there but, sister, rest them on the way back.'

An answer to prayer! Relief flooded through Dominica - she had wondered how they would get to the town before the King had moved on. Perhaps now she could catch him in time.

The Abbot must have sent word to the trader that evening, as just before dawn he was there. After breaking their fast they set off heading up onto the hills, following in strict single file wherever the trader led with his pony.

The almost invisible track the trader followed led them along the side of valleys, where fast water could be seen and heard crashing around rocks below. The valleys wound around the hills, so much so Dominica wondered if they were actually travelling forward, not just side to side. Often, as they rose towards the top of a rounded hill, they picked their way through beds of rushes, or between flat green patches of wound-moss, each pony leaving hoof-prints filling with water as a trail. She could see the trader leaning forward, scanning the land before him at these places and, more than once, he glanced back to check they were alert to following him carefully. Then, once through, he'd straighten and they'd drop a little from the high ground and continue their winding way again until they needed to circumvent a waterway or bog too dangerous to cross.

Dominica was fascinated to see this land up close. Before, she had only seen it as a vast area of hills at a great distance, from the heights of Tamerkam, or as an edge of lowering mounds, from St. Rumon's. Many of the hills they wound around had pinnacles of the grey rock the trader called moorstone, some massive blocks standing proud from the hill against the sky, some seeming like piles of giant beans balanced upon each other, some extraordinary in shape and form looking like faces or animals. Other hilltops seemed to have less of a solid cap, but their slopes were scattered with the great grey rocks, right down to the stream-beds.

Twice they had descended to the rushing water, instead of rising. Both times the river was wide enough to ford carefully. Another time they crossed a series of smaller streams running cleanly down a hillside. Shortly after this they stopped to have a bite to eat in a strange small circle of the moorstones leaning their backs against the rock to shelter from the wind that had been picking up as the sky had begun to go grey.

The rocks are carefully placed, Dominica thought, as she went further into the undergrowth to relieve herself, and came upon other similar circles, half sunk into the ground, the space inside lower than that outside. Returning she noticed the men sitting within the circle, and wondered aloud if it had been a small house? Made of stone instead of wood?

The trader said it most likely was, as it was a common way to make a hut on the moor, where timber was scarce and rock plentiful. Brannon took more interest all of a sudden, feeling the quality of some of the looser rocks. Going so far as to balance some together to see how they could fit, how they gripped each other with just their roughness.

'These would make fine stones to re-build our church with one day,' he mused, 'and there is so much here.'

When they got going again the wind was much stronger, though at least it was pushing them along rather than fighting them, and she could almost taste the rain in the air. And then it came, like a shroud of grey, blotting out the landscape, moving from big wet drops to a drenching wall of rain in moments. There was no shelter to even consider running to, but there was no going forward, almost blinded by the torrent. The trader stopped, hunching himself down, so they all did, gathering the three ponies together as if for comfort.

Then, as fast as it came, the wind blew the rain away, and they could watch its progress as a line marching across the hills. The wind, however, stayed, chilling them where the wet had soaked into their clothes – but there was no time to stop or change. If they wanted to be off the moor by sunset they had to press on, the trader said, and so they did.

The valley they looked down into was already in deep shade, though up on this last ridge the sun still glowered behind them so that they cast long shadows. Below, in the distance, they could see a myriad of red stars – camp fires and watch-fires - the trader said. He also said he'd take them to where he hoped there was still an inn, in a village just outside the town and so, steadily, they began the descent into the darkening valley.

Chapter 54

Two-edged Vision - *circa AD 710*

The trader had gone quietly ahead to see what remained of the village he hoped they could stay in, and returned to say the inn was there, but stripped of anything that could be taken, down to the bare earth, and he didn't think it a safe place. Instead he led them back along a tight coombe to an outcrop of rock where he said they could make camp more safely. There they rubbed down the ponies with handfuls of wiry grass, made sure they had water to drink and time to graze before being hobbled, and then made their own supper and some sort of sleeping arrangement. He said, with him guarding the entrance, Dominica and Brannon could probably sleep a bit.

Dominica barely slept. It wasn't the cold or the hard ground; it was that she spent half the night in prayer, seeking some comfort, some assurance - but no answer came, and she doubted herself all over again. *Yet, what else can I do, with that promise he gave me, I must try.*

The next morning they brushed down their robes, which they had changed into from their wet clothes the night before, and were up and on their ponies heading towards the main camp before dawn. The trader said he'd go back and wait for them at the coombe for three days, and if they returned he'd take them back over the moors.

They could see a red and gold pennant flying high in the mass of tents and headed towards it. As they reached the first gap in the already foul-smelling ditch that surrounded the tented camp, a squat, muscular, scar-faced warrior, holding a spear taller than himself, stepped into the space and barred their way.

'Where do you think you're going?'

‘I have business with King Ina, please escort us to him,’ Dominica said in her best Anglisc.

‘He’ll have no time for the bleating of nuns.’

She changed her tone, using that she had heard in her own father’s court, ‘He will have time for me. I am as high-born as he and he has a debt to me. Who is your thegn?’

The warrior looked wary, ‘Herewig Axe-warrior.’

‘Call him!’

‘He’ll not ...’

‘You *will* find him, you *will* tell him to come and speak with me - I will not speak to any lower than him.’

‘Wilf!’ he called, glancing behind him, ‘Guard here – don’t let them through.’ As Wilf appeared the man handed him the spear and turned away and went out of sight. He returned after a while with a tall flaxen-haired warrior by his side, and Dominica smiled. *Thank you, Lord.* He was older and wore his hair a little longer, but she knew him.

He looked directly at her, ‘Sister – what is it?’

‘Herewig Axe-warrior? I am Prioress Dominica, sister to Saint Indract of Glestyngabyrig,’ she tilted her head and peered at him, ‘and I believe I saw you there, maybe ten years ago? You were one of six escorting the King into the Martyrs’ Mass?’ She could tell from his face that he remembered the occasion – if not herself. ‘The King told me then, just after the Mass, that I could come to him whenever I needed to – I need to see him, today. Please escort us to the King.’

‘I will, my lady. I believe you did a great service to the Lord King that day - not that any speak of it,’ he added with a smile.

Herewig gave a sign for Dominica and Brannon to follow him. They wound through the camp, Dominica glad she was on a pony as in places the mud was thick and maybe not just mud. Nearer the tent flying the red and gold they were stopped again, by another tent which completely blocked the way. Herewig ducked his head in speaking quickly, and a robed clerk appeared, his fingers ink-stained.

'Well?' the clerk said, looking them up and down.

'I want an audience with the King. Today,' she said boldly.

'You can want it all you like, but I doubt the King, or anyone, will see you today.'

'Your name, man?' Dominica tried again, determined to use everything she had learnt about how those with power talked to get their own way.

'Cenred,' he said, adding, 'my lady,' as a tentative after-thought.

'Cenred, you will take a note!' He looked startled, half bowed and backed into the tent. Dominica gave Brannon her reins and slipped off the pony to land as close to the dry matting that had been laid on the floor of the tent as she could. She followed him to his desk where he was preparing a small odd-shaped piece of parchment. 'Write, Prioress Dominica, healer, daughter of a King of Eriu, sister to the Holy Saint Indract of Glestyngabyrig ...' she paused, whether to beg or to request? 'requests an audience with King Ina. Underline the word healer.'

The clerk looked up at her. He'd just about squeezed the words onto the scrap of parchment.

'I presume you can make sure the King sees that note today? This morning would be best.'

The clerk gave a sort of smile, 'It will be with the other letters for this morning,' he said.

She wasn't quite sure what that meant. 'I shall wait here then,' she announced, casting a glance around for a stool - there was none. 'Have someone fetch me a seat!' she instructed. The clerk looked startled again, but went to the other side of the tent and called to someone outside. After a long while a man came carrying a seat, a strip of leather suspended between crossed frames of wood, and gave it to the clerk. It was enough. She said to Brannon, 'Brother, please take the ponies and make sure they are fed and watered.'

Hours passed. Brannon had returned and tied the ponies to the tent ropes where he could see them and settled himself on the floor next to Dominica.

More hours passed. Used as she was to fasting she still began to feel hungry, so she told the clerk to bring her and Brannon a drink. He looked as if he would argue, then changed his mind and called out to the back of the tent again, and shortly two cups of weak ale were brought.

The clerk's tent appeared to be a sort of gateway to the King's tents and court behind, one that was used only by messengers and the like. As the light began to fail Dominica asked the clerk whether the King had yet seen her note.

He said he had no idea, as he passed all the messages on to the King's clerk who sorted them for priority. 'You had best go back to your lodging, my Lady, and try again tomorrow,' he said with a small self-satisfied smile.

'I shall not! I shall stay right here until the King sees me,' she replied, noticing how his smile faded.

That clerk was replaced by another, and something about Dominica and Brannon was said, as attested by the glances made towards them. Despite this the night clerk came over and introduced himself as Garwig, and was more accommodating, telling Brannon where they he might get something for them to eat. As it grew dark Brannon brought in their blankets and they wrapped themselves to be as warm and comfortable as they could. Each time they woke to pray, Garwig was still at his desk, though sometimes leaning heavily on it, his head resting on the board.

In the morning, before the clerks changed back, Dominica asked Garwig to write almost the same words and have them sent through. This time, at the end, she had written. 'Your servant asks if your foot is healed?' thinking it might jog the King's memory.

Afterwards she sent Brannon out to look after the ponies and settled herself on the seat to wait for her audience again. The day-clerk was not pleased to see her. He glowered at her but said not a word.

'Good day, Cenred,' Dominica said sweetly. 'I hope today I may see the King.'

'Hope all you will ... my lady. It is not for me to know or say.'

'Of course not. Yet you will write again for me. You will need a larger piece of parchment.' He hesitated. She stared him down. Reluctantly he selected a piece about twice the size of the first scrap. She shook her head. He picked up a piece double that. She shook her head. He turned around and picked a piece almost double that, she nodded. Now to fill it! She changed it all round. Opened with, 'My Lord King will remember our meeting at Glestyngabyrig and the promise you made to me then, for the healing of your ailments. It is essential I tell you of a vision vouchsafed to me' ... and concluding with her plea to be granted swift audience, her titles and her kinship to Saint Indract.

The call came just before dusk. The night clerk had arrived and he was talking with the day clerk when another bustled in from the rear of the tent. He glanced in Dominica's direction and spoke with the clerks. It was Garwig that came, all smiles, to ask Dominica to follow the newcomer.

The King was eating when she was brought to him, and he was almost alone. He turned to the warrior who stood just behind him and with a tip of the head told him to stand further away.

'Prioress, come sit here. Forgive me if I eat. It has been a long day. Would you take some food? Drink?' Not waiting for an answer he beckoned, and a young man came from somewhere and brought her a cup and a plate. She sat. Wine was poured into her cup, and the server disappeared again.

'Thank you for seeing me, Lord King, tell me, how is your foot? Is it healed?' Glancing to see what food he was eating. Fish, some kind of white meat, beans – nothing over-rich.

'The Lord be praised, it left me the day you prayed for me, and has not returned.'

'The Lord be praised,' she repeated.

'But you do not come just to check on my health?'

'No, Lord King, I come to ask for the promise you offered. As you know I am a Prioress of a monastery on the banks of the Tamer, in the part of Dumnonia known as Kernow. We are a God fearing and active monastery, both men and women working for God and for the community he has placed us in. Rumours come that even monasteries and churches have been sacked in this campaign. I could not believe this, knowing yourself to be a good Christian King, yet we are now told it is because we are excommunicated for not following the pattern of Rome.'

'I regret the damage done to churches and monasteries, yet they stood against the Church of Rome, and must be brought into line. We have a papal mission to do this.'

'No word of this excommunication had ever reached our ears, and there is no cause for it where we are. We brought with us the Roman timings of Pascha, accepted many years ago in our part of Eriu, and the people just followed our lead as they were unministered.'

'So what is it you want of me?'

'Immediately after your healing, and your promise, at Glestyngabyrig, the Abbot there brought two of the hermit brothers to speak to me. They had both received the same vision and said it was meant for me. Separately they had been given the same vision, and only when it troubled them so much as to mention it to their Abbot, did they learn of the other. So they broke their usual silence to tell me. In this vision they saw a monastery hard by a river, and they saw the slaughter coming. They saw a pennant, a flag of red and gold, at the entrance of the monastery and they witnessed it grow and grow until it covered the whole of the grounds of the monastery ... and hid it from the slaughter.' She drew breath and looked directly into his eyes, 'Lord King, this meant nothing to me back then. Only now, as I hear of your army so near at Escancastre, and of the destruction of monasteries, the vision makes sense ... and I come to beg for your protection, for something that your men will recognise and respect when they come, so that they leave our monastery and all our people unharmed.'

'Where is your monastery? Again, exactly?'

'On the banks of the river Tamer. Tamerkam, the place in your tongue would be the bend in the Tamer.'

'On which bank?'

'Across the river, on the other bank from here, in Kernow,' Dominica said, curious about his question.

'So their vision also affirms that I will conquer beyond that river!' he smiled.

Dominica had not thought of that!

Chapter 55
Pennant *- circa AD 710*

She had been given a place in a women's area to sleep that night, but she was back in the clerks' tent waiting with Brannon when, late in the day, a large and heavy bag was brought to her. The clerk that brought it said, 'This is the King's promise for you – one for each face,' and bid her farewell.

'Convey my thanks to my Lord King,' she said as he turned away, feeling folded fabric through the outer bag. Swiftly they loaded the bag onto a pony and turned to leave in the hope they would reach the coombe before the light failed.

The sun was dipping close to the hill as they headed into the sunset, half blinded by the same golden light they needed to see their path.

They felt sure they had reached the small valley that led into the coombe as the light turned to a gloom barely relieved by the light of a finger-nail moon, and so followed the track as best they, and their sure-footed ponies, could.

The journey up the coombe seemed to take much longer than they thought it should and they were just beginning to whisper to each other that they maybe they had taken the wrong track when a man stepped into their path.

'Almost too late,' he said. 'I would have been gone at first light.'

They were all gone by first light and, as the ponies had rested well, they made their journey in one day. Once at St. Rumon's, Dominica unpacked the bag to have a good look at the king's gift. It held pennants, not just one but four, and not the smaller ones meant for the tops of poles riding into battle, but those meant to fly over the king's tent. Each was just more than half her arm-span at the widest and over her full arm-span to the point. The cloth was red and a bright yellow image of a beast, dragon like, with a long curled tail, was sewn onto it. The King had taken the vision literally; these were to be his protection for her. All at once she felt she should try to protect those at St. Rumon's too, should the fighting get to them. *One for each face, the clerk said, but one of our monastery faces is towards the river. We can spare one, can't we?*

The next morning Dominica asked to speak with the Abbot, and was bid to come to speak with him.

'Thank you so much for your help, and for your guidance.'

'And the King heard you?'

'He did, and he,' she gave a half-laugh, 'he took the vision as it was, and has given us royal pennants to protect us. More than one,' she sighed. 'He also saw in the vision his victory – which I hadn't. Yet on our journey back I have been thinking. You recall we had been celebrating Pascha according to our ways in Eriu when you took us in, and that we agreed between us to stay as we were to save confusing the people, for we did not know there was a dispute here, that the old ways on working-out the day of Pascha were still in use. It is that, apparently, which gives a Christian King papal license to sack churches and monasteries, because they follow the old ways and not the ways of Rome. The King accepted that we brought the Roman way with us from Eriu, and his protection was made easier by this. Please, take one of the pennants and fly it if they come to you, and profess to follow Rome, for the sake of the souls in your care – for in truth, I do not believe God or his Son cares which day we remember his passion and glory, but only that we do remember.'

The Abbot was silent for a few long minutes. 'Thank you, sister. I must pray on this. I will send a man with you to bring back our ponies. Get yourself prepared for the journey and we will speak shortly, in plenty of time for you to return to Tamerkam, I promise.'

They arrived back at Tamerkam before dusk, one pennant fewer than when they had arrived in St. Rumon's. Dominica left Brannon to see to the ponies and the lay brother that had come with them, and immediately sought out Keynae to tell her the news.

*

In the time they had been away the boundary had been marked quite well, but Dominica wanted it to be absolutely unmistakable, so she said the work should continue, building it up higher and wider all around, including where anyone could easily beach from the river - though there was really only the one place, where they had first landed themselves. She also asked for three stout poles to be cut and set into the ground ready to take the pennants. One beside the entrance to the monastery grounds, one each side of the grounds, facing upriver and down.

Shelters were also still being built - a multitude of smaller round houses in wood and wicker with reed roofs had sprouted near the newly enclosed edges. Off to one side, in an area yet unused she decided they might as well build another two larger, permanent round houses that could be used by the monastery after the war, hopefully, when the people could safely return to their homes. *But the vision gives King Ina the victory – and I haven't shared that insight with Keynae, have I? What will happen? Who will rule here? What will happen to the people?*

**

News came. Though Geraint's men had been defeated at the battle that gave Ina Escancastre, they hadn't been wiped out. They had dropped back, regrouped north of the Great Moor and were ready to fight to keep Ina's men from taking all of Dewnen.

Keynae, and the old men who advised her, got the people to gather any food-stuffs they could, albeit too early in the year for much to have grown that was planted; there were still wild plants that could be picked and dried to be used later, fish and birds to be hunted and preserved – all to be stored down in the monastery, ready for when it was needed.

Some muttered that they would take to the woods and the hills - as they had in the feuds - and had not even built anything within the monastery, so they had no need to lay up stores. Keynae told them - if that was their way they had best not come begging to be let in. Dominica was unhappy, but Keynae was adamant. They had chosen to defy her when they would not have defied Cador this way.

***

Dominica sent a message with a river-man to Cormag at Tamerunta, warning him of the way that monasteries had been treated at Escancastre. He did not send a reply. She worried that she should have sent him a king's pennant, and prayed he had understood all she had said about telling the Saxons they were following the Roman way.

****

News came slowly to Kellyventon, from wounded men who would never fight again, and trickled down to Bo Barr, and ran down to Keynae.

Keynae came to Dominica. 'They lost that battle to stop them still in Dewnen, but Geraint pulls them back to fight again. I do not know where this is, but the war has come right to this river border, they say. They say he gathers our men on the high-ground beyond the great crossing of the Tamer.'

'The crossing closest to here?'

'No, a man from Kellyventon would know it and say if it was the crossing to Lamburn. I think it is a wider place, where you could take an army across.'

'Was there any news of the men from here? They were all in Cynan's band of warriors too, weren't they?'

'I have only the second-hand tale. I will send a messenger to my brother's wife to see if she knows any more – but I think if she had news of Cador she would have sent word.'

*****

The monastery grounds were now very well marked, nothing that would stop a war-band set on breaking through, but enough to mark off the area the pennants would fly from. People began to bring down pots, stores, stones for the hearth, and wicker and bracken to raise bedding from the floor - simple things they could make more of, or spare, so when they came running, they need only carry what they could.

****

There was no more news. Two of the warriors who had struggled back to Kellyventon had died and the third was most like to, his wounds so bad. Rannoeu and her elders had set men - old men and boys in pairs - to watch from the great hill, and some to watch the rhyd across to Lamburn - in hope of knowing when to run and hide, she said. The woods were thick in the valley below Kellyventon, easy to hide in, and they could wade through the Linar river there and follow it to the sea if need be - there was little else those left could do.

***

Keynae set her own watchers, pairing old men with boys too, so the latter could run swiftly with the news. She had them at the stronghold and the signal point of Pensinys, on the high road above, and at the rhyd below Bo Barr, looking out for any signs of war on the move towards them.

**

The people of Bo Etherick and Bo Barr were the ones to start the move into the monastery. Not all of them, but those weakest or with the youngest. The quiet of the place was lost immediately, the smell of smoke from home-fires was always in the air unless there was a good breeze blowing up the valley. There was even, sometimes, a line at the well. It was as if they could sense the war coming nearer but, as the days passed, there was no more news from the battle front.

*

On a clear and cloudless morning smoke was seen from Bo Barr. At first it rose straight up like a tree, billowing out at the top. Kellyventon was burning! The cry rang around Bo Barr, a boy sped along the way toward Bo Etherick – another over the hill down toward Tamerkam – fear flowed through the people as they gathered all they could carry and fled towards Tamerkam - and into Saint Indract's monastery.

Chapter 56
***War** - circa AD 710*

It was chaos! What had appeared well planned, with shelters built and some stores laid in, soon showed itself to be far too cramped when all the rest of the people came with their children – and animals. *Why didn't I think about the animals? Most likely because what livestock we have is with the other monastery – as we have little grazing here because that land was provision for here too.*

As the day came to a close the smoke from so many extra home-fires hung thick over the monastery and, already, there had been arguments, mainly about animals wandering into other people's shelters. Tempers were short; the anxiety of what was to come making everyone on edge.

Keynae set extra watchers, looking over the way down from Bo Barr and from Bo Etherick, also looking over the other two rhyds, the shallow places through the streams of The Cut and The Pil. She'd also arranged for their animals to graze on nearby Tamerkam grassland to be fetched in as dusk came.

*

Dawn came, with no sign of the King Ina's men, for which Dominica gave thanks. She sent her monks to the Tamerkam monastery to bring back more supplies, as much as they could without leaving the other monastery too little – and to make the offer again; to come to them under the protection of the pennants. It was refused and, though Godric would not speak with her monks, Matuid told them, with a supercilious air, 'We have plans should the Saxons not understand the holiness of our place.'

The day passed. No news came from Kellyventon, and still no Saxons came their way. There were murmurings of returning - to the Tamerkam homesteads, at least. 'They were close, more comfortable, their livestock could feed better, they could run back here if need be.'

Dominica left all that to Keynae, as her people were her responsibility. Dominica had done all she could, led by the vision and, truth be told, even a handful fewer households and their livestock made it calmer within the monastery boundaries.

**

The next morning the boy from Bo Etherick came running in as if his heels were on fire. Smoke had been seen, across the upstream winding of the river this time, great plumes of it. They thought it was from Kalesak, the stronghold high above another tight loop of the river - on their side of the river.

Word spread and those who had left the monastery for their homes in Tamerkam poured back in.

Not long after, coracles drifted past as the falling-tide drew them down the narrowing channel. Seeing people on the bank, some of the people in the coracles shouted to them, 'All at Kalesak is put to the torch!' 'Everyone else - put to the sword - or taken!' 'Best run and hide - or take to the river!'

Run and hide? The woods were thick across the Pil, but that wasn't Tamerkam land. Take to the river? Only a few could take that option; there were only six or seven coracles laid up on the bank below their monastery, if that. Or stay and trust in the Lord! Dominica knew what *she* must do. She prayed that she had not just gathered everyone else for an easier slaughter.

Time passed, the river began to fill again, the wind dropped and people cooked and ate, argued and fretted. Dominica and Brannon walked around the hastily made perimeter. It was a marker only, nothing to stop determined men, easily burnt or climbed over. But there were the pennants. That was the vision.

She had drilled her monks in some simple Anglisc, they could shout, 'King Ina protects us!' and now the time seemed right to send them to the edges of the monastery, to stand on the raised points they had made, where they could be seen, and where they could see, either side of where the pennants flapped bravely from their poles.

The boy from the rhyd watch on The Cut between Bo Barr and Bo Etherick came first. A war band had crossed the rhyd and was climbing cautiously up the steep path between the two Bos.

The boy from the Bo Barr rhyd came in next, gasping fit to retch, his dusty-face marked with tears. He had only just got away, urged on by his grandfather. They had been over looking the rhyd below Bo Barr when they heard noises behind them, coming from the other side of the Bo. Dominica gave the boy water, and Keynae pressed him for details. How many men? Had they torched Bo Barr? He did not know. He hadn't wanted to leave the old man but he had run as his grandfather had ordered, screamed at him - run and do not look back.

Brannon stood by the main entrance to the monastery. They had debated whether they should try to throw up some kind of barrier but, it had been decided, they would merely stand there. A monastery's gate should always be open. He was alternately praying under his breath, and repeating the words in Anglisc, so they would be on the tip of his tongue when he had to call out, no matter how fearful he felt.

Suddenly he heard shouting and a scream from down-river. He turned to look but, of course, could see nothing as there were still trees between them and the Tamerkam landing place. He wasn't the only one to have heard it though. Some came out of their shelters, some dived in. A hubbub rose and died; now each ear strained to hear more.

For a moment it seemed that the river made more noise than the people.

Snatches of voices from across the way, nothing intelligible. A baby began to wail nearby - the mother's voice hushing it with an urgent low tone. Nothing for a while. Brannon's skin prickled as if he was being watched, but he could see no one in the cleared area outside the boundary.

One of Keynae's tree-watch boys suddenly appeared through the bank of trees, running fast, curving up to get to the new gateway. 'They're at the monastery!' he called as soon as he was close enough, but without slowing his racing legs until he was inside the boundary.

Keynae met him just inside the open gap, 'Here!' she ordered. He stood gasping before her. 'Which trees were you in? What did you see? '

'I was in the big tree where the three paths meet, on the corner where the men's monastery is.'

'What did you see?'

'Saxons! Most had helmets! They came right under me. Lots of them, many on ponies, lots of swords and axes!'

'What were they doing?'

'Going to the monastery.'

Keynae glanced at the sky in the direction of the stronghold. 'Did you see any smoke, or flames, from our stronghold?'

'No, I smelt smoke though. They carried torches, stinking of smoke, but not flaming, you know?'

'I know,' she said, she knew they'd just have to stick them in someone's hearth to light them up again, 'And the scream we heard?'

'That's when I ran! They were shouting at the Prior, he was shouting back. Strange words, didn't understand anything – but they were all angry. Then this big man stepped forward, fast as a snake, and speared him through. I almost fell out of the tree.'

'Speared him? The Prior?' The boy nodded. 'Go, get a drink. Well done.' Keynae stalked over to Dominica where she was talking to the other nuns. 'The boy says they put a spear through Godric.'

Dominica felt a chill run round her frame. Much as she disliked the man, she'd not wish this on him. 'Dead?' she asked.

'The boy ran. He'd been brave enough. They'd passed right beneath him!'

There was a sudden shouting and then people rushing towards the river. *Lord preserve me - let it not be an attack from the river?* But no, the crowd soon swarmed back, with two men dragging a half naked man between them towards Keynae and Dominica.

'Who are you?' Keynae asked, but by the time the words were out of her mouth she could see his tonsure.

'Maban, monk - from there!' he glanced down river.

'Let him go!' Dominica snapped as she recognised him, 'Maban! What happened?'

'I stripped and ran into the river. The, the Saxons! The big beast he stuck Prior Godric like a pig. He was doubled up over the spear - he had to shake him off it, like, like,' he shuddered, 'in a heap.'

'Why did they do it?'

'They were speaking in Anglisc. Prior said it would protect us, so he'd been teaching all of us to speak it - though I had much already. They wanted to search the church - but Prior Godric wouldn't let them, shouted they were sinners, said they'd have to kill him first. And - they did.'

'The rest of the monks?'

'Some stood as if stone, some ran for coracles - I ran into the river - the tide's going up so I swam here. God saved me,' he began to shake uncontrollably.

'Quick, dry him, get him warm, find him a habit,' Dominica instructed.

Then it came, a slow rhythmic thumping, clashing sound. Spears on the ground? Swords on shields? A guttural wo-ha! Wo-ha! accompanied the noise, making hearts beat faster. Sunlight glinted here and there from the dark line of trees, but there was no one to see.

Around Dominica people huddled together, held children tight, cried, stared, prayed. Dominica glanced round at their 'protection', the pennants, to realise that the breeze had dropped and they now hung limply from their poles. *Maybe I should have pulled them out from the points to be displayed even when there was little wind? Is it too late?*

Then the warriors came into view, stepping out of the surrounding tree-line, an assault on the ears and fearsome to look at, sun glinting on helmets, weapons, shield centres and edges. They spread their line to face the make-shift boundary at all points. Dominica tried counting the men she could see – forty, maybe forty-five? They started to move inwards, slow steps towards their monastery boundary, a short step per thump.

Most people shifted to where they could see, but stayed well inside the monastery grounds. Brannon ran to the entrance and started yelling in Anglisc! 'King Ina protects us!' pointing with his staff to the pennant, 'King Ina protects us! King Ina protects us! King Ina protects us!' He couldn't hear his brothers at the other posts over the war-band's noise, and wondered if the Saxons could hear him. 'King Ina protects us! King Ina protects us!'

Dominica came to his side, 'I will go and talk to them.'

'No! No!' he grasped her arm, 'Not after ... Godric! You heard what Maban said!'

Dominica touched his hand, he dropped his grip and his words dried in his mouth. She nodded.

'I must,' she said and, giving a grim smile, added, 'pray for me,' then walked forward - towards the advancing warriors.

Chapter 57
Saxons - circa AD 710

As Dominica stepped forward she heard cries from the people behind her, and she prayed, she prayed she could identify the leader so she could speak directly to him.

There he was. The man just to the right of the centre, a man who lifted his hand and, at which sign, the thumping and shouting stopped in a ripple left and right, until all she could hear were the sounds of sobbing behind her and the brothers shouting in Anglisc, 'King Ina protects us!' all at different times, a jumble of words.

And all she could see were the fired-up eyes of warriors focused on her. The brothers, raggedly, stopped their chanting, and she could have sworn she could hear her own heart beating. It certainly felt like it was beating so hard that it was making her tremble.

She looked at the man. He was not the biggest man there. A giant of a man stood at his right shoulder with a long spear in his grasp. She tore her eyes away from its point, gleaming wetly, back to the man with the assured stance.

'I am Prioress Dominica,' she spoke clearly in Anglisc as she drew to a stop facing him, leaving a good sized gap between them, 'and this monastery, by grace of God, is under the protection of King Ina.'

He stepped forward a pace, the warriors at each of his shoulders paced with him. It took all Dominica's will-power to stand still. She lifted her chin.

'We know nothing about monasteries being protected. They are ours to take. We are to clear out any resistance behind the King's victories.'

'The Lord King Ina gave me his pennants. Look! You can see them there! They are to show *any* of his men that we are *not* to be harmed!' She swallowed the ache in her throat,

‘And within here there is no resistance to the King’s rule. All those who *could* fight, you have already met elsewhere, and they have not returned.’

He turned to the huge warrior, ‘Fetch that rag here!’ He, and two others, stalked towards Dominica - she felt sick, but they swept past her.

She glanced after them to see them marching towards Brannon, he scrambled back inside the boundary. A cry went up behind him, and there was a movement as everyone shrank back well out of reach of the spear carrier. He stopped at the pennant, reached up and cut it down. Screwed it in his fist and turned back towards his leader, the other two guarding his back as he did so.

Shaken, she turned back to the leader, swallowed, said, ‘I have told you my name, but you have not told me who comes here in the name of the King - but does not know his will?’

‘I command these men - that’s all you need to know.’ Dominica heard the warriors come close, but steeled herself not to turn to look at them. They stomped past. The warrior held out the pennant. It looked smaller in his hand than it had when she had held it in her arms.

The leader looked at it - she could see, by a shift in his countenance, that he knew it was authentic.

Her voice rising, ‘You can see it is real! And we have *three* of them! Were you with King Ina at Escancastre? That’s where he gave me the pennants!’ And rising again, ‘For *our safety! We* are under *his protection!*’ she shouted.

There was a movement from the right side of the semi-circle. A warrior wearing more armour than most, a shining helmet and carrying an axe, had left his position and was striding over to them. He went right up to the leader and said something but, with his back to Dominica, she couldn’t hear what was said. Given a nod the warrior turned and swiftly headed straight for Dominica. She slightly shied her gaze away from his advance, but then he turned sharply to stand beside her - as if to take her prisoner.

‘It’s her!’ he said.

What now? She glanced up at the man who stood there, then she looked, then looked again. His face was partly hidden by the leather cheek protectors, but ... ‘Herewig Axe-warrior?’ she asked, wonderingly.

‘It is,’ he said, loosening his cheek-pieces, ‘I recognised your way of speaking Anglisc when you shouted at him! Wulfstan is in charge of our war-band. There’s four of us thegns, with our men - mopping up.’

‘Is the war over?’

‘The King has called a halt at the next river. Geraint has fled - we think dying.’

Wulfstan strode over, ‘Enough! We will see everyone in your camp, and we will search it!’

‘But you will not lay a hand upon any!’ Dominica retorted, ‘*Everyone* in *this monastery* is under my protection, and so under the King’s protection.’

Wulfstan glanced at Herewig and grunted, ‘Get it searched!’ and turned away.

Herewig escorted Dominica back to the monastery opening, his men falling in behind her. She led him towards the middle where a preaching stone and wooden cross had been set up. The people shrank back, some ducking into their shelters. She stood on the stone and called out to the monks and nuns, ‘We need everybody here so I can speak to them. Call everyone out, we’ve been promised they won’t be harmed.’

When they had gathered she told them that the monastery would be searched. That they were to stand where they were while the place was searched for fighting men. ‘If any of your family are still in your shelters go and fetch them, bring everyone, even the sick, the sick can be carried to the infirmary where the sisters will look out for them.’ Up on the stone she was as tall as the warrior. She turned to him. 'Herewig Axe-warrior, will you please search the infirmary first before we bring the sick in?'

'Which hut?'

She pointed and he sent two men to check inside.

'Why did you kill the Prior at the other monastery?' she asked quietly while the hustle of people being moved went on around them.

'Huh! Well you should have heard him – and Wulfstan hasn't much patience, doesn't like being insulted by anyone, or told he can't search where he wants to. This whole area was so deserted, we suspected they were all holed up in the church, maybe an ambush – it's big enough!'

'It is big – it was built for the community to worship in.'

'But that Prior, he told Wulfstan – the trouble makers you want are all hiding in the other monastery – go and deal with them. Wulfstan didn't like it – sounded to him like a trap. He said we were going to search whether they liked it or not – and your man said – over my dead body. Wulfstan just flicked his finger at Bear and your Prior was dead.'

'And there was no-one in the church?' Dominica said.

'Not a soul.'

'And the other monks? There weren't many.'

'They all - got away. You know, we don't really like killing monks. It doesn't sit right, when you fight you know death can come any day – most of us like to be – more sure of our souls.'

The invalids were taken to the infirmary, and all the other huts were searched. The chaos of possessions turned over, animals let out and barking dogs was endured so as to give no reason for offence.

Dominica watched from the preaching stone, ready to intervene if there was a problem before it could cause trouble. Over by the monastery entrance she noticed Herewig, the other thegns and Wulfstan gathered. They were talking animatedly. Wulfstan laughed, and shrugged, and they parted.

Men returned to report on the search and eventually Wulfstan was convinced that there really were only the old, the young and women there, apart from the monks, and, with bad grace, admitted they would be left alone – for now.

'Who is really in charge of the people in this place?' he asked her.

'I am. Just me,' Dominica said. *Well while they are in the monastery, it's true.*

Wulfstan stepped up onto the preaching stone, and she jumped down to get out of his way. 'Tell them what I say!' he snarled at Dominica then, looking around, he addressed the crowd, 'I will leave men here until the King decides your fate. There will be no treachery from you people here. We will take your Prioress as hostage to your good behaviour.'

As the translation of his words ended there was an eruption of cries and muttering. He gave a half laugh, 'We seem to have chosen our hostage well,' he said grinning. 'Get up here!' He gripped her upper arm and hauled her back up - there was an audible intake of breath from the people. The stone was not really big enough for two, her nostrils filled with the stench of him.

'Now tell them this. My men and horses must be fed tonight and again in the morning - then we will go to continue the King's work – leaving Herewig Axe-warrior and his men to guard you.' He glared round while she translated. He must have seen something in their faces he didn't like, 'We *will* be well fed – otherwise we will *take what we want*! You understand? *Anything* we want!' he growled. Dominica could see that they understood already but, as she translated this last bit, she looked hard at some of the old men who might have glared resentfully at Wulfstan's demand and caused this outburst.

'She's all yours,' he said, looking at Herewig, and stepped down, 'we're making camp at the other place,' he added, 'that church is a good shelter.'

Herewig watched him leave, then turned to Dominica, 'Don't worry, I've made sure it is me and my men who are left here. They'll not trouble your people if your people do not trouble them. Make sure your people understand this. And, now, get them going on food for all of us and ale if you have it - you do not want to provoke Wulfstan. He is in no mood to be crossed.'

'Thank you. May the Lord bless you.'

'Oh, it's in my own interest. I *know* the King values you,' he said.

Chapter 58
***Hostage** - circa AD 710*

In the morning the Saxons at the Tamerkam monastery were brought food to break their fast. After they'd eaten, and taking whatever was left over with them, they wasted no time in leaving.

Herewig watched them go too and turned to Dominica, 'Are you packed, ready to go?' She nodded. The evening before he'd told her he was taking her to King Ina as the hostage, but gave her the evening time to sort out who would run the monastery in her absence, and lead the people. She spent time with her monks, nuns and lay workers, making sure they could continue the work without her and leaving Brannon and Yowann in charge. Then with Keynae, comforting her as best she could and encouraging her to take this small victory - their lives without slavery or slaughter - and make the best of it. She didn't have to remind her of the awful report from the coracles drifting down from Kalesak.

With a change of habit, her mother's faded brat, and her healing scrip, she was as ready as she could be. Most people in her monastery were hanging about the centre, watching and waiting.

Herewig brought one of his men's pony for her to ride. He then jumped up on the preaching stone and shouted for all to come close to hear.

'Elsewhere – you will hear, soon enough, those not slaughtered, those fit to work, any over five years, have been taken as slaves - men, women and children. Your fate is in your hands – your Prioress has saved you, so far, and you will save *her* by causing my warriors *no* trouble. If any harm comes to them – not a soul will live here again for a thousand years. This is my promise.' His axe glinted in the sunlight, and the silence was complete. 'My men have been ordered to treat you well, *as long as you treat them well.* They are to be fed and given ale each day. I shall return shortly and I shall know just how much I can trust you in the future.'

As she finished translating Dominica nodded, and added, 'Do as he says. May the blessing of Christ be upon you all, in the name of God, bless you all!' There was a murmured 'Amen' and Dominica turned, with tears in her eyes, and followed Herewig to where their rides stood.

They rode out, up the ridge highway towards Bo Barr, with Herewig asking her to tell him about Tamerkam and the extent of it - which she did as best she could. They didn't turn off for Bo Barr, but followed the highway out of the Tamerkam area and joined the wider highway which passed Ventonpemps and headed towards The Hill. As they passed the turn-off that led into Kellyventon, Dominica thought she could smell the tang of smoke in the air. 'Were you and your men here?'

He turned and looked back, then looked around towards the hill, shook his head, 'No, we didn't come this way – we were told to follow the river down towards the sea – others were sweeping inland. Why do you ask?'

'People I knew lived there,' she said quietly. 'What will happen when we get to the King?'

'With luck we will see him quickly.'

'And then?'

'I will ask for recompense, for all your lives saved from slavery. Wulfstan was *so* angry,' he gave a short laugh, 'a day wasted, he said, and nothing to show for it! So when I volunteered to take on the duty he thought I was crazy. Laughed, said I had the hots for an old nun! But I knew about you and the King at Glestyngabyrig – he didn't!' He paused, added, 'Besides, sister - you are my lucky talisman.'

'So you hope he will reward you for making sure we were not hurt?'

'I do! Do you know how being in the King's service works?'

She shook her head, though born the daughter of a king, none of that had been explained to her.

'A thegn who fights well and survives can be rewarded by his king with silver or with more land. As a thegn you are duty bound to provide yourself as a warrior, and *other men*, according to the amount of land you hold. Other men, trained, armed, and ready to fight for the king.'

'I see.'

'Ah, but you don't. Before that day in Glestyngabyrig *I* was just one of those *other men*, a nobody, a man sworn to a thegn. The bright armour I wore that day was just borrowed from the man who should have been there, but was sick, doubled up over his guts. The King asked for a warrior to be found to match the others. He needed his full number that day to surround him as he was in such pain. I was chosen because I was the right height and colouring. The man had to give me his armour – it was provided by the king, but his sword was his own so I didn't get that. Ha! And that was the day I got my name too, because I was, I am, an axe-warrior. It was a name given as an insult by the other king's men - but I embraced it. Never had the proper training in the sword before. Made up for that now, and I can use both, very well! So I carry my axe with pride – because many of *them* can't use an axe half as well as me!'

They rode in silence for a short time as their mounts negotiated a slippery path where a stream had crossed the way.

He continued, 'After you did – whatever you did – and the King was better, he was in such a good mood. He gave the others silver, but he gave me five hides of land near the border between his kingdom and your king's. Owning five hides of land makes you a thegn, did you know that? Makes you a lord over people who you have to care for, but who owe you labour, produce and coin. So for the past, what? Ten years? I've worked with my people and our place has grown well, prospered, but then came the war – and I knew I had a chance to advance myself. I'd always been planning, that's why I took in suitable boys to train as my men. I didn't have to – at five hides I only needed to bring myself, a horse and a manservant. It costs to have fighting men in your service. Weapons, shields, helmets, their keep – it all costs, but then if I can be of service to the king, I get my share of plunder based on the number I bring - and this time - I may get silver instead of land.'

'So why did you choose to guard us? Under the King's protection there was no plunder.'

'Because the King owes you, and I hope he will reward me for making sure you are safe.'

'Is that all?'

They rode in silence again – Dominica could tell Herewig was debating something with himself.

'Maybe – maybe because *you are* my talisman,' he muttered.

'Your talisman? Maybe, but I would say God had brought us together for a reason. It may just be to have saved our mission – or it maybe more – I do not know, but over the years I have recognised His hand shaping my world.'

'Well we shall see, sister. I, for one, have no idea. God hasn't figured much in my life so far.'

Dominica laughed, 'Ha! So you say! '

Though they'd stopped only briefly on their way, it was getting late by the time they saw the encampment. They had passed a high point, which Herewig pointed out as being occupied by the king's men, but had then veered right, along a wide, well beaten, track which he said led to the great ford.

Though Herewig found a place for each of them to stay, found a man to care for the mounts, he'd also discovered that there were many petitioners, both Saxons and Britons, all wanting to see the King - it was obvious he wasn't going to get to stand before the King easily, or soon.

'Why not get the clerk to write a note to ask for an audience?' she suggested, 'That is what I did at Escancastre.'

He shrugged, then smiled, 'Why not? We can try,' he said, and led them both through the maze of tents towards the King's tent. As before there was the outer tent, and in it, the same clerk. He obviously recognised Dominica - his face betrayed him.

'Cenred!' she said, as she approached his desk, 'It is good to see a face I recognise.' He looked taken aback and puzzled, but before he could open his mouth she went on, 'We need you to take a note to the King.' He didn't bother objecting, just turned and picked up a piece of parchment showing it to her with eyebrows raised. She nodded.

'Please write; Prioress Dominica congratulates you on your visionary victory. Here as a hostage to fortune I request an audience for myself and your thegn Herewig Axe-warrior. Praise be to God for his mercies.' She waited while his quill scratched down the last words, then added, 'Underline the word visionary. Good, now, make sure it gets before the King this time, and remind the King's clerk of how pleased the King was to see me last time. We shall return here in the morning.'

They left and sought food and drink before settling down for the night. They were so early next morning that the night clerk had not left, and he actually smiled when he saw her. 'Sister, Prioress, I was told you had returned, I have brought you a seat,' he said, indicating where one stood waiting for her.

'Thank you, Garwig. So thoughtful.'

'Sister,' he looked a little abashed, 'Last time you wrote that you were a healer?'

She smiled, 'In God's grace, I am.'

'I, er, I am troubled with an aching in my knees and worse, sister, in my fingers – as a clerk this is worrying as well as painful. I have asked at a monastery before, but what they gave me did nothing to help. Will you help me?'

'Brother, I hope I can. I can make up a balm for you to rub on your joints to ease them and a drink to take, but only when most painful. Let me see if I can find the herbs I need hereabouts and I will see what I can do *after* I have seen the King – I dare not leave in case he calls me.'

'And I, sister, will speak urgently with the King's clerk on your behalf.'

Whether it was the words of the night clerk or the remembrance of her previous visit – before the end of that day they were called.

The King was not alone this time, sitting below and to one side were two clerks, and another presiding above them. Two king's men stood guard, and one seemed to give Herewig a stare and slight twitch of his lips. Dominica could not discern if it was a suppressed smile or a sneer.

Dominica and Herewig bowed.

'Prioress, I am glad to see you are well.'

'And I am glad to see you are well too, Lord King. I thank you for your protection that you gave us - our community are now within your conquered lands – and I am hostage to their well-being.'

The King looked sharply at Herewig, 'Why have you taken the lady Prioress hostage? A woman of the church and under my protection?'

Herewig, for once, seemed struck dumb, then stuttered out, 'I, I haven't, as such...'

The King cut him short, 'You have brought her here as a hostage! You will answer for this!'

'Lord King, he has brought me, but it was not he who demanded me as hostage!' Dominica said quickly, 'That was one named Wulfstan who was leading the war band. If it were not for Herewig our community may yet have been desecrated. It was Herewig who remembered me from

Glestyngabyrig and from Escancastre and stepped in to defend us.'

'Then why are you still a hostage?'

Dominica looked at Herewig – he seemed to have lost his tongue, head down. 'Because, he volunteered his men to – protect our community from others, and, and as Wulfstan had claimed me as hostage I had to be brought to you, Lord King, for a decision.'

The King drew in a long breath. 'So. I hereby release you.' He glanced at the clerks and raised a finger, one began scratching away on the parchment. Dominica felt like they were about to be dismissed, and Herewig still stood mute.

'Lord King, I pray that you will consider rewarding Herewig? Without him our community would surely have been sacked, our people taken as slaves. We know this! Before they came to our monastery, Wulfstan confronted the Prior of the old monastery – and had him brutally murdered, the rest of those monks fleeing for their lives. Even with your pennants flying at our monastery, Lord, he was reluctant to give up his plunder until Herewig stepped in and took responsibility.'

'Ah! Yes, my pennants! Tell me! How did one of those I granted *you*, for *your safety*, end up flying at a monastery beside the Great Moor?'

A chill ran around Dominica, 'Are they? Is the monastery – untouched?'

Chapter 59

***The King's Hand** - circa AD 710*

'I asked you, how?' the King repeated, his voice cold and low.

'Lord King, I gave it to the monastery that has taken us under its auspices. They send a priested monk to bring us our Eucharist on the Holy days. Lord, I had only need of three pennants. Our monastery lies hard against the river one side. I wanted, I hoped, your protection would stretch to them? Forgive me if it was wrong – it was done for the love of God, for they are gentle and holy men at St. Rumon's,' the tightness in her chest had increased so she could hardly breathe to speak, 'Are they – well, Lord King?' she said her voice barely above a whisper.

Ina looked at Dominica, then sighed, 'You are an extraordinary and brave woman. They are well, my thegn who scoured that area recognised my pennant and left them be, but reported the matter.'

'Thanks be to God!' Dominica sighed, the ache in her chest dissipating. She gave a bright smile, glanced round at Herewig, standing beside her.

The King looked at Herewig too. 'You said you recognised the Prioress?'

'Yes, Lord,' Herewig found his voice, and straightened, 'When she spoke, shouted at Wulfstan, I recognised the way she speaks Anglisc, and remembered her from Escancastre and Glestyngabyrig, where I was, for that one day at the martyrs' mass, one of your King's guard.'

The King paused, 'Ah! I remember. You had no sword so you held your axe! I gave you land - five hides?'

'Yes, Lord, five hides - but I brought with me, to this war, four trained men in my service,' Herewig said quickly, now standing tall with his head held high.

'Good man! Good man!' He glanced at the clerks again, 'Prioress, how many fit and able men in your community? How many women, how many children over five?'

It was Dominica's turn to go dumb as she tried to count up families, 'Lord, not many men, all those who were of fighting age went to fight - and have not returned. We have old men, fit only to talk of the past. Women, about ...'

'Take you time. Be honest as I am sure you will. Come back and send me a note by my clerk tomorrow and Herewig Axe-warrior will be rewarded in silver for all those who would have made coin.'

'Thank you, Lord,' Herewig said with a bow.

The King looked thoughtful for a moment, 'I will hold this land, but you, Herewig, will be my gerefa, to stand as Lord for me in this place – what is it called?'

'Tamerkam,' Dominica said, 'It means bend in the Tamer river. It overlooks a tight bend in the river,' she added.

'Tamerkam.' A glance at the clerk who was busy writing everything down. 'How big is it – this place – how many hides?

Dominica looked at Herewig – she had no idea.

Herewig said, 'I have only ridden two parts of the border,' he gave a small shrug, 'perhaps around half a hide?'

'Half a hide? It is small, and a long way from your property, so you, yourself, will only need to sit as Lord for justice each quarter day, but must ensure it is well run and protected, even when you are not there.'

Herewig bowed, the clerk scratched down the information and the King's decision. And then they were dismissed, to await Dominica's assessment of her numbers, and to receive the reward in silver.

'I can't believe this,' Herewig said as they stepped into the open air. He gave a small laugh, 'seems you were right, God wants me at your place – yet I am to be rewarded too.'

'God be praised!' Dominica said, smiling as they walked through the camp.

Dominica worked out as best she could the number of people in the community as asked, and added herself and the monks and nuns at the end of the list separately. She returned to the tent with her numbers, to be written on a note to be given to the King's clerk, that very evening – happy to hand it to Garwig to ensure it got to the right person, assuring him she would now be able to go and seek out the herbs in the morning.

The countryside around the camp had plenty of ash trees, for their leaves, and the yellow flower the locals called piss-the-bed, both good against aches in the joints. Then there was the white fluffy-headed bittersweet for pain and, lastly, some nettles which, along with the dried herbs she carried, was all she needed.

She tore all the herbs into pieces and crushed them between stones, then steeped them in hot fat, begged from the cooks, and kept it warm for a time, stirring now and again. When she could see the fat had absorbed some colour she poured it through a small rush mat she'd woven while waiting, to catch the pieces and let the greenish fat trickle into a pot. When it was cooled and firm in the evening she brought it to the clerk, telling him to rub it on his joints daily, morning and evening, and dictated the recipe for him to get more made up by someone else when this pot ran out. She also gave him her own parchment packet of bittersweet powder, to take in a little wine for when the pain was unbearable.

The next morning Herewig was sent for - to receive his silver. The King's clerk made him put his mark beside a line of writing and told him he would also receive the stipend for being the king's gerefa each year upon his written report on the prosperity of the place.

Another man, of a much larger stature but still wearing clerks robes, handed him a money bag which felt pleasantly heavy as he received it. 'The King told me to say that you had done well to bring so many men from such a small holding, that is also rewarded in there, and to say that he will be watching you and how you fare,' he said.

The king's clerk added, 'You are to escort the Prioress back to her place – and remain there for a month and await orders.' He proffered a sealed piece of folded parchment, 'and you are to hand this to the Prioress.'

'I am honoured,' Herewig said, though wondering exactly how he would be watched, and why.

Herewig handed Dominica the King's note and said that, as it was still early enough, they would prepare to leave. Dominica glanced at the note and tucked it away safely, she didn't want Herewig to ask her what it said.

They talked for a lot of the journey back, Herewig about how he ran his holding and Dominica about the way Tamerkam was run before the war. She wanted him to understand the place and how it worked together under Cador and Keynae, and how a knowledge of the individuals was so important.

When they arrived back at Tamerkam late that day, the news flew around the monastery with people gathering at the monastery entrance to welcome Dominica back. Keynae came forward to welcome Dominica as she dismounted, giving her a hug.

'Sister, is all well?' she asked as she stepped back and searched Dominica's face.

'All is well. And here?'

Keynae's eyes welled, 'Cador was killed, and Drustan ... he's back,' she whispered, 'what is left of him,' and the tears overflowed. Dominica took her in her arms and held her.

'I will come to you. Are you back in your own home?'

Keynae tipped her head towards Herewig, now dismounted and with two of his men obviously reporting to him. 'His men wanted us all to stay in the monastery until he came back – I understand – it was easier for them to check on us.'

Dominica went over to Herewig, 'May I come and speak with you later ... lord?'

He smiled, 'Yes, there's still time before dark.'

Keynae took Dominica into her hut, so small compared to her place on the hill, and there, lying asleep on the bed was Drustan. When her eyes adjusted for the light, Dominica could see he was wan and sickly. He had lost his right ear - and the hand of his right arm. It was a miracle he was alive, that he hadn't bled out.

'How did you get him past the guards and into the monastery?'

'The guards brought him. Found him sitting by the river, and just brought him over.'

'Amazing! They did not harm him?'

'No. That monk from the river, Maban, helped translate - it seems they didn't want to kill him in case their lord wanted him alive, but they didn't know what to do with a man that was looking so sick, so damaged, so they brought him to us.'

'Has Eiliwedd or Avan looked at him?'

'Yes, both. Avan cleaned-up everything. The stump – it's been treated with fire – she says it may have saved him, but it has cooked his flesh,' Keynae shuddered. 'She's given him something to help the pain and to let him sleep.'

'She's done well then – but Keynae, if the flesh is cooked it cannot heal properly, I will look tomorrow, let him sleep now.'

Later, after they had eaten and washed, Dominica passed Herewig's guard, the pair of them either side of the entrance, and made her way over to the old monastery.

Herewig and one of his men were in the church, the other stood guard at the door and pushed it open for Dominica to enter.

'Ah! Prioress, come in,' Herewig said. Dominica looked around the church. She could only think of it as a church, but she noticed the altar was gone. Then, with a small shock, she recognised it as the table that Herewig was sitting behind. Bereft of its altar cloths and set up differently, the altar did seem like any other table.

She stood across from Herewig, 'May we talk about the people?'

He nodded, 'Go ahead.'

'They have been cooped up in the monastery long enough. Can they return to their households, to their land?'

'I can see this would be a good idea – but how may we be sure they will not rise up against us. We are few.'

'The people do not know the King made me free – as far as the people are concerned, I am still hostage to their behaviour, whether in the monastery grounds or at their own homes. Besides – you will have to return to your home at some time, will you not?'

'That is up to the King,' he said, 'but yes, you are right – I must work something out before that time. I have decided that over the days to come, you will make yourself available to show me the whole of this area, I shall meet the people in their homes and understand how this place works.'

'That is a wise choice,' Dominica smiled. 'We can let the people go home tomorrow...'

'After I have spoken to them all,' Herewig cut in.

'After you have spoken to them all,' Dominica agreed.

Part Five

In a different kingdom - on the same ground

Chapter 60

Dwale *- AD circa 710*

The next morning everyone fit enough was called to the preaching stone of the monastery. Herewig came, with an escort of all his men, dressed in his best warrior's attire, polished and oiled, his sword at his belt but his axe in his hand. He stepped lightly up onto the preaching stone and lifted the axe. A silence fell upon the people, they even stopped their shuffling and looked up at him.

'The Lord King Ina of Wessex has claimed this land as his and you, and it, are under his protection.' He paused to allow Dominica to translate. 'He has also seen fit to place me in his stead as your Lord. You will be permitted to return to your life as it was. Be sure that dissent will not be tolerated. My orders stand as before - you are on your honour and the honour of your Prioress. I shall visit each of your households, Prioress Dominica shall be my guide - so go now - and make your homes and holdings ready.'

He stepped down as the translation finished, and smiled briefly at Dominica as a hubbub broke out amongst the people, some turning and heading to their makeshift homes immediately, gathering their belongings to leave.

When the majority had left the monastery Dominica had time to go and see how Drustan was doing. He was sitting up when she entered. He glanced at her and dropped his gaze to his one hand resting in his lap.

'Drustan, so good to see you awake and sitting up!' she said brightly.

'What's left of me. The pain, the smell. I can barely stand it.'

'You are alive. There is much to thank God for.'

'Huh! What use am I? I should have died!'

'Tell me, what happened?'

'A bastard sliced me!' He shook his head, 'Sorry. Our lines had broken. The horn sounded to reform a line further back, so we were running to that place and suddenly, my ear is burning and I was dragged down by my right arm – it was his sword slicing through my wrist. Ha! I watched my hand and axe fall away! I never even saw his face – he rode on, slashing into our people from behind them. I don't know where they came from, a horde of riders slashing all of us in their path,' his voice cracking.

'The others from here?'

'Dead! All of them I think – Father, certainly. The battle sort of swept past me then – moved fast across the land, I was left behind, amongst the dead. I, I was kneeling, gripping my own arm, hopelessly trying to stop the blood from draining away – a monk appeared, he bound up my wrist with a leather strip and a stick to twist it until the blood stopped pushing out.' Drustan blew out a long breath and shook his head. 'There were a couple of them going through the battlefield turning over bodies. They took me, with a few others, walking but – damaged, back to their monastery. There they strapped my arm down and put this hot metal on the stump – I ... Oh! The pain! I woke later. The stench hit me first and then the pain, again and again! It still comes and goes – unbelievable.'

'The brothers – they saved you.'

'I know. But, huh! What for? I'm useless – and every man, everywhere I go, will think me a liar and a twice-time thief,' he raised his stump, setting it gently down again. 'So I made my way back here, where I hope people may not judge me that way. I didn't know what else to do.'

'Your mother is happy you have survived. You did right; you can be useful here. You have other skills – you can read and write...'

'Read sister - but not even write any more!' He lifted his stump again, looked at it, 'And anyway - what use is that?'

'You can learn to write with your other hand - not easy, but you can. In the meantime – I must look at your wound and see if I can make it so that the flesh does not corrupt, and the skin can grow to cover the wound properly.'

Later that day Herewig called on Dominica for her to show him the boundaries and to point out the settlements, so they set off back up the highway out of Tamerkam.

'I can point out the boundaries roughly,' she said, 'but you'd have to walk beside the streams to really know. Like here, we are just under the brow of the hill on the highway track, but over the brow the land goes down by really steep wooded slopes to the stream they call the Pill. And it is the same all round as far as I can tell. The Tamerkam land is surrounded by steep, wooded stream valleys.'

'That's good. Plenty of building material, good defences.'

'I think there's some places that need watching more than others, and part of the highway that goes from Kellyventon to – I don't know where - but it passes here, that is also a border.'

'Kellyventon?'

'The place that had been burnt - near The Hill, where I asked if your men had been there? It was where the Big Man of this area lived ... before,' she paused, 'You know, there is one who could tell you everything you need to know about the land, and about the defences.'

'One of the elders? Would I understand them, or they me?'

'Not one of them. The injured warrior who came back.'

Herewig looked round sharply, 'He is alive? My men thought he must surely have died.'

'Near to it, but he was a strong young man and – rallies. He'll never be a warrior again, he has lost his axe-wielding hand.' Out of the corner of her eye she caught the involuntary wince Herewig made.

'And, no doubt sister you have ministered to him.'

'Of course. He's a bright young man. He can read and – could – write. I will encourage him to learn to write with his other hand. He knows a little Anglisc and would soon learn, I promise. But best – he knows everything you need to know – he was the son of the Chiefman here and is Keynae's son. She can advise him too. He is perfect to be your steward when you must be away – they, the people, will look up to him and he knows them all, rascals and right-thinkers, hard workers and shirkers, and he knows the defences and the land.'

Herewig rode in silence for a time. 'But he may also be a leader of trouble against me.' There was a small note of inquiry in his words, but not quite as much as a question.

'Why would he, if he has everything he could gain from causing trouble, given to him as your man?' There was no response. Dominica held her tongue for a while, but she couldn't let the chance slip so she added, 'And he is – in despair, believes he should have just died with the others – no longer able to wield his axe, he feels he is - nothing. *I* know he is not, I know he is beloved by the Lord, by his mother, by - me – yet he does not see this, feel this. But he would be a loyal man to you - for you can give him back his worth – you can make him *someone* again – and only you.'

By the time they rode back down from Bo Etherick to the monastery they had looked at the stronghold at Pensinys, the rhyd below it and the settlement behind it of Bo Barr. They'd stood at the top of the track that came up from the rhyd across the stream called the Cut, which Herewig realised was the one he and the other men had crossed into Tamerkam by, and circled Bo Etherick to spy out the extent of the land.

“I think a bit more than half a hide after all, though much is steep,’ Herewig said, half to himself, then turning to Dominica, ‘So, two strongholds, three settlements, and a few scattered homesteads?’

‘Yes, the homesteads are attached to one or other of the settlements and, of course, we did have two monasteries.’

‘You will still have one. I will be keeping the other as my court. I need a proper base when I am here - and for my representatives to work out of. The old chief’s home and the meeting house can remain in their family.’

‘And the land around the monastery? It was supposed to support our monastery?’

‘You can keep that, I will take my, and the King’s, due from all, I will not need to work that land. My steward will have to work hard,’ he smiled.

‘Your steward?’

‘No promises, sister, but I will meet with your wounded warrior, then we will see.’

The next day Dominica decided that Drustan was strong enough to withstand the work she had to do on his arm. She had sharpened her bronze blade to a fine edge, had boiled the thread and needle ready, read and re-read the recipe for dwale that trader Joseph has presented to her, then prepared the concoction in its copious amount of wine.

She prayed, as she always did before doing a difficult thing, even more so with the untried dwale as her main hope of painlessly cutting away the cooked flesh and preparing the stump for a chance to heal – without this it would surely rot and lead to a horrible death.

Avan was to help her, and Eiliwedd came down too in case both were needed. Drustan was brought to the infirmary and seated on the edge of a refectory table which was covered by a clean cloth and set up where the light from the door fell upon it. He was given the dwale to drink.

Drustan sniffed the cup, 'Smells like wine?' he said, a little confused, 'are you just going to get me drunk?'

'The medicine is in the wine,' Dominica said, '*apparently,* it is best when working with wine,' she raised her eyebrows as if she didn't quite believe it, and thought it an excuse to drink wine anyway. 'And the terrible thing is,' she added, 'you have to drink four cups at least!' That made Drustan smile a bit and show a little of the usual twinkle in his eye.

By the end of the third cup Drustan was grinning like a fool. The fourth cup almost slipped from his grasp as he tipped it up to drain it – the cup was caught by Avan as he slipped into sleep, and the others caught him and laid him down on the table top.

Even after Dominica had cut away all the damaged, cooked flesh - already looking greenish - and then a bit more until the wound bled fresh and clean, even after she had folded and sewn the biggest vessels while the flow was stopped, and then cleaned it all and bathed it in garlic water and an oil of self-heal, even after she'd gently stretched and drawn the ragged ends of skin to cover all she could of the flesh, and used skins of navel-wort and honey to seal it before wrapping in nettle-cloth bandages - even after all this he still snored on, oblivious. The only holding that had been necessary was to steady his arm for such delicate work.

She thanked God and thanked the fact they had in store such a powerful medicine that meant she could work so carefully and so long and yet the patient would feel no pain.

All that they could do now was wait to see how he fared when he recovered from the effects of the dwale.

Chapter 61

***Drustan** - AD circa 710*

Across Tamerkam the harvest was being made, and everyone old enough to help was there - even small children who would, another year, have done little but glean, were gathering-up and learning to stack tied sheaves into stooks with their slightly older siblings.

Dominica understood every family mourned the young fit men who had not come back for the harvest - but it still made her heart glow to see everyone working together. Including everyone from the monastery - and even Herewig and his men, and she felt foolishly proud that Herewig didn't shirk the manual work.

*

The days passed swiftly, Drustan's stump began to heal, though he had to keep it safe, clean and dry yet, but soon he was well enough to talk with Herewig. Dominica brought him into Herewig's hall. The makeshift fire pit had been replaced with a large neat stone edged hearth. A long side table, with a bench beside it, had been made and stood along one side of this new fireplace – somehow looking as if it was just waiting for a matching one to lie opposite it.

Beyond it, the old altar, the new lord's high table, stood facing them. Dominica brought Drustan to stand before that table, as Herewig sat behind it.

'Lord Herewig, this is Drustan son of Cador, the man I was telling you about.'

'Welcome. Prioress,' he smiled, 'will you translate for us?'

'Willingly, when needed - I have begun to teach Drustan some more Anglisc.'

'So you are an axe warrior?' Herewig began.

Drustan's head came up, 'I was. A good one too,' he replied slowly in Anglisc, then added, 'Lord,' as if he'd just remembered who he spoke to.

'My favourite weapon too, as I am sure the Prioress has told you. How is your – wound?'

Dominica translated that for Drustan as Herewig had not spoken slowly.

'Healing well - thanks to the Prioress.' Then added ruefully, in Cornish, 'I dare say I'll not wield an axe again though.'

Herewig nodded slowly as Dominica translated the last bit, 'Yet our friend here thinks that you could do well wielding a little power in the community, that you could lead, guide them in the right path, keep them safe and that they would listen to you.'

Dominica took over translating all from then on; it was too important to be misunderstood.

'I would hope that the people of Tamerkam would listen to me, would know I had their best interests at heart for they know me - and they knew my father who led them well for many years,' Drustan replied.

'And how would you feel reporting everything back to me? Owing your allegiance to me – and to King Ina – who you so recently fought, whose war has taken your friends, and their fathers too?'

'This is what happens. Men make war, and those who lose must make peace or go. And, from what I am told by my mother and by the Prioress, without you, there would not be a community here to lead. So why would I not want to work for you, Lord?'

'Can you still ride?'

Drustan lifted his stump, 'This won't stop me riding, Lord.'

'Then tomorrow we will see if, and how, you can help me. I want to get to know the people, and you can come with me. Prioress, can you accompany us, unless there is another who can translate?'

'If it pleases you, I would prefer to remain with the mission. There is always much to do, but we have one monk, Maban, who has quite a bit of Anglisc, maybe he will be able to do what you wish?'

'Send him with Drustan tomorrow and we will see.'

**

Keynae visited Dominica about seven days later. Dominica, so glad to see her friend without grey-rimmed eyes at last, welcomed her and prepared a herbal drink for them both. They sat in the sun outside the herbarium.

'You would think that those two had been friends since young, to hear Drustan tell of it,' Keynae said, a smile on her face.

'And the people? How do they take to Herewig as their chief?'

'Well, they do not venture their opinion too loudly, but those who have met with your Herewig seem to find him fair and - interested,' she laughed, 'a bit too nosy, is how one put it, but admitted he had a right to be. He did himself no harm working in the fields as he does.'

'It is no more than Cador would do – but I can see how it might have helped. From his own account he has made his place in Somersaete prosperous through taking an interest. I believe him, otherwise he'd not have the wealth to train and bring four fighting men with him.'

Drustan's opinion of Herewig was confirmed to Dominica the very next day, when Herewig came to see her.

'Prioress,' he said as found her between the chapel and the herbarium.

'Lord Herewig. Is all well?'

'Indeed it is. Now that I have met with all the heads of the main households, and understand the defences and the possibilities of this place, I believe Drustan is the man for the job as my steward here – and he has accepted. My thanks go to you, for suggesting him.'

'My thanks go to the Lord and to you for considering Drustan,' she was smiling broadly. It did seem all God given.

'Well, we seem to get on very well,' he grinned, 'and he picks up Anglisc quickly.' He added, 'Many of the heads of the households are women, until their sons gain age. However, they seem to know their business well.'

'The women of this place are as equals with their men-folk in many ways – and some know even more than them as they have the household knowledge too.'

'So I see,' he smiled and looked directly at Dominica, 'You know you are well favoured amongst the people, don't you?'

'I am blessed to have been of service to many, healing is a gift from God,' she said. She had a nagging feeling he wanted to say something more – but was finding it hard to put it into words.

He turned away, as if he meant to go, then turned back and took a step closer to her, 'Drustan can read and write you said?'

'He can read Latin, and I am sure he could learn to write again with his left hand.'

'Latin? So how long does it take to learn Latin and to read and write in it?'

'That depends on each person. My healer Avan surprised even me, but others, monks even, take many months, some years.'

Herewig looked up at the sky, as if looking for writing on the clouds, then returned his gaze to Dominica, 'I would like to try to learn, though I may only have a week before my orders come from the King ...'

'Well, we could start, Lord, see how you get on? And maybe we can find a way to continue your lessons when you return to your own place?'

He smiled, looked to the ground, then back, 'Let's try then, Prioress.'

'Lord Herewig, please call me sister when we are not in a formal meeting. Everyone else does.'

‘Then, likewise – sister, do call me Herewig.’

The people were told that Drustan would be Herewig’s steward, and would also hold the court while Herewig was away. The people seemed to approve, and there was very little muttering or argument, for which Dominica was thankful.

***

The King sent a messenger to Herewig about two weeks later. It was one of Wulfstan’s men, which made sense in that he would know where he was going, but Herewig didn’t like the way he looked around eagerly as if judging the place for opportunity, nor the way he insisted on a meeting with the Prioress the next morning - alone.

Dominica heard the messenger had arrived and had set about writing to the King as he had commanded her. She didn’t know how she would give the note to the messenger, but waited for an opportunity. She’d also been told of the way the man had ‘stalked around the place as if surveying their defences’, wondering if that was his intent, or if the King had asked him to report back too.

Herewig met Dominica in the chapel and explained that he had been called, that Drustan had been given command of his warriors, and of the Hall, should there be a need to call a court to deal with any problems. It would, Herewig said, be a good start – as he was sure to be back soon. He then added the messenger’s demand and left the man with her there - yet stood outside anxiously. The messenger soon came out and they set off taking one of Herewig’s men, Rinan, with them.

****

The days passed and Herewig did not return. Dominica prayed for his safety, the thought of Wulfstan not far from her mind.

Nearly a week later Herewig and his man rode back into Tamerkam straight to his house and nigh-on fell from their mounts. Shortly after a boy ran to Dominica to say Lord Herewig was sick.

Herewig was laid out on his bed, looking flushed – his skin hot, red and shiny, his eyes bloodshot – in the outer space of the house lay his man on a makeshift bed, in a similar condition. Herewig managed to tell them that the King's camp had moved away from the ford, and the new place was a much longer ride away to the north. On their way back they had stopped at a village on the edge of the Great Moor for the night and from dawn-light had felt sick, both of them. They thought it was something in the ale or the food, so they rode, between desperate stops to be sick or to shit water, as fast as they could to get to where they knew they had the best chance of recovery.

Dominica asked what the vomit looked like, exactly how they felt, trying to glean anything that could help her know what had caused this. Did they see any sick people at the village, hear of any? *It might have been bad food or ale, but something about their colour doesn't accord with that.*

Immediately she sent for cooled boiled water, there was usually a freshly made pot each day, covered and set aside in their infirmary. Whatever it was, she knew she had to make them drink clean water and plenty of it. Many sicknesses were worse when people stopped drinking as the ache from voiding or vomiting became too painful.

Bringing masks and aprons for herself and Avan, and the cups with a fine shaped edge, she and Avan got both men to drink, with a bowl ready to catch the eruption when it came – and then, more drink, until eventually the vomiting subsided, and they slept.

Dominica prayed that Herewig and his man would be saved. Having him as their protector was the best outcome for Tamerkam. He was someone who cared and listened; to lose him now would leave them open to attack that the King would be too far away to do anything about. She hadn't forgotten the way Wulfstan's man had eyed up all he could see while he was delivering the King's summons.

The next morning they were difficult to wake and to get to sit up, their colour was still high, their skin tight and shiny. Something was not right. Dominica was confused as to the nature of their sickness but began to wonder if it was not just bad food or ale - whether it could be poisoning? She asked if they had eaten any berries from the hedgerows on their way, Herewig shook his head, and then vomited, watery and greenish, a bit garlicky but not evil-smelling.

The coincidence with their stop now made her worried they'd been poisoned deliberately. After all, they were Saxons travelling in a recently conquered land. So she decided to try treating it as if it were poisoning, besides much of sickness from bad food or ale seemed to be some kind of poison made in the belly anyway – so it was a worthy plan.

She sent Avan to collect two handfuls of avals, the fruits of eve, telling her to pick those that looked ripest, for it was early yet for them, and to set them to stew in a pot. She herself turned to her dried herbs and measured out a spoonful of powder of ramsons, another of bittersweet and a hefty pinch of salt, all of which she added to the pot. When it had all gone to a mush she sweetened it with a little honey.

When the men had drunk more cooled water and been able to keep it down, she and Avan spooned a little into them at a time, washed down with more cooled boiled water, until it was all gone. They both had the shakes and felt cold, so they covered them with linens and furs and let them rest again.

Before nightfall they were worse, unable to sit-up or move even with help, and were both vomiting and shitting a watery mess where they lay. Dominica and Avan did all they could to clean their bodies and the area, but it was an impossible task.

Dominica feared she was losing them both, that they would not see the dawn – the thought of losing Herewig hurt her heart more than she could comprehend.

She prayed fervently that they would live – yet was acutely aware that she had not been overtaken by the Spirit as she had for Indract and the King.

Eventually, exhausted, she fell asleep against the wall, on the floor where she sat.

Chapter 62

Halhtun *- AD circa 710*

Dawn seeped into the hut, the candles had long burned out, and Avan and Dominica had slumped into sleep just as they were. The light from a gap by the door traced a line across the floor and woke Dominica. She remained very still and held her breath, listening. There! A wheezing breath! Alive! She shook herself and clambered to her feet, her bones aching. She pressed her lips together. *I feel so old this morning, not so much forty-odd years - more like sixty, hah!*

She opened the door for more light and went to look at the men. Both were breathing, if a little wheezily, but their colour was paler, the skin maybe less tight looking. Despite all the vomiting and voiding, still much in evidence in the light of day, there wasn't the stench of rot that usually came with it. She shook her head - this was something she had never met before.

'Herewig?' she tried to gently wake him. He stirred and opened his eyes. 'How do you feel?' she asked. He closed his eyes again and sighed, his breath making a whistle.

'I think you may be past the worst,' Dominica said brightly, more brightly than she felt. 'We will get you water,' she added and turned back to wake Avan and to try to rouse the man, Rinan.

After cleaning up themselves and the men, Dominica sent Avan to collect more fruit and set it to stew. This time Dominica added some ground oats and mixed it into the fruit and herb pottage, letting it cook until it was all soft. The boiled water had stayed down, so when the fruit porridge was cool enough they spooned it into the men.

Dominica was glad to see the high colour did not return to their skin. She still didn't know what caused the illness, but she felt more confident that it was not a contagion, as some of these vomiting illnesses were – and that they were on their way back to health.

It was another two days until Herewig was able to stand, his man taking yet another day.

*

'Sister,' Herewig said as he stood at the door of her infirmary a few days later, 'thank you for your ministering. I have never felt more ravaged by sickness.'

'I just thank God you are recovered. I still do not know what caused it – it was not the same as any illness caused by food or ale that I have met, nor from drinking foul water – those bring with them a stench that this did not have. Are you sure you met with no sick people at the place?'

'None. In fact, the women who served us had really clear skins, like some high-born ladies, yet these were not pale, they had pink cheeks, even the older woman. Anyway, whatever caused it, you made it go away, and I am grateful,' he said, touching his hand to his chest with a small bow of his head. 'I have also got my orders from the King. I am to go to Kellyventon and report to him on what I find there. It seems he had given that land to the thegn who took it, but that man has suddenly died, and others have told him it is worthless land, cursed land, and won't accept it. He wants my opinion, and I know you knew that land. You told me you had friends there once.'

'Yes. Before it was burned to the ground,' Dominica shot back, then closed her eyes, and shook her head. 'Sadly, they didn't have a Herewig to speak up for them, nor the King's protection.'

'Ah! That reminds me, the King has renamed this place, like others he has now in his hand, he gives it a name in our tongue - welcome sister to the 'tun on the halh' - Halhtun.'

'Halh-tun?'

‘It means settlement on the bend - of the river, obviously. See, he listened when you told him the name before.’

‘I don’t think it will make any difference to the people, they’ll still think of it as Tamerkam.’

‘Probably true!’ He gave a quick grin, ‘I renamed my tun because it was called by the name of the previous lord, I named it Seolfor-tun, as it was my ‘silver’ from the King.’

‘It is a good name.’

‘Yes, and it is written in the king’s records, I’m told - but few of the people call it that, they still say they are of Herves-tun.’

Dominica smiled, she was glad Herewig had survived.

**

It was another week before Herewig felt able to make the journey to Kellyventon to survey it for the King, and when he was ready he came to ask Dominica to join him. She had already spoken to Keynae, who had grown up there, and agreed that she would join them. Drustan saw them off, giving his mother a one-armed hug before she mounted up. The journey wasn’t long by horseback, even at an amble, but the difference between the untouched homes of Tamerkam and the sight that met them as they turned off the highway and towards Kellyventon was stark. Keynae gave an involuntary cry and tears ran down her face as she looked around her.

Where there had been a fine palisade were charred stumps, and beyond, the chief’s house, large as the meeting house in Tamerkam, was gone, a bare blackened area showing where it had once stood. Elsewhere there were bits of buildings just about still standing, spared the fire for some unknown reason. All else was devastation. It had an unnatural silence too, as if all the birds and beasts had also left - as if it *were* cursed. Even Dominica shivered.

'Help me understand what I am seeing, Keynae,' Herewig said quietly, glancing at Dominica for her to translate his words, 'Please.' She nodded and did so.

'Destruction!' Keynae spat, 'Wanton destruction – why?'

'Maybe they put up a fight?'

'I don't know, but they were as we were – just the women, the young and the old. I don't think they fought – their plan was to slip off down the river Linar, even as far as the sea. So why this?'

Herewig shrugged, 'Some war-bands do – destroy if they feel – thwarted. If you are right there'd be no spoils here – no slaves to take, nothing left of worth.'

Keynae dashed her hand across her eyes and down her face. 'I hope that is it! What do you need to know?'

'Show me. Explain why this is a good place for a settlement to be restored.'

'Come,' Keynae said, turning her pony and winding through the debris. They heard it long before they reached it, the sound of water pounding into a pool.

'This is the spring, sweet water for all, and it has never failed. It is told that when the first people came this way this was all woodland, and as they walked by beside the high land,' she waved her hand towards The Hill, 'they heard the call of this spring from where they were and followed it to here to drink. The great spring in the woods – Kellyventon. What more did they need? A forest to hunt in, wood to build and burn, plenty of sweet water and, of course, the ancient highway nearby for trade. Now this place is beside where ways cross, with tracks leading to the fordable places across the Tamer, and across the Linar, and of course, that way,' she pointed sunwards, 'the highway to the river or the sea, and the other way, to the moors and beyond.'

'I see this now.' Herewig said, gazing around, 'And farming land?'

'Land is all around, a lot of good land back toward the way we came, the woodland strip stopped you seeing the fields, but they are not too steep, good soil and they serve the community well.'

'So it is only missing its people?'

'Yes - *my* people.'

They returned to the centre of the settlement, picking their way carefully. Dominica was looking for bodies, praying not to find any. She tried to orientate herself. *If that was the Chief's house, and that the meeting house, then the healer's hut would be* – she stopped. There was a burnt body, more skeleton than form – somehow still standing! A cry from Keynae told Dominica she had seen it too. She turned to see Herewig cross himself.

'Is this the curse?' he asked.

'Maybe,' Dominica said, 'what were you told?'

'That the thegn that took this place – tried to get the old-magic woman to tell him where the silver was buried – and she cursed him – and he died - horribly.'

'The old-magic woman? Meduyl?' Dominica looked to Keynae. 'Why would she stay and not go with the others?'

'I don't know. But she was ever strange. Yet, to be burned alive! For what? If everyone had gone – they would have taken everything of value anyway.'

'Would she have cursed them?' Herewig asked.

'Oh yes! She would have cursed them!' Keynae said in a vengefully pleased tone. 'She was good at that!'

'And could the curse be lifted? For people who were not her killers?' Herewig asked, still staring at the blackened figure.

Keynae looked around at the devastation, 'I would say the *only* people who would *ever* thrive here again would be the people who were driven out. Meduyl would have woven it well - the curse will smite *all* others, but not them.'

Dominica kept her head down so her small smile could not be seen; she had recognised the clever answer that only someone grown in a great chief's house would think of so quickly.

'Then this is what I will tell the King, that if he wants this place to thrive he must find the people who lived here before.' He looked at Keynae, 'Would you know how to contact them?'

'Truth be told, I do not know – at the moment. But let me ask around and see if anyone knows where they travelled to. This land runs right to the Linar. I understand that your king stopped at that river?'

'So I am told.'

'Then I should be able to find someone over that border who knows.'

***

A week later and it was time for Herewig to leave Tamerkam, the new Halhtun. Keynae had sent out people to slip across the Linar and seek news of Rannoeu and the people, but so far she had not heard back.

Herewig said he would be leaving one of his men, Rinan, the one who had been sick when he was, and who also had no wife back in Seolfortun, to help Drustan.

He also planned to take with him three boys, one from the Bo Barr family, one from the Bo Etherick's and one of Keynae's family, a nephew.

When Dominica heard she was surprised and annoyed so went swiftly to speak with Herewig. She swept into his hall saying, 'Why are you taking hostages? I thought we had given my assurance here!'

Herewig looked up sharply, 'I am not, sister! I have chosen three boys who show promise. They are not hostages. I will train them to be warriors and they will eventually come back to support Drustan at Halhtun. A place needs some protection and I cannot spare more of my own men.'

Dominica subsided, 'Ah! I understand now. Forgive me, I shouldn't have doubted you.'

'A little doubt doesn't hurt. And thank you sister for sending brother Maban with me. I may never get the hang of Latin and writing, but I now have my own clerk and monk - the King will be impressed. On my way to Seolfortun I will report to the King that Kellyventon is a good place and well situated for a trading place, but that it must be given back to its people to lift the curse and do well. When Keynae finds her people, send word with Rinan to me – and I will seek the King's blessing on this.'

So it was, with a small regret, Dominica saw Herewig's party ride out, each of his men with a boy sharing his mount, and Brother Maban on a pony bought from a trader further down river.

She watched them disappear over the hill and turned to Keynae and Drustan standing beside her. 'May the Lord protect them all,' she said.

Keynae stared after them, 'Amen,' she said quietly.

Chapter 63

Rannoeu *- AD circa 710*

When Rannoeu slipped into Tamerkam late one evening, Keynae brought her straight down to see Dominica. The three women sat round a table as Rannoeu told of their escape from Kellyventon just before the Saxons had swept in. How their lookouts had warned them, how well they had been prepared and so took everything they could carry and slipped away down to the river. It was as Keynae had suspected. Meduyl had chosen to stay, had said her 'time had come, that she would make them pay'. Nothing would dissuade her.

That she had cursed the Saxons so vehemently at the end did not surprise Rannoeu at all - through tears she said she was proud of Meduyl.

'The thegn that killed Meduyl died – horribly, I believe – so much so that no other man wanted to take his place. Herewig says they call the place cursed,' Dominica said.

'Good! Filthy Saxons should not live in our home!'

'But the King thinks it is a good place, a good position. Keynae told Herewig that the curse would affect all who tried to live there – except those who had been driven out.'

'Who is this Herewig – he sounds foreign?'

'Ah!' Keynae began, 'Herewig is the warrior who recognised Dominica when she was risking her life to face the enemy. Yes, Saxon - but it was only his intervention that saved us from the man who would have plundered Tamerkam and taken us all for slaves!'

'*But still a Saxon!*' Rannou shook her head in disgust.

'A good man,' Dominica began, but seeing the fire flame in Rannoeu's eyes added, 'Really, a good man. The King has made him his steward, to rule for him here.'

'There is so much to tell. We *have* been lucky - not one has been made a slave, harmed or taken from their place,'

Keynae said, 'And Drustan,' she swallowed, 'of all our men, he alone survived, but badly wounded - lost his hand, his right hand. But Herewig has made him steward, like our Chiefman here, when he is away at his own tun - which is most of the time.'

Rannoeu looked from one to the other. Her lip curled, 'You talk like you are grateful to be the servants of a Saxon lord – little more than slaves. Is that what our men died for? Yes, most of *our* men died too! We heard it from the few who made it home - only to die in the arms of their wives. All our fighting-age men, yes Keynae, your brother and nephews too – all gone – and we are to accept these, these – *bastards* as our overlords?'

Keynae went to Rannoeu and hugged her as she wept, deep sobs. She tried to shake her off, but Keynae held tight. As the cries eased she said, gently. 'We accept it for our lives, the lives of our old and the lives of our children still with us. I am sure in some places the Saxon will grind the people down, but we can see *we have been lucky here.*' Rannoeu shook her head. 'Yes, we have. And I sent word to you as Kellyventon can be yours again, and you can share in this luck – for I think, and Dominica thinks, King Ina will ask Herewig to be king's steward for there too.'

The next morning Rannoeu told Keynae that she understood, she did, but she had to speak to Dominica again.

Dominica emerged from prayers to find the two women waiting for her.

'I understand,' Rannoeu said, 'sleep seems to have cleared my mind. I need to ask, do you think we can say yes, but say we only agree if it is the same steward as the one at Tamerkam?'

Dominica looked at her. She longed to say yes, but instead said, 'I do not know. We can but try. We could send a letter from you to the King with Herewig, asking for this to be the case. After all, you still have the choice between returning or not – and the King may have other ideas. I was only guessing when I said Herewig might be the steward, but I know for a fact that the King is taking an interest in the man and how he does.'

Dominica sent word to Rinan that she would have a message for him to take to Herewig at Seolfortun soon and to get ready to ride. Rannoeu and Dominica wrote the letter and sealed it to be given to the King and Dominica wrote a separate one for Herewig alone, though conscious that Maban would be reading it out to him, she tried to make it as business-like as possible even while telling him of the developments and her hope that he would find the King's favour and be the gerefa for Kellyventon too. With an arrow prayer she sealed her letter and put it together with Rannoeu's to give to Rinan.

When she went over to the old monastery, to the great hall, she saw Rinan standing ready with his mount and speaking to a girl from Tamerkam. The girl handed him a bag of some kind, and stayed close to him, gazing up at him, until she stole a glance around and spotted Dominica. She took a sharp step back and dipped her head, then looked up again at Rinan and with a small wave of her hand headed back up the hill. Dominica smiled. Well maybe Rinan would be coming back here after all, it seemed he'd found an admirer locally.

'Rinan, here are two letters - give both to Lord Herewig, though one is for him and one for him to give to King Ina. Please keep them safe. I pray you have a good journey. Have you all you need for the journey?'

In answer Rinan held up the cloth bag, 'Thank you, sister, I have plenty to keep me going on the way.'

'I look forward to seeing you back here sometime,' Dominica said with a real smile. it was good to have a few young men about the place and Rinan certainly pulled his weight.

Rannoeu left the same day to return to where her people were sheltering, near where she herself came from

– she'd told them it was an abandoned settlement above the place where the Linar and the Teudhi rivers became one. It had been left empty for many years as the people had moved and made a new settlement nearer the trade routes.

The old place was safe and defensible but it was also one you could only escape from by going across deep water. This made Rannoeu uneasy. There was only one other way out, to race past the invader up the banks of the Teudhi and hope the river was low enough at the rhyd to escape further into Kernow.

When they'd been offered it, it was the best their homeless tribe could hope for. A few huts still stood, some even with roof timbers - but it was not home.

*

The weather remained mild through to December and, a week before the great celebration of Christ's birth, Herewig returned – bringing Rinan, two other men and news.

'Prioress,' he gave a slight formal bow as he greeted her.

'Lord Herewig, it is good to see you back in – Halhtun.'

He smiled, 'Thank you, sister. It somehow feels good, much as I value my own tun I think this place has made its way into my heart,' he said, looking a little puzzled even as he spoke, 'and thank you for your letter, it was helpful.'

'Have you taken, I mean, have you had time to take the other letter to King Ina?'

'Indeed. And he was interested, and questioned me further.' Herewig paused and looked at Dominica. 'I have his reply here for you,' he proffered a folded, sealed, piece of parchment.

Dominica took it and broke the seal. Unfolding the stiff letter, she scanned it quickly, then read it properly, a smile broadening across her face. 'You *will* be the gerefa! Ah! That means Rannoeu will come back with her people! Bless you! Bless King Ina for seeing this.'

'It's a lot of work, and I fear this place may have to help with some of the work and support - they'll need somewhere to live until homes are built.'

'They will want to help – some are kin. Kinship is very important here.'

'And I have brought with me two men skilled in building to help too. They can remain until harvest. Please let Keynae know to send word to Rannoeu for all to come back as soon as they can,' he smiled, obviously pleased with his plans – and Dominica smiled back – it was good to see him back in Tamerkam.

Keynae was told and immediately sent a messenger to Rannoeu.

**

They arrived four days later, bedraggled and carrying all they had taken with them.

Drustan had arranged with Bo Barr and Bo Etherick that their meeting houses would be used to shelter families, along with that of Tamerkam. Keynae took Rannoeu and her girls into her own home, and some other families, related to those in the Tamerkam area, were offered space in their homes. The huts in the old monastery were repurposed; the monks' and the nuns' houses, the refectory, the healing hut – all became homes for the people from Kellyventon. Even some of the hastily made shelters thrown together at Saint Indract's monastery were strengthened and made ready to house people.

The next day was the celebration of Christ's birth. Early that morning Dominica had sent out Sister Aylwyn with Brother Yowann to Bo Barr, and Sister Esselt with Brother Resmen to Bo Etherick, to say prayers and lead a Christian celebration service, whilst she and Brother Brannon served at Tamerkam.

People had already decorated their homes and meeting places with greenery, holly and ivy, inside and out. Even though the meeting houses were now homes for families, the inner areas were cleared and into each a huge well dried ash log was brought, marked with the figure of the old year, and lit. Each family brought hot food and ale to share for the celebration, as did those at the monastery of St. Indract the Martyr – but only after significantly more prayers and worship in the chapel. Both Keynae and Dominica had invited Herewig and his men to share the celebration - they chose to be at Tamerkam.

Later in the day Herewig arrived at the monastery, and was welcomed into their quieter celebrations in the refectory. He looked a little flushed and spoke a little louder than usual, and began to get expansive about how he envisaged the new Kellyventon, or Kelli-Wic, as the King had renamed it.

Dominica persuaded him to come and sit on a bench against the wall.

'You know, King Ina listened to everything I said,' he continued, 'everything about the good points of its location and declared it *would be a wic*, a trading place, with his mark upon it! Mind you, with some of the trade taxes being his share - rather than all from the land - which means now I have to make it work - but I know little about trade. Plenty about people, but little about trade,' he shook his head, and added again, 'Plenty about people, but little about trade,' ending in a yawn and, resting his head back, he slept.

Chapter 64
***Kelliwic** - AD circa 711 - 718*

Dominica smiled and rested herself against the wall too. With its own people back it would always be Kellyventon, she thought, but to be a trading place under the King's hand would be a bonus for them as it meant protection of sorts – and she felt sure that Herewig's understanding of people would show him the way with traders and trade even though it bothered him now.

*

AD 711 - 712

There was so much to do to clear and rebuild Kellyventon, and little that could be done over the winter months on the land at home, so many volunteered to go and help Rannoeu's people rebuild.

Herewig had been thinking hard about the place, and he brought out a sketch of what he thought the new Kelliwic should be like. It wasn't quite the usual arrangement of a settlement, but it planned for a proper market area with a large enclosure for livestock fairs beside it and for the highway to be between the homes and these areas, keeping the bulk of the strangers out of the settlement itself.

Once a meeting house was built Herewig bought in food and a kitchen was set up. Now many stayed overnight there and were fed for their work, and the place grew - and so more were able to stay and help.

Herewig stayed until almost Lady Day. The weather had remained mild and drier than usual, so when soft rains fell towards the middle of March they were welcome - and turned the minds of all to tilling the soil and sowing seeds. He sat at court in Halhtun to hear any grievances or issues

Drustan wanted dealt with at a higher level, then left for Seolfortun the next day, taking Rinan back with him.

Life in Tamerkam returned to as much like normal as is possible when your fit older and your young men have been taken. Those who had been helping at Kellyventon returned and everyone worked harder to prepare the land for growing. Dominica insisted that the monks and nuns not only worked their own land, but helped with all those who struggled, especially those where the family had mainly the old and infirm and the very young, where just to keep going was difficult.

The year was punctuated by the great feast days, with special services and sometimes merry-making and storytelling, and the return of Herewig each quarter day – always staying a few weeks at a time as he now had Kelliwic to check up on as well.

The year was also consumed by hard work, but the harvest was good - and by the next Christmas there had been no great disasters or losses, bar a few old, to be expected, and some young, unfortunately lost to sudden fevers or mishaps.

By the end of the second year all those who came from Kellyventon lived back there again and the homes and meeting houses of Tamerkam felt empty.

**

AD 713 - 714

Life in both Tamerkam and Kellyventon settled into the routine of farming and living, much as it had been before all the upheaval, destruction and loss of war.

At his visit for the previous Christmastide quarter, Herewig told Dominica he had recently taken a wife,

Osgyth, a daughter of Lord Osgar from a nearby tun in Somersaete.

Since then he'd left her to run Seolfortun whenever he came to Kernow, so no one had seen her yet. But this Christmastide, his news was that she was with child, so was not about to travel anywhere soon.

***

The following year the word went out about the new market and fair to be held at Kelliwic. Messages were sent to all the settlements between the moor and the sea and anyone who passed by Kelliwic was told the news of a new market to be held there, two weeks after midsummer.

So it was that the first proper livestock fair was held at Kelliwic. From a day or two before the date chosen people began to arrive with a few cattle, sheep or goats to sell or barter. Others arrived closer to the day, bringing young geese, fowl or ducks, and then the artisans; the potters, wood carvers, weavers and basket makers, and lastly those who made trinkets and delicacies for which a person would be willing to part with a small coin, a fine cheese or a pot of honey.

The first market and fair was a success. The new wic made coin so the king would get his share, but the people of the place also profited, in silver or goods, by putting up the traders who needed accommodation or selling ale, bread, their local honey and other food stuffs.

Later, news made its way to Tamerkam with Rinan, that Herewig' wife had given birth to a son, whom he'd named Herewig, and that he'd given Rinan leave to wed the girl from Tamerkam that he'd been courting for so long.

****

AD 715 - 718

The four years that followed were blessed. The summers fine and the winters mild and each spring the flowers came earlier and each winter they were able to keep more livestock alive, feeding on the slowly growing grass, allowing their herds and flocks to grow year on year.

*

Only one thing marred Dominica's life – Brannon. He was ailing. She had no idea what was wrong or how to cure it. Nearly four years after the first Kelliwic market he had come to her just after Pascha, when he found he could no longer write, his hand trembling each time he tried to do so, even when it was still before he tried.

'I haven't complained before,' he said, 'but often at rest, or during prayer, my hand and arm will shake, but it has got worse, and now even if my hand is still, if I try to pick up the quill the ink just flies from the point as the shaking begins.'

**

She tried a number of herbal remedies to relax the muscles, as she thought they may be tight, or to help sleep, as she thought he was, perhaps, overtired.

None of these had helped. And now, the harvest in, the days shortening, he had come back almost in tears – his other hand had begun to shake too. He'd learnt to use that hand to eat with but now, he was lucky if it would obey him in this task.

She promised she would try harder to find something that would help and she prayed with him, fervently hoping that this would be a time that God intervened, would flow through her and heal - but her prayers remained in her mind and mouth alone.

As he left she noticed how old he was looking, not just the way his red hair had faded to a dirty white, but how he stood, no longer upright, but stooped, his gait unsteady. *Brannon, the lively and quick, my milk brother, my little light of optimism when things looked dark – and a good person, a good and kindly person, how could God let this happen?*

She went with one of the old fishermen in his coracle down river to Tamerunta. She knew already from the river-men that Tamerunta had fared better than many on her side of the river. The drive of the war had been to cross the Tamer and sweep up everything right up to the next barrier. Tamerunta was now under Saxon rule, but it was much as before – they just owed their allegiance and dues to a new master. Though they had lost their fair share of fighters, many had come back and retained their liberty, such as it was.

The news about the mission was not so good. It was reduced to just Prior Cormag and three others. They prayed, led services occasionally for the community, but otherwise kept quiet and in their own area, but it was not them Dominica had come to see. She was seeking out Liaden to see if she had ever met such a condition as Brannon had. She prayed she had, and that she knew what might help.

Liaden seemed a lot older too, but she had lost both of her sons, and though Eudaf had returned, he was a broken man. Dominica, not used to thinking how she herself appeared, found herself wondering what others saw when they looked at her. She knew her dark hair, when it grew so as to have to be cut off, was now well mixed with grey for she saw it on the floor but, apart from Avan, no one else saw that. Her face felt different, softer, looser, yet as she'd not considered how she looked to others for so many years, these were strange thoughts.

Liaden greeted her warmly and they settled to talk with small-ale and fresh bread. After a while exchanging news Dominica said, 'You remember Brother Brannon?'

Liaden's eyes lit and she smiled, 'The ever excited and cheerful one?'

'Indeed!' Dominica grinned, but then almost at once frowned, 'He is not well, and I have no idea what it is that is wrong,' and went on to describe how it was with him.

Liaden listened carefully. Frowning, she shook her head. 'Has he had a bad fall, hit his head, or someone hit him on the head?'

'No, not that I know of, why?'

'There was a boy, young man really, here who fell from a lookout place and landed awkwardly on his head. He was never the same and he trembled so that he could scarcely hold anything still.'

'Did you find anything to help him – to stop the trembling?'

Liaden shook her head again, 'No, I tried many herbal concoctions, things that would relax the body, things that would make the body lively, but nothing worked.'

'What happened to him?'

Liaden shook her head yet again, 'He was so – saddened by his life he didn't care to live any more. He tried to kill himself, but it didn't work, just crippled him more. After that he would drink as much ale as he could get, even stealing it, until he fell into a stupor. People understood, to a point. One night he drank of a brew left unattended – and was found dead beside the overturned pot.'

'Poisoned?'

'You are not the only one to think that might have been the case. Perhaps, whatever it was a blessed release as it seemed to be getting worse. I know he'd asked me for something to end his life, but I just couldn't do it - it would never end well if a wise-woman used her knowledge to kill someone not naturally near their end.'

'Hmm, true.'

'Did you try the healers hemp? I didn't even know of it back then.'

'No, I didn't think of that for this – but, maybe?'

'Worth trying.'

'Though I have very little left ...'

'And I have none, I am sorry to say, for the Trader does not seem to come this way any more – if he lives that is – I don't know where we'd get more.'

After sharing a meal with Eudaf and Liaden, Dominica said she must visit the mission before she went back up-river with the tide. She took the short walk from the settlement to the monastery. The area looked rather unkempt, but with so few to work the land and maintain the buildings she supposed it wasn't surprising.

'She arrived at the monastery entrance and called, 'Brothers? Brothers?' She could hear thumping from somewhere. After a minute or two she walked further in and tried again. A minute later she heard a voice and then saw one of the monks come hurrying from behind the group of huts.

'Brother, it is Prioress Dominica from Tamerkam, come to see the Prior.'

'Welcome Sister, we are all beyond,' he waved his hand and she followed him back to where the four of them had been threshing in the sunshine.

Cormag came over, limping but at a speed that suggested he wasn't in pain. 'Welcome Prioress. You will forgive us if we just complete this last bit before the sun leaves our floor.'

'Of course,' she said and rested herself on a rock to wait while they flailed at the sheaves laid on the flat area. It was hard work and they all had a sweat on them, but they worked as one, each flail striking the stalks in a rhythm, one after the other. There was a stop now and again to rearrange the stalks.

They finished and Cormag came over to Dominica. 'Shall we talk while the brothers gather up the grain. What brings you here?'

'I came seeking help for an ailment - from Liaden.'

'Ah! She has been good enough to make up the recipe you gave me last we met. I was a fool to resist help.'

'So much has happened since.'

'So much,' he replied.

'It's Brannon!' she said, it came almost as a cry. 'The ailment I cannot help – it's Brannon.'

'Brother Brannon? Oh no. That is – sad news indeed. What is it?'

'I don't know! I cannot find anything that helps – he shakes, his arms, his hands, both now, shake violently – especially if he wants to do something – like – eat!'

'He is the only one who came back from Rome,' Cormag said almost to himself.

'He did,' Dominica sighed.

'Sad news, but I thank you for letting me know. I will add him to my prayers.'

'I thought, I thought you should know – there are so few of us left now.'

'I know – and I am sorry.' He paused, looked up then back to Dominica, 'I feel – I have asked God's pardon, but I feel, no, believe I must ask your forgiveness too. I was harsh and driven by evil thoughts and did much to harm your ministry at Tamerkam – and worse. Can you forgive me?'

Dominica stared at him, her voice lost to her. She shook herself, 'Brother Cormag, if God has forgiven you – I can do no less.'

'Thank you sister. Thank you.' He drew in a breath and sighed it out. 'Please send word if there is any way I can help in the future.'

'I will. I will, farewell,' she raised a hand as if to bless, nodded and turned to leave.

'Please send word on how Brother Brannon fares,' Cormag said suddenly, his voice sounding thick with emotion.

She turned back and, with a sad smile, nodded her assent.

Chapter 65
The Dry Time *- circa AD 719 – 720*

Dominica tried a little of the healers hemp on Brannon. She crushed it, soaked it, drained it and gave it in a drink, tipping it a little at a time into his mouth.

Brannon needed a help-meet most of the time now when he needed to eat or drink, for each time he tried to do it himself the shaking afterwards would make it impossible even for someone else to help him.

Brannon said the healers' hemp drink made him feel light-headed and later sleepy, but it did not stop the tremors when he tried to use his hand for something, like reaching for a cup. Dominica was disappointed, though if it had worked she would have struggled to get more, but she didn't say as much to Brannon. Instead she said she would have to think again; there must be something that would help.

*

Herewig brought both is wife and his son, now four years old, to Halhtun for the first time for the Feast of St. John's quarter day at midsummer. The former Prior's house had been prepared for them, as Herewig had already said he hoped his wife would come, and with Keynae's advice had been made more fit for living in by a woman who had been brought up as the daughter of a thegn, than it had previously been.

When they arrived the weather was warm and dry, as it had been for weeks, the crops were growing in the fields, maybe not as tall or as vigorously as usual as the rainfall had been sporadic since the end of April, but Halhtun looked beautiful and the river, glimpsed as they rode down towards it, sparkled brightly reflecting the blue sky.

Keynae and Drustan, both in their best clothes went down to Halhtun Hall, as the old church had become known, ready to greet Herewig and his family. Dominica, when told they had been seen coming in by the highway, had freshened her face and put on a clean lighter-weight robe, her wooden cross, her red-cord belt of office and a fresh veil – it was as if she wanted to make a good impression, but did not really know why. Herewig had seen her with her robe mud-caked, or with her face reddened and pouring sweat at harvest, so she assumed it was because he brought his wife that she was so concerned.

She stood next to Keynae as Herewig's party appeared from the main track, finding herself with a broad smile on her face as Herewig escorted Osgyth over to meet them all, little Herewig tagging along behind.

Osgyth looked pale, made paler by her light coloured hair maybe, but she was an attractive woman who held herself well and had a warm smile for them.

'Prioress Dominica,' she said, 'I have heard a lot about you from Lord Herewig, he speaks highly of your healing skills.'

'He is very kind. It is a pleasure to meet you and your son, we have also heard much about both of you,' Dominica said. *She **is** paler than she ought to be.*

Later in the week Osgyth sought Dominica out, and asked if she could speak with her.

'Of course,' Dominica said, let us go to the herb garden, there is a bench in the shade there,' and began to lead the way, 'we keep a seat here for those who are feeling a bit better to sit on outside the infirmary and get some sun, as we feel it does them good.'

When they were both sitting in the dappled shade surrounded by the scents of the herbs and the hum of bees on their flowers, Osgyth spoke, 'I hope you may help me, Prioress Dominica.'

'Just call me sister if it is easier. Within our own walls it is usual. What is the problem?'

‘Since little Herewig was born I have had two – losses, the baby more than three moons but not yet kicking.’

‘And are you tired all the time too?’

Osgyth looked a little startled, ‘Yes, more than I let Herewig know.’

‘And how are your moon-flows?’

‘Since little Herewig was born my moon-flow is heavy, very long too.’

‘I think I know how I can help your tiredness. We will begin with that. Go and relax now - it is pleasant by the river. I will come and find you when I have made a preparation,’ she smiled and both women stood and walked arm in arm out of the herb garden.

Dominica stripped fresh leaves from the parsley that grew flat to the ground and crushed them in a pestle with a small handful of the small red strewberries. It was this greeny-brownish pulp that she put in a covered pot and took, with a small scoop made from a hollow plant stem, to give to Osgyth.

‘See,’ Dominica demonstrated, ‘just take what will fit into this scoop each day. Come and ask me for more when it is gone,’ she said, emptying the scoop onto a spoon for Osgyth to eat.

‘It’s sweetish?’ Osgyth said, sounding surprised.

‘The herb isn’t but the berries are, and they work together in other ways too. Just let me know when you need more – and I will show you how to make it,’ Dominica added.

Over the month that Herewig and Osgyth stayed at Halhtun and Kelliwic, Osgyth’s colour improved and she reported feeling less tired already. She proved to be an able pupil when shown the amounts and way to make the preparation and the alternatives as the seasons changed. She asked after other simple remedies as, she said, although they had a wise-woman at Seolfortun, and even at her parents’ tun, they did mostly the births and the laying out, and had only a few remedies, and those seemed to have to serve for all conditions.

When they left, taking the joy that was little Herewig with them, Dominica missed them far more than she expected to.

**

The year continued dry, forcing an early harvest, the grain ripe but not as plentiful as had been hoped for, the root crops not swelling in the dusty ground, the grass slowing in growth so that they knew they could not keep so many animals on it through the coming winter.

Herewig came alone for the following quarter days, but reported that Osgyth sent her good wishes and had told him to tell Dominica that she was much restored.

Brannon continued to live and continued to deteriorate. His gait, when he managed the strength to try to walk was perilous - so stooped, each step only just prevented him falling, each step a little faster than the previous one. He couldn't use sticks to help as his hands would not hold or control them. In the end he stopped trying except when necessary, and then his help-meet would support him, pressing back on his shoulders to slow the steps. It was agonising for Dominica to watch, and when Brannon begged for relief that she did not know how to give, her heart broke for him.

***

AD 720

The following spring the rain came in due time, but lightly and not as often as was usual. The air seemed to be heating up early and the wild plants flowered profusely making the whole area a beautiful sight. However, Dominica was concerned. She had already taken baskets of food to some of the poorest families where signs of lack of enough good food were showing in ill health.

After much prayer, Dominica offered the mothers a place in the monastery for either boys or girls to be fed, cared for and taught - if the mother wished. And so it was she welcomed seven children in, four girls and three boys between the ages of seven and ten – all of them the youngest in the families. She also welcomed three widows and one man, who had lost the use of an arm, to the laity and taken on another promising trainee to learn how to be a healer.

****

When he came at Michaelmas, Herewig quietly told Dominica that Osgyth was with child and was now into her fifth month, so they prayed all would be well.

Dominica sent word with a river-man to Prior Cormag to let him know that Brannon was much worse – she hadn't expected him to accompany the man on his return, but he did. He brought with him all he required for the Eucharist, and took it upon himself to hear Brannon's confession, give absolution and communion. Dominica, whilst glad of this, was worried that Brannon might think she had given up hope for him, and give up himself - but he seemed little changed in his way.

***

All was still well with Osgyth come the Christmas quarter day – but all was not well at both Halhtun and Kelliwic – nor, reportedly, anywhere in the wider area – all were husbanding their resources, praying to have enough to get them past the hungry gap in the coming year.

**

By the Feast of Christ's Presentation Brannon was in great pain. He'd long stopped trying to walk anywhere beyond the infirmary, where he stayed now for constant care, but something else was moving through him – his whole body thrown into convulsions that left him exhausted yet at the same time unable to sleep. Added to this he also found it hard to take solid food; he could only take small sips of broth.

Dominica felt helpless and distraught. She prayed and she prayed, but the healing prayer wouldn't come; it was just like with Nuala all over again. *What good is healing some but letting others you dearly love die – and in such agony? What was God doing! Where was He?*

Suddenly she thought of the dwale. It could give sleep, perhaps with only a little taken it could give a restful sleep to Brannon. There had been about two cups left from the mix made up for Drustan which she'd put in a pot and stoppered well – maybe it was time to see if it was still there, or if it had gone to a paste.

It had gone to a paste! But maybe with a little more warmed wine it could be revived? She warmed some wine and added it to the pot, stirring it well until she felt no resistance. She continued to stir now and again as it cooled, then took some to Brannon.

His eyes greeted her warmly, but his face had long lost its full expression.

'I've brought you something that may help you sleep,' she said brightly, sitting beside him and offering him a spoonful of the dwale.

'Wine?' he said, after a sip, his voice scratchy.

She nodded, 'Yes, it is in some wine,' and smiled. After two more spoonfuls his eyelids began to droop. Enough she thought, and made sure he was comfortably supported to sleep.

The next few days went in the same way, he said he felt a little better now that his muscles were not hurting all the time, and though the spasms continued they seemed to be less violent. Dominica's only worry was that there was such a limited amount of dwale to be used.

The evening before Shrove Tuesday Dominica had to face the fact that there was barely any dwale left, a couple of spoonfuls maybe, so she stirred it well and tipped into a thin edged cup. It was little dark and slow to pour, like honey, but didn't appear to be much more than a few spoonfuls. She helped him drink it, wondering what she could do tomorrow to help calm his tremors.

Next morning she went into the infirmary with her answer, a drink that she'd prepared the evening before and strained off after she awoke that morning - mead infused with dried bittersweet and powdered root of valerian – nothing like as powerful as dwale but maybe it would be enough to help him relax and sleep.

She sensed his stillness before she reached him, for even in sleep there were often twitches. He looked at peace, eyes closed. She gently rested her hand on his chest – there seemed to be no movement. She felt for the blood-thump, *his skin feels cool,* and found none. *Did I give too much dwale yesterday evening? Was there more pape in the dregs than I knew? Surely not?* She stood up straight and breathed slowly, then resting her hands on his lifted them and placed them across his chest and, as tears ran down her cheeks, prayed that God would welcome him into heaven - *and that I have not committed a mortal sin.*

Chapter 66

Drought - *circa AD 721*

Brannon's body was wrapped and psalms and prayers said in the little stone church he had dreamed of and made real. They carried him up to The Monks' Field on the higher side of the old church that was now Herewig's Hall. There he joined the slowly growing rows of monks, nuns and lay members of the monastery.

Prior Cormag came for the funeral and led the prayers, speaking well of Brannon, of how he had humble beginnings but had risen in Christ to be a wise man. With difficulty, Dominica spoke of his God-given way seeing God and finding joy in everything and everyone – and then they laid him in the earth and began to cover him up.

As the earth filled in the grave, Dominica felt as if it was being thrown in on top of her, her chest ached with the weight of it and, as she turned away, an anguished cry broke free from her and she staggered a little, but was caught by Aylwyn who was at her side. Sobs wracking her body, barely knowing where she stepped, they returned to the monastery - where she insisted on going into the little chapel again - and being left alone.

She had to be alone, she couldn't let anyone else see or hear her just now. It was all too much.

Lord, why have you taken everyone I love away? Is it me? Was it me? Did I give him too much dwale? How could I know? I do not understand. Such good people, Lord, I'm always seeing good people hurt and die and – wicked – survive. Small children, babies, they have had no time to sin, yet they die – so sadly, sometimes in misery, they die. How can I do your work when my heart is so heavy? How can I praise you when I want to blame you? It all feels so wrong! Lord help me, it makes no sense!

She ran out of energy, ran out of words, sat with her head bowed and let the acid run out of her spirit. After a while she sighed. A spirit of calm had filled her, and for now, that was sufficient. It had to be sufficient for now - she had a monastery to run, people to care for.

*

Herewig came for the Lady Day quarter sessions, bringing news of Osgyth and the safe birth of their daughter Heregyth and a gift for the monastery – a polished bronze cross, shining like warm gold, to replace the wooden one on their altar.

The spring had been quite dry but the land had been tilled and the crops sown as usual, waiting on the rain they hoped would come.

**

The first report of a well-spring drying up came just after the late Pascha. It was already noticeable that the low tide in the river was lower than usual, and that the higher banks didn't seem to get covered by water as they used to at high tide.

The trees had budded up, but few leaves appeared, and those only on the lower branches, the higher buds eventually turning brown and dropping. The grass in the full sun on the crowns of the hills didn't grow again after it had been eaten, so the animals were taken to the margins of the woodland where the sporadic shade allowed better growth.

***

As the year moved into summer it was really hot. Day after day, the sky blue from horizon to horizon. The crops had barely shown themselves, and many had just withered away, except where they were near a water source. There the people took water and trickled it around the plants at night – and those grew. Dominica instructed the herbalists to do the same for the herb garden, as it was important to keep their healing herbs growing.

One by one reports came in of well-springs drying up. The spring that fed the baptism pool and fish ponds turned to a thin trickle that barely kept the top pool level, and without that overflowing the fish pools grew still, the fish gaping at the surface and at great risk of just dying - so they were netted out, eaten or dried before that could happen. People began to have to walk a long way to the next spring and queue to fetch home a jug of water.

Arguments broke out about people taking water from well-springs that were close to other people's homes, even though any water not taken flowed away. Drustan had to step in. They made a time for others to collect, and made plans so that water was collected and stored in any container that could hold water, even all through the short summer nights. This way people managed for water to drink, even managed enough for some plants to be watered, though almost individually.

****

When Herewig came at midsummer he was shocked to see how parched the land appeared. He had thought it was only over the north of the moors until he had started down into what were usually lush green valleys filled with rushing streams - and instead found narrow strips of green beside thin trickles. Dominica spoke with Herewig, asking how the crops were in his own tun, and was surprised to hear the rains had fallen more there, that their crop was growing.

The main spring at Kelliwic still poured out water, maybe not as strongly, but they too had chosen to collect water overnight, to take out and try to water crops, especially the crops that showed the greatest benefit for the least water.

More well-springs ran dry in Halhtun. Harvest came early, but pitifully. Much of the grain had formed but not swollen to a good size. There was discussion about what they should keep to sow the next year, and bitter words were said. Grain was sorted by size – and the best stored for seed grain – yet even then it looked nothing like enough. That there may not be as many mouths to feed was left unvoiced – but those who had known hard times before knew it. There had been deaths already, exacerbated by lack of food, or lack of water. There was not much of a harvest festival, more like a vigil.

***

The next quarter day came, but the rain everyone prayed for did not. More well-springs ran dry. Dominica and her healers found they had to deal with something new, a vomiting sickness. It was as if people had forgotten the wisdom they'd learnt at their mother's knee. As the springs dried up it turned out that some people, rather than make a long trek and have a long wait at a distant spring, had taken water from the streams that surrounded Halhtun. All of which were used by the animals to drink from - now more than ever – and almost all those people had fallen sick. Two children and one old man died and many were weakened.

**

There was not much to celebrate Christmas with, but Herewig brought some bags of grain, enough to make fifty to sixty loaves, which were a treat by then, even when mixed with some pea-flour to make it go further.

He also brought back the boys who had been training with him, men now, to help Drustan and release Rinin to go and assist Rannoeu at Kelliwic. There was some joy in Bo Barr, Bo Etherick and Tamerkam as their grown boys came home.

*

There were now only three springs providing a good flow of water in the whole of Halhtun: the one at Herewig's court, one near the rhyd below the 'old place' at Bo Barr, and one near Bo Etherick off the track towards Halhtun. At each well-spring people queued day and night for water.

Lent arrived and all at the monastery restricted their own food to one very small vegetable meal with a small piece of the bitter peasbread each day, taken after sunset. Dominica, however, began a stricter time of fasting and prayer; a black fast as is usually only followed on the most solemn days of Holy week - water and one small piece of peasbread with salt and a few herbs only, each day - taken between sunset and sunrise.

She would fast and pray - for rain to save her people, all the people, and for her sins – for she still felt she had hastened Brannon's death. After all, everything had been going well since the war, but ever since they buried Brannon, death stalked their land - and she was helpless in the face of this death. All she could do was offer her full penance and prayer.

Besides – there was something else. She could feel the weight of it bearing down within her, but she could not face up to it while she felt so spiritually burdened.

Chapter 67
Lent *- circa AD 722*

Every Lenten day Dominica woke for matins, between midnight and dawn, and prayed until the light began seeping into the sky. Her prayers were for the people, for forgiveness and for the much needed rain. What she didn't understand, nor could control, was the weeping. Her heart ached so, as if being crushed, and tears leaked from her closed eyes wetting her sunken cheeks and even her robe.

When she roused from prayer she would dry her face and take a cup of water, before the sun rose fully and she was joined by the sisters for Lauds, the dawn prayers.

One morning they came upon her still in prayer, her face wet with her tears, and she had to explain how they just came while she was praying for rain, and even laughed, that her tears wouldn't do much to water the crops or fill the springs.

Each day after Lauds she'd then see to the beginning of the day in the monastery. First to the infirmary and the herbarium, then to the herb garden and the school.

She had a good number of healers and assistants now; Avan was in charge of the healers and took one or other of the trained nuns out with her whenever she had to attend someone, and the other remained at the infirmary for those who came there, always knowing Dominica was to be found if required. Eiliwedd continued as the wise-woman at Bo Barr, a widow now, but with children that were her consolation, but she too knew she could call on the monastery whenever she had need.

Merewin dealt with the herbs in the herbarium at the edge of the herb garden. There she made up the potions, and taught the new lay sister studying under her as herbalist - one who was quick to learn and took no offence at Merewin's brusque manner. Between them they also looked after the growing, collecting and preserving of the herbs they needed all year through.

Apart from Dominica, the full nuns numbered six now, and between them they taught the two new novitiates and the new herbalist Latin, reading, and writing. Sister Aylwyn taught the novitiates their scripture, and Sister Esselt their prayers.

The men's half of the monastery needed little input from Dominica, ably led by Yowann, though his years were beginning to tell on him and he said, more than once, how much he missed his right hand man, Brannon. However, he had appointed others to take on some of his work, and another to know all that he did.

*

Three weeks into Dominica's black fast - she woke to a roaring sound.

The wind was battering her hut, lifting the edges of the roof, blowing in. Dressing quickly she tied her red cord belt and pushed her way out. As she rounded her hut the strength of the wind took her breath away and, gripping the edge of her veil, she stepped back into its shelter.

All around, in what little moonlight pierced the clouds, she could see that the wind was tugging at the edges of the roofs, a basket rushed past her to bounce off another hut and roll onwards. She headed towards the other nuns' hut, her habit dragging her sideways as she tried to cross the wind direction, one hand on her head. She battered at the door, calling to them to pull back the bar. Suddenly the door was pushed open and she dived in, dragging the door closed behind her. Despite the early hour the other nuns were all up, getting dressed and looking round each time the wind howled.

'There's a huge wind!' Dominica shouted over the noise, 'It's blowing anything lightweight away. We need to get what we can inside and safe. But take care, I fear we may lose some of the roofs! Leave your veils, the wind will only take them,' she added removing hers and leaving it there.

They all left, struggling off in different directions to secure what they could. The healers and lay sisters were next, the same message, especially for securing the herbarium.

The monks and lay-men appeared – as blown by the wind as the nuns. Dominica battled her way over towards them, pausing in the shelter of the chapel between the nuns' and the monks' sides of the monastery. There was a sheet of fine dust being whipped away from the chapel by the wind and it stung as she stepped through it. She made a dash towards where Yowann had just disappeared behind a hut and stepped into the semi-calm where he was catching his breath.

'I've never known a wind blow like this!' Dominica shouted above the roar.

'Me neither. There's not much we can do – apart from get any stuff inside that might end up blown into the river, I've sent for the coracles, if it's not too late. This wind seems to be channelling down the river, it's coming from the wrong way! We're usually sheltered from strong winds here.'

'Yes, you're right! We're all built for the wind from the other way, and not usually this bad either.' As she spoke the sound changed, a deep rumble came too and the sky, that had been getting lighter seemed to dim again. Looking up and behind her she could see the sky beyond the roof had taken on a blue-black hue. She peered around the side of the hut and could see the rest of the cloud – from side to side the valley was filled with a threatening mass, trailing beneath it a black-grey veil. Even as she looked, it advanced. Stepping back she shouted at Yowann, 'Get everyone under cover – it's going to rain!' And dashed off to shout the warning to her charges.

No sooner than she had reached the last of them up by the herbarium, still bringing in pots and bowls that had been used outside, or had carried water but had already blown over, than the rain began. Heavy, stinging, driven rain that felt as if it wanted to go right through you. Certainly it went right through her habit, cold wet darts that soon drenched, head, habit, shoes and had her shivering.

All of the nuns were back in their hut, shaking out their sleeves, wringing the hems of their habits when the first jag of lightning struck, turning the roof and walls to a pattern of fine bright lines and, almost immediately, the crack of thunder shook them to their core. They stood still, waiting for the next. It came, the lightning striking not so close, but the thunder almost just as loud.

The rain came sideways – driven by the relentless wind – drenching everything in its path. No matter what they heard – or what they could see when they peeped out – a single step outside would have a person blown along skidding on sheet mud as the dust of months, years even, turned to a slime that flowed wherever the land-slope took it.

The air was full of bits of water reed, whether from roofs or from the reed beds it was hard to know. The air was also full of sounds, rushing, roaring and crashing sounds – and the deep rumble of thunder that seemed to fade, then restore itself to frightening proximity, then fade into the distance again.

And then another sound, one that was felt, a tremor felt through feet. They each looked at their feet and then at each other. Dominica took a peek outside. At first she saw nothing – and then she saw what was missing – the top of their chapel couldn't be seen. Had the roof blown off?

She remembered what Brannon had said after their trip to Glestyngabyrig – how the masons had laughed at him for sticking his slabs of stone with clay. *At least his stone church had still been standing when he left this world.*

The storm seemed to bounce around the valley for a while, then it was gone. The sky behind it was clear. Like frightened animals they began to emerge from their places of refuge – and look at the devastation.

Taking great care not to slide they ventured further. Dominica found Yowann standing looking at the chapel - the remains of the chapel. It was as if someone had pushed it sideways and all the stones had slipped, the whole place was now just a loose pile of slabs, with a few tipped up where they had found resistance to their line of slide – the roof a little distance away, upside down and its back broken.

One pile of slabs was near where the altar had been and Yowann started towards it, sliding precariously as he stepped over slick slabs.

'Take care, Yowann!' Dominica called, but then she saw what he had seen, the glint of the cross. He reached it and managed to get it out, wiping it with his muddy hand, he carried it back to her.

'It's a bit bent where a slab landed on it, but it can be worked on to get it flat again!' he said, a small note of triumph in his voice. Dominica smiled at him, it sounded so much like something Brannon would say at a time like this.

Drustan came later that day to see how the monastery had fared and was shocked by the damage. When the storm hit he'd been staying in the stewards hut provided for him near the Hall, and he told them that the wind had done little damage there where it was more protected by the hill that the Tamerkam stronghold stood on. He'd already been up to there to see Keynae was safe and, apart from some old roofs losing part of their thatching, they had survived the wind and rain surprisingly well.

'It looks like you got the worst of it, with the wind channelled down the river and you being so close to the river, but,' he added, 'at least we have had the rain we were all praying for! Now all we need is some more rain, gentle rain, to soak the ground properly.'

The rain we were praying for! And that thought is so Brannon too! And all I was seeing was the destruction.

**

Herewig had been held up a bit by the weather, as it had been raining all the way from Escancastre and it made the journey slow, so they'd diverted and stopped the night at St. Rumon's rather than try to make it in failing light. The next day Herewig arrived for the Lady Day quarter, going first to his Hall, where Drustan's servant boy was able to tell him that Drustan was at the monastery.

He left his men to unload the pack ponies and rode on down to the monastery, his horse picking its way through runnels and puddles of muddy water. As he neared the entrance he saw the damage and sat looking around for a few minutes. He caught sight of Dominica treading carefully across a gap between buildings, so rode on in, following the way he thought she was headed. When he nearly caught her up he called to her, 'Sister Dominica!'

She turned towards him. He was shocked, she looked so drawn and pale, her habit soaked to her knees and with a thick trim of mud along its hem. He slid from his horse and walked it to her, 'Sister, they told me you'd had bad weather - but this?'

'Oh! Herewig! Of course, quarter day. Yes, a mighty storm, and running down the valley. We were in its path.'

'The chapel?' he said looking round.

'Gone! But we thank God for the rain!'

He wanted to ask how she was, but couldn't bring himself to do so. She seemed brittle as if she might break if put under pressure of answering. He smiled, 'What can I do to help? I have two of my fighting men with me but they can be useful in other ways too.'

The next two days were taken up with a community effort to get the monastery cleared and cleaned up. The weather was dry, and for the time being they were happy not to have to do this work in the rain.

After recognisance, Drustan reported a whole swathe of trees on a riverside slope had been blown over. 'Flattened like a man trampling barley,' he said.

Herewig asked what Dominica intended to do about the chapel. Were they going to rebuild with the same stones? She told him the tale of Brannon and the masons of Glestyngabyrig, and explained they would not.

'Then,' he said when she finished her tale, 'if you wish it, you can use the timber that has been provided, ready felled by God's own hand.'

God's own hand? Was this the answer to her prayers and her penance combined, rain and the loss of Brannon's chapel?

'It is very kind of you, so much timber has a great worth. I will gladly put building a new chapel with this timber to the monastery, thank you, Herewig.'

The next day it began to rain again, soft gentle rain and, as Dominica stood in it at the top of the herb garden, the rain falling on her face as she looked down-river, she knew it was coming from the usual direction, and she felt in every fibre of her being that all would be well with the monastery, after all.

Chapter 68

Lammas - *circa AD 722*

The rain soaked in, the people set to work, tilling the ground and sowing seed. Herewig had brought some more bags of grain for both Tamerkam and Kelliwic, this time for seed, bought on the King's behalf – enough to top up their own carefully hoarded seed so that there would be enough to sow the main fields.

The following weeks provided just the right mixture of rain and sun for the seeds to start to grow, a green haze appearing quickly over the tilled soils.

Dominica maintained her black fast and pre-dawn prayers until Pascha, as she had vowed to do, her prayers now being full of thanksgiving - and dry-eyed. They held a joyous service up at the Tamerkam stronghold, one of true thanksgiving to God.

*

The springs began to flow again, the first at the monastery, then others. One here, another a week later there, slowly at first then stronger, until by midsummer all were flowing to some extent. The work to clear up and repair the damage at the monastery went on steadily and all but the rebuild of the chapel was done before midsummer.

After Herewig had returned to Seolfortun Dominica sought out Avan one evening and asked her to walk with her.

'Avan, dear sister. I believe that between you and Merewin you know all I ever did, and far more. When I go I know the care of the people of this area will be in good hands.'

'Where are you going?'

Dominica walked in silence for a little while. In the end she said, quietly, 'I suppose, I hope I am going to my Lord Jesus, to God.'

Avan stopped walking. 'What?'

'I am ill, Avan,' she said turning to look at her.

'Surely not, I would have seen,' she began.

'Truth be told, not a week ago I had thought God had given me my life back, I ... I felt better. But now I know it is still there.'

'What is there? What is it?'

'It is like a heavy bag that is growing inside of me, taking up space where my breathing comes from, and causing pain. I know this ailment – when I was a child, maybe seven or eight, there was a dear man who guarded our place, he used to make toys for us children,' she smiled, remembering. 'Then one day as he was helping me up onto a pony, ah, he taught us to ride too, I felt his pain – this illness. When I asked her, Mother Nuala explained it to me. She made a potion that she said could not clear it, but would ease the pain a bit, and told me I had to pray for him while he drank it, as I had felt his pain and it would help him.'

'And?'

'And, well, I do not know really. The words for the prayer just flowed out of me, but I didn't feel like it was me, and I felt a heat leave me and – *go to him. He* said it moved the lump, made it slide away. He lived! He lived longer than Mother Nuala – and he was older than she.'

'A miracle?' Avan wondered.

'When Mother Nuala was dying she reminded me of that, told me it had been a miracle, told me I seemed to be aglow. But then I prayed *so hard* for *her* to live – and she didn't! It seems it only happens when God has a plan. It wouldn't work for my dear Brother Brannon either, and you know how much his ailment grieved me.'

'I do, that.'

'Well! I have been remiss. We must train a monk, or a lay man to be a healer for the men. It would be good to have another person trained anyway. Remember Fergus and Kellagh? I thought them the most unlikely men to become healers, but they were good! So, will you take on the training of a monk or lay-man for this? For me?'

'Of course, Sister Dominica, but surely you'll be able to do this yourself?'

'I may. It is enough that you agree. I will begin the process – I may finish it even, but I am glad you are willing.'

Dominica already had a boy in mind, Ruan, who with his reddish hair reminded her of Brannon as a boy. He was one of the boys who had come to the monastery in the dry time, then he was only just eight, but now he was ten and had shown himself to be quick enough to learn to read and write already. She knew Yowann thought him a candidate for being a monk, but she thought he might be better trained as a healer first, leaving the boy options at such a young age.

Dominica sought Ruan out and talked to him about being a healer, and when he showed interest she took herself to Bo Etherick where his mother lived with her other children, and suggested that this was a good path for Ruan to take.

His mother cried. But not that he would be a healer, but that she was worried he might have wanted to be a monk and she would not see him as often, and she thought Dominica had come to tell her that. Her older boy, now nearly fifteen summers and quite the man of the house, taking responsibility for his mother and his slightly younger brother and sister, said that it was for the best, and that seemed to be that. And so Ruan's training began, working with Dominica for the signs of sickness and the possible treatments and Merewin for the knowledge of herbs, how to preserve them and how to make the potions. It was not long before they could see he would become a careful and sensitive healer for the monks as he matured.

**

Harvest began. The higher fields first as usual; they got more sun and ripened earlier, the fields in the monastery grounds grew well and were south-facing, but were also lower and slightly more shaded and tended to be among the last in the Tamerkam area.

Since the war the monastery had helped as much as it could with the Tamerkam harvest and the people had helped the monastery get in their crop – and so it was this year, but this year Dominica, who would usually help with tying and stacking of the stooks with the best of them, found it too hard.

By the time she walked up the hill she was out of breath and holding herself as if she had a stitch, yet only she knew this was not from exertion. So she quietly took on the task of helping brew and bring the small ale to the workers in the field, along with the other older women who were past helping with the hard physical work of the harvest – no one made comment and they welcomed her into their group.

The greater harvest was the longest season, taking in grain, peas, beans, roots, fruits and nuts, counted from Lammas, traditionally the start of harvest, to Michaelmas. As for the grain harvest each handful of stems had to be cut with a sheaf hook, wielded by a bent-backed man or woman, and laid aside carefully - gathered up with other handfuls to make a sheaf and tied with a long-straw by another hand. Then these sheaves gathered to stand in stooks of a dozen or more, each leaning against the others so they would not fall, to let the air blow through the heads of grain to dry them. Behind them came the young gathering up any heads of grain that had broken off.

Later would come the gathering of the stooks into a well-built thatched rick to save them from the weather, and later the gleaning of seeds lost while this happened. Harvest would be in but the work still not all done. Even later would come the flailing and winnowing, the grinding of the grain to make the flour, and the making of the bread

– but for now it was all about the grain harvest – the bountiful harvest.

***

At the end of the first field to be cut Dominica had taken seven long stems of the grain to weave her harvest cross, which she usually placed on the altar. When it was finished there were three heads at the top, two each side and three strong straight stems - making the long base of the cross - and, at the centre, a circle woven from the other stems keeping it all together. Without the chapel, so without an altar, she placed it carefully on her work table before the bronze cross. After all, her table had been used outside as the altar for their Paschal Eucharist - with the restored cross shining in the sunlight.

Before that Eucharist service she had spoken with Abbot Kenver, at this very table, and told him of her belief that she would die soon, most likely within a year.

He'd looked hard at her, 'I find it hard to believe, but you – you know more about healing and death than most.'

'I only tell you this, in case I do not survive until the next Great day - I would that you hear my confession now, and give absolution, then the Paschal Eucharist will be my last communion and no one else will think anything different, I do not want all to know that I am ailing,' she said and smiled at him. He nodded, stood and began the ritual words to hear confession.

****

By about four weeks into harvest, everyone was tiring, but while the weather held they worked as this was the last grain field to be cut, the monastery field – though they knew they had many more weeks of other harvesting to do.

If the dew had been heavy – or if there had been a shower the work could not start until the field began to dry, leaving time for other, less back-aching work, or rest. This day had been the third in a row of dry days, the dew minimal, the sun warm and the breeze light. Most went to the harvest field early.

Dominica held prayers with the nuns at dawn as usual. Together they thanked the Lord for the good grain harvest which would sustain the whole community, for the coming harvest, the ripening peas, fruits, nuts, and garden roots that were swelling in the soil - and then everyone had gone their own way to whatever work bid them.

Dominica felt so very weary. The bittersweet and valerian potion she'd designed to give to Brannon, she now took herself for the pain, sometimes necessarily often - but it also made her drowsy. *It's early yet, perhaps I'll just lie down - just for a minute or two.*

It was not until mid afternoon when Avan asked one of the women bringing drinks whether Dominica was back at the brewing house, that anyone knew Dominica was missing - the women had just assumed she had other, monastery, work to do.

Alarmed, Avan rushed back to the monastery.

Chapter 69

Amen *- circa AD 722*

Avan hitched her skirt and ran as soon as she was out of sight of those working in the field, ran straight for the Prioress' hut. She pulled open the door, dashed through the outer area where Dominica had her table and met with people, straight to the divider behind which Dominica's cell-sized bed space lay. Only then did she hesitate, long enough to knock on the upright that was part of the division, and call, 'Sister Dominica? Sister? Are you well?' No answer, so she pushed away the cloth flap. In the dimness she could see Dominica, fully dressed, lying on her bed, eyes closed.

Avan started forward, hesitated, then reached out a hand and gently shook her shoulder, whispering, 'Sister Dominica? Sister?' There was no response.

Her training kicking in, Avan brought her cheek down to feel for a breath and looked for any movement of the chest. Nothing. She straightened a little and felt for the life thump. Nothing, yet the skin was not cold.

She felt something like panic rise in her and shook Dominica by both shoulders. Nothing - no sudden awakening. After a moment of just staring, memories racing through her head, she gently lifted Dominica's hands and placed them one over the other and, under them, laid Dominica's wooden cross. She would have to get Aylwyn – Aylwyn would know what to do next - for the church.

She turned to go, then turned back and kissed Dominica's forehead, whispering, 'Goodbye mother. I will always love you.'

Aylwyn could scarcely believe it when Avan told her. She stared gape-mouthed, questioned, Are you sure? at least three times. They both went to see Dominica, and even then, standing beside her body, Avan could tell Aylwyn was struggling to accept it. However, she pulled herself together, said a prayer and said she'd go and tell Yowann.

Aylwyn knew what they ought to do, but also wanted to discuss and plan with Yowann what was possible to do. The weather was warm and so the burial *had* to be soon, but they both felt that there would be people important to Dominica, who should know, who should be there, and the king's steward, Herewig, was one of them. However Lord Herewig was most likely at Seolfortun – so it was impossible for him to come in time, the shortest round trip to Seolfortun was five or six days.

Then there was the Abbot of St. Rumon's - and Prior Cormag. They thought their Prioress and the Prior of Tamerunta had settled their differences, but were not sure. On the other hand they were concerned that the Abbot may not get to them soon enough. They took a decision. That very evening they sent a messenger to the Abbot.

Eiliwedd came as soon as she was told and then helped Avan wash, prepare and wrap Dominica's body for burial. As they worked Avan revealed how Dominica had told her she was dying and made her promise to tell no one. Eiliwedd listened and comforted Avan, telling her she did right, to do as Dominica asked, all the while her own heart feeling crushed in loss.

Once wrapped, they laid her in a shroud and gathered it up and sewed together all but the face covering – leaving that so it may be covered or open.

Candles were lit, one placed at her head and one at her feet and, taking turns, two of the nuns stayed in the hut with Dominica's body at all times, keeping vigil. So that they could see her body on the bed through the doorway at the back of her hut, her table was moved to one side. With the restored bronze cross standing on it and her harvest one laid in front, it looked like an altar set up in there, as if her hut was now the church.

The whole community was shocked when it became known. People went about speaking quietly, remembering times Dominica had helped them or their families - but the work of harvest continued - it had to. Keynae came to pay her respects early in the morning, helped down the hill by her nephew and her stick.

She looked at Dominica's face, so pale yet somehow looking smoother and younger than in life, shook her head and cried, saying to the nuns sitting vigil, 'She was my best friend! The best! And such a blessing to this place!' and wept more – but still only leaving the hut when she was composed again.

Others came: Rannoeu, Drustan, and each member of the monastery, to stand in silence, or murmur thanks or say a prayer. Then her shroud was sewn closed tight - for fear of flies. Finally they laid her faded blue brat over her lengthwise - as everyone knew her by it whenever she wore it, and so it seemed right.

The Abbot arrived late in the day. He was tired, but Aylwyn and Yowann wanted to talk to him and plan the funeral. After he had eaten they sat together.

'Prioress Dominica was well loved by the people, but we believe others will want to recognise her passing to glory,' Aylwyn said.

'Like our Lord Herewig,' Yowann added, 'though we cannot hold the funeral any later as it is so warm we,' he glanced at Aylwyn, 'believe he would have wanted to be here. We want to hold another service later, to remember Prioress Dominica and all God did through her here.'

'And we would like you to preside, if you would?'

Abbot Kenver took a breath, 'It is unusual, but I can understand the position, with your Lord Herewig not living here and all he has done for this monastery. When would you want do this?'

'We will send him a message about Prioress Dominica tomorrow, but we expect him to be here in about three weeks anyway for he usually comes about a week before Michaelmas – would that be a suitable time?'

'I agree. Please do arrange it for Michaelmas.'

That settled they decided the time and order for the funeral the next day. They also sent for Keynae's nephew, and told him to ride back to Seolfortun in the morning with a message for Herewig telling of the death of Dominica and the plan for a memorial service at Michaelmas.

The next morning word had gone around the settlement, Prioress Dominica's funeral would be at noon, but that it would be simple and there would be a different service at Michaelmas to remember her.

Abbot Kenver said prayers with the members of the monastery outside the Prioress' hut, then the four most able monks carried her covered body on a bier towards the old monastery, the monks and nuns followed reciting the psalm, The Lord is my shepherd, over and over, with the lay brothers and sisters following them.

As they walked other people just joined them, until there were more than fifty or sixty following the monastery procession. When they reached the monks field they brought the bier beside the grave that had been prepared that morning. The monks stood on one side of the deep trench, the nuns on the other, behind them the lay members of the monastery, and beyond them the people, finding whatever vantage point they could

Abbot Kenver led prayers and said the words for burial.

The small silences were punctuated by sounds of weeping and the snuffling sound of people trying not to cry. Her body was lowered into the hole and, as they began to fill in the grave, more prayers were said. No one seemed to want to leave the spot, so they stayed until the grave was filled and all the earth that had been removed, replaced.

Eventually Abbot Kenver nodded to Aylwyn and Yowann and he led the monastery procession away. Leaving the people of Tamerkam to mourn in their own way, with hugs and murmured words.

The next morning, Avan felt drawn to go to The Monks' Field early. She, who knew best that Dominica had died, still found it hard to believe. The turf had been placed back on the raised mound, she could see that from a distance, but there was something else.

The mound and all around it was strewn with wild flowers, mostly single flowers, but sometimes a small bunch, tied with grass. It was strangely beautiful and moved Avan to tears. Looking round she could see she'd have to walk quite a way to find a flower of her own, and suddenly then realised what she had do.

Avan went to where the old herb garden was, on the edge of what was now Herewig's court. There the herbs were growing wild where odd roots had been left when they moved to the new monastery. She pulled some of each, roots and all, then found any herbs that had flowers on them, gathered them into a bunch and tied that with grass. She picked up a stick and broke it to give it a sharp point and walked back to The Monks' Field.

There, she poked the herb roots in around the edges of the grave, placed her bunch of herbs on top. She stood and composed herself, held her hand out over the grave and, aloud, spoke the wise-woman's blessing that Dominica had told her about.

Now, she felt better. Now it felt right.

Chapter 70

Amen, Amen! - circa AD 722

Herewig arrived a week before Michaelmas as predicted and dealt with court matters at Kelliwic and Halhtun in that time. When he went to the monastery he was a little nonplussed, not knowing who was now in charge. In the end he went to find Yowann as the most senior person there.

'Lord Herewig!' Yowann said when Herewig turned up where he was working.

'Brother Yowann. Thank you for sending word of dear Prioress Dominica's ...' he hesitated, 'passing into glory,' he finished using their words in the message.

'She is greatly missed.'

'She will be, I am sure of that! Tell me, have you chosen a new ...'

'No, not yet. We ought, but we are loath to do so yet. It isn't essential you know. The Prior or Prioress is more for those from outside to know who to deal with. They are merely first amongst equals in the monastery.'

Herewig nodded. 'So I should talk with you? Or?'

'I will do, or Aylwyn as senior nun, best both of us together.'

'Then that is what I will do. For now, tell me about this service.'

Herewig offered his Hall, the old church, for the special service, and his table once more looked like the Lord's table, the Altar. It was planned to welcome as many as would like to come, but certain people were invited personally, and so it was that the two benches were filled by Lord Herewig, Drustan, Keynae, Prior Cormag, Liaden, alone as Eudaf had died in the spring, Rannoeu, and Brother Tethion from St. Rumon's. What felt like just about everyone from the whole of Halhtun lands seemed to then squash into the remainder of the big building and even so some had to stand outside.

The service began with the words and responses for the Eucharist, with flat-breads being blessed and passed hand to hand, a small piece to be torn off and held up until the word was spoken to consume it. Then the words were spoken and the Abbot took the cup for all. Once the Lord's prayer was said and the blessing given Abbot Kenver addressed them all.

'This is when I would give you a sermon, but today we remember our dear departed sister, Prioress Dominica, gone to glory.'

There was a sound like a collective sigh.

'I have only known Prioress Dominica since shortly before the war. She came to help us when our monastery was beset with an ailment we did not know, and which was taking our brothers. She worked tirelessly to cure those who were sick, and succeeded. She was a remarkable healer using her God-given skills and knowledge.'

Prior Cormag suddenly stood up, 'I ask leave to speak,' he said, his voice sounding thick and heavy. Abbot Kenver looked at Yowann, who shrugged. Kenver, nodded, and Cormag came to the front.

'I am Prior Cormag, now the only one left of those of us who came from Eriu to this place, I am Prior at Tamerunta,' he said. Liaden was staring at him. 'And, and, I need to say something about Sister Dominica, Prioress, and how we came to be here.'

He looked around at the people gathered and nodded a few times before drawing a deep breath. 'Back in our home monastery in Eriu, Indract and Dominica were the son and daughter of the King of that place, before they joined the monastery there. They were brother and sister by blood as well as in God. So when Indract became ill - I do not know the name of this ailment but it had already taken another brother - and Indract was so sick our infirmarer said he would not last the night. Brother

Brannon went and told Sister Dominica and, against the rules, she went into the men's infirmary. There, while the infirmarer was at vespers she prayed for Indract. Indract told me this himself, he opened his eyes and saw her shining in the darkness, pouring the Holy Spirit of healing into him – and he was restored!'

There was a murmuring around the hall.

Cormag lifted his voice again, 'And that is not all I want to say. When he was fully recovered, Indract had a vision! He was to go on pilgrimage to Rome to thank God for his miraculous cure through Dominica, and that was not all. In the vision Dominica was there too. Despite many obstacles, he would not leave without her going too. Without that, she would not have come to this place. God wanted her to be here.'

Herewig stood, Cormag looked at him and stood aside as he also went to the front, 'Prior Cormag has spoken about Sister Dominica's prayer working miracles. I, I will tell you about another, about the King, King Ina.

The first time I saw Sister Dominica I didn't know her; she was just some nun at the church where her brother, Saint Indract, had been buried. The King was invited as it was the special Martyrs' Mass for them all, and he happened to be in the area. I was part of the king's escort. Six of us surrounded him as he entered the church, remained with him until he was comfortably sat at the front, and only then stepped away.

He needed six of us to shield him from being seen as weak and in pain, because he was crippled with such pain in his feet. At the end of that service he sent everyone out of the church, except Sister Dominica. Within a short time he and Sister Dominica stepped out of the church. His crippling pain completely gone, him in a joyous mood! And this, this *miraculous cure*, is why the King provided Prioress Dominica, and this place, with his protection when she asked for it.'

Avan, standing in the front row, put up her hand. 'Sister?' Abbot Kenver asked.

'Prioress Dominica told me ...'

'Come up here sister. You are one of Prioress Dominica's healers, are you not?'

'I am, which is why she told me that she knew she had not long to live, because Sister Dominica knew what was going to take her life – because she had, as a child of about seven years, sensed this same canker inside a person who they all loved and who was ill. The healer of the place said it would kill him soon. Then she said Dominica should pray while the man took a simple easing potion as she had 'seen' his ailment - and so she did. Afterwards he said he had felt the lump inside of him slide away. He didn't die, and lived for many, many years. Much later, when the healer herself was dying, she told Dominica that she knew Dominica had important work to do – as she had seen her glow when she was praying for the man all those years ago. I believe *that* was her first miraculous healing.'

A great deal of murmuring followed this revelation.

Esselt just stood in her place turned round and sang out, 'And her prayers - prayers with tears she couldn't control ... her fasting and prayers broke the drought so that we could live, so that we had such a bountiful harvest!' The murmuring increased.

Keynae stood and, using her stick, hobbled to the front.

The murmuring subsided.

Keynae stood tall, pushing up from the stick, 'Prioress Dominica had visions too, she told me, that before their boat even landed at Tamerunta she was shown this place in a vision and so when the mission was set up at Tamerunta she shared this vision with Indract so that they could come here too.' She nodded.

'*This* was the place God sent *her* – to us – and she loved us so much, she was *so brave for us* -' she stopped to swallow a sob, 'the way, the way, even after she knew that man had killed the other Prior – the way she strode out to face him, to demand he respect those pennants the King had given her! She *risked* her life *for us*!'

There was a silence - and then people began to clap and cheer.

Abbot Kenver, stepped forward and rapped the end of his staff on the bench – the noise quietened. 'I can confirm the words said about her visions, for she told me these and she vouchsafed another vision to me – that the place they first landed should be where their new mission would be, as it came to pass.'

Drustan called out from where he was sitting, 'I remember that day, I was lookout – when we saw her through the trees round the clearing, she was standing with her arms up, looking up to heaven - and there was a glow about her! I thought it was a trick of the light – but not now.'

Abbot Kenver said, slowly and thoughtfully, 'It seems quite a few here knew about her visions, as visions need to be shared to become reality - but the *miraculous* healings, she kept them close without us knowing - for she did not really talk about the miraculous healing God did through her. Yet others witnessed some of them and have vouched for them to us – how many more may God have used her to perform?

I believe we have all shared this holy place with a saint. *A true saint.* Prioress Dominica was gifted with healing by miracle though the Lord God and the Holy Spirit - as well as being gifted with healing through her knowledge and her hands,' raising his voice he ended with, 'And we are blessed to have known her! *A true saint – Dominica!* Amen. Amen!'

At which everyone replied, 'Amen, Amen!' and once again broke into applause and cheers, with the words 'Saint Dominica!' being said by many. '*Our saint* - Dominica!'

Part Six
The Manor of Haltone
- the year 1089

Chapter 71
Epilogue

The great harvest is half-way through, yet this day there has been little or no work done, for it is the feast day of Saint Dominica, the saint of this place that is now known as the Manor of Haltone.

What do we still see of the place? The river has not changed much, but the main settlement is now nearer the river, not much left up on the hill overlooking it now. There are some new buildings crafted from stone, notably the new Manor Hall, but they are all still thatched with reed. Most of the rest of the buildings are rectangular now, even those of wood and wattle, not circular as they were.

Of course, the land is worked for a new master too, a Norman overlord, half brother to the late King William they are told, but that makes little difference; it's been one lord or another forever, what matters where he came from?

To begin with the new steward was very demanding. The income for the Lord was not as much as it should be, he said, this much land should provide more – but the people had worked with him, and all was settled; the land made its due - as long as the weather was kind and the harvests came in reliably.

This is one of the reasons they observe this day, for Dominica is the Saint they pray to for a good harvest in springtime, during Lent, and to whom they offer a thanksgiving on her feast day, which falls in the middle of the great harvest – exactly halfway between Lammas and Michaelmas.

The monastery holds a special service on Saint Dominica's day, then, bearing a cross made from seven stalks of the first cut field, they set off on a great procession with the people following them, visiting all the settlements, and gathering more people on the way.

They go first up to Bohudrek and there say prayers at the praying place, under the ancient oak tree. Then they move on to do the same at the stone cross near the cross roads.

Their last stop is at the small wooden church built beside Saint Dominica's old place at Babur, where the procession circles the building chanting the psalm, 'The Lord is my shepherd'. Then, placing the wheat-stalk cross on the small altar in there, said to be made from her very own table, they finish with more prayers, before the procession returns down to the monastery.

Food and ale will be provided for all who would share in it - and there will be singing of harvest songs but, most importantly and before all that, the telling of the story of Saint Dominica and her brother Indract.

Come on, come and sit on the hill-slope, the story teller is about to begin. He is the latest in a long-line of storytellers in a family that can trace its lineage back beyond the tale of Saint Dominica. See, how they settle themselves down and a hush falls as he stands before them all and lifts his hand – *listen!*

'A long, long time ago, in the year six-hundred-and-eighty-nine, two strangers from a foreign land came to this place in a coracle. Their names were?' his voice rises in question.

The people respond, '*Indract and Dominica!*'

He pretends not to be able to hear them, repeats. 'Their names were?'

The people sing back louder, 'Indract and Dominica!'

'Yes! Indract and Dominica - and they were son and daughter of a King in Hibernia, a holy monk and a holy nun.

They came because a *vision* told them to come here, and your great, great, great forefathers took them in and made them welcome, setting aside land for them to build the first monastery here. They were not alone in coming from Hibernia, they had left other brothers down at Tamertone, where they had started another monastery.

After a while, when all was settled and both monasteries flourished, nine of the brothers set off on a pilgrimage to Rome, Indract leading them - but who *chose* to stay here with *us?*

The people call out, *'Dominica!'* The story teller repeats his question, miming that he can't hear.

The people shout, this time with gusto, ***'Dominica!'***

He laughs and settles back into his story again. 'Now, on their way back from Rome our Holy pilgrims stopped at the great monastery at Glastonbury, to pray at the tomb of the blessed Saint Patrick of Hibernia.'

He drops his voice low, yet harsh, so people strain to hear - yet cower in their hearts.

'News came with the one brother who *escaped.'* He looks around. 'The holy brothers had been set upon by *evil men*, warriors driven by *greed*, who saw them carrying their bags as if they were precious and saw their staff-tips shining like gold - and *plotted murder and plunder.*

Listen, all who have covetous thoughts, the staff tips were but bronze polished to a shine, and the bags just bore seeds of strange herbs from distant lands.'

His voice rises. 'Yet for *this* our holy brothers were *slaughtered* and buried in the mire to *hide their murder!*

He allows the silence to stand a moment or two.

'But did God let this terrible evil go undiscovered?'

The people shout, *'No!'*

'Did God let this terrible evil go unpunished?'

The people shout, *'No!'*

'No! God set pillars of light at night over every place where a body lay. Word reached the King of this miracle and - of - the - *terrible deed.*

Now, the King was a pious king, a very pious King, who had the bodies taken out of the mire and taken up into the church and buried there properly, with a tomb to match Saint Patrick's made for Saint Indract.'

He shakes his head as if in sorrow. 'When our Saint Dominica heard of this she was sorrowful and named the monastery here after her brother, Saint Indract the Martyr.

She vowed to go and visit the place her brother lay, finding great favour with the King there.

Though she was sorrowful, though she had found favour with the King, did she leave us?' he asks.

'No!!' the people respond.

'No! She didn't, she returned to us and continued to serve our community - with humility, with godliness.

With her God-given healing powers – did she cure our people?

'Yes!' the people respond. The story teller puts his hand up to cup his ear, and asks again.

'Yes!' they shout back

When danger of *war* threatened us – did *she risk her own life* to protect us?

'Yes!!' they shout back, warming to the theme.

When the springs dried up one by one – did she weep until they began to fill again?

'Yes!!'

'Yes! When famine threatened to starve our people to death - she fasted and prayed so that the rains came in time, the crops grew and the harvest was so great - that she made a cross from the first stems and laid it on the altar, *as we still do today! Alleluia!'*

'Alleluia!' the people sing back.

His voice drops again, 'Having given *all of herself* to us and to God, she was transported to glory on *this* day, exactly mid-way between Lammas and Michaelmas. It is even said that the very land in the Monks' Field where she was laid to rest grew sweet-smelling herbs and beautiful wild flowers in remembrance of her.'

His voice rises again, becomes authoritative, 'Such was the love of our forefathers for Dominica that a great ceremony was held in her honour where, from testimonies and to great acclamation, she was named *Saint for this place!'* He stoops to pick up a cup and stands tall, raises his voice and his cup, 'Saint Dominica! *Our saint*, Dominica!'

This is what the people are waiting for. They scramble to their feet, ***'Saint Dominica! Our saint, Dominica! Saint Dominica!'*** they shout, and drink from their own cups.

'The feast may begin!'

***** *finis et principium* *****

Author's Notes: The Legends and Other Notes of Inspiration

This *novel* is about the *Cornwall-based* Dominica. However I did read any of the legends that named Indract as well.

In general there is not much to work from for our Dominica, but I have paraphrased here the main legends relating to Saints Dominica and Indract, especially those touching on Cornwall, the Tamar river and Halton in the parish of St. Dominick.

With all the following legends, bear in mind that ***there is documentary evidence*** that the Parish Church of St. Dominick, very likely the biggest building in the whole of the two manors (Halton and Ashton) which made up the, probably *relatively* new, parish was dedicated to Saint Dominica, albeit in Latin, by Bishop Walter de Bronescombe in October 1259.

There is also contemporary documentary evidence, dated the 10th of September 1445, to show that St Indract's saint's day was celebrated on May 8th in this parish, probably at the Chapel dedicated to him (as well as at Glastonbury) but that St. Dominica's saint's day was 'on the day after the decollation *(beheading)* of St. John the Baptist' which is the 29th August - **making her original saint's day the 30th of August** (in the middle of the great harvest).

This primary evidence is from the granting, by Bishop Lacy of Exeter, of a request from the rector and parishioners of the Church of St. Dominica for a change of Feast Day for St. Dominica - because it was 'inconveniently in the middle of harvest'. They suggested it could be moved to the day after St. Indract's feast day – hence to the 9th of May. If it being in the middle of harvest seems unimportant today – we must remember that no work would be done on your parish saint's feast day – what with the solemn services and the observances of the day, to say nothing of the 'feast' which would be as it's name suggests, and as it was a Holy day – it was a holiday.

It also seems that there was frequently, amongst those who have never heard of our Dominica, a confusion with St. Dominic (Spanish founder of the Dominican Order) and so in most *national* lists, *if* she is included, she is sometimes given the same date as him *August 4th. *(*this was his date pre 1970)* or her 'modern' date in May.

There is also documented evidence that a chapel dedicated to St Indract, *(sometimes rendered Ildrieth or Indracht or Indractus - depending when written)* was first mentioned as early as 1351 and was recorded as being licensed in 1405 and in 1419 in the area now known as *'Chapel' (pronounced Chaypul locally)* in the Parish of St. Dominick - the small remains of which still stand on private land right beside the river.

It is also to be noted that, very close to these chapel remains, is St. Indract's Holy Well, also on private land.

In this *story*, I have set Dominica's monastery, which she dedicated to Indract in this *'Chapel'* area. Whereas the Tamerkam monastery is placed in the area where the manor house of Halton Barton is situated today.

So to the simple and short legend that puts Dominica and Indract in this place, where the Tamar loops almost back on itself, a place easily recognised on maps if you follow the river Tamar in from the sea – today known as Halton in the parish of St. Dominick.

"Indract and Dominica, son and daughter of an Irish King, came up the Tamar in a coracle to this place and made a religious settlement here."

Now we must acknowledge and add the legend from Tamerton (Foliot). This village is situated at the end of an estuarine creek on the *other* side of the river, just below the confluence where the Tavy joins the Tamar. They, too have a legend of Indract and Dominica, and say he founded the original church there – though their current, much rebuilt church, with 12th/13th century origins, is dedicated to St. Mary.

Indract with his (nine) companions and his sister Dominica, on their way to Rome, stopped at a place called Tamerunta. There Indract drove his staff into the ground, causing an oak tree to grow, and there he caused a pond to provide a plentiful supply of fish. (There is an extension to this legend, added later perhaps, concerning the stealing of fish and a parting of the ways between Indract's group, who went on to Rome, and the remaining group)

The rest of the legends concern the dramatic end of Indract and companions on their return from pilgrimage to Rome following their stop-off at Glastonbury – these are linked to Glastonbury Abbey, and give the saint's day – the day of martyrdom as May 8th.

Indract and his nine (or seven) companions had gone to Rome on pilgrimage and on their return journey they decided to visit Glastonbury and the tomb of St Patrick there, staying for the night at a place called Hywisc afterwards. King Ine, of Wessex, was staying nearby at 'Pedred'. A king's thegn named Husa (or Huna), with his men, attacked and killed the pilgrims believing they had gold (some versions add 'they thought their staffs were tipped with gold, and their bags full of treasure – but the 'gold' was brass and the 'treasure' was seeds, particularly celery seeds). They buried their bodies, but at night columns of light appeared and the King, being shown this miracle, had their bodies taken up and re-interred at 'The Old Church', St. Mary's at Glastonbury, setting Indract's tomb on the left side of the altar opposite St. Patrick's. (some versions add – 'but one body was never found – though a light appears there each anniversary of their martyrdom')

This tale was recorded a number of times, with many variations and elaborations, but a copy of the 'Passio sancti Indracti' by an anonymous 12th century author, who claimed it to be based on an earlier 'Old English' work, is the earliest surviving example.

The 14th century St. Alban's monk, known as 'John of Tynemouth' in his Sanctilogium Angliae, repeated much of the Passio sancti Indracti, but also included the legends involving Tamerton (Foliot) and St Dominica – and so I have based my story more on this version.

I think I should mention that there is yet another version. This one is restricted to Shapwick in Somerset, a place quite close to Glastonbury - relating a tale of Indract *and Drusa* (who is said to be *'also known as' Dominica*, in this version).

In the Shapwick tale it is suggested that the people of Shapwick themselves mistook the pilgrims for wealthy merchants and it was they who killed and hid their bodies (though another telling of this does say it was 'Horsa, a thegn of King Ine, and his men'). Also in this tale Drusa is sometimes designated as Indract's wife and they are not from a monastery but just on their way back from a holy pilgrimage - and so still considered martyrs.

However, the Shapwick version also states their saints day, from their day or martyrdom, as February 5th. I have not used this version in my novel as evidence tells that the Cornwall based Dominica had a different saint's day – and so she would not have been amongst those martyred with Indract - whether that occurred in February or in May.

Among the variations between all the versions are the number of companions going with Indract to Rome (after their time in Cornwall) - this ranges from seven to nine *(if we discount the 100 suggested by Worcester)* – I chose to send eight companions with Indract – so, nine travelling altogether. In my story this leaves Dominica and one of the brothers to hold the fort in the two religious settlements they have established.

Very Local Legends

Then, there are the very local, never-written, legends. Like the one that is passed down from one owner of the Halton Barton to the next.

"The field, known as 'The Monks' Field' is never to be ploughed - as plague victims were buried there and/or the monks were buried there"

Mentions of **the Plague** in this story are not to be confused with the Black Death of the 14th and 17th Centuries. The Plague in this story is the Justinian Plague which ravaged Europe mainly between AD 541 and AD 543 but with reoccurring outbreaks until around AD 750 in many places, including in Britain and Ireland. The Justinian Plague was a bubonic plague but, though caused by the same bacterium Yersinia pestis, is now known to be a different strain which died out – rather than mutated to become the Black Death plague.

Of course the legend *may* refer to plague victims of the later date – but by then that area was definitely just behind the actual Manor House and therefore a very unlikely burial place for plague victims at all.

And then we have the other very local tale that says:

"St. Indract's Well was refilled/made by Dominica's tears at a time of dreadful drought."

Told to me by the current owner of Chapel House in which the remains of the chapel, dedicated to St. Indract and licensed in the 15th century, stand, and also by the owner of the land on which St. Indract's well is situated.

You will have found both of these local legends incorporated into this story.

OTHER NOTES
and some of my sources of inspiration

<u>Historic Weather Events</u>

Finding that reports of weather events and trends have been found in documents relating to specific dates and (mostly large) areas, I chose to use these as a background to this story – so there really was red rain reported across southern Britain and Ireland in AD 685 (now thought to be caused by activity at both Etna and Vesuvius). Subsequently the general weather did get wetter and cooler for years – then became dryer and warmer year on year – culminating in a severe drought in the South West of Britain in 721.

<u>Lords of the Manor</u>

According to the Domesday book, Halton, prior to 1066, was held by Earl Harold (otherwise known as Harold Godwinson, Earl of Wessex aka King Harold - though obviously not named as the latter in the Domesday book in 1086) as was Callington. Both places were in the Hundred of Rillaton, an area roughly covering what was later known as the Hundred of East Wivelshire, and is the area the Cornish part of the novel is set in.

Incidentally in the story, when King Ine / Ina of Wessex decided he'd take Halton 'under his hand' and be its Lord I didn't even know he was going to say it! So, I also did not really know that it had become part of the King of Wessex' holdings, and passed down the Wessex line to King Harold - to be taken over post 1066 by William - until I paused the writing and researched to check out the possibility. Out of the 53 places named in the Domesday book for the Hundred of Rillaton, only seven were held by Earl Harold so the odds were not great - and for one of the other seven to be Callington was a bonus for me.

Ley Lines

Having mentioned Indract's well above, let me add here that there is also a recognised Ley Line which begins on the Bere peninsular, crosses the river Tamar and passes just beside St. Indract's Holy Well (where the line has been much studied by a local dowser). It continues in a straight line passing diagonally through the parish Church of St. Dominick, St. Dominica's, over 2.7km away, through the south-east corner, diagonally encompassing almost all the church, and out via the north-west corner the other side, before continuing onwards through St. Samsom's church at South Hill and St. Torney's at North Hill - ending up on the top of a rocky outcrop, surrounded by cairns, on top of Bray Down some 20.5 miles (37.9 km) from it's beginning - and always on a 54 degrees NW bearing.

Inspiration for the Stone circle at Bo Barr

About fifteen miles away from St Dominick Church, at Duloe, is one of a very few stone circles using only Quartz stones, though a single significant quartz stone features in others.

It is common in the wider area around St. Dominick to find quartz stones edging the paths around churches and old farms. However, there are a *lot* around this particular church, some rounded, some angular, fist-size and larger, but none of them are of a huge size. However, whether brought in from elsewhere or just found 'lying' around, the much larger quartz and pale grey tall stones in the old rectory gardens (most as part of a rockery) right next to the church, inspired the idea of a small stone circle, a 'place of the old people' at Bo Barr. A place where Dominica would preach and pray with the people - and at which, much later, the church would be built. Added to this, dowsers have described a very strong 'feminine' energy emanating from the middle of the nave, aligned with the north and south doorways, and within the width of the Ley line.

There is no current evidence for this particular place having been the site of a stone circle previous to the building of the church, but such places were frequently 'taken-over' by the 'new religion' of Christianity - so it is not beyond belief - and became my inspiration.

Many have said that this church does have that very special feel of a 'thin place' - one of those Celtic places where God's love and presence feels closer than usual.

Author's Notes: Place Names
Which place names I used and why

Writing an historical novel was always going to be difficult, but to write one that crosses linguistic borders, both in geography and in political dominance, made for some interesting challenges. Obviously I would not be writing each in their original language – yet I wanted to give some idea of the language that our protagonists were using and hearing as the story progressed.

Like other aspects of this time in history I found I knew a lot less than I expected, and of Ireland only headlines, and those mostly from different times than these. I researched, I learnt – but then I didn't want to bog down the story with the learning – so I endeavoured to give a feeling, the light touch of words they would have used for a few everyday items, the names of herbs or clothing or landscape features. Hopefully a lot of this was successful and you were not left completely puzzled by a term. However names of places are more specific and here I set out the reasons for the choices I made.

In Eriu (Eire/Ireland)

Eriu – Name of this country as probably used *by the natives* at that time. Outsiders may have been calling it **Hibernia.**

Drom-Eanaigh *(anglicised as - Dromana)* – the name and location of the low-king of the Deisi's stronghold and court (partly fictional).
Drom-Mohr *(anglicised as – Dromore)* the name of the location of the (fictional) monastery of St. Declan and St. Brigid

Having researched the known monasteries operating at that time and in the area above the mouth of the Blackwater River, Co. Waterford, I found none suitable for my story.

Why, you may wonder, must the monastery be in this area? Well, if I wanted our pilgrims to end up near to the mouth of the Tamar, then the best way was for them to be leaving from the harbour near the mouth of The Blackwater river near Youghal (*Eochaille*). If they left from the east coast, even with the storm and the prevailing currents, they'd most likely have ended up on the north coast of Devon or Cornwall. Yet it was also still quite reasonable for them to leave from a harbour at the mouth of this river to go to Saint David's *(San Dyfd)* in Wales as travel by water was quicker than by road. These two places are almost lined up with each other if the first part of the journey followed the coast. There is a small query over the port's actual location at the time, as to which side of the river mouth it was, yet there was definitely a settlement at Eochaille, as the church there was founded in the mid 5th century by St. Declan.

Lacking an extant monastery and stronghold that suited the story, I decided to **create the court of the low-king Conall of the Deisi Muman at Drom-Eanaigh** and **the monastery of St. Declan and St. Brigid** at **Drom-Mhor** - a geographically suitable land formation that was within the kingdom of the *Deisi Muman* of the time, and overlooking The Great River.

There *are two* ridges – one called Dromana *Drom-Eanaigh (Ridge in the marsh) the other, a*cross the valley (through which the little river Goish winds, probably causing the eponymous marsh) and on which I sited the monastery - Dromore *Drom-Mohr (Great Ridge).*

Powers, in his 1903 book, Place Names of the Decies, says "Within this parish was the chief seat and stronghold (Dromana) of the Lords of Decies" and, indeed, from the 12th century there has been a significant stronghold at Dromana which is claimed as that of the Lord of the Decies, and which *could* have been built on an older occupation site.

There is no archaeological evidence that I can find of anything previous to this, but it is within reason, as I endeavoured to site them both as would suit such settlements - strategically for one and in suitable isolation for the other - within the real landscape.

Added to this, the location of Ogham stones on the lower slope of Dromore, at Kiltera, is suggestive of a very old Christian presence on this ridge – and these are dated to times contemporary with this story.

The monastery in the story is referred to by either its saints' names, Declan and Brigid, or the ridge name of Drom-Mohr.

There is nothing else of significance shown as having existed on these ridges overlooking the river Blackwater. The only other place of significance nearby is Villierstown, a relatively new build founded in the 1740s by John Villiers, which is at the foot of Dromana in the, now drained, marshy valley.

St. Declan's monastery at Ardmore *(of which my monastery in the story was originally a daughter monastery)* is real and located near the coast about 14 miles away and is reputed to have been set up by Saint Declan – who was also of the Deisi Muman family – in AD430.

Our pilgrims travel down to *Eochaille* via *An Abhainn Mhor* (**The Great River** - now called the Blackwater river) as it would be the fastest way to carry themselves and their supplies to the vicinity of the harbour near the mouth of the river.

In Dumnonia: (Cornwall & Devon)

Dumnonia – The area ruled by the tribal king of the Dumnonians stretching from Lands End up to, at the time this story reaches Britain, roughly the current Somerset and Dorset border with Devon.

Cornish Place Names:

A note on Cornish place names – when a word contains two elements, the first is last and the last is first.

For instance the place name in Cornwall 'Redruth' is made up of two parts. The *'Red' comes from Rhyd* meaning *Ford* and the *Ruth part comes from Rudh* meaning *Red* (the colour). Red-Ruth actually says – Ford-Red, meaning – the Red-Ford)

Cornwall Council have 'approved' Cornish names for places in Cornwall. I could have just used these, but in quite a few cases they have chosen words with Old English elements and names from an historical list that are in, or post, the Domesday Book (1086).

However, when looking up a very old place I used to live in, I noticed they had named it without reference to the *actual* landscape, or maybe, even without reference to earlier renditions - (an earlier rendition of Radland from the 1300s is *Redelond).*

They had decided the place name 'Radland' would have been Anglo-saxon *(with no actual evidence)* and as *'Readan-land'* - meaning a red strip of land. So they then translated this as 'a red strip of earth'. Suggesting *'rudh'* meaning 'red', and translating 'land' into '*gweres*' meaning 'earth, soil' giving it as '*Gweresrudh*'.

Whereas, I *know* that this land is *not* on a strip of 'red earth or soil'. However *it is adjacent to where there was a ford* (Old Cornish, *Rhyd).* To be the land by the ford makes far more sense of the reality.

And if we are looking at 'land' rather than 'earth/soil' we have the farming terminology, in Cornish of, 'len' or 'lenyow' (piece of land or pieces of land) which would bring us closer still to Radland - with Ryhd-len (ford-land = the land by the ford)

In Kernow: (Cornwall)

There were many place names I felt couldn't use – as they are too Saxon to be used when the story is in the pre-Saxon-occupation of the area we are set in.

The modern **Halton** was one of these (*until it actually changed from a Cornish name to the Saxon Halhtun, within the story*). From the Old English (Saxon) O.E. *Halh* (corner – as in nook/a bend in a river) *Tun* (homestead/town). So I worked with that name backwards to create ***Tamerkam*** (Brythonic-root spelling of Tamar + O.C. for bend - kam) while also reflecting the name of Tamerton *as it is in their* Legend, ***Tamerunta***, where the river's name is used as part of the identifier.

Tamer – for the river Tamar, using the Brythonic root Tame – dark flowing – and to be in keeping with Tamerunta, essentially on the other side of the same river.

Bo Etherick – is **Bohetherick** A 'Bo,' 'Bos' or 'Boh' is an Old Cornish word for a home or homestead. Etherick is a Cornish name of the time, likely a contraction of Petherick. Nothing to be changed here really – just to separate the two words. Etherick's Homestead. (Though the name may have been Hudrek, Hydrek or any other similar – Etherick has persisted down the years)

Bo Barr - hopefully those who know the parish see where I am going with this. This area has been known as **Baber** (or similar - *Barbur 1327*) for a *long* time which is not too far from the idea and sound of Bo Barr – the homestead of Barr. 'Bar', in O.C., means the the top or summit of a hill and the Baber area occupies a small shallow valley between two hill tops - so the name of the first person to live there *could* have just come from that word too. St. Dominica's Church stands on the edge of the wide end of this valley, just before the land drops more steeply down to the stream which cuts across the end of the valley and marks the border between Tamerkam and Ventonpemps.

Pensinys: The Cornish Archaeology walking survey team suggested there had been an iron-age fort* facing the one still showing at Bury Farm, across the valley *(*recently confirmed by LIDAR)* - and there is a lane running behind this area to a small field identified as 'pensingers' on the Tithe Map – hence the name of the lane is known as Pensingers. My inspiration in using this name is that Pensingers ***may*** have been a corruption of *Pensinys* - *Pen* in O.C. meaning *headland/point* + *sinys* being cornish for *signal.* Maybe where a fire was lit to signal to other parts of the territory, or further afield.

Ventonpemps - is Ashton - the place called the Manor of Aissetone in the Domesday book 1086. It is generally believed where this occurs it was a Norman spelling of *Aesctun* (O.E. Aesc = Ash trees - the homestead where ash-trees grow) ***Ventonpemps*** in this story I derived from *Venton* - Old Cornish for spring + *pemps* O.C. for five, meaning Five Springs. I chose this name as there were at least that number that were used as domestic water sources in this hamlet to my certain knowledge. As well as being a place occupied from the stone-age, and water sources being more important and fixed than the type of trees.

Kellyventon (situated where **Callington** is today) O.C. *Kelly* (woods) *Venton* (spring) – meaning spring in the woods (the spring that flows at Pipe / Lady's Well is still strong!)

This is my idea alone – and I refer anyone who would know the many and accepted theories on Callington's name to the book Callington by Sheila Lightbody.

I was not entirely convinced of the origin idea from the approved list that says it was *Kellygwig* (Kelly = woods) and (gwig = forest settlement) and then that becoming Kelliwic - all while still being in Old Cornish - when the first written reference to any place called this comes from the late 11th Century.

Especially as Wic was also a Saxon designation of a market or trading place. Then, somehow, this Kelliwic turned into Kellington/Killington. So I *chose* to suggest that the name Kellyventon remained in the memory of the people beyond the Kelliwic of the Saxon to re-emerge as Kellington and morph to Callington.

Kalesak is what I have called **Calstock**. Again, trying to make sense of the name of the place pre Saxon changes. The approved 'Cornish' name (Kalstok) is a version taken from 1270 and they suggest no reasoning – saying the origin is 'obscure'. 'Stock' is a O.E. word, and Stok does not appear to be a Cornish word at all.

Kales, however, is an O.C. word meaning Hard (and knowing, as we do now, that that area had been occupied by a Roman fort, including a Roman road into it – it was not only a superb spot defensively, but also had a lot of 'hard' areas. The '*ak*' ending has been added as being the O.C. suffix '*ak*' - meaning the place 'located' or 'found'. Kalesak – the location of the Hard place.

In Dewnen: (Devon)

Tamerunta - **Tamerton (Foliot)** - as taken from the legends.

***Tafvi* river** River **Tavy** - *Taf* also being a Brythonic root word meaning dark, with most water courses running from peat being 'dark water', it is fitting. *I included the f and the v in the spelling just as an indicator of pronunciation.*

St. Rumon's on Tafvi is my precursor to the Saxon monastery built* two hundred years later and below St. Rumon's position on the hill *(*on what would have been flood-plain at this time, though which, by the 10th Century, had become a safe place to build)*

I believe there must have been a monastery here long before AD 974, when Bishop Ordulph established the Benedictine monastery of St Mary and St. Rumon, mainly because they included St. Rumon as a secondary saint.

St. Mary was obviously well known, but Rumon? A fairly obscure Breton-Cornish saint of the 5th Century said to have set up a monastery at, and been buried in, Ruan Lanihorne (*Ruan Lanryhorn - 1270*) Lan (holy place) *ryhorn - believed to be a co*rruption of Rumon, as well as Ruan being the Cornish version of Rumon. Had there not been a tradition of a monastery in Tavistock being dedicated to St. Rumon already, why would Ordulf have included him in the dedication of a totally new Benedictine monastery?

However, if he was already the established saint of the place, then Bishop Ordulph certainly made sure of his connection when he had most of Rumon's remains removed from their resting place in Ruan Lanihorne in the late 10th century and transported to his new monastery at Tavistock.

In this story a monastery already existed, a 'British' monastery, maybe even set up by Rumon himself, on a bluff above the river Tavy and its flood plain, maybe around the area of Kilworthy Park.

(I was convinced of this location hypothesis from studying the article by S. Gedye. 'Hydrology and Tavistock's Saxon Abbey')

Porthkudh is what I have renamed the harbour at **Mount Batten.** It was here that the first international port was located in the great bay at the mouth of the Plym on one side and the Tamar, Tavy and Lynher, on the other. There had been a settlement at this place from the Bronze Age, and it continued as a port and trading place for the Roman Empire.

The oldest name I found for this port, tucked away behind the promontory, is 'How Stert' (a name superseded by 'Mount Batten' in *very* recent times). 'How Stert' is an O.E. construct meaning 'Hill Promontory' beneath and behind which lies this small ancient natural harbour, safe from the waves.

Porthkudh is a pairing of words in Cornish which means *'hidden port'* – for, from the sea, you'd not know it was there – and Cornish would be the closest to the language used across Dumnonia that we have.

***Escancastre:* (Exeter)**

I struggled with naming this as so many sources seemed to think it virtually had no name after the Romans left and before Athelstan formally named it Escancaester in the 9th century. There is some mention of it being known as Moncton, as there were so many monks there, and some of a Roman-Saxon blend of Iscachester.

Then I found that in the Life of Saint Boniface (of Exeter fame) written around 750AD, it was named as Escancastre – and, as the closest I can get to the right name at the right time, I have gone with that. It seems it took another 800 years to contract to the name Exeter we know today. **information from The English Place Name Society. University of Nottingham.*

In Somersaete (Somerset)

Glestyngabyrig - as in Saxon hands the Saxon term is used - we will know it as **Glastonbury**

Hywisc – now **Huish Episcopi** in Somerset - about 11.5 miles walk from Glastonbury - would have been on a small rise in very low lying and wet land, hosting both the River Yeo and the River Parrett and their tributaries. However, it was also near a route towards the Fosse Way, the old Roman road running straight towards Exeter.

Seolfortun O.E. for Silver-town (Herewig's tun in Somerset). **Forton,** in what is now Dorset, is in the right area and a plausible contraction – but *I just made up the name Seolfortun.*

On the Journey to Rome and back:

I will not go into all the place names here – but I tried to use the names current at the time, though in truth some were in flux even at that time.

I also, where mentioned, tried to use the 'country' or 'area' names as would have been used. This, however, makes tracing their route in today's geo-political landscape a bit harder for anyone who would want see where my set of pilgrims trod.

The length of time taken was supported by written evidence of the time taken to travel from Rome back to Canterbury in a, nearly contemporaneous, pilgrimage diary – however, the conditions are mostly from my imagination.

Author's Notes: Further Reading

For those of you who like to follow up an historical novel with some further reading, or are curious as to what I based *some* of my ideas on, I have included here a *short* list of some of the books, papers and other sources that I used - or found interesting, as they shed light into the darker parts of the early medieval age.

NOTE: Anything that looks like a web page, if the words here are put into a search bar as set out, it ought to bring up the relevant pages – however, to read all of the information on some of them may need scrolling through pages or signing up to the host site.

On Places and building styles:
For where I sited the stronghold and monastery in Ireland:
The Place Names of the Decies - Rev. P. Power 1907 (Principalities of the Decies within Drum)
Also ref: www.logainm.ie for spellings, ancient and anglicised, and meanings.

Early medieval ages - roundhouses with partitions:
Early Irish Farming – based on the Law texts of the 7th and 8th centuries AD – Fergus Kelly (p360 on) 1997

Early medieval roundhouses – with added roundhouse 'rooms':
Early Medieval Dwellings and Settlements in Ireland, AD 400-1100 Vol. I Aidan O'Sullivan, Finbar McCormick, Lorcan Harney, Jonathan Kinsella and Thomas Kerr.

Early medieval Re: 'wind holes' and possibility of shutters (re: iron age round houses)
swheritage.org.uk/Avalon-archaeology

On Medicine and Medicinal Herbs in 6th / 7th centuries:

Antifungal antibacterial properties of spices. Specifically the tables within this:
pmc.ncbi.nlm.nih.gov/articles/PMC5486105/

Celtic Provenance in Traditional Herbal Medicine of Medieval Wales and Classical Antiquity
ncbi.nlm.nih.gov/pmc/articles/PMC7058801/

Dwale
pmc.ncbi.nlm.nih.gov/articles/PMC1127089/

Early medieval herbals cures (Bald's Leechbook – Anglo-Saxon) As an example of efficacy.
AncientBiotics - medieval medicine conquers MRSA superbug – The University of Nottingham

Monastery medicines
researchgate.net/publication/328415886_Medications_of_medieval_monastery_medicine

On 'the buried grains' *(which would have had the desired effect, but for which no evidence exists for their being* <u>*traded*</u> *as a cure, as there was no written system in Nubia at that time)*
researchgate.net/publication/16196663_Tetracycline-Labeled_Human_Bone_from_Ancient_Sudanese_Nubia_AD_350

On the history of the birthing stool, which was used widely and as early as the Egyptians.
Simple overview: en.wikipedia.org/wiki/Birthing_chair

<u>On Ecclesiastical matters:</u>

Irish monasticism in 6th 7th centuries: Also overview of Columbanus:
Christian Monasticism – wikipedia (an extraordinarily well sourced overview)

On confession and the types of penances:
Medieval Handbooks of Penance: A Translation of the Principal "Libri Poenitentiales" and Selections From Related Documents by John T. McNeill; Helena M. Gamer.

For early history of canonisation – how saints were made by acclamation, until the 10th century.
Encyclopedia Britannica: Canonization: ref: The early history of canonization.

A Land of Saints – ref webpage: *Wilcuma.org.uk (wessex, the history of cornwall, a land of saints)*

On the infrequency of The Mass:
The Mass in monastic practice c. 400 – 1200 – Fiona Griffiths.

On the written legends of Saint Indract and Saint Dominica – Cornwall – history and interpretations.
The Saints of Cornwall – Nicholas Orme – Oxford University Press. 2000.
Saint Indract and Saint Dominic. Canon G H Doble, D.D. Cornish saints series No. 48

On Glastonbury - early history:

Research by Reading University – re: The Old Church and the new Saxon Church 700AD
research.reading.ac.uk/glastonburyabbeyarchaeology/

On King Ine of Wessex and the Saxon stage of the book:

King Ina's record in the Anglo-Saxon Chronicle:
The Anglo-Saxon Chronicle, edited, from the translation in Monumenta Historica Britannica and other version, by the late J. A. Giles 1914

On becoming an early medieval Thegn.
The five-hide unit and the Old English military obligation. By C. Warren Hollister.

On Saxon hostage taking and on Saxon slavery:
Perceiving and Personifying Status and Submission in Pre-Viking England: Some Observations on a Few Early Hostages : Ryan Lavelle, in Hostage-Taking and Hostage Situations: The Medieval Precursor to a Modern Phenomenon, Editors: M. Bennett and K. Weikert. 2017

Slavery in Anglo Saxon England. Ref: webpage: Octavia.net

On Wessex expansion into Dumnonia.
Wicuma.org.uk – Anglo-Saxon Englisc Heritage: Romans, Celts and Saxons
wilcuma.org.uk/wessex/a-history-of-devon/saxon-devon/

On the invasion beyond the Tamar – to the Lynher.
Early History Saltash: *kernoweb.neocities.org/saltash/bhsearly*
AND *intocornwall.com/features/cornwall-history-timeline.asp*

<u>Other findings of interest or relevance:</u>

On the Ley Line that passes beside St. Indract's well and, diagonally, right through St. Dominica's Church, which stands in the place where Dominica led services at Bo Barr in this story.
Ley Lines of the South West by Alan Neal. Bossiney Books 2004.

On place names in Devon and Cornwall:
Place-names in Devon and Cornwall by Arthur Grigg. Published by The College of St. Mark and St. John, Plymouth.

On Kingship in Early Ireland :
On Kingship in Early Ireland paper by Charles Doherty: University College Dublin.

That Ireland was 'aceramic' (no native clay vessels) between the Bronze Age and the Viking age.
EMAP Report 4.2 EarlyMedievalSettlementsVol1 by A O'Sullivan et al University College Dublin research repository

On the symptoms and treatment of arsenic poisoning
jsstd.org/dermatological-manifestations-of-arsenic-exposure/

The Good the Bad and the Rotten: How the Living Dealt with the Dead in England
C. 600-1200. Medieval History Masters Dissertation. Norwich 2017

On formation and spontaneous ignition of marsh gas.
Soil in the Environment. Daniel Hillel.

The weather in the past.
premium.weatherweb.net/weather-in-history

Antibiotic found in Soil in Northern Ireland. (*Just for interest*)
smithsonianmag.com/science-nature/astonishing-medical-potential-soil-northern-ireland-graveyard-180973741/

Author's Notes:
Thanks and Acknowledgements

As always, with the writing of a book, there are those who have helped enormously in various ways.

My thanks are due to my beta readers, Steph, Gill, Nina and Sally. Thank you all for reading this before its final proofing for spotting those bits that can only be seen by fresh eyes - plot holes, dangling threads and sentences that just don't quite ....

Thanks too, to Simon for some medieval history-error snagging, to Nina for final proofreading and to my husband, Mark, who always reads the finished book before it goes to press. Any remaining errors I own.

As always thanks go to my friends and family for their support and, who for so many long years, have had to put up with my going on about Dominica, or the information that caught my interest in any of the weird and wonderful rabbit holes the research lured me down.

And finally, many thanks to Fiona who, when I was just over two thirds in and feeling that it 'might not be exciting enough to be a good novel' read the raw, totally unedited, work ... and fed-back enough positive remarks to give me the impetus to keep going, and to speed up to keep ahead of her reading ... just.

Also with grateful thanks to Diana and Keith Greene of Halton Barton, Hilary and John Davis of Chapel House in Chapel, and Mary and, the late, Derek Scofield (both dowsers) of Greenhill, also in Chapel - for discussions, Legends, Ley-line identification, and permissions to visit the sites located on their properties.

And my thanks also extend to you – the reader!
If you have enjoyed this book, please recommend it to others you know. You can also do this for a wider audience by leaving a review on Goodreads or Amazon.

Other novels by ANN FOWERAKER

Nothing Ever Happens Here
Living in London suddenly becomes too uncomfortable for the attractive Jo Smart and her sixteen year-old son, Alex, after he is beaten up. so when they are offered the chance to take an immediate holiday in a peaceful Cornish town they jump at it. But not all is as peaceful as it seems as they become involved in a murder enquiry, drug raid and abduction.
DI Rick Whittington has also escaped from London and the reminders of the death of his wife and child, and through his investigations finds himself meeting Jo and being drawn into the events surrounding her.
This is a light thriller, set in the early 1990s, which combines the historic Cornish love of the sea and smuggling with romance and hard faced twentieth century crime and detection.

Divining the Line
The first time it happened it felt like stumbling across another avenue to an ancient monument, but this one pulled at more than just his head, there was a tightness in his chest, the lights twinkled and flashed inside his mind, the intensity giving Perran a firework of a headache.
Following the line - years later in the early nineties - leads him into Liz Hawkey's ordered life, and together they discover the source of the line.
A story of family, love and loss, Divining the Line brings the ordinary and the extraordinary together into everyday life.

Some Kind of Synchrony
Faith Warren, married mother of two, is a secretary in a newspaper office. It wasn't what she'd hoped for, but her dreams of university and becoming an author were lost long ago. Telling stories to entertain her lifelong friend

on their journey to work and back is all that is left, until she tells The Story.

The real trouble began with the minor characters, just unfortunate co-incidences, but when do you stop calling them co-incidences and begin to wonder what the hell is going on – and how it can be stopped.

The Angel Bug

'These memoirs may be the only evidence left of what really happened, where it came from and how it spread.'

When Gabbi Johnston, a quiet, fifty-something botanist at Eden, was shown the unusual red leaves on the Moringa tree, she had no idea what was wrong. What she did know was that the legendary Dr Luke Adamson was arriving soon - and that he would insist on investigating it.

This is the unassuming start to a maelstrom of discovery and change - with Gabbi swept up in it. What starts out as an accident turns into something illicit, clandestine and unethical – but is it really, as Adamson claims, for the good of all mankind?

'The Angel Bug' is set mainly at the Eden Project in Cornwall, UK. This is a contemporary novel combining science fact and fiction, told by the people at the heart of the discovery.

A Respectable Life

Art enthusiast, magistrate, village do-gooder, Cordelia Steadman is the epitome of respectable country life ... until her past catches up with her. Even then she thinks she has it all under control ... until she starts to receive the emails ... and the demands.

A psychological thriller set in the tranquil Tamar Valley, Cornwall.

About the Author

I am poet, teacher, mother, author ... and each incarnation has had an ascendancy in my life – now is the time of the author.

My first writing passion was poetry - and this is still with me - story writing grew later.

I became a teacher when it was more of a vocation than an occupation; gaining my BEd degree in the seventies.

Marriage took me from Berkshire, where I was born, to live in glorious Cornwall and the novel writing blossomed while taking an extended break from teaching, to bring up our four boys - but only came to fruition as they left the nest.

Please follow my blog on annfoweraker.com where you'll get an insight into the things I'm in to - from belly dancing and local history to health and nutrition and, of course, writing.

Follow or Like my Author page on Facebook 'Ann Foweraker author' if you'd like to keep up to date with my writing adventures

Blessings and All Good to You All

Ann Foweraker – 2026

www.ingramcontent.com/pod-product-compliance
Lightning Source LLC
La Vergne TN
LVHW050910080826

845145LV00001B/34
9781909936331